SHADOWFACE

A DARK COLLEGE ROMANCE

RHEA RYAN

TRIGGER WARNINGS

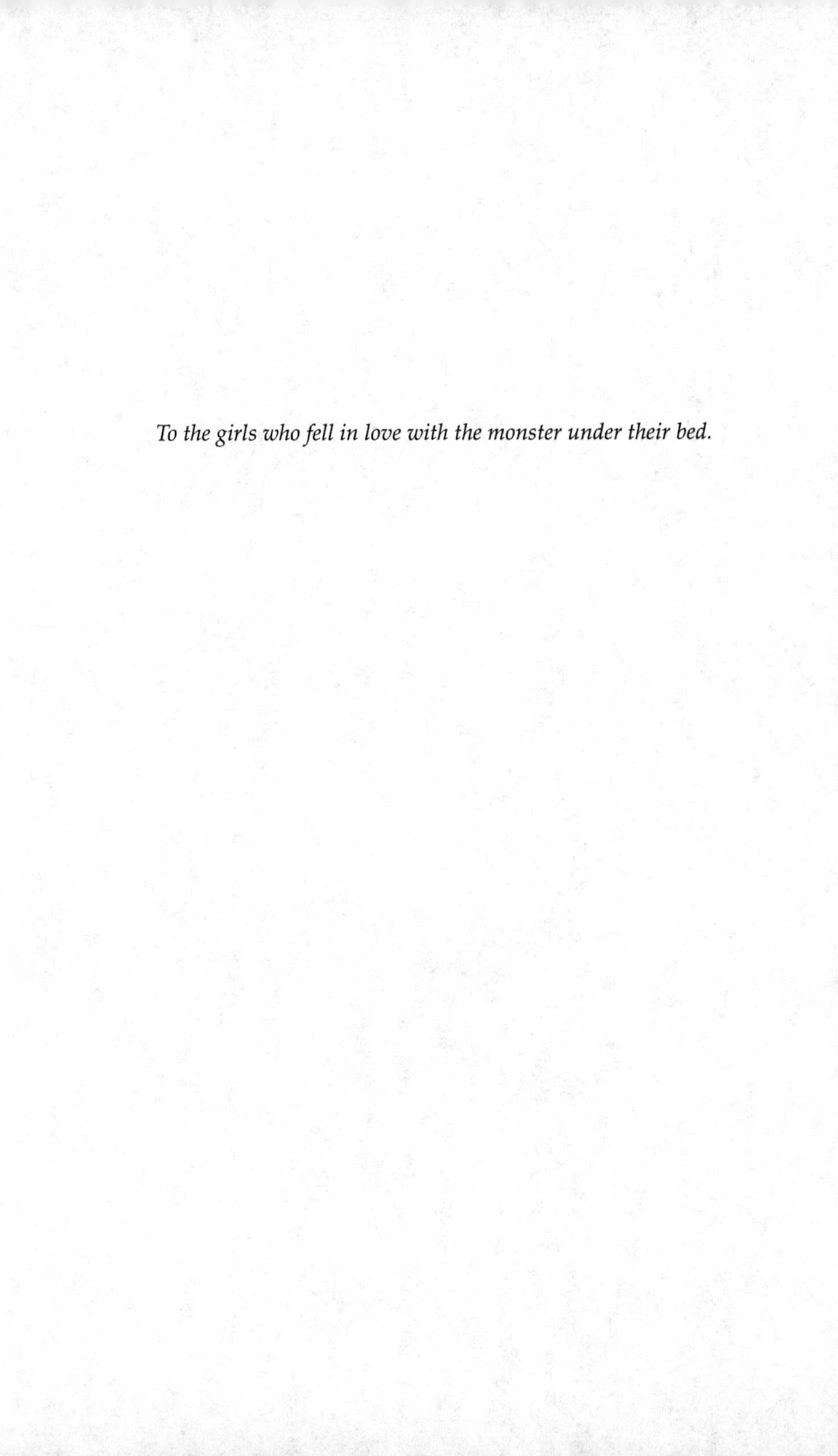

To the girls who fell in love with the monster under their bed.

Umbra Mortis
(The Shadow of Death)
From The Shadow Codex (Babylon)
(rewritten and decoded 1751)

Prefix:
Shadowface

"Enlightenment is found in the perpetual dance of order and disorder, control and liberation. Just as stars are born from the collapse of darkness, so too must order yield to chaos for the light of true knowledge to shine."
Creed I: Those who seek nirvana must embrace this collapse.
Creed II: Those who wish to enter must do so with their bloodline.
Creed III: Silence or death.
Creed IV: Each member must sacrifice their one true love.

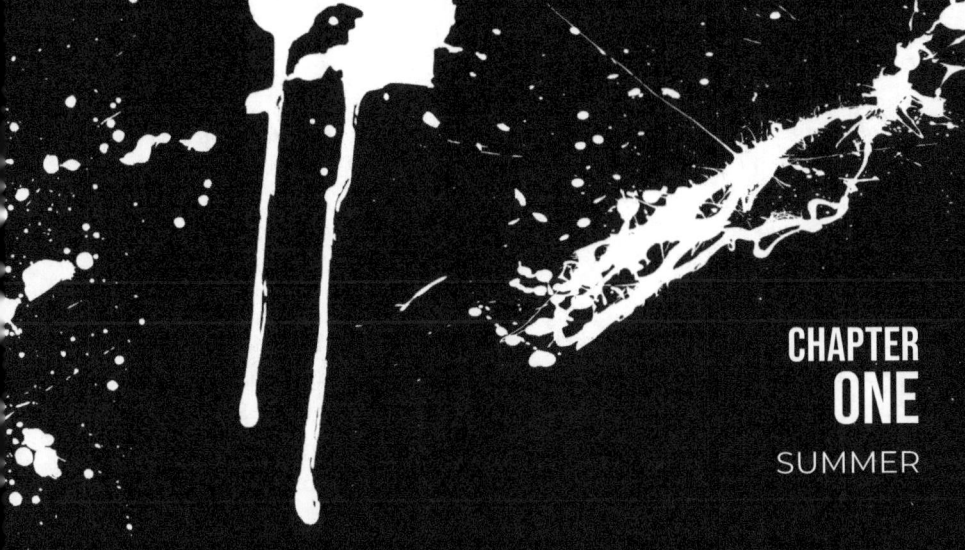

PYSC 100
Fall 2024
Monday, Wednesday, Friday
Kinsmen University
Department of Psychology
Course Syllabus

I nstructor: Dr. Talia Garcia
Teaching Assistant: Lincoln Kennedy
Required Textbook: *Science of the Mind: An Introduction to Psychological Principles.* Third edition. 2022. *T. Garcia. K. Landry. L. Kennedy.* Petticoat Publishing.

Optional Textbook (Strongly Recommended): *The War of Emotions: Fear, Anger, and Loathing. Second Edition. 2020. K. Landry. T. Garcia.* Petticoat Publishing.

Course Description

This course was created to break you, to help you understand all parts of yourself: the good, the bad, and the parts you'd rather keep locked inside. If you progress along the semester and don't drop out after the first month, you will transform. You will rebuild yourself with a deeper understanding of your inner psyche. To succeed in this course, you must plunge into the darkest parts of your mind and connect with the world around you. Psychology is the scientific study of the human experience, and mastering yourself is key. You will gain insight into your true identity and apply that knowledge to gain a deeper understanding of your life and what drives the behavior of those around you. You will probably fail this course. Welcome to Kinsmen University. Welcome to Psychology 100.

D r. Garcia's high heels click against the marble floor to the front of the lecture hall as everyone—at least, those who have read the course outline—immediately hushes their conversation. She's a tiny woman with an extraordinary presence and a reputation that precedes her. I barely see her, so small against the vastness of Smith Hall, the university's most famous lecture hall.

I've seen her before on the news, heard her on crime podcasts as the leading authority on child psychology. Her photo is on the wall in my father's study next to his desk—although, she was much younger in that photo. My father knew her; she was his supervisor while completing his PhD program at this very school, and he worked with her off and on for years after.

My breathing stalls as she takes her place on the podium in front of the room. Her salt and pepper dark hair is pulled back, and an elegant silver streak marks her forehead. She rises to the podium; behind her, a grand black curtain hangs over marble walls. While this room has a modern feel, this institution is nearly three hundred years old, and I wonder how many students have sat here listening to her.

I can't believe we are actually here. It feels like yesterday we were sipping wine in Paris, riding bikes in Belgium, and scooting around to different hotels in Amsterdam. My best friend Dani and I traveled through Europe for the summer after doing a year at community college in our hometown. I only got my scholarship letter in June after thinking I didn't get in. Oddly enough, it was days after my father died. Dani deferred a year so we could go to school together. And now, here we are.

She lifts herself on a riser and clears her throat. What's left of any murmur of the two hundred people seated immediately silences as this tiny Italian woman commands the room.

You can hear a pin drop.

Dani elbows me. "Holy shit, she seems intense."

I elbow her back as a few people turn and glare. "Shh, Dani. We can't talk right now."

People pay thousands of dollars for their kids to attend this private university—which rivals Harvard and Yale in prestige—and many attend just to hear this tiny woman speak.

Three screens light up on the wall behind her. One giant wall of screens, unlike anything I've ever seen. Those dreaded words are written in various ways all across them.

Tiny, large, intertwined, as if taunting me.

You will fail.

As if she knows I'm not good enough to be here. That I am a fraud, thinking I can follow in my father's footsteps because, deep down, I know I'm not smart enough and he must have pulled strings to get me in here. I'm nothing like him.

"Welcome to Kinsmen University." Dr. Garcia's voice booms across the lecture hall. She seems ageless, timeless in her beauty.

I'm not sure how old she is, but she's at least pushing seventy, given she was at least twenty-five years older than my father.

My head spins at the words in front of me. Failure is not an option since I'm here on a scholarship I barely earned. Failure will get me kicked out.

Why did I sign up for this class for the first semester? I must derive pleasure from torturing myself.

There are over two hundred students in this class, and half are vying to major in this program since psychology is what this school is known for. It has the best program in the country. It was the part of my father's life he never brought me into, until now.

"What emotion do these words invoke in you?" she asks the room, and I swear... I swear her eyes land right on me.

I get it, people usually stare. My hair draws attention, especially in a sea of mediocrity. Few people can say their hair is as naturally white as snow. It's so clear, it crystallizes under the light. Describing it as blonde doesn't do it justice. My father used to tell me I was a vision of an angel. My hair was a gift, my birthright, and I should be proud of it because I got it from my grandmother.

"It makes me feel all tingly inside," someone yells and chuckles.

Dr. Garcia pauses as if she wants to retort, then her lips merely twitch into a small smile. "Clever. I hope we can keep up that level of humor throughout the semester. Although, thin jokes will hardly help you pass this course."

The room collectively chuckles.

"Scared," someone else yells out.

Her eyes light up. "Ah, yes. Fear. That is a very natural emotion to failure. Show of hands; how many of you are scared right now?"

At least half the class puts their hands up, me included. Although, that's not exactly how I would describe how I feel at this moment.

Feelings aren't something that comes naturally to me.

She scans the room, then clicks something in her hand and a new slide pops up on the wall of screens behind her.

"Fear," she says, waving her hands theatrically, striding to the center of the stage. "Fear is instinctive, fear is powerful. Fear can both protect you and paralyze you, motivate and haunt you." The note in her voice gives me pause. "Fear is what we will primarily focus on throughout this class. Your response to fear will either lift you up to extraordinary heights or cause your demise. I find fear the most…fascinating of all human emotions."

Fear… What about anger and loathing?

My father became the world's leading expert on fear. Fear, in the context of the class textbook, belonged to him.

She sighs, and for a moment, she finally shows her age as her fingers pinch her nose. "Indeed, some of you will barely pass this class, as you will find out after your first major paper. This is to weed you out, as we only want the brightest minds in our program. I will not be reviewing the syllabus with you—assuming since you're in this school, you can read—but I would like to point out we expect short weekly reflections, which are due on Fridays."

The class groans, and Dr. Garcia waves her hand like she couldn't be bothered to hear it.

"I'd also like to introduce you to your TA for the class, Lincoln Kennedy. Lincoln will be grading everything this semester and will be holding office hours on class days: Monday, Wednesday, and Friday. This class is incredibly lucky to have Lincoln. He's one of my PhD students and knows this material very well—after all, he helped me write the textbook. I'll encourage you to take up any grievances with Lincoln before you come to me."

My eyes drift to a guy with dark hair sitting in the front. I can only glimpse the side of his head, but he keeps a tight look on his face. Glasses so thick, I wonder if he isn't completely blind.

L. Kennedy.

Lincoln Kennedy.

A flash of recognition hits me before he turns his head back toward the front of the class. But it's enough of a view that my stomach squeezes so tight and shoots right to my core.

"Wow, look at Professor Hottie," Dani teases in an obnoxious whisper. "He looks too young to have written the damn textbook."

I squint to get a better look. His name precedes him, as I merely stare at an entity in my mind. My father talked about him so much, but I never had the pleasure of meeting him.

He sits like a stone, not budging in the first row, even though the entire room is looking at him.

Jet-black hair, skin a pale glow. He's wearing all black, a turtleneck, and has a gothic look to him. An aura of arrogance, as if he is too smart to be bothered to engage with any of us in this class. A creepy kind of sexy that words can't describe.

Dani, of course, has already googled him.

"He finished his degree at nineteen and jumped right into his master's. He's only twenty-five and is about to finish his PhD." Dani looks at me carefully. "So, do you know him?"

The back of my teeth grind together. "Why would you ask that?"

She narrows her eyes, jerking her head in his direction. "Well…he wrote the textbook with your father."

I keep my gaze on Lincoln, darkness shrouding him. "No. I don't know him." My father believed in the separation of church and state—his work being church, his family being state. Lincoln was like the son my father never had, a relationship I had no part of. An entire part of my father's life I could never tap into.

"I've never met him." I keep my voice low as we start to catch the attention of Professor Garcia. "He was my father's protégé." I can't hide the hint of jealousy that laces my voice. "He helped my father with research and stuff."

Which is part of the reason I'm here—I never had the chance to share that with my father. We lived only an hour away from here, so my father commuted all the time for visits. It's like he lived a double life. When he was home, the dinner table was always about how brilliant *Lincoln* was. How much potential *Lincoln* had.

And I was just so…ordinary.

It was never my path to follow my father, even though I was fascinated by it all, too. But Lincoln…he was always top of mind for my father.

"You don't have to follow his footsteps, Summer."

My mother hated that I came here—hated it even more when I was awarded the scholarship and accepted it. My mom, for whatever reason, wanted nothing to do with this place, even though this is where my father grew up.

Evidently, my father has entrusted me with his legacy, and it is now my responsibility to seize it. He pulled the strings to get me here. He must have...

Dani looks at me and frowns. "Weekly reflections? Well, I'm fucked."

I smile tightly as my nerves fire on end. "You'll be fine. You just have to pass; it's not like you want in this program."

Dani plays with her braid falling over her shoulders. "You'll be fine, too, but honestly, I can't wait for office hours with Lincoln." Her eyes flicker as she watches my reaction.

I can't help but look at him again, the familiarity of him. It's like he can sense me and looks right at me, and his soft features seem bored. I give him a weak smile, and I almost wave before he shifts his attention back to Dr. Garcia without returning it.

I am very curious as to what rumors she's heard about him, though. From everything I can see, he's extremely rigid. Awkward, even. Like he's so nerdy, he doesn't realize how attractive he is.

"Well, he seems fun," I joke, and Dani laughs. Probably because I never joke.

Dani gives me a mischievous grin. "Maybe you could help him loosen his turtleneck."

I can't help but snicker.

Dr. Garcia clears her throat and glares at us, as if speaking to me. "You will do well to pay strong attention and keep up with your course readings. Don't overthink your weekly reflections and use at least one external source to back up any claims. Each reflection should focus on the material for that week. This is an introductory class, but we will dive into the five major perspectives of psychology over the next twelve weeks."

I catch Lincoln looking at us again as a blush hits my cheeks. He looks serious, too serious...and he's staring right at me. I understand academia enough. Most professors or wannabe professors are doing this for the research, and grading papers is annoying for them.

And Lincoln, in all his Alt-Gothic glory, looks really fucking annoyed. As if being in this class is beneath him.

Dr. Garcia starts her lecture about research methods and the importance of study groups, and I scribble down everything she says.

I can't take my eyes off Lincoln, and for whatever reason, he keeps glancing at me, too, like he knows he's going to fail me. Unlike Dani, I not only need to pass this course, I need to excel in it. Because psychology is the major I've decided to pursue.

I can't go home to my mother as a failure. She's still angry at me for accepting this scholarship and for running off to Europe with Dani. Especially since she never approved of my friendship with Dani to begin with.

Dani's family name is soiled. Her father went to prison when we were sixteen, but Dani won't tell me for what. All I know is all the court records and proceedings are confidential, which means whatever he did was really bad.

I glance at the clock. Only ten minutes left, and I can't wait to get out of here. I have hours of reading to do. I look down at my thick psychology textbook, the author's name bleeding out of the pages, slapping me in the face.

K. Landry.

Suddenly, my attention is caught as my phone buzzes. Not just mine, but everyone's phone in the vast room buzzes simultaneously. A soft murmur flows through the crowd. Intrigued, I grab it out of my bag, wondering if it's an emergency text message. As I open the message, a shockwave courses through me, nearly causing my eyes to pop out of their sockets. It's me... Someone sent a photo of me.

No, not me. This isn't me.

But it could be me. There is an uncanny resemblance as I stare down at the photo.

"What the fuck?" I whisper and glance over at Dani, who is staring at the same photo.

It's a picture of a picture? The photo has distinguished black edges and is placed on a table. A dead girl, arms bound, wearing nothing but her white bra and underwear. Her face is covered by a burlap sack and her knees are up, as if she's displaying herself for the camera.

She's a blonde like me... Curvy and beautiful.

And dead. Clearly dead.

Dr. Garcia pauses her lecture, looking almost bored, as the class erupts into chatter. "Relax, everyone. It's only a prank. These old photos get sent out every year to this class to scare you. It's unfortunate, but a certain group of people on this campus don't seem to have respect for the dead. You'll get used to it."

A reminder, I realize. Someone is sending out a reminder.

I understand why my mother was so against me coming here. I know the lore of what happened at this school in the 1970s, and again in 2002, because I read about it when I got accepted.

I glossed over it, because what happened, happened so long ago, it didn't really matter. I guess I was wrong.

After all this time, it should be left alone and not brought up again. The stain on the campus should have faded into oblivion with how horrible it is.

"Holy mother of fuck," Dani whispers, staring down at her phone, her eyes bulging out of her head. I can't rip my eyes from it, either.

Dani tilts her head and squints, inspecting the photo closer. Dr. Garcia speaks into the microphone, realizing she's lost the group. "This class is officially over. Don't forget your readings and try not to get caught up in the madness. The lore of what happened is quite alluring, but he's a distraction, and you'll get behind if you pay too much attention to him."

Him...

The person who did this all those years ago, and the entity that came before him. His trademark name now haunts this town. He signed every taunting photo and left them in public places across campus for everyone to see.

The name he gave himself corresponds to the whispers and legend that haunts this town. The photos he left instilled fear in every student who attended this institution. Rumor has it, he carved out their eyes and hid their faces behind a burlap mask.

The mask is a symbol of a secret society so wicked, they had prohibited all fraternities and sororities on campus since the 1970s because of it.

And is the creepiest name I've ever heard.

Shadowface.

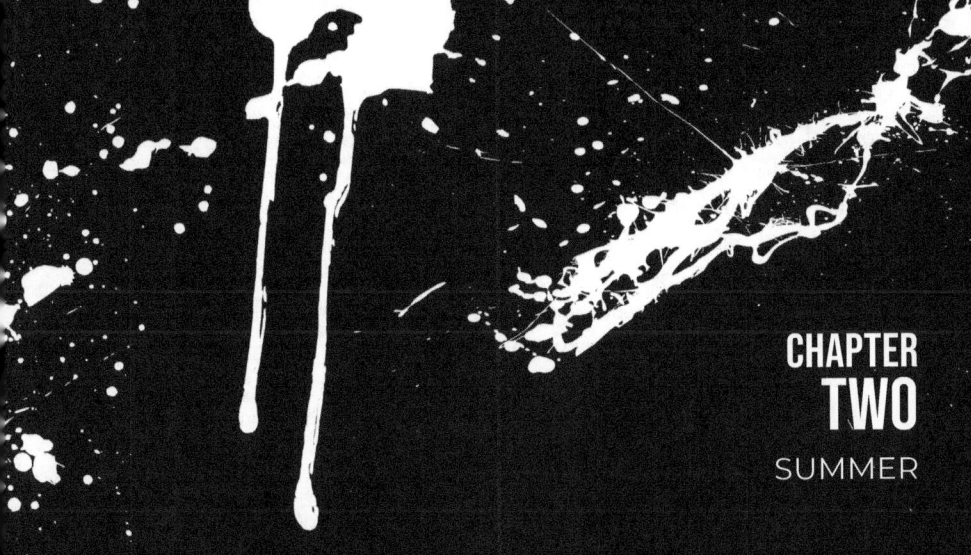

Dani and I came home after class to our quaint, two-story house in the middle of town we are renting together. Dani's mother didn't want her living in the residence hall, so she found us a house instead. I tried to ignore the ickiness building in my stomach after seeing the photo sent out to the class. Everyone was talking about it when we left, whispers of Shadowface reverberating throughout the school. This unknown entity…this familiar demon in my mind.

I now understand why Dani and I saw a few students wearing burlap masks. I thought it was a weird freshman thing, but I now understand it's a symbol of Shadowface.

They idolize him here.

It also makes sense why my mom was upset I came here.

After spending a few hours unpacking and getting ready for our new roommate to join us, I head upstairs to my charming room that also serves as the attic. It comprises my bed, a slim armoire, a desk in the corner, and a dresser beside the large square window under the arched ceilings. It's small but has a beautiful view of the outside, where I can stare out into the canopy trees of the park near my house, and the tree-lined street beyond. Kinsmen is known for its dark, massive trees, which only adds to the crippling ambience of its history.

This semester is already proving intense, so I open my literature textbook and start reading through some of the material, avoiding my psychology readings altogether.

I lean my head against my headboard and stare out at the moon and a cloud hovering over it. A cool breeze hits my face, but I don't close the window. I always keep my window open, and that's what I love about these old houses. Windows without screens, where people can crawl into your room at night.

The idea of being watched excites me...always has.

Eventually, I grab the computer and pull up the list of today's readings I have to get done for psychology. Three online articles and the entire first chapter on research methods. I run my thumb over my father's name.

K. Landry.

My heart swells when I remember him, and I allow myself to feel the pain of his loss. After running away immediately after he died, it remains a lingering wound in my heart. I stare at the textbook on my desk and my vision blurs, as if my subconscious won't let me read his words. My jaw tightens, realizing that book is the only significant part of my father I have left.

Defeated, I place my computer on the edge of my bed and grab my phone and message my mother and ask how she's doing. She doesn't respond—she never responds to me right away. She's been devastated, and in her mind, I abandoned her to come to school here. Leaving her after my father's body gave out on him.

Cardiac arrest in his early forties. It was quick and dirty. One minute he was here, the next, he was comatose on life support. I haven't really had a chance to process it.

I pull up the photo of the Shadowface victim and stare at it. I squint, trying to get a view of the eyes behind the burlap mask, trying to imagine them cut out.

I inspect the photo closer and let out a huge breath to release all the tension rising in me. She's been delicately placed on the bed, her arms tied up behind her head, her breasts perky and on display. It's like whoever was behind these photos took pride in making sure she looked perfect. And although her face is covered, I can imagine the serene look in her eyes before she died.

Like she was about to be fucked.

It's the hair falling in gentle waves over her breasts that catches my attention the most, her ivory skin so smooth and tight.

It's like looking in a mirror.

A spindly sensation shoots down my spine, landing between my legs with a pleasurable intensity.

My breath lengthens as I lift the hem of the sweater dress I'm still wearing from earlier and look at the similar white panties I have on, and heat pools in my core. I slip my hand beneath my panties and press down on my clit, moving my fingers in a gentle circle as a slight cool wind blows through my open windows.

It's a coincidence—it has to be. White lace bras and panties are timeless.

It's not him. It's not my nameless monster. This photo is from twenty-two years ago, when the copycat killer slaughtered those women. I wasn't even born when it happened.

I think back to two years ago...to the last night my monster came to me when I was in my senior year of high school. It was rare I saw him, even though he was a constant presence in my mind. The silly teenage me actually fell in love with him—or at least, I thought I did.

He is a ghost. A man I only saw in my dreams, and even then, it was only a couple of times a year. I'm not even sure he was real.

The pressure builds in my core as I think about him, then it starts to burn. Despite the fresh air coming in through my open window, the room grows hot.

Ping.

I snap myself back to the present and pull my hand from between my legs as if someone just caught me in the act. My pulse is racing, my fist curling the blankets beneath me.

What am I doing? Dreaming of a masked man fucking his victims.

Shadowface never indicated he had sex with those girls. Why would I even think that? That was never what it was about for Shadowface. He killed them for sport, and because he could. And I have no clue why my natural response is to get off on it.

Overwhelmed by disgust, I quickly adjust myself and strain my eyes to locate the origin of the noise on my computer. I notice a red circle on the chat group in my online class forum.

Someone sent me a message.

Dr. Garcia strongly suggested we form study groups, and I antici-pated studying with Dani, so I'm surprised I have an unread message in our classroom chat group.

I pull the computer to my lap and lay my head back.

I created a fake username earlier. The professor told us we can remain anonymous if we choose to. In fact, she encouraged it due to the personal nature of the course.

I click on the message and my eyes narrow when I see the display name.

SF: *Hi there.*

I hover the mouse over the name.

Oh, for crying out loud. Subtle.

Fuck. It's as if he knew. Like he was watching me through that screen and smelled my arousal. I pause for a second before answering.

Bikiniqueen: *Hi*

SF: *Want to study with me?*

Feeling silly for being freaked out, I blow out a breath. This is just psychology class, and this weirdo must have a sick sense of humor. But the thing is, it doesn't freak me out like it should, given the symbolism of it all and this town's obsession with Shadowface.

Bikiniqueen: *I don't fraternize with serial killers, sorry.*

A pause and my lips curl into a small smile. But my heart...the rhythm of the beat tells a different story.

SF: *You don't like my name?*

Bikiniqueen: *No. I do not.*

I scan the class list. There is zero indication who this could be. And even though this seems innocent enough, someone at this school sent that photo. Joke or no joke, it's really messed up. And who's to say this SF wasn't the one who sent it?

SF: *It's a joke. And it could mean something entirely different, you know.*

Bikiniqueen: *Like what?*

Another pause on his end. Or her end, because I have no idea who I'm talking to.

SF: *It could mean several things. Super flirty, perhaps?*

Someone is flirty, so I guess I'll play. I'm a good flirt. It comes with the territory of being me, even if I'm a prude at heart. And all I ever do is flirt, even though what I just did is the opposite of prudish.

Bikiniqueen: *Why are you assuming I'm a girl, or are you into guys, too? I could be hideous, and you might not want to be my boyfriend when you see what I look like.*

SF: *I bet a girl with a name like Summer must be gorgeous.*

"What the hell?" I mutter. I'm tempted to slam my laptop closed, instantly regretting logging on here. I don't need some creep bugging me during my first week.

Bikiniqueen: *How do you know my name?*

SF: *Your attempts at anonymity are cute. I figured it out from your nickname. It wasn't that hard.*

Okay, he has me on that one.

Bikiniqueen: *Smart ass.*

SF: *I try. I bet you like people seeing you in your bikini, don't you, Summer? You enjoy people looking at that tight body, don't you, pretty girl?*

Pretty girl...

The little hairs stand on my neck and my head lifts to the window, only to be met by moonlight and darkness. No creepy masked man standing outside looking at me, but the blinds are wide open, and I'm splayed out on my bed for anyone outside to see.

I pull my sweater dress over my knees. I'm too curious now to end this conversation, even though I should. So far, my interactions with people at this school have been strange, to say the least. That's what I get for choosing such a stupid username, I guess.

Bikiniqueen: *Come again?*

SF: *Maybe you'll show me what's underneath that little sweater dress.*

Nope! No. No. No.

I get up and slam the window closed. Settling my heartbeat, I sit back down. He's just fucking with me. I wore this outfit to school today.

Bikiniqueen: *Who am I speaking to? It's only right that, given you have my name, I should have yours.*

He doesn't respond right away. A few minutes go by, and I stare up at my pitched ceiling.

Finally, a response.

SF: *Fairness is a social construct, identified and articulated by your worldview and limited by experiences you had as a child. You will learn this when we study personality. Life isn't fair, Summer, and it's not in my best interest right now to tell you who I am. You didn't tell me your name, I figured it out. I never asked you for it, so how is it fair you're asking for mine?*

I suck in a breath. It's like listening to my father speak or scold me at the dinner table. Always psychoanalyzing. It's like he couldn't help himself.

Bikiniqueen: *You seem to know a whole heck of a lot about our class.*

Lincoln kept staring at me today, like he recognized me... Would he message me like this?

SF: *I read ahead. I like to understand what I'm getting into.*

I shake my head. "So stupid," I mutter to myself. Why would a guy as established as Lincoln want to play some prank on me? It makes no sense.

SF: *So will you answer my question?*

I bite my bottom lip and smile, typing back a response.

Bikiniqueen: *What question?*

SF: *Will you study with me?*

Bikiniqueen: *I think I'll pass.*

A few seconds go by before he or she finally says,

SF: *Have a good night, Summer.*

Their circle turns gray, indicating they've logged off, and I slam my computer shut, shaking my head. I turn off my bedside light and curl up in a ball, trying to calm my senses. Every nerve in my body is fired up. This school, this town, this obsession with masked men...

Officially. Fucking. Creepy.

All I can think about is some psycho wearing a potato sack mask, fantasizing about me in my bed. Worst of all, I am so sexually frustrated right now that a pulse hits between my legs again. I have to admit, for the first time since that night, I'm really fucking turned on.

T*he Order of the Shadows.*
    "I don't know much about them, only that they killed lots of people," Dani says as we walk through the well-manicured pathways that meander around old Gothic sandstone buildings that make up the fabric of Kinsmen University. A campus as old as the trees. The trees must keep all this town's secrets, given how old they are.

I am already familiar with the Order of the Shadows, as is everyone else. However, their true identity remains a mystery. All we know is that they used to live here.

Rumors, stories, myths of monsters.

A secret society—so secret, it's as if they don't exist anymore.

Dani loves this kind of thing, and I'm curious about it, so I asked her about them.

"What happened to the Order? Do they still exist?" I ask as I run my gaze up to a heavy mist in the sky starting to break as the sun begins to peek through. I guess the sun doesn't like to shine in a place like this, as if it knows evil resides here.

We head toward a break in the trees, and sit side by side on our jackets on the lush lawn and sip our coffees.

Dani continues, "They disappeared without a trace. No more pranks, no more whispers. They went from wanting everyone to know they were here to utter silence."

I stretch my legs out in front of me while staring up at the canopy and get lost in its beauty of the fall colors I can finally see through the mist. "What kind of pranks?" Admittedly, I've not heard much about them.

She arches a well-manicured brow and smiles. She's so into this lore. I've not seen her this interested in something for a long time. Ever since her father's conviction, she lives on the edge.

"Well, in the seventies, they used to wreak havoc on campus—burning buildings down, lacing drinks with acid at parties. The more word spread about their movement, the more people panicked. But it remained a mystery who exactly was in charge or what their purpose was—that was always a secret. They used to spray paint the name Shadowface on the quad. That name has been in this town a long time; it was always used to scare people here, like he was a boogie man or something. But it's the name of the god they worshipped. Then the slaughter of 1979 happened, and everything changed. They went quiet." She means the mass, chaotic killing spree that took the lives of seven people at a campus party in the woods.

I take a sip of my latte. "Were there any suspects?"

She shakes her head. "It happened at night, and witnesses only say they saw a group of people wearing burlap masks holding torches. Really creepy shit. But it was the same mask Shadowface used to cover the girls' faces in the photos over twenty years later. They've got to be connected somehow. But the 2002 killings were much more meticulous than the ones in the seventies. Four girls went missing over the course of a year. All that was left of them were the pictures of their dead bodies; their actual bodies were never found. Fear crippled this campus for months until it just...stopped. The Order was behind it, too. I don't believe they ever left."

Ever since her father got put away, she's been obsessed with anything related to conspiracy theories. She would be a great candidate for a flat earth society or a cult.

"It sounds like you got a lot of your actual homework done last night," I joke. Although, it's not like I was any more productive, especially with this stranger messaging me, drumming up all sorts of feelings and memories.

And urges.

Thank god Dani didn't notice the resemblance of that girl in the picture.

My insides start to turn, and I can't stop thinking about the mask on the girl in the photo. I'm convinced my nameless monster wore one just like it.

I vividly remember waking up to the scent of scarecrow and a hint of spice, the scratch on my face while he was deep inside me and the gentle kisses he pressed along my collarbone. The threats he whispered while taking my virginity; the vile words that didn't match his intoxicating actions.

Dani spent her evening finding out as much as she could about the Order, while I spent my night staring at the photo sent out to our class, masturbating to it, dreaming about my nameless monster and why he never came back. While Dani was obsessing, I was wholly consumed by *him*.

Breathe, Summer. It's just a hallucination. We lived an hour away from here; there is absolutely no way this is connected.

I grab my phone, open the photo, and gaze at it, just like I did for hours yesterday. My nose crinkles.

"What's wrong, Summer?" Dani asks.

This girl looks like me, but there is something else bugging me about it. "This photo wasn't online," I whisper. "I don't remember seeing this picture before."

The victims' photos are easy enough to find in the underbellies of the internet, and we glanced at them before I couldn't stomach it anymore.

Dani leans over to look as I hand my phone to her. Her bohemian braid tucked to the side of her head, falling over her slim shoulder. "I'm sure it was, and we just missed it. It sounds like people at this school like to instill fear. So fucking sick, if you ask me. But it's kind of exciting."

I give her a tight smile, cross my legs, and play with my hair. "Yeah, I'm sure you're right."

I wish I could go inside that photo and see what she was seeing. What she was experiencing while staring up at the face of her killer.

Dani continues, "Do you want to hear the freakiest thing about all of it?"

I put my phone down and face her, trying to not go *there* in my mind again.

"Rumors are that the killings were actually happening at this school for hundreds of years. That there were way more victims over time, and the slaughter of '79 and the copycat of '02 were just the finale. People have been dying in this town for centuries."

I whip my head up. "What do you mean, hundreds of years?"

Leaning back on the grass, Dani holds her phone above her head, eyes glued to an article on the screen. "Well, how old is this university?"

"The giant stone bench at the entrance of campus says 1742," I retort. "That's how long."

I frown. "I don't know, Dani... That sounds like a bit of a conspiracy theory."

She scrolls down her phone. "The data shows an abnormal number of mysterious deaths and disappearances. They went missing in the forests that surround the town, but it's hard to say..." She turns and gives me a wicked grin. "People believe the town was cursed, Summer. I wouldn't be surprised if it was haunted, too."

Curses don't exist, and bad things don't just happen. People make bad things happen because humanity is insane. But hundreds of years? That just sounds absurd.

"Your father went here, didn't he?" Dani asks, casually sipping her coffee.

Fighting down a wave of emotion, I direct my attention to a red leaf that fell on my shoe. Dani gives me a sympathetic look. She regrets mentioning my father, but they are valid questions, given my family's connection to this town.

"Yeah, he did all his schooling here. Then he moved back to Mystic, and he only came back through a fellowship and some research he did with Dr. Garcia. My grandparents grew up here, though, but they moved to Mystic after college."

Mystic is where I grew up, an hour away from here. I love my grand-father, who I call Papa, but I never had a chance to meet my grandmother.

She presses her lips together. "So, he went here during that time? During the Shadowface era?"

I blink at her, silently doing the math in my head. "Yeah, I guess he did." I never really thought about it, and he never spoke about it. Although, I can understand why he wouldn't want to talk about a serial killer with his little girl.

"And you have no other family in the region?"

I shake my head. "No. My father was an only child. I'm the only one left on that side, other than Papa."

A shadow looms over us, and I glance up at someone standing a couple of feet away, holding a piece of paper in his hand. "Hey ladies, wanna come to a party?"

Dani shoots up and rips the invitation from his hand. "What's this?"

He shrugs, but not before checking me out. "It's the harvest party. You ladies up for it, or are you too chicken shit? Happens every year on the first weekend of fall. It's a tradition."

I grab the invite from her and stare at the image of the mask on the front as annoyance tugs at my gut.

"A Shadowface-themed party? Really?" I roll my eyes and he grins. I can't say I'm surprised. This campus, this town, is obsessed—whispers are everywhere, and that text message was just the beginning. Calling it a harvest party is a joke when it's obvious what it is.

Everyone speaks about Shadowface as if he's a god. As if he's a deity that walks among the shadows of this town, infiltrating his evil into every stone. In actuality, he killed people. Very *real* victims. He wasn't a god; he was a fucking coward who hid his true identity.

"We'll be there," Dani muses, ignoring the guy, but excitement gleams from her face.

For whatever reason, the guy lingers for a moment, his eyes on my legs, and I wave him off. "Carry on." I frown as I play with the invitation between my fingers and stare down at the picture representing death, chaos, and evil. I shoot Dani a look as soon as he leaves. "I'm not going to this."

"Yeah, you are," she responds. "Don't be such a stick in the mud."

More people walk by, and a familiar face comes into my periphery, and I drop the invite to my lap. Black hair, a pale white face, contrasting against otherwise dark cold features...thick glasses. Sexy as fuck.

Lincoln Kennedy.

Dani notices, too, and she nudges me and loudly whispers, "Professor Hottie."

Fuck. It is him. And he's even better looking up close.

He walks toward us, his face a cool glaze. He's wearing a black T-shirt sculpted to his arms. Pants that should be illegal, given he is staff and his students are milling about. His face is so pale, he looks like a vampire.

Not a professor yet, I remind myself. *Technically, he's still a student.*

I hate that I'm looking... I hate that he has *any* of my attention. I can't help but feel a familiarity about him more than just his name.

Like maybe I've met him before, seen him before... But I distinctly remember not meeting Lincoln Kennedy—and how bitter I was about that.

I try to appear calm and avoid making direct eye contact with him. I can't help but imagine what it would be like to possess the same level of intelligence as he apparently has.

Writing a textbook...

As he strolls past me, I awkwardly adjust my posture, crossing my long, bare legs, wondering if it's possible he was my mysterious messenger last night.

He gives me nothing, no sign it was he who contacted me. He walks right by me, doesn't even spare me a glance until the very last moment. His gaze lingers on me for half a second.

My heart nearly stops as he tilts his lips to a small smile and, for the first time, he proves there is at least some warmth behind those cold, dead eyes. He turns his head and keeps walking, and I realize I'm smiling. Like really smiling back at him.

"My god. How can a nerd be that hot?" Dani's mouth is hanging open. "He totally checked you out."

"He didn't check me out," I tell her as the heat in my face rises. But a flash of recognition hits his eyes, and the inside of my belly squirms. His eyes, the way he looked at me, even if it was for only a moment...

And he's not alone, I realize. The people he's with are dressed in black, too, because apparently, it's the trendy thing to do at this campus. The two girls in his group are showing lots of skin: low cut jeans that can barely count as pants, loose, ripped T-shirts, and... Is that girl wearing a collar? I nearly choke on my tongue.

"Wasn't the Order of the Shadows banned from campus?" I mutter.

"They were," she says. "What do you mean?"

I glance down at my pink nails. I purse my lips and glance back at them, at Lincoln looking dark and broody. *This* is who my father was so fond of?

My expression flattens. "They seem satanic. And weren't they devil worshipers? They seem to fit the bill."

She snickers. "I suppose. But no dead bodies have been found recently. Whoever the Order was, they've stayed hidden."

I want to believe that...

The girl in the collar walks past us and glares. Behind her is a silver chain, and on the other end is an attractive, very muscled guy with tribal tattoos that cover each of his arms. He walks by with the cockiest grin on his face and chews on his bottom lip. His attention lingers slightly longer on Dani than on me.

"Jesus," Dani breathes, and I'm pretty sure she's drooling.

This guy has at least half an inch on Lincoln and about twenty pounds, and Lincoln's not exactly a small guy. The guy's dark features are menacing, and he looks much scarier than Lincoln.

He gives Dani a wink, causing her to seemingly lose her ability to breathe. Although none of them directly communicated with us, a lot was said. They all continue walking, giving very few fucks about the fact that *everyone* is staring at them.

"I can't imagine humiliating myself like that in public," I say, watching as they all sit in a circle close to us, the girl with the collar sitting on her knees like an obedient pet.

Dani bites her lip. "It's so hot. He's so fucking hot. That is *sooooo* fucking hot."

"It's not."

She scoffs. "Well, you're not overly sexual, Summer."

I jab her in the ribs. "I am sexual; I just haven't found anyone I want to have sex with. There's a big difference."

She cocks a brow and finally tears her gaze away from the group. "I just don't believe you're a virgin."

I'm not a virgin, but I can't explain it, so I don't say anything.

I watch as Lincoln grabs his backpack and starts reading his textbook, away from the others. He keeps pushing his glasses up, as if they might fall off.

I fold my arms. "It's disgusting. Those girls are humiliating themselves for someone else's sick pleasure."

"Deliciously disgusting," she echoes, but can't keep her eyes off them, either.

The insides of my belly squirm watching them.

"So, I couldn't help myself... I did some digging last night, and found out more about Lincoln," Dani says.

I smirk at her. "Of course you did."

"Here's what I found out. Lincoln Kennedy and his posse are rich as shit. And elitists...*super* snobby. And he's very smart, but he's not just Dr. Garcia's PhD student; he's her adopted son."

My eyes shoot up, watching Lincoln from this new perspective. How could I have missed this? But that would explain my father's affinity to him, given his professional relationship with Dr. Garcia. My father never talked about him, only the work he did with him. He was a mentor to Lincoln, and apparently, was for a long time.

"Do you see the really hot one holding on to that leash?"

How could I *not* see him? His hulking presence is hard to ignore.

She smiles. "His name is Xander, and he's Dr. Garcia's grandson."

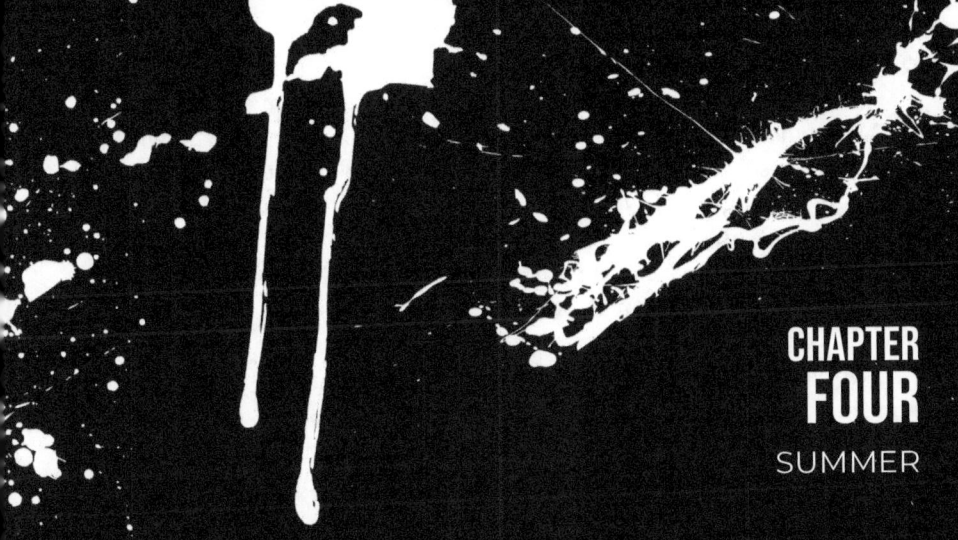

"Why do you want to go to this party so badly?" I ask Dani as we drive back to the house after class.

"Because we get to wear one of those creepy masks all night." Dani says it without shame and with a devilish smile. Shame, however, rises from the pits of my stomach and blooms in my chest.

We cruise through the windy roads of our town as we pass giant brick houses, rows and rows of homes of people who seem to be thriving here, despite the endless fall and dreary weather. Opulence is evident, with luxury vehicles parked in each driveway.

I fiddle with the party invite, running my hand along the devilish face with eyes that seem to jump out of the picture—eyes that haunt my dreams and seep into my soul.

Shadowface is everywhere.

I grab the overhead handle to keep my balance because Dani drives so erratically. She always drives like a maniac and seems to thrive off fear and danger. Always forcing me on the scariest rollercoasters and cliff diving, doing whatever she can to get a thrill. It's a wonder I'm not dead already just by driving with her or spending the summer in Europe with her.

"So we have to go worship him and dance around? I don't really want to wear a mask all night. It's weird memorializing him, given what he is."

She seems utterly unconcerned. "That's exactly why I'm going. It will be so exciting hooking up with a stranger."

My stomach tingles, but not in a bad way...more like the way when you're doing something naughty and don't want to get caught.

"Ugh. Dani, gross. I would never fuck someone when I don't know what they look like."

Even though that's exactly what I did...at least, I think. I'm still not convinced that night was real, but I remember his flesh as I dug my nails into his skin.

Two years ago... That night was two years ago, and I haven't seen him since.

My nameless monster who tormented my nightmares for years before he finally had sex with me. Every few months, I'd sense him lurking in the corner. Watching. Waiting. Protecting.

I never once saw his face.

She turns her attention away from the road and gives me the most obnoxious smile. "I'll bet Lincoln and Xander will be there."

I press my lips together. "Lincoln is our TA. Why would he be there?"

"Ahem... PhD student. Emphasize the *student*, Summer. And he gave you eyes, I saw it. And he's not that old; he's only two years older than you."

I don't argue with that; he did give me eyes. Something passed between us when he walked by me and in class. Recognition maybe? My father must have spoken about me to him. My last name is also apparent. He would have seen it on the class roster and potentially made the connection.

"Fine. But Xander seems like he's taken. Or did you miss that?"

A distant expression flashes over her eyes, and a hint of something predatory flickers in them. "From my perspective, that girl doesn't own anyone. He was watching me the entire time she was kneeling in front of him. He doesn't seem interested in her."

I don't argue with that, either. When Dani sets her sights on someone, men don't stand a chance.

I cross my arms in one last act of defiance. "I seem to be the only person in this town bothered by the fact that some creep sent a photo of a nearly naked dead girl to everyone. Why does that not upset you?"

Her hand finds mine on the console. "Shadowface is part of this town, Summer. Don't fight him; just have fun for once. And girl, you need to get laid. Now quit looking at that invitation like you're going to throw up on it. We're going to that party. At least it's not for a week and a half, so you have lots of time to mentally prepare yourself."

A spark of heat settles into my veins and starts to build in places it shouldn't, so I clench my legs together to make it go away. I don't say anything as desire pulses inside me the rest of the ride home.

We finally pull up on our street and she parks the car in front of our house, pulling the keys out of the ignition. A small Mini Cooper is parked in front of us with heart-shaped bumper stickers on the back. I already don't like her.

"Relax, Summer. Don't be so uptight. This party is a tradition, and students have kept it going for years. It's obviously non-sanctioned, but the university can't do shit about people getting together in the woods. Apparently, it gets wild, and I'm not missing it."

The real reason Dani wanted to come to this school is because the parties are epic. We heard everything about them growing up.

I can't help the nagging sense that something about this is different.

Someone is watching me. Whoever was messing with me last night could identify my exact outfit as I laid in my room. But she's probably right; whoever Shadowface was, it was a different time. Over twenty years later, the game has changed, and whoever did it wouldn't get away with it today. Not with wi-fi and surveillance cameras everywhere.

That was a different era. Now we just have mass shootings. Same sick fucks, different method of madness.

I sense Dani's intense gaze on my cheek. "Are you going to be okay? You haven't had a chance to process everything about your father."

I give her a heavy smile and let out a sigh. "I'm trying, I really am. I'll be fine."

This town holds a piece of him, a side I'm unfamiliar with. My scholarship letter was like a sign from him for me to follow in his footsteps, and I had to seize the moment. After a year of community college upgrading, I was supposed to transfer to a completely different school on the opposite side of the country. This was a last-minute decision. The fact Dani was transferring here was just icing on the cake.

She places a consoling hand on my arm. "You said that last week, but you really don't seem okay."

Darkness flickers inside me, planting its deep roots, simmering like hot coals. I'm not sure I'll ever see the world in rose color again. I had to watch my father die over the course of three days. And I sensed...nothing. The same emptiness inside I had for years. I only ever seem to feel alive when I'm dreaming.

In fact, the only real emotion I've experienced in years was the arousal last night from the mysterious messenger and the anticipation that my nameless monster was coming back to me.

I force a tear, since I'm good at displaying fake emotion for the sake of others. It seems to put people at ease. "People lose parents, Dani. It's a part of the cycle of life. I just lost one early. I'll be alright."

My eyes draw back to the Mini Cooper, trying to avoid her stare, hoping she can't tell I'm faking.

"Come on," Dani says, reading my mind. "Time to go meet Misty. And you need to be nice to her."

I stick out my tongue at Dani before following her inside.

I'll attempt to be pleasant. I'm not sure why I am the way I am, letting very few people in. I have the perfect life; I had parents who loved each other. I grew up in a nice house in the quiet suburbs, where people left the doors unlocked and the windows open at night.

It's like I'm battling internal demons, except I'm uncertain what caused them. I can't pinpoint what the problem is. I'm a perfectly put together puzzle, except the last piece is missing, so the entire thing is soiled.

Without that missing piece, I'm soiled.

Our tiny house still smells of used boxes as we walk in as we've been taking our time unpacking. I startle when I see Misty, at how similar she is to me, her hair not quite as white, but still a shimmering blonde.

She's pretty…not beautiful. But pretty.

She's bent over, grabbing something from a box. Her eyes light up when she sees us, and I try to repress my immediate sense of jealousy. Of course she has to be blonde and well put together. I put on a fake smile, the one I've eloquently practiced my whole life.

"You must be Misty!" Dani hugs her, and I can already see her driving a wedge between us. Dani looks right at me. "Summer and I have been looking forward to having you here."

We have not looked forward to her moving in, Dani has. The house isn't big enough, but Dani likes to take in strays.

I smile sweetly. "Super excited. We get to share a bathroom." Dani, of course, has the master bedroom with an ensuite since she's paying more.

I took the loft bedroom, which means Misty and I will share the main bathroom, and I'm not happy about it.

Misty looks over at me and frowns. "Thank you for letting me stay here. There is literally no place to rent at all in this town, and the dorms were all full by the time I decided to come here."

"No problem at all," Dani assures her. "Right, Summer?" Dani responded to a last-minute plea for a roommate and offered our spare room. So here we are...

"Right."

"I saw you in psychology," Misty says, parting her perfect heart-shaped lips. I take in her appearance, evaluating her. She's pretty, just not as pretty as me. Her frame is more boxy than curvy. She shifts uncomfortably, noticing me looking at everything but her eyes.

"Oh man," Dani says, "that course is going to be brutal."

She darts her gaze uncomfortably. "It's going to be interesting. Dr. Garcia is fascinating, and did you *see* the TA?"

Dani gives me a wink and I ignore it.

He smiled at me, Dani. Relax.

"What did you think of that photo?" Misty asks.

Dani grabs our leftover take out Chinese food from last night and takes a bite. "Creepy as fuck," she says, chewing with her mouth open. "But we're going to that party on the twenty-first if you want to come?"

Misty's eyes widen. "Yeah, I'll go to that."

I walk to the fridge and grab a bottle of water, avoiding all of Misty's annoying boxes, and my phone lights up on the counter beside me.

Dani looks at me and smiles. "See now you have to go, Summer. Misty's coming, too."

I glance down at the phone and swipe open the message. My world dims and I can barely register Dani's voice. This time, there is no mistaking it...

It's a similar photo as the one sent to the class, but it's zoomed out and there is no mask on her head. And this time there is no mistaking the arched ceilings above me.

It's a photo of me sleeping in my bed, my breasts hanging out, the blanket hanging off my hips. My heart nearly bursts out of my chest. It was taken in this house...the one I've lived in for less than a week. Dani and I only moved in on Saturday.

"Are you okay, Summer?" Dani and Misty stop their conversation and both stare at me.

My breath catches in my throat. "Yeah," I lie. "I'm going to go study."

I excuse myself and burst into my bedroom and immediately slam my window shut.

CHAPTER
FIVE
SUMMER

I barely sleep, nightmares plaguing my mind as I toss and turn all night, still not used to the creaky house or the eerie silence of this smaller rural town. I'm used to noise. Mystic is much bigger than Kinsmen.

Here? I can hear a pin drop. Or someone scream.

I didn't hear anyone scream, although I screamed in my dream. The kind where no sounds come out.

I roll over in my bed and realize I'm sticky with sweat dripping down my back. I've slept with my window open for the last six years, and last night was the first night I slept with it closed. Moonlight streamed through my window, making the trees sparkle with an ethereal glow.

Six years… It's been six years since I first saw him in the corner of my bedroom in that burlap mask, six years since he started visiting me at night. Two years since he stole my innocence, with no sign of him since. Before then, he only watched me, and sometimes he touched me, but it was mainly desperate whispers in my dreams of how much he hated me.

After years of visiting me during the darkest parts of the night, he finally fucked me. His body was pressed against mine, and I opened my legs, inviting him in. After the initial shock of what was happening, and the first jolt of pain from when he pushed into me, my body absorbed him.

I died a little inside at how good he was. His hands were soft, inviting. He lifted his mask only to kiss me, and his kisses were intoxicating.

37

I wasn't scared. At that point, I had already fallen in love with him. I simply couldn't accept that he hated me, especially considering his actions didn't align with his words. Over the years, whenever I had my recurring nightmare, he seemed to be there at the edge of my bed with that creepy mask, caressing my hairline with his thumb, telling me it was going to be okay.

It makes me wonder how often he was there, and I was unaware.

Then he was gone and never came back, and I had no proof he was real—other than the blood on my sheets when I woke up the next morning. I waited for him the next night, and the days and weeks after. I left the window open, hoping he'd return, but he never did.

He ruined me.

Over the years, I've convinced myself he was not real; I could have easily made myself bleed while dreaming of him.

I grab my phone and see a missed text from Dani.

Dani: *You good up there?*

It was from three hours ago. It's now three in the morning, so I don't respond.

The air in my room is suffocating, so I rise and open the window, inviting the cool crisp fall air into my room. I glance outside and see the outline of the dark firs and the stars in the clear night. No masked man, nothing but a hint of mist and the twinkling morning dew.

He's not real...my nightmare. My dreams are not real.

That missing fragment of a memory I keep replaying in my head but can't quite grasp. The cause of nightmares I've had since I was a child.

I pull up the photos *again* and stare at them, as if I didn't stare at them enough last night. There is no question now—the girl in the first photo is me, both pictures were clearly taken the same night.

My hand moves to my breast, to my small and tight nipples. I run my hands over them like he used to, kissing my skin with my fingertips, driving my body crazy.

My body becomes ravished at the memory of him...the longing I can't get rid of.

Taking a deep breath, I open the text and respond to the unknown number. My head begins to swirl. I should call 911, but my emotions are overriding my better judgment.

Summer: *What do you want from me?*

My body slumps forward, and I remember that dream. The soft whispers, the deadly aura that surrounded him.

Unknown Number: *I missed you, pretty girl.*

Pretty girl. My nameless monster used to call me that. He never used my name, it was always, pretty girl.

My hand whips to my mouth. Tears sting the backs of my eyes, and it takes a few seconds for me to regain my composure.

My nameless monster is back.

"Fuck me," I whisper. The sick fuck is real, even though I've spent the last two years convincing myself he wasn't. And now he's here. Watching me, waiting for something.

Summer: *Were you the one messaging me on the class site?*

Unknown Number: *I was just trying to help you, Summer.*

I scramble up and shut my window again, checking to make sure it's locked. I creep downstairs as goosebumps pebble my exposed flesh and I head into the kitchen.

Tripping over a box, I stub my toe. "Fuck's sakes," I grumble as a debilitating pain shoots up my foot, and I kick the box out of the way.

A draft hits my skin and I turn my head to find the drapes flowing over the window. Dani must have left it open. I rush over and shut that, too, before checking the front door, making a note to give her hell for leaving a window open.

I turn the light on, half expecting someone to jump out at me, but our tiny house is vacant. Just Misty's mess still strewn about and Chinese takeout boxes littering the counter and two empty wineglasses they neglected to wash before bed.

I let out my breath and head upstairs, locking my bedroom door as a precaution before pulling the covers over me entirely.

Not that covers ever stopped him before… And now it seems like my stalker from high school is in my psychology class.

I wake up in a daze a couple of hours later, my throat dry and lips parched. The sun is streaming into the room now, and it's like a sauna. I rise and open the window; the sunshine increases my sense of security. He never came to me when the sun was shining, as if he belonged to the night.

I stare at my tiny desk in the corner, and the pile of textbooks beckons me to read. Luckily, my first class doesn't start until ten today, so I have some time to catch up and do the reading I wasn't able to last night. My sleep was fitful at best for obvious reasons.

I swallow hard and grab my computer, pulling up my first weekly reflection, which I haven't been able to start.

My phone is on my nightstand taunting me, but I ignore it. SF never texted me back last night, and I never responded to him, either. But that's not unusual. The text message was the first time I've communicated with him other than with my eyes.

All those nights, while I was in a sleep-induced haze waiting for him, when I tried to say something, his hand caught my mouth, and I couldn't breathe. The first time I screamed, I thought he might kill me, so I learned to stay quiet.

I open my computer and log onto the class site and stare down at the email address listed for Lincoln Kennedy.

He is the only person left linking me to this place. He knew my father, and I can't rule out the possibility he's behind this. What I can't fathom is why?

He's so...coveted, accomplished, and brilliant. It's hard to comprehend his motivations for stalking and tormenting a teenage girl who lives in another town. Why would he threaten everything he's built here? I can't, however, ignore the obvious connection to me.

My stomach sinks, remembering the basis of his research. He and my father studied fear, anger, and all the other ickiest emotions, and he would have had easy access to me. Especially since my father was so close to Dr. Garcia, who is his adoptive mother.

An inkling in my stomach tells me I'm missing something. The flashes of familiarity that passed between Lincoln and me. Nothing concrete enough to really remember him, though.

Just a feeling.

I open an empty Word document and can't seem to put words on the page. It doesn't help that I haven't started the readings beyond the articles on research methods in the social sciences, and I'm utterly determined to make it the best it can be, knowing who is grading it. That is, if I can bring myself to pick up my father's textbook and actually start it.

The fresh aroma of coffee seeps into my room, distracting me, and my mouth salivates. I throw on some yoga pants, some mascara, a tank top with a denim jacket, throw my hair into a messy bun, and head out of my room. When I'm down the steep steps, Dani and Misty are huddled around the phone at the kitchen table, both of their faces etched with concern. Neither of them acknowledges me.

A pot of coffee is almost empty, and the delicious scent is wafting through the room.

"What's going on?" I ask, pulling out a mug from the cupboard. Dani, looking fresh in baggy jeans and a cropped shirt showing off her tight and toned belly, finally notices me. I see they both have fresh cups of coffee, and no one bothered to call me down as I pour myself the burnt bit at the bottom.

Dani narrows her brows. "You look like shit." Dani isn't anything if she's not honest.

I merely huff and take a sip, watching them.

"Summer, come watch this. This is seriously scary," Misty says, being nice enough. I only join them when Dani turns up the volume and the name Shadowface hits my ear, catching my attention. The mere mention of his name piques my curiosity, just like everyone else who has caught the fever of him.

Only a few days at this university, and I'm already just as obsessed as everyone else is. His compulsion is strong, and I have a weird desire for more. To understand it all...even the dark parts I shouldn't be so interested in. And now, I need to find out if I am somehow connected to it all.

It's a live press conference, the red banner at the bottom of the news feed.

Breaking News—

"Remember yesterday when you said that photo was new?" Dani asks. "That you didn't see that photo online when we were checking out the Shadowface victims?"

My heart falters. "Yeah."

"Well, you were right. The news just broke this morning. That photo has never been seen before. She's new and wasn't part of the four victims of the 2002 copycat."

Bile hits my throat and I stand in stunned silence.

Rather than respond, I take a moment to savor my coffee. It's as if my brain understands what I need to do but can't.

Misty shakes her head. "I doubt she's new. She was still killed over twenty years ago. It's just fresh evidence."

My throat goes dry. "Are you sure about that?"

How can I possibly describe the inexplicable? I am absolutely certain that the photo is me. It seems like the first photo has spread everywhere.

My lifeless body is displayed like a doll. At least the second photo, the one he only shared with me, is all mine.

The taste of ash lingers in my mouth. The entire campus gazing at me in that way was already distressing enough, but now it's being broadcasted on the national news as well?

Dani's eyes meet mine. "It must be old. It has to be. They haven't found any other evidence. Someone out there would have missed a girl who looked like that."

Misty quirks her head, studying her, then looks directly at me. "She seems so...sexual. It's all so erotic."

Red blurs my vision. "Shut up, Misty. Have some fucking respect for the dead."

Misty's mouth gapes open. "Sorry...I didn't mean anything by it."

I slide in next to Dani, attempting to steady my trembling hands. Dani shoots me a glance, but I choose to ignore it, focusing on the reporter who is positioned in front of a building on campus. The place will be swarming today. Authorities are looking into the origin of the text message on the first day of class and are advising everyone not to panic but remain vigilant.

"This is so messed up," Dani whispers as the reporter shifts gears.

More breaking news—

"Look," Misty says, pointing at the screen, her eyes bulging. "They found a connection. A girl went missing at a community college a few counties over three days ago. They believe it's connected to the photo that was sent to our class. Like a copycat killer."

This catches my attention...

I shuffle closer to get a better view of the live footage. The missing girl is blonde, of course. I can't help but run my fingers over a lock of my hair. The color is eerily similar to my platinum white.

Her name is Cali, and she went missing while running in the woods. I guess it didn't make headlines until now. Her friends and family can't locate her, and the media from her town questions if this is connected, although the local police haven't confirmed it. She was officially declared missing this morning, but the problem is, without the body, they can't tell for sure.

Heat singes my neck and face, and a pain develops in my jaw from my clenched teeth.

"I was so sure," I whisper under my breath, my heart leaping beneath my skin. The face in the photo that was sent to the class was covered in the mask, so it's possible I might have misunderstood everything. Or perhaps the first photo was Cali, and I'm his next target and the picture he sent me was a warning?

I'm completely lost now. My mind is spiralling.

"So sure of what?" Dani asks, but I shake my head.

"Nothing. Forget I said anything."

"It's not the same girl," Misty points out. "The hair color is similar for sure, but the body type is a touch different. The girl in the photo is curvier, like an hourglass. Kind of like you, Summer."

My lips part slightly and I try to stop my voice from coming out wobbly. No words escape my lips, no matter how hard I try.

Dani looks at me carefully, watches the slight quivering of my hand. She rests hers on mine. "Girl, are you okay? Don't worry, the police are saying not to jump to conclusions. You know what this town is like."

I flip my eyes up to Dani and Misty, their gazes locking on mine as I brush a strand of hair from my eyes under their scrutiny.

Tell her... Tell someone about him. Show her the photo he saved just for me.

But I don't, because if I do, it will be over. It will stop, or he will hide, and I will never find out what he wants from me.

"But they aren't certain of that," I remind her.

"Who do you think sent it?" Misty asks.

Dani says, her lips pressed together in a tight line, "If you want my opinion, I suspect the Order's behind it. Their whole ideology was about creating disorder and chaos, and I'd say this is creating disorder and chaos."

I observe her closely, wondering how she knows that, and ask, "Will they cancel the party because of this? I mean, a girl is missing."

Dani shrugs. "I bet it's all just an elaborate prank someone orchestrated to set the mood. They are trying to make everyone scared. And personally, I like to be a little scared."

Yeah, scared...not tied up and erased from existence.

My hand finds the back of my neck. "Yeah, you're probably right."

Dani smirks and leans her elbows on the island. "Good, then you're still coming?"

No. I'm not going to that fucking party. Not when there's a potential copycat killer targeting me, or the fact I couldn't be bothered. I don't want to glorify murder.

"Fine, I'll go." I immediately regret my words. My willpower with Dani is non-existent, and I know she won't let up. I'll shoot my shot with the slim chance someone actually wants to murder me. And maybe, just maybe, he'll finally reveal himself to me. If there was ever a place, that would be it.

I gather my books and head out the door with a shaking sense of dread that going to this party is a really terrible fucking mistake.

CHAPTER
SIX
SUMMER

D riving through the outskirts of Kinsmen is a stark contrast to driving in town. It's truly remarkable how much darkness encompasses this place, with its quiet, old houses scattered among the never-ending trees. Time has lost its significance, with secrets that predate the Bible.

I relax in the passenger seat. It's so still, with a silent mist hovering in the air. The weather is so dreary and quiet, making me wonder if the birds have abandoned this place. If the lore is real, then these woods are indeed cursed.

Dani took the long way to campus today, wanting to check out some places in town we haven't seen yet. Eventually, the trees and houses thin out into barren, rolling hills and grasslands.

My heart leaps as she turns onto a dusty road, and all my senses tingle like we're being watched. "Maybe we should turn back," I tell her. "Something about this area gives me the creeps."

She points up ahead through the mist as raindrops fall on the windshield. "Over there, it's some sort of store. The abandoned warehouse I was looking for." She drives closer. The roads out here aren't even paved, as if the wealth and privilege stopped at the tree line and there is nothing enchanting about this place.

Everything is dusty.

We drive toward the abandoned building, the name *Fresh Mart* still sun-bleached on the side of the building, even though the sign has long been taken down. Something about it is familiar. My Papa used to talk about the *Fresh Mart*; he used to go meet my grandmother there, because that's where she worked. I had no idea it looked like this.

My palms begin to sweat as she drives past it and carries onto the road beyond. "Where are we going, exactly?" I ask her and glance back at the abandoned general store, which looks nothing more than an abandoned warehouse. At this point, it seems like we are driving through tall grass that leads to nowhere with a few scattered trees that look like they got rejected, too.

She fires me a devious smirk. "There is an old, haunted house out this way, and I wanted to check out in the daylight hours."

My heart leaps. "Dani, really? We're going to be late for class."

"Relax. We have lots of time. We are going to do a quick drive by for my research."

Research? What kind of research is she doing?

"I'm trying to piece together all the weird things that have happened in this town. Plus, this place gives me the creeps, and I want to find out what happened here. I need ten minutes, then I'll take us back to Kinsmen."

I can't stop her. She's hellbent on doing this, and it's not long before I realize we are going to a place that holds a piece of my history. My grandmother lived in a house near the *Fresh Mart* and used to walk there for work. The house, from what I've heard from my Papa, had bad things happen in it before she lived there. It must be the same place.

We carry on, and it doesn't take long for us to find the skeletal remains of a home deep in the grass, as if the grass has taken over it. Its walls are crumbling, broken and haunted, and if we weren't specifically looking for it, we could have easily missed it.

She stops the car, and we both stare at it. I'm sure as shit not getting out of the car if that's what she's expecting.

"How creepy is that?" I mutter. "There isn't even a road that leads up to it."

"They call it the Old Sheffield Place," Dani says. "Apparently, a man in the 1950s ended up going insane and killed his wife and daughter in this home. They found his body face down in a field a few months later. Rumor has it, everyone who lived here after him lost their minds, too. They ended up condemning it in the 80s after more bad things happened, so no one wants to go near it in case they end up going insane, too. So now it's here, rotting away…"

My grandmother wasn't born into wealth like my grandfather was.

She lived in this house after the Sheffield family died; she was here during the slaughters of 1979. This was her home. Dani doesn't realize she's speaking about my family.

A prickle shoots down my spine and a haunting image pushes into my vision. This fragment of an image, the same in my nightmares. The memory I can't quite grasp then shifts into an image of my beautiful grandmother going insane.

Everyone who lives here goes insane.

I take a shuddering breath, staring at this old house that's part of my ancestry.

I turn to face Dani, who is white as a ghost, as if she can sense the intensity of this place, too. "Can we go now?"

She nods and peels away, kicking dust up as we head back into the affluent, and much safer, part of town.

As soon as we drive back into town, I relax. That is, until my phone vibrates, and I hold my breath as I swipe the message open and read it.

Unknown number: *Good morning, Summer.*

Summer, not pretty girl.

I lower my gaze and frown, but my skin starts to buzz with excitement. I don't answer, but I do insert the number in my contacts under SF. A few minutes go by before he texts again.

SF: *Ignoring me already?*

Not knowing what to say, I nibble on my lip as a burning heat settles between my thighs. I scroll up and see the picture he sent of me a couple of nights ago.

Dani is oblivious to what I'm looking at and turns the music to an uncomfortable level as she zips toward campus as drops of rain patter around us. I stare out into those trees, although my heart is taking a beating.

SF: *Have you decided yet?*

What the hell do I even say to that?

Summer: *Have I decided what?*

He responds quickly.

SF: *If you want my help?*

I grimace at the phone. That's what he wants to talk about right now? Not about why he snuck into my room and took a photo of me sleeping. I stare down and admire how pretty I am as a dead girl, and that thrashing pulse hits me again.

Undeniably turned on by it.

Summer: *No thank you. I've found someone else to study with.*

The rain dances across the windshield while the breeze gains strength outside. The drops grow in intensity, pounding on the glass with such force that it reverberates inside my head. Dani calmly increases the volume of the music and taps her hand along to the beat on the steering wheel.

SF: *Is that so?*

My manicured nails tap against the keyboard.

Summer: *That is so. That is what you get for being creepy.*

Fuck, I'm playing with fire. And why isn't he saying anything concrete... Why isn't he calling me pretty girl?

He always calls me pretty girl.

SF: *You mean nice? I've been very nice to you, given the circumstances.*

Dani turns down the music and nudges me. "Who are you talking to?

I jerk away and place my phone on my lap face down, hoping she didn't catch me admiring the photo of myself. "No one."

Her eyes widen and she reaches for my cell. "What are you looking at?"

I yank the phone out of reach. "The photo, okay?" She obviously saw me looking at it. She doesn't have to know it's an entirely different photo than the one sent out to the class or that it's a much more revealing one.

If she notices my bare breasts, she doesn't say anything. "Okay...you don't have to act so skittish. I was just asking."

"Focus on the road, will you?" I yell as she swerves into the oncoming traffic lane. "It's honestly no one important."

She narrows her eyes. "Doesn't seem like no one. You're scowling."

I cross my arms. "It's some guy from psychology who wants to study with me."

Her grin grows to ridiculous heights. "Some guy? You've met a guy already and haven't told me. Spill the details... Now."

I let out a huff. "I don't know who he is. We made plans to meet up, but I'm breaking it off."

She turns the music down. "Sounds scandalous. How did you meet him?"

I lean my head against the window and watch the water drip down in spirals. "It's not scandalous. I met him online on our class site. We were just chatting a bit, but now he's being creepy, so I'm cutting it off."

"What's his name? I'll look him up."

"I don't know."

She slams on the brakes and looks at me. "You don't know?"

I grab the handle on the top and hold on tight. "Jesus, Dani. Please watch the road. He never told me his name, which is why you're reacting for no reason, and also why I'm not going to meet him. With everything going on, I'm freaked out."

"Good, because I think you should go get some extra help from Lincoln."

I frown. "Will you stop?"

She gives me a scandalous grin. "Stop what?"

"Being horny all the damn time. All you think about is sex."

She shrugs. "And you don't think about it at all."

I raise my eyebrows. "That's not true. I'm just picky." I realize the reason behind my pickiness is because my nameless monster ruined the experience for me. Losing my virginity to him meant everything to me. It was a high I never thought I'd experience again. The idea of being intimate with someone else was painful, so I chose not to have sex again. Simple as that.

She whips around a corner much too fast, considering we are in a residential area. "Well, I think he's hot. I'm personally not into the hot nerd goth vibe, but I could see you with him. And girl, you really need a good healthy dose of dick. Plus, if he's a genius like everyone says he is, imagine what kinds of things he could do between the sheets."

I huff a breath and lean back in the seat.

She tilts her head and says softly, "I wish you were sexual, Summer. You have to give people a chance."

I am sexual. I'm just turned on by things I shouldn't be. Things I can never verbalize that make my toes curl.

"You're insufferable, but you know that," I tell her.

Dani looks at me and frowns, but doesn't push the subject, even though I can tell she wants to call me out on my bullshit.

My phone vibrates again, and I turn my gaze downward to a new message.

SF: *Are you still there, or did I lose you?*

I type out a quick response to him.

Summer: *Impatient much? Please stop messaging me.*

There...I said it.

We pull into the parking lot of campus and my stomach drops when he sends me a link. My eyes narrow as I click on it, and the news link of the missing girl comes up on my screen.

The blonde girl from the news today.

My doppelgänger.

SF: *You better play nice with me, Summer.*

I let out a small gasp, but keep my phone hidden and quickly recover before Dani notices. Even though my face has gone completely white.

Summer: *This is enough evidence to incriminate you.*

SF: *You won't tell anyone, because you never did. You need my help. I'm the only one who can protect you from him.*

Him? Who is he talking about? *He's* the one doing this to me.

SF: *See you at the party.*

My palms break out in a cold sweat. This entire conversation played out differently from how I imagined it would go. The tone of these texts is very much how I'd picture Lincoln speaking, but this is not how I remember my nameless monster. This is not the man in my dreams.

Despite his mask, his raw emotions always found a way into my heart. The person on the other end of this line is far more calculating and logical—I'd say he's almost soulless.

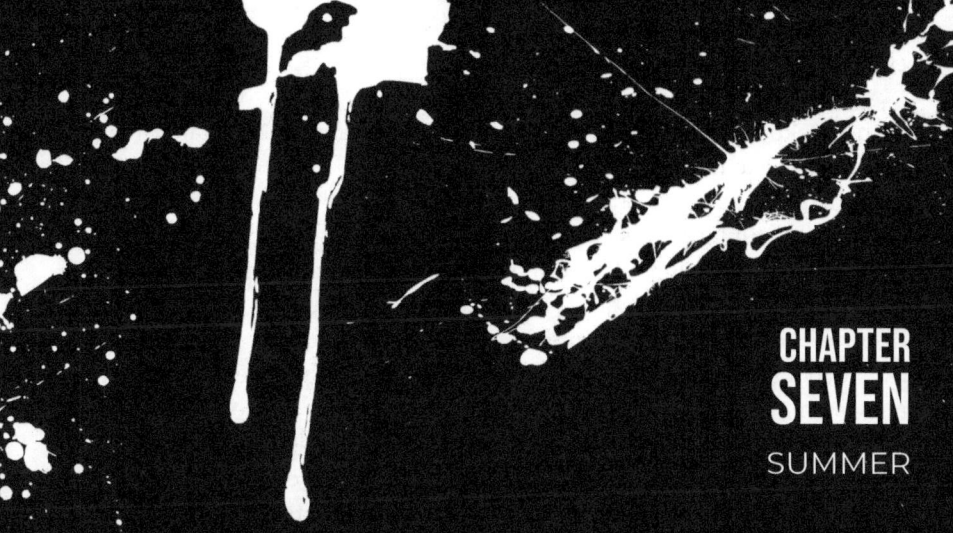

CHAPTER
SEVEN
SUMMER

My body is frozen during my hour-long English-lit class as we study Shakespeare. The chill underpinning my bones is penetrating, and it's not from getting caught in the icy rain with Dani as we bolted across campus speckled with the endless brick gardens and gargoyles. It's because I am finally realizing how much danger I'm in.

I'm still contemplating everything swirling through my brain after the initial shock of SF sending me the news link, insinuating he's behind Cali's disappearance.

Normal people would be scared shitless with such a threat. Normal people wouldn't have a hit of arousal at the thought of a serial killer targeting them. Normal people would experience guilt for possessing evidence about a missing girl's potential abductor and doing nothing about it.

A missing girl… There is a missing girl, Summer. A girl who looks like you.

I head into the dark and damp lecture hall for psychology class. A dull, persistent ache throbs in my jaw from the hour I spent clenching my teeth, haunted by the vision of her pretty face. The thought of her with him is a vice around my mind.

Seeing Dani wave from the back, I make my way to the back row. Lincoln is directly in front of me when I turn. A dark ripple cuts through me when our eyes connect and that excitement bursts through me.

The moment is fleeting. A darkness settles deep in my core as he stops in front of me. I freeze as I take him in close up. His sexy onyx hair contrasts with his pale face, his eyes behind his glasses look like stone, with cheekbones that could slice me open. He's a good foot taller than me, so I have to lift my head to look at him.

When I do, recognition pours through me.

I have definitely crossed paths with him before, I am certain of it—a quick meeting in a dimly lit room. However, a distinct image of someone else, with a sharp and clear face, suddenly comes to mind. It is a distorted and long-forgotten memory.

He looks me up and down, and the two hundred people in this room are watching me gawk at him and clam up like I have a schoolgirl crush.

He smiles at me, and even his teeth are perfect, along with his juicy lips. His hand finds my arm and my heart rate soars to incredible heights. "Excuse me," he says, his voice deep and inviting.

My thighs clench and I nibble on my lip as I look at him, trying to imagine him on the other end of that phone.

"Excuse me, what?" I breathe, recalling the countless nights my nameless monster caressed me and the night he was nearly my undoing.

He adjusts his glasses and leans in. "I have to get by you."

Heat blooms to my face as a couple of people watching us chuckle. "Oh…yeah. Of course." I shift over to let him by, and he grabs my hand briefly as he slinks past, as if apologizing for me making an ass out of myself.

He didn't recognize me. Of course he didn't recognize me. There was nothing in his eyes that indicated he knows who I am. Because why would he?

It's someone else, then. It's got to be someone else. No one is that good of an actor.

I bolt up the steps and take a seat next to Dani as I watch Lincoln take his usual seat down below.

Dani shoots me an incredulous look, her eyes wide with a mixture of amusement and concern, but before she can comment on my foul mood or how I was just caught gawking at our TA in front of everyone, someone slides in beside me, a welcome distraction.

I peer over and find a tall, athletic, cute guy in the chair next to me.

"Is this seat taken?" he asks.

My heart pounds and I force a smile and steal a glance at him. He smells good, like a mixture of spice and sweat.

"No, go ahead."

He sits next to me, placing his arm around the back of my chair as he makes it obvious he is checking me out.

A nervous flutter hits me—not from the proximity of the attractive stranger, but from the chilling certainty of unseen eyes on me. I keep my eyes on Lincoln, his profile sharp against the dim light, but he doesn't turn to face me.

"My name is Grant. What's your name?"

I cup my hand into his to shake it. "Summer," I say with a shaky breath.

His eyes flicker as they draw down to my chest, and I can't help but tuck my hair behind my ear in a flirty gesture. If SF is watching, I want him to see this.

Dani leans over. "Hi, I'm Dani, and this is Misty."

Misty is grinning at him like an idiot, and he smiles back at her, his gaze lingering on her for a second longer than I want before directing it back to my chest.

"How's your semester going, Summer?"

He has eyes on me. Dani and Misty are irrelevant to him as I work toward keeping his attention by straightening my back and pressing my chest out. I highly doubt Grant is my nameless monster, but the knowledge that SF is potentially watching fills me with a thrilling, nervous energy.

I avert my gaze playfully. "Super busy so far. You?"

He chuckles. "That's an understatement. This course is going to kick my ass. Where are you girls from?"

"Upstate."

He leans further into me. "I'm from New York State on a football scholarship. Do you like watching football?"

A football player—typical.

As a child, I dreamt about my future, and I always pictured myself with a football player. But now, the thought of being with someone like Grant is just plain boring.

"Not really," I reply.

He frowns. "Are you going to the harvest party?" Even his questions are boring. I immediately dismiss the idea that he is the one behind those texts. I'm just not getting the vibe. He seems too nice, even if he can't stop staring at my tits.

I shrug. "I'm not planning on it."

Dani elbows me while Misty cranes her neck, trying to hear what's going on.

"Yes," Dani says, chewing on her pen. "She is."

Grant's gaze drops to my chest again—his eyes are thick and merciless—his tongue grazing his lip.

Ugh. Why?

The lights dim, and Professor Garcia clicks onto the stage with her stilettos. Grant nudges me slightly. "Do you want to meet up sometime? I'd love to show you a good time."

Dani leans over my seat. "She'd love to."

Grant pulls his hand from around me and grabs his phone, laying it across my lap. Too close to places his hand shouldn't be close to. "Here, put your number in."

I glare at Dani and grab Grant's phone, inserting my phone number, and immediately, he texts me back so I have his number. "Great." I feign a smile. "I'll text you. It will be fun to meet up at the party."

Perhaps a football player could be useful to have along. I need a certain level of protection from the psychopath.

Thank fuck the party is still over a week away.

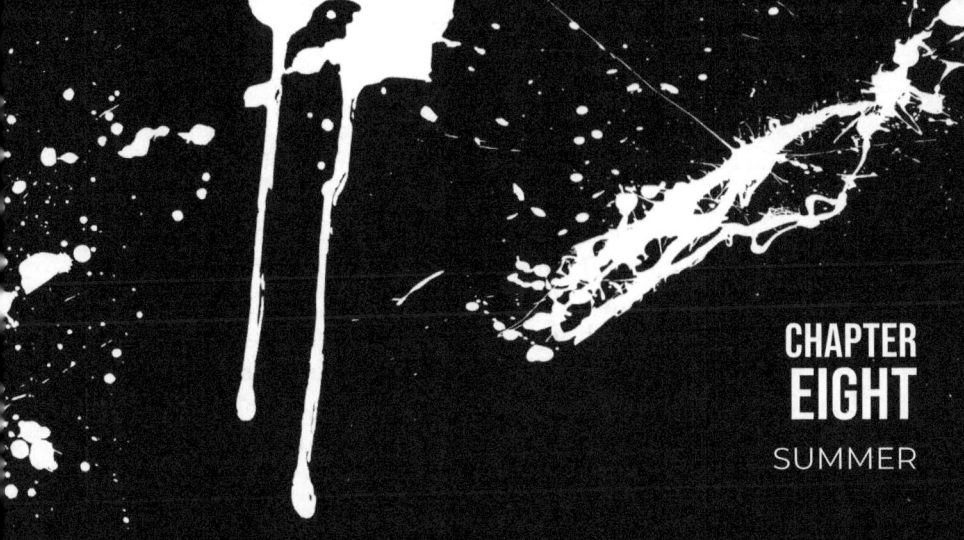

CHAPTER
EIGHT
SUMMER

It's Friday, the last lecture of the week. The last two days have been quiet, with no texts from SF, and I'm still not able to bring myself to write my first weekly reflection, even though it's due at midnight.

Lincoln is absent today—perhaps he doesn't need to attend every lecture. I don't want to question or think about it meaning anything. I can't assume there is anything unusual about it.

Grant sits next to me again, and Dr. Garcia starts her lecture. All chatter in the room ceases, and I keep waiting for my phone to do something, like buzz. For SF to say something, even though we haven't communicated since Wednesday. His haunting aura is suffocating me, his presence heavy in the room.

Silence. No text, no message. Nothing to indicate he even exists or cares. I've been pretending to flirt with Grant for the last hour as we whisper into each other's ears and I give him all the wrong signals.

I sit up straight, sensing his eyes on me—the eyes behind that cloth mask. He is here, somewhere, I think. His essence is washing over me.

"Congratulations on completing your first week," Dr. Garcia says at the end of the hour. "Before I let you leave, I want you to look around. At these walls, the seats you're in, everything around you, including your peers." I swallow hard and drift my gaze across the room and everyone else does the same. "Now, I want you to look at the person directly beside you."

My eyes shift to Grant, who has finally decided to drift his attention to my face.

"Now I want you to imagine this person is on the brink of death. In fact, every single one of you is about to die. I want you to imagine this hall is burning behind me. The fire is shooting from the stage across the room."

It's scary how fast I imagine Grant's face beaten and bloody, his wandering eyes carved out. I blink a couple of times as the image crystalizes.

"What the fuck?" Dani whispers. "This lecture just got weird."

I turn to face Dr. Garcia and try to get that image out of my mind.

"That very thing happened to 150 people in this room," Dr. Garcia continues. "Smith Hall burned down in 1976. The fire started up here on this stage, right behind where I'm standing now. The room went from calm to chaos in seconds."

"I heard about this," Dani whispers. "The Order used to do really messed up stuff, like starting fires in public places."

"What makes you say that?" someone asks.

Dr. Garcia grins, the white streak in her hair shimmering under the light. "Because, child, I was here when it happened. I was one of the 150 people in that room and almost lost my life that day." She shuffles papers in front of her eyes, flashing to that dark place. "Our in-depth study of human emotions starts next week. Fear is the emotion I talk about the most, but consider all the human emotions and which ones might be triggered right before you die."

"It was the Order who burnt this building down, wasn't it?" someone asks.

Dr. Garcia merely nods, a contemplative look in her eye, as if remembering every sordid detail. Dr. Garcia went here, so she must have known my grandparents growing up. She taught my father, but I hadn't realized how deep her roots were.

I fight back a swell of emotion and push it out of my mind. She was here. She was a part of something, even if she wasn't one of them.

Dr. Garcia frowns. "So they say. I barely made it out alive. It was pandemonium, chaos, and darkness. The smoke was so thick and black, it filled the room in seconds. I truly thought I was going to die."

"Why would they do that?" someone asks. "It's so messed up."

She releases a heavy sigh and the sound echoes in the quiet room. "The Order employed tactics that were far from ideal and, not to mention, against the law. But I understand at the most primal level what they were trying to do. What their purpose was." The room is so quiet, you can hear a pin drop. I hang off every word.

"For thousands of years, and all throughout humanity, we've witnessed vast empires rise and crumble. Over time, we rebuild, restore, rejuvenate, and peace is restored. This has happened time and time again: the Romans, the Greeks, the Egyptians, and…Babylon. The Order of the Shadows believed those who sought nirvana must embrace this collapse. Powerful empires rise because of it. Empires with more wealth and power."

A girl in the front puts her hand up. "I hear they worship death."

"You mean *worshipped* death," she muses. "There has been no evidence of them for forty-five years. And while death is a necessary part of the cycle, remember the rise is just as important. The rise is the symbol of rebirth. Now, I'm not saying what they did was right, but before my near-death experience, I had no real sense of self. It was only after almost losing my life that I gained true clarity. Don't get me wrong, I'm not endorsing setting fire to this beautifully restored building, but I do want you to empathize with them." She tilts her chin and looks at the class. "Perhaps this can be the basis of next week's self reflection. And don't forget to submit your first week's work by midnight tonight. Be prepared to dig deeper into the concepts next week."

Yet another assignment.

I haven't even started the first one yet. I suppose it's time to delve into the textbook I've been avoiding. And I really need to understand why I'm avoiding it.

As I bend over, packing up my stuff, strong arms suddenly wrap around my waist, making me jump.

"So, will you call me sometime, beautiful?" I nearly jump out of my bones. I forgot about Grant.

I take my time and turn to face him, smiling sweetly. "Yeah, sure thing."

He smirks and turns away, and I watch him check another girl out in front of me like he just can't help himself.

Gross. Utterly gross.

On my way out of Smith Hall, Dani, wearing her usual bohemian braid, loops her arm into mine. "So, are you going to call Grant? He's been pining over you all week."

I give her a flat stare. "I'm not sure I'm into him."

She arches her brows. "He's athletic, cute, from *New York*—"

"And stupid," I interrupt before she can carry on the thought. "And he's not my type. I'm not sure what my type is anymore."

If I even have a type… I literally feel nothing. Devoid, like the upper portion of an hourglass. That is, except for the moments when I reminisce about the nights my nameless monster came to visit me.

At night… I seem to experience everything while I'm asleep.

Dani gazes down at the phone I'm gripping, my knuckles nearly white. "You like the mysterious types who don't have a name."

My eyes shoot upward.

"If you don't want to go out with him, I will," Misty says in a cheery voice from behind us.

I snap my head toward her. "He's not into you; he's into me." My face turns as red as a cherry as I continue, "I mean, Grant was actually talking to me, Misty. He asked me out, not you."

Misty freezes in her tracks and takes two steps backward, stammering, "I'm sorry, it's just…you just said you weren't interested in him."

I run my hands through my hair and rest them on my hip. "I haven't decided if I'm into him or not," I tell her. Reflecting on my words as they come out of my mouth, I barely recognize myself.

It's not me.

Dani releases my arm and frowns. "Summer, don't be like that." My gaze flickers between Dani, who's scowling, and Misty, whose tear-filled eyes betray her efforts to remain composed.

As I watch the campus slowly empty, I breathe in the peaceful late afternoon air, savoring the stillness that envelops the trees. "I'm just stressed out about school," I tell them quietly. "It's more overwhelming than I thought it would be, and I miss my dad."

I contemplate the late night I am about to have, thinking about the morbidity of what we are being asked to write about next week, and the fact that Dr. Gracia was here during the fire. I stomp off ahead, a flush hitting my cheeks, not wanting Misty to see me flustered.

"You didn't mean what you said," Dani yells. "It's a forty-five-minute walk, Summer, and it's raining! Let us drive you."

I ignore her and keep walking. I'm unsure why I have these outbursts of jealousy. It's like my nameless monster left a hole in my heart, leaving me with nothing but my insecurities I'm desperately trying to hide.

"I'm sorry, Misty," I call over my shoulder without looking back as tears start to form at the back of my eyes. Maybe if I walk home through the woods, under the cover of the trees, he will finally show himself.

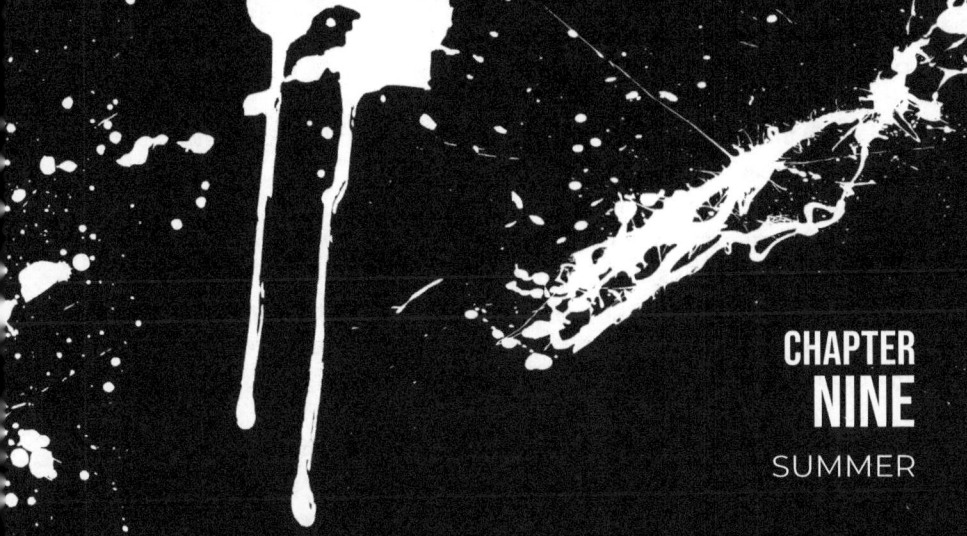

CHAPTER
NINE
SUMMER

I walked the path through the woods toward the forest near Dani's and my home, yet he never showed himself. It was stupid to think he would, that he would chase through the forest and claim me.

Or kill me…since that was what he always said he'd do.

And that's what Shadowface does.

He kills people.

He kills girls…

So why did he fuck me that night instead of killing me? That decision point I saw in his eyes through his mask, his hatred pouring out of him before something shifted and he became my lover instead.

Dani and Misty are both locked away in their rooms when I arrive home. I'm cold, tired, and utterly dead inside. The chill from earlier has settled deep into my bones, and I can't seem to get rid of it.

I hover outside Misty's door, ready to apologize, but I hear her on the phone, so I let it be. Instead, I head into the bathroom, discard my clothes, and run the shower as hot as it can go. Once finished, I wrap myself in a towel, step out into the hall, and dart up to my small attic bedroom.

I don't bother shutting my blinds as I bend over and try to find something warm to put on. The cool air pebbles my nipples as I wring out my hair, realizing my window is open, though I distinctly remember shutting it.

A cool wind hits me as I stride to my dresser and pull out the lace bra and panties I bought three weeks ago that matches both pictures SF sent out. I pick a comfortable sweater dress that hovers just over my knees and settle into my bed, grabbing my computer and laying my head back on the soft headboard behind me.

I start clicking away on another assignment, but it's not long before I hear a buzzing from my nightstand. I unconsciously reach for it, a small smile escaping my lips at the sight of his name.

I run my hand through my hair and take my time, not reading it right away. After a few minutes, my curiosity gets the best of me. I swipe my thumb on the message that's waiting for me.

SF: *You can do better than him.*

I lean my head back on my headboard with my knees up, letting my dress hang loose over my thighs, and start clicking my response.

Summer: *You won't even tell me who you are. At least Grant formally introduced himself. What's wrong with him? He's athletic, attractive, smart, and most importantly, real. You're just annoying.*

SF: *Are you trying to make me jealous, pretty girl?*

My heart jolts at that pet name. I didn't realize how much I missed it.

There's a change in his tone from before. Small things that suggest his moods swing dramatically.

Summer: *Maybe.*

SF: *Well, it's working. And that's not very nice.*

I shift and tilt my head at the screen.

Summer: *Are you going to tell me who you are?*

SF: *Where is the fun in that?*

I pause and rest my hand on my bare thigh. As usual, a hint of warmth begins to build inside me. Only he can arouse me so intensely. In fact, only he can arouse me at all. My thighs part and my gaze shoots to the window, at the open blinds and the inky darkness outside.

Is he watching me right now?

Summer: *So you were watching in class. I thought I told you to stop messaging me.*

A pause... I also stop to consider Lincoln wasn't in class today. Not that it means anything.

SF: *We've never stopped watching you, Summer. We've been watching you for a long time.*

My pulse ticks a little faster, and I stare at the word on the screen.

We...

My memories of his visits are few and far between. His soft hands caressing me and the honeyed whispers in my sleep. There was never a *we* in the equation...it was only ever *him*.

It's possible, I guess, if there's more than one person in the secret society, and if they are behind this. It's too intimate, too sensual for a group to be involved.

Whatever this is, it's bigger than the Order of the Shadows. This is about *him*, not about them. And the only connection point is that burlap mask.

I press my lips together, my fingers drawing circles on my thigh, instantly regretting what I'm about to ask him.

Summer: *Are you watching me right now?*

He doesn't answer. Two long minutes go by and nothing, and I think I scared him off. Until—

Incoming video call

Shit.

I throw my phone onto my bed like it's on fire, my heart racing as I fix my gaze on it. He's actually calling me. No, he's video calling me. I guess I wanted to know who he is, and this is my opportunity to find out. I snatch the phone and answer the call, making sure the camera is facing toward the bed. I remain silent, yet his breathing is audible on the other end.

"What do you want?" I finally say in a voice that's weaker than it sounded in my head.

His voice is robotic and distorted, as if filtered through a machine. It reminds me of a horror movie.

"To watch you," he says. "Do you want me to watch you, Summer?"

Those stupid butterflies… Why do I like the thought of him watching me so much?

"This isn't normal," I respond. *I'm* clearly not normal. That missing girl still hasn't been located, and whoever is on the other end of this line is directly responsible. He's indicated as much.

He snickers. "Define normal. Are you normal? Or would you prefer I were *Grant* right now, because he's pretty fucking basic, isn't he? Admit it, I am way more exciting."

I can't deny that.

"Let me see you," he says softly. "I miss your pretty face and those soft legs."

The ones I wrapped around him so tightly two years ago.

I guess there is no harm in showing him my face since he's already seen it. He clearly already knows what I look like, so I turn the phone around, resting it on my thigh with the camera angling up at me. My cheeks burn, and he, of course, has his camera off.

"So fucking pretty," he whispers, and my skin tingles. "And look how worked up you already are. Your cheeks only get pink when you get flustered. Turn the camera around. Let me see your legs now, baby."

Baby... He never called me baby.

I grind my teeth. "I don't think so, asshole, and I'm not fucking flustered. This is really messed up, and you don't get to call me pet names."

"Turn your phone around, Summer," he says in that chilling robotic voice. "I want to see what you're wearing. Trust me, you don't want to piss me off."

My mouth gapes as my stomach starts to roil and twirl, and the room spins around me.

"Now, pretty girl, before I cut that sagging tongue out. It's not like you're naked. I don't think it's a big ask."

I snap my lips together and he laughs again, that robotic sound sending chills up my spine. As soon as my fingers twirl the camera, my dizziness subsides.

The words of a legend, and this is how he speaks to me.

Thank god I'm not naked.

I flip the camera around and lift it up, showing off my toned legs under my dress, which has now ridden further up my thighs. He's quiet, terrifyingly quiet, and my heart races, unsure of what he's doing beyond the camera's lens.

His breath deepens. "Lift your skirt a little more."

Enough. Enough games. Enough teasing.

"Listen... Who the fuck do you think you are? You disappear for years and expect me to do whatever you ask. I am not showing you anything else until you tell me who you are."

I click off the camera. He no longer gets to see me. I should hang up, block him, and at the very least, report it to the school. I have more than enough incriminating evidence now to get him thrown in jail for years.

But I don't. I can't bring myself to do it just yet. The anticipation of what he is going to do next stirs something between my legs. I grab my scalp and pull my hair, trying to resist the immense pleasure building inside me.

I swallow, breathe, and wait for him to say something as my body vibrates.

"You have a stick up your ass, don't you, baby?"

"What?" I breathe, releasing the tension on my scalp and my hands drift to my stomach.

"You've always been so stuck up, Summer."

He knows every naked truth about me, and I know nothing about him.

"So what if I am?" I snipe, finally finding my voice with this creep. "I'm worth much more than being someone's entertainment on call. You're going to have to do better than this. You're going to have to earn me."

He takes off the app or whatever he's using to distort his voice. His voice comes out deep and dark, and so familiar, it takes my breath away.

"I'm going to take that stick out of your ass and make you fuck yourself with it. And once you're begging for my cock because your pussy has splinters, I'm going to fuck that filthy mouth of yours."

My heart beats and heat sears straight to my pussy.

I sit upright and scramble my legs up, slamming my hand over my mouth. My stomach coils in on itself. No one, and I mean *no one*, has ever spoken to me like that. The phone falls to the floor with a *thud*. I want to flee, but I have nowhere to go. This is the safest place for me.

Somehow, the darkness outside intensifies—as if his evil spirit is out there, watching me. I stare at the phone, then close my eyes. I dry heave, my body freezes, vision blurs. Finally, my body reacts how it should. Frightened like a kitty cat.

That voice... I know that voice so intimately. Every dream I'd hear him, feel him, experience him. This isn't a joke. This isn't some guy with a weird crush trying to ask me out.

He touched my most vulnerable places, talking to me in my sleep, making me experience things. And at an age where I was just innocent and confused. He made me fantasize about things no girl should ever fantasize about. He's been stalking me for a long time, saying things to me that are so utterly vile, so messed up...

And it led to me falling in love with him.

A dark laugh echoes from the phone. A twisted, cruel, and utterly sexy voice. "I wish I could see your face right now. How rosy those pretty cheeks must be. Don't worry, pretty girl, we're just getting started. Before I'm done, you will be the one begging to take your clothes off for me."

It takes a moment to compose myself, to find the voice I so confidently had only moments before.

I choke out a stuttered breath. "So, what are you, then? Are you Shadowface?"

A pause.

"It's physically impossible for me to be Shadowface, if that's what you're thinking. He would be in his forties, depending on which one you are referring to. Do I sound like I'm that old? I'm not your father's age, Summer."

My head spins, my throat dries up as the words form like ash in my mouth at the mention of my father.

The insinuation is not lost on me.

A memory floods my brain, the one that's been in the periphery since I got here.

A face. A boy a few years older than me, sitting across from me as we eat our usual Sunday roast. My heart stutters and a sickening feeling falls over me.

I can't remember how old I was—the memory is fleeting. He was older, that much I remember, but the years blur.

My father said he wanted this boy to experience a happy family dinner because he lost his own family. He was so insignificant, I never gave him another thought.

I'm positive it wasn't Lincoln, even though he had similarities to Lincoln. Lincoln didn't come into my father's life until after. And that boy was timid; he didn't act like Lincoln does now. My father often volunteered with troubled kids, helping them recover from trauma. There could have been more than one orphan he was working with.

He wouldn't look at me the entire dinner. My mom tried to talk to him, and he'd only give one-word answers, his eyes downcast, pushing food around his plate with his fork. He stole glances at me, though. I only looked him in the eyes once, and I started to feel itchy. Something was off about him.

He spent the night in the guest bedroom, and I never saw him again.

I suddenly feel very dirty... My skin starts to itch all over at the thought of my nameless monster being that boy.

What was his damn name?

Mikael... I think it was Mikael.

I can hear his familiar breathing on the other line, like he's waiting for me to ask him something. "I've been asleep, Summer," he finally says, and I have no idea what riddles he's spewing. "That's where I've been."

Asleep. I was asleep when he whispered to me for the first time, and all the times after. It always started out in a state where I couldn't move. I was helpless, my body was paralyzed as if caught between sleeping and waking.

He must have crept into my room that night and watched me. Then he found a way into the house during the years after, and as I got older, he got bolder. His whispers became more intense.

My father was barely home; it wouldn't have been hard.

A heavy anger ripples inside me, but I hate what he's insinuating about my father even more. "You're nothing but a pathetic orphan who decided to sneak up to my room and take advantage of me."

A deafening silence settles as I wait for him to respond.

"Do you know why Shadowface covered the faces of his victims?" He's so composed, yet his voice is sharp as a razor's edge.

I refuse to dignify that with a response. Tension grips me as I inhale deeply.

His deep relenting voice continues, "It's because he cut their tongues out and mutilated their faces. Probably because they talked back to him like you are right now."

Bile rises in my throat at the visual, but I also can't control the heat building in my stomach. As if two opposing forces are pulling me apart from the inside.

"And if you don't watch your mouth, eventually I will cut your tongue out, too. I hope we don't get to that point though, pretty girl. Your mouth is too precious."

I kissed him once. The one night we were intimate, I couldn't stop kissing him. It was the only time he ever touched me. Eventually, I craved his touch more than I needed to breathe.

"Where have you been all these years?" I finally whisper. My voice comes out shaken and broken.

The line goes quiet again, and I can't bring myself to blink should I miss his response.

"I told you, I've been asleep," he says in a soft voice, and I blow out a shaky breath. His voice is back to normal—not that I have a clue what normal is with him, but at least his tone sounds less nefarious. "I want you to turn the camera back on."

This time I do what he says, losing all logic as to why I am listening to him.

"You're really fucking sick and demented," I say, turning my camera on.

"Yeah?" he says, and I hate how hot he sounds.

"Yeah," I repeat back to him.

"Come on, Summer, you're into this, so don't deny it. You like when I talk dirty to you." His demeanor shifts erratically between sophisticated and adolescent. My mind and heart have whiplash.

"Only because you whispered it for years." The death threats, mixed with the soft, honeyed whispers after. My body is vibrating at the thought of it—memories, I realize now. The line goes silent for a heartbeat.

"What now?" I breathe, focusing the camera back on my legs, thinking that's what he wants from me. My head pounds as I pull up my dress, showing my lace panty line.

Another small sob escapes me. Maybe if I just give him the show he wants, he will leave me alone and find someone else to target. Either way, as soon as this phone call is over, I fully intend to call the cops and report him. That's the sane thing to do.

His eyes penetrate me through the phone. It's like he can see into my soul.

"Show me, please," he demands, almost sounding desperate. "Show me how slick your fingers are when you touch yourself."

Please.

Such manners for a perverted psycho.

I lengthen my breath and move my hands in between my legs and gasp as I make contact at how sensitive I am. It doesn't take much to make my entire index finger wet.

"Lick them, baby," he whispers, and a sinking pit hits my stomach as the realization dawns on me that I currently have no control over my own desires. It's disheartening to think about how degrading this is. It's as if he has complete power over my thoughts, manipulating them as he pleases. I stare right into that camera and stick my finger into my mouth, and I can't deny how good I taste.

"Now what?" I whisper as arousal bubbles up inside me.

Another lengthened pause, and I nibble on my lip, thinking about the next demand he is going to make and if I'll actually do it.

Silence. I wonder if I've lost him.

"Hello?"

A cosmic shift through the phone. He's done with whatever game he was playing.

"I want you to open your psychology textbook you're so scared of."

I squint my brows together as I come back to my senses. "What?" I ask him. I almost don't recognize the voice…almost.

"Open it and start reading chapter two. Take your time, Summer. I'll watch and wait, then we can talk about it."

A heaviness hits my stomach at the sudden change in his voice.

Two orphans. Two. Is it possible there are two behind this? Are they working together?

I frown and wipe away my tears as I grab my textbook.

"Don't look so confused, Summer. I want to help you—I wasn't lying about that—and this is my favorite chapter. It's an introduction to ethics."

The week goes by. No texts or photos, just a swirling media presence on campus and a statewide search for Cali, who is still missing. Local authorities are refusing to connect Cali's disappearance with the photo or Shadowface lore, stating there is no proof the two are connected and the distance between the towns is a driving factor in that decision.

It's like they don't want to admit what's blatantly obvious to me.

The party is tomorrow, and even though no one knows who actually plans it every year, the rumor is it's at the abandoned *Fresh Mart*.

Kinsmen is a secluded, quiet place. The woods run for miles and miles, very easy to get lost in. None of this sounds like a good idea.

I didn't call the police after the dirty threats. We read together, then he tested my understanding of the subject matter.

For the next hour, I could almost imagine he was normal, and we were only talking about class. That he wasn't pretending to be Shadowface and getting off on the pure fear he instilled in me. That he wasn't controlling my every move by exploiting the persona of a serial killer.

I couldn't stop listening to his voice as he talked to me, obsessed with every word and how different he sounded from earlier in the conversation. How deep and composed he was, how certain and confident. I pictured that boy in my kitchen but couldn't place the two together.

As much as I hated it—the thought of it being him—I can't deny that I finally read it and forced myself to start my paper, and even submitted it on time. It was nice having someone to work through the material with.

It's psychology class again, the last of the week. Dani, Misty, and I take our usual spots in the back of the lecture hall. Lincoln is in the front row, ignoring everyone with his usual grace and sophistication. He hasn't looked at me all week; I might as well be dead to him.

I can sense my nameless monster watching me, though... He's somewhere in this room, even if I'm not entirely sure it's Lincoln.

Grant and a few of his friends join us. He's sat next to me all week. His eyes are on my chest during the entire lecture. I'm leaning into him and smiling, flirting more than usual. Not for Grant's sake, of course, but for *him*. I'm sure he's looking, and I'm desperate for some sort of reaction from Lincoln.

The lights dim and Dr. Garcia clicks to the microphone. At just five feet tall, the woman dominates the room. The hall falls silent, as it always does when she's on stage.

"Congratulations. You've made it to the end of week two," she says. "I hope you all understand the basic concepts of research. If you don't, I suggest figuring it out quickly, as you will need to grasp the concept to be successful in this class. Your first reflections have been graded and will be available to view. Unfortunately, some of you failed. So let's pay attention to instructions." She waves her hands. "And keep up with your readings."

My heart stutters. There is no way I failed. I submitted a decent paper. I stayed up so late working on it, and I worked with him on it.

"Students who wish to discuss their grades can meet with Lincoln during his office hours on Monday. You are free to argue about it with him, but I promise, he's difficult and generally, I agree and trust his assessments. You may be better off focusing on your first paper due in a couple of weeks and your reflection on the burning building example due tonight. Today, we are going to finish our discussion on ethics, and next week we will dive into basic principles of psychobiology, otherwise known as the nature side of the coin, which we will discuss at length over the next couple of weeks."

Burning building example, as if it wasn't pure debauchery and evil, as if it didn't really happen. Like it's some theory in a textbook.

I spend the next hour feverishly writing everything she says in my notebook. I'm behind on readings, so I don't join the conversation she facilitates at the end of class. No one leaves once the class ends. Everyone opens their phones, tablets, and computers, and checks their grades, including me.

My heart sinks.

An F. I got a fucking F?

Dani nudges me. "How did you do?"

My eyes shoot up at her, bloodshot, I'm sure, as the room crashes in on me.

Her eyes widen. "That bad?"

I press my lips together. "This must be some sort of mistake." I steal a glance at Misty, who is watching me as if we are in some sort of unspoken competition. "How did you do?" I ask her.

"I got an A-minus."

Dani gives me a half smile. "I got an A."

"This is absolute bullshit," I mutter, a deep tightness forming in my belly. I'm used to Dani excelling at everything, but the fact that Misty managed to outperform me just infuriates me. Failing would mean losing my scholarship, which is the only reason I'm even able to attend this school. I'm well-aware I lack the smarts to be here on my own, but this isn't right.

Misty gives me a flat look and twists her hair. "I'm sure you can make it up on the next assignment. How bad did you do?"

My lip curls. "Bad."

Dani's eyes sparkle. "Well, I guess you have a good excuse to go talk to Lincoln now," Dani jokes. "Tell me how he is in person."

I give Dani a half smile as blood shoots to my face. Misty just stares at me inquisitively, and Grant freezes beside me, clearly listening to our conversation.

Misty's eyes draw over to Lincoln, and my stomach burns at her looking at him that way. She's gone to see him nearly every office hour.

I slam my laptop shut and shove it into my bag. "Yeah, I suppose I have to. I'll meet up with you girls later." I strut out of the lecture hall without looking back. I guess I'll spend most of my night studying and prepare myself to face Lincoln on Monday.

I 'm in a mood.

Not a good one, nor a bad one, but definitely a vibe.

Dani came barging into my room around three PM and forced me to stop studying. I peeled myself away from my computer after slaving away on my first real paper most of the day, taking advantage of the fact it's now the weekend.

We are about to study psychobiology. Basically, it's the argument that people are the way they are from birth, instead of attributing brain development and personality solely to early life experiences.

Real fascinating stuff, and considering I have a real-life psycho messaging me, I can't help but reflect on what made him the way he is.

What childhood trauma did you go through, SF, or were you born this way?

The campus was still buzzing all week about the rumors that Shadowface was back. The media is hanging around, interviewing students about what they think is really going on.

"Summer, drink up." Dani shoves a shot in front of me. I stare at it, my vision already blurred from the two afternoon cocktails we had while listening to music, dancing around our living room, and doing our hair and makeup.

It's the first time I've had a little fun since being here, and I have to admit, it's nice, amidst my reluctance to have any since my father died.

Now I'm dressed in all black. High-waisted leggings and a tiny black lace top that shows my mid-section. My hair is curled in pretty waves, the blonde a stark contrast to the inky dark fabric.

Yup. Definitely a vibe.

I feel sexy, probably for the first time in a while.

"Everybody cheers." Dani raises her shot glass in a toast, and I mirror her movement. Swigging down the dark liquid and clinking it on the granite island in front of me, I slide it over to her in triumph.

My triumph only lasts for a second as that dark liquid burns and stays in my stomach for all of a second before rising back into my throat. My eyes water and I force myself to swallow it back down.

The smell. Ugh, the smell. "What the hell was that?"

"Something to set your insides on fire," Dani jokes.

I wipe my watering eyes as black mascara smudges onto my hand.

Dani frowns as she leans over the counter across from me. "Girl, don't. You'll ruin your makeup." Dani took charge of applying my makeup, using an excessive amount of black eyeliner and eyeshadow—far more than I typically wear. I kind of like it instead of resorting to pink blush and natural makeup like I usually do. Not that anyone will see me under the mask I'm being forced to wear. It gives me a sense of satisfaction knowing if I'm going to get slashed up tonight, I will look damn good doing it.

"It doesn't matter, anyway," I say, grabbing a glass of red wine as Misty slips in beside me. "We have to wear those disgusting potato sacks all night."

"The slutty makeup is not for the party, silly girl. It's for whoever we end up coming home with after." Dani throws me a wink.

The party's tonight, and my stomach has been laced with butterflies all day at the thought of finally seeing SF.

My limbs grow heavy, and my fingers drift to my thigh as my pussy clenches at that thought. This longing I have for him is cracking away my innocence, piece by piece, and it makes me nauseous.

I grab my red wine and take a sip. If I'm going to this party tonight, I'm not doing it sober.

All three of us are wearing black outfits, so I'm hoping it will make me invisible because I want him to have a hard time finding me. He needs to work for it after what he's put me through.

Dani shakes her head as the wine simmers on my tongue, and I make an orgasmic face and smile at her.

Probably because I'm drunk...and very horny. The heat of the liquor intensifies everything, and I've not experienced a true orgasm in years.

"I don't know how you drink that stuff. Red wine makes me loopy," Dani says as she walks to the fridge and grabs a bottle of white and pours her and Misty a glass. It seems she also has a little strut tonight.

Red wine is my drink of choice. I always thought my parents looked so sophisticated when they drank it, my father especially.

The doorbell rings and Misty's eyes light up. "I'll get it." She gracefully slides off the barstool and saunters over to the door while I keep my back straight and face the kitchen.

I hear three male voices, and bile rises in my throat as I get a whiff of the cheap cologne Grant usually wears. He sneaks up behind me, and I nearly choke on the smell as he slides his hands around my midsection.

"Hey, Summer."

My body convulses.

Dani arches her well-manicured brows as I scowl at her. "I invited Grant and his friends so they can take us to the party. I thought it would be safer showing up with them."

She has a valid point, so I turn and smile sweetly at him, knowing

Misty is watching. I'd rather Misty think I have a crush on Grant, which couldn't be further from the truth.

"You look good tonight," he tells me, and I can't help but notice Misty's shoulders slump a bit.

"Thank you," I respond, straightening my back as his eyes veer down and I really take him in.

He looks cute tonight—dark curls, tanned skin, all-American face. I realize just how big and muscled Grant really is, how perfect he *should* be for me.

From what I recall of my nameless monster, his body was lean, but he wasn't a giant. Every time I close my eyes, Lincoln's body is the one I dream of. So perhaps if I walk in with a football player that will get the attention I need from him.

I gently place my hand on his muscled thigh, finally meeting his gaze. My three-inch heels brush against his legs, playfully tickling him. Despite my slightly blurry vision, his eyes sparkle with excitement from our connection. Deep down, I'm aware I'm toying with danger.

The six of us cram into Grant's SUV. Grant opens the door and I slide beside him in the front, while the rest pile in the back. He turns the music up and we drive out of town as the sun fades in the sky. The usual autumn mist swirls in the air as darkness descends.

Electronic music blasts out of the speakers and the girls dance behind me, giggling as we make our way deep into the woods. My stomach swirls and so does my vision, and I regret drinking so much. Grant's hand finds my thigh in the dark and my face heats, but I let his hand linger there for a moment.

The touch of his skin shoots butterflies into my belly—not SF-level chills, but enough to know that at least I'm normal and react as I should when a cute guy makes contact with me.

Someone who acts like a normal college guy, not a guy who stalks and threatens me.

My head bobs from the alcohol and my hand finds his. He relaxes and squeezes my hand.

I'm a terrible person, and I'm definitely drunk. He'll want a piece of me tonight, and with how much I'm teasing him, I'm not sure I can stop it. I can tell by the look in his eye he has something planned for me.

I can't let him, but I can't push him away, either. My curiosity about SF is tempered by my desire to not die tonight.

A delicate dance.

I'll have to navigate both guys: one for excitement, and one for protection.

We take a minor road through the woods as moonlight slithers through the canopy above, casting long shadows on the road in front of us. The crisp fall air is calm and still, the trees are motionless giants.

Dark woods, a legendary slasher, a secret cult that kills people. What could possibly go wrong tonight?

We pull up to what looks like an abandoned warehouse in the woods, with black silhouettes and an obscene amount of glow sticks everywhere. It looks as though the entire school is here, even though the police and administration warned everyone not to do this.

My stomach turns, realizing it's at the old *Fresh Mart* Dani and I saw last week. Surrounding it are barricades and a broken sign saying: *Stay Out.* As if my grandmother is screaming at me from the grave.

The place is already bustling with activity.

We park and all step out into the night. Music pulses from the inside the building, everyone lining up to get in.

My skin crawls as someone pushes past me. Whoever it is stops and stares at me, wearing that hideous burlap mask. He tilts his head, and I gasp.

"Hey, fucker, watch out," Grant threatens, and I look up at him. I grab his hand to stay near him, but only because of the overwhelming amount of Shadowfaces consuming me.

Dani loops her arm with mine, sensing my unease. "It's fine, don't worry so much."

Everyone is wearing a mask, with creepy eyes and gaping holes over their mouths, and I wonder which grocery store the campus must have infiltrated to get their hands on these potato sacks.

Scarecrows... Everyone looks like haunted scarecrows, and I don't understand the appeal. These aren't even the sexy masks like Ghostface, or the kind that glow in the dark. This is truly disturbing and has an occult feel.

Dani hands me one. "Come on, Summer. If you can't beat em, join em."

With a deep breath, I secure my mask in its rightful position, anticipating some sort of sensation. The rough texture of the burlap against my skin is abrasive and uneasy. His eyes on me—in front of me, behind me. It's like he's everywhere. His essence is seeping into my skin.

My heart stammers as a wind cuts through my thin layer of clothes, and Grant, who senses my nervousness, grabs my hand. "Just stay with me, beautiful. You'll be alright."

"It's just fun," Dani reminds me. I have to do a double take at her. Her eyes are shadowed, and she has a rope tied around her neck, reminding me of the collar Lincoln's brother had on that girl. Morbidly hot, Dani would say, so it doesn't surprise me she added that accessory.

My eyes grow wide, and she stares back at me.

Here, everyone is equal. Everyone's the same. Everyone is *him.*

A unifying ceremony, Dani had called it, and I wonder just how much research she's done on the Order.

"It's like we've been reborn," she says as Misty walks up beside her, looking just as deranged. Dani twirls around in a dance and squeals. "It's like we can do anything we want and be anyone." Those words chill me to the core.

Death. He represents death. We shouldn't be glamorizing this.

This is supposed to be fun, I tell myself as we head toward the *Fresh Mart,* where the walls are shaking from pounding music inside.

The warehouse is one massive room, with a dark hallway in the corner leading to a few rooms in the back. No bathrooms that I can see, and the lack of air is suffocating. The place is packed, with barely enough room to walk. And the music is so loud it would mute any sounds, should anyone need to scream.

I keep my hands on Dani, but she slips from my grip and Grant takes over.

Dani turns to face me with that creepy mask. "Let's dance," she yells over the music.

Grant's hand moves to my lower back, and I immediately get lost in the room. Sweat, alcohol, and limbs are everywhere.

Everyone is grinding on each other, shrieks of laughter and yelling over the pounding music. It's not the drinking, partying, or the sex that makes my core vibrate. It's the masks that make my toes curl and make me want to combust.

I blink a few times as *he* infiltrates my senses, captivating people's attention and making them feral.

I jolt when Grant grabs my hand, as if sensing my unease. "It's alright, Summer." He leans down so his mouth teases my ear. "Here, take this."

My stomach curdles.

I fall into him, trying to regain my composure amidst the chaos, and he slips something into my mouth. My eyes widen and I stare up at him. He gives me a comforting nod, and I realize it's a pill, which I swallow without thinking.

Shit…What was that?

My phone buzzes in my purse, and I pull it out. I squint, realizing that somehow I only have one bar, yet here he is.

SF's name appears on the screen and a burst of satisfaction blooms inside me. I was wondering when he was going to make his presence known. Despite my intention to ignore his texts, I can't help but read it.

SF: *If he doesn't take his hands off you, I will break his fingers, one by one.*

I spew out a laugh, and Grant tilts his head at me as I freeze and stare down at my phone. The liquor from before blurs my ability to give a shit about him anymore. Let him squirm. Let him threaten me.

Let him fucking watch.

Summer: *I'd love to see you try. Come out, come out, wherever you are.*

He takes a couple of seconds to respond.

SF: *Is that a dare?*

I respond the only way I can in my drunken state.

Summer: *Fuck you.*

SF: *I plan to, pretty girl. Real soon.*

Good. He's kept me waiting for two years.

I gently nibble on my lips, a smile forming on my face. This is exactly the version of him I had been hoping for. The side of him that is playful, the one who lovingly calls me his pretty girl. It's this side of him that never fails to make me squirm.

My mask gets hot, hotter than simmering coals, and my skin heats like molten lava.

I slip my phone into my purse and turn to Dani, who's dancing with some guy, who has a suspiciously similar build to Xander, looking like she's about to rail him right on the dance floor.

Even in her drunken state, she's always been the protector of my things. I nudge her shoulder and raise my purse in her face. She knows what I need without me even having to say it.

She tilts her head, sensing that something is amiss, but grabs my purse and casually slings it over her shoulder, resuming her grinding. I lost my purse that had my credit card and phone in it one night when we were out in Amsterdam. This shouldn't be a surprise to her, especially since I'm a cheap drunk.

I glance back at Grant, who's waiting for me, and I stare down at Grant's poor fingers. I don't like Grant, and I'm not ready for Grant to lose a limb, but I also don't appreciate SF's attempt at sabotaging my date.

Knowing that SF is watching, I step toward Grant and twist my body so my ass is pressed into his center and flip my hair to my side.

Closing my eyes, I sway to the music. I smile because, as tough as SF thinks he is, there is no way he would try anything right now.

There is nothing he can do.

We don't talk. I grind on Grant the way every girl here is grinding on every guy, giving an added thrust and sexual oomph. I'm not sure how much time goes by, and I seem to get swept up in the music.

Grant's hands, which are already around my middle, begin to roam to places they shouldn't, and I can't move. I can't say no, I can't do anything. My body is foreign to me.

I turn to him, but a wave of tingling and nausea washes over me. Whatever he gave me is kicking in, hardcore. I can barely see. The lights are dancing. Masks swirl everywhere and his body is nice. Really nice…

"I need some air," I tell him and push away before he can protest, disappearing into the crowd before he can follow me.

If I stay near him, he'll do something, and I can't let that happen.

The music is so crisp as I float through the crowd, through the sea of masks and limbs and sex. Just a swirl of blurry burlap faces until my head spins and mouth dries up.

I stumble to the side of the room, suddenly regretting my choice of footwear. I lean over and what little I have in my stomach comes boiling into my throat. My heart is racing a million miles an hour.

Fuck. Fuck. Fuck. I'm so high.

I can't stand still. My body needs stimulation, it needs to move. Almost speedy, like the pill was laced with something.

I run my sweaty hands over my head and face, and deepen my breath as the panic sets in. I yank the mask off and suck in a breath, gasping for air. My hair hangs over my face, and my hairline is drenched with sweat.

The drugs are too much. The room is spinning, the walls closing in, and an overwhelming thirst consumes me—all I can think about is water.

I squat down and rest my hands on my knees, and when I lift my gaze, in the swirling lights and motion, my soul is vibrating.

My mouth goes dry as I whip my head up, and that's when I see someone watching me.

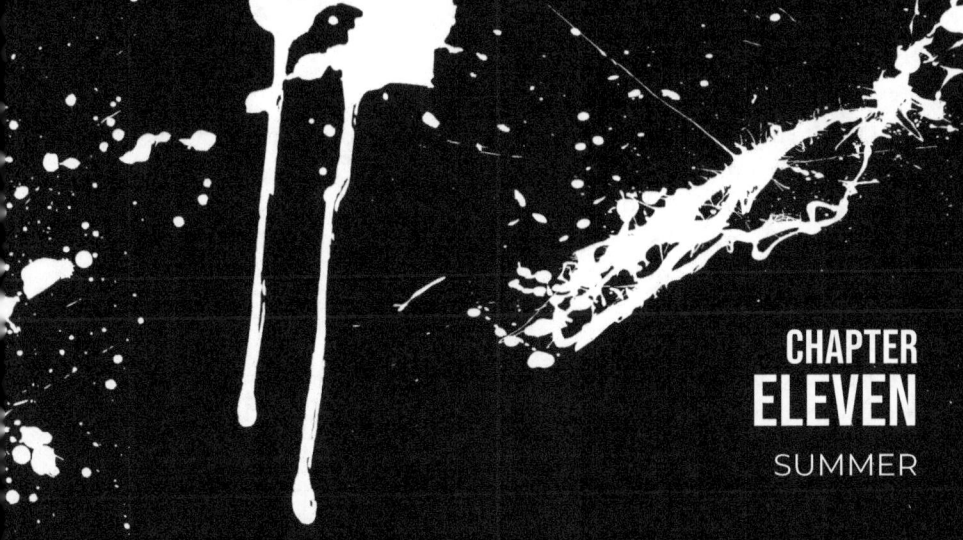

CHAPTER
ELEVEN
SUMMER

He is leaning against a wall, approximately ten feet away, with the mask over his head like everyone else. His arms are crossed, biceps flexed, and he is wearing tight-fitted black pants, his shirt showing off his toned, pale arms. His head is tilted down.

My breathing stalls as I behold him. Evil is rippling off him like a sexy shadow, because that's exactly what he is.

He is death.

I stay squatted down, my three-inch heels sinking slightly into the sticky, warm floor. A sharp, sickeningly sweet smell stings my nostrils; the drugs made the stench overpowering to my senses. Yet, I can't bring myself to rise or face him. He slowly raises his head, and my heart jolts as we make eye contact.

I'm still wildly out of breath, my heart pattering. I can't stop staring at him, and my pussy clenches at the thought that this could be the man who took my virginity two years before.

The pulsing is like fire in my veins.

I miss it—I miss him. I miss his constant presence in my dreams.

He doesn't move, either, so we stare at each other for a few long seconds. The swirl of burlap masks surrounds my vision, but I keep my attention focused solely on him. For a moment, I think I'm just being crazy, and he's not really looking at me. Then he raises his arms and gives me a little wave, and his lips curve beneath the mask into a cruel, evil smile.

My nameless monster.

Panic sets in.

Despite my desire for this...*entity*, he is dangerous. There is a missing girl, and he's hinted she's within his clutches.

If I wasn't so high, I'd run. But running is futile, and I want him to come speak to me. His goal doesn't seem to include killing me, and I won't be some cliché by running out into the woods so he can chase me and get off on it.

I will *never* run from him.

He walks toward me and all my confidence shatters. I pull myself up, wobble on my high heels, steadying myself on the wall behind me. I want to be sure-footed for this.

He moves with grace and ease, and with a self-assurance I don't remember from the nerdy kid sitting at my dinner table all those years ago, if they are indeed the same person.

His body is incredibly attractive. Tall, lean, and filled out in all the right places, but not in a jock way like Grant's, where he was born with size. SF seems more...*deliberate.* Not at all like the scrawny nerd I thought he would be.

I scan his body, thinking back to class. Thinking back to Lincoln.

Their resemblance is uncanny...just not his movements, but his motions.

The lights are flashing, and it's as if I merely blink and he's stalking toward me, towering over me. He smells like spice, and after being on a sweaty dance floor for the past hour, his aroma is incredible.

And exactly how I remember.

I close my eyes and breathe in his scent, and when I open them, I meet his heavy stare with one of my own.

I'm staring at a devil—a really sexy devil who threatened to cut out my tongue. My heart is hammering now; his mere presence suffocates me and my body is like jelly.

I'm so close to him, I can make out his eyes through the holes in his mask. Dark brown, the blacks of them so black, yet in the flashing light, they are almost translucent.

His eyes seem different. Or maybe I'm just extremely high, and my vision is flickering.

I tilt my head up, and my mouth falls open as I actively study him. I'm mesmerized by him and can't help but reach out and run my finger along his collarbone, playing with the edge of it, testing how far I can pull off his mask and expose him.

One more inch...

He leans down, cupping my hands with his. "You're high, Summer." His voice is exactly how it was on the phone

That deep, sexy voice.

Except...*this isn't him.*

A crash of disappointment before a wave of euphoria hits me, as I'm reminded of how flawed I am for wanting the monster so desperately. The one who threatens. The one who kills.

His hands grip my waist and I sway into him, toppling over on my heels I clearly can't handle wearing at the moment.

I look up and press my hand into his abdomen, petting him with my fingers as I stare daringly into his eyes. Just as I suspect, his abs are rock hard and his shirt is soft.

So soft...

His body is delicious.

"Yeah. So?" I breathe, the waves hitting me at full force now. The flickering lights make it seem like I'm in outer space. Even if I wanted to fear this man, I don't think it's physically possible right now.

His chest rises and falls as he takes in my sorry state. "You need water. Come with me."

I yank my hand away. "I'm not going anywhere with you."

Oh, the lies I tell myself. I'd follow this man into the depths of hell right now if he asked me to.

He grabs my hand softly, the calluses of his hand teasing my soft skin. His softness lasts for only a moment before I fall into his muscled body and all the memories come flashing back again.

His warmth and breath mingled with mine. The soft whispers. The deviant threats.

I run my hand through my hair.

Something tugs at my gut, my intuition spiking.

This isn't him...

This is not the same man who snuck into my room at night. Nothing about him is familiar, other than the voice.

The voice...the same voice as when we were studying. Tears prick the backs of my eyes as confusion settles in.

He runs his thumb softly over my brow and leans into my ear so I can hear him. "I wasn't asking, Summer." The moment of intensity is over. I part my lips to say something, but I have no words as he pulls me into the crowd.

I stumble behind him as he effortlessly weaves through people, and they move out of his way as if he's liquid. He keeps his grip firm on my hand as he pulls me through the hordes of masks and half-naked bodies dancing and grinding.

People bump into me from every angle, so he wraps his arm around my lower back and pulls me through, as if protecting me, keeping me close.

I clutch onto him as if he's my saviour.

Everyone here is high, I realize. Just as messed up as I am following my stalker.

Except him. He doesn't seem messed up at all. At least not with the help of any substance. He's got that down all on his own.

He leads me to a bucket of ice near the side of the room and grabs a bottle of water, then leads me to another hallway. He corners me, presses me into the back of the room where I can't see anyone and no one can see me. I'm pretty sure there is a couple fucking somewhere close to us. A girl moans over the music.

He moves in close, his lips teasing my ear. "Drink this," he orders. "The whole thing."

I glare at him but down the entire bottle, closing my eyes and enjoying the cool liquid in my throat. When I finish, I lean my head back against the wall, enjoying the reverberations of the music while he merely watches me through the darkness.

The tension between us is blistering hot. My heart rate jolts with every moment that passes, mirroring the beat of the music pounding around me.

I suck in a breath as he reaches out and plays with a lock of my white hair and moves his hands to my hip bone. His fingers are like fire as he runs his thumb over the bit of skin I have showing on my hip, and heat swells between my legs as I open them slightly for him. Like he is going to touch me down there.

He's holding back. Not touching me the way I think he wants to.

I stare up at him, wide-eyed and curious. "Say something," I demand.

His lips curl beneath his mask. "I don't like that he gave you drugs, Summer. And I like it even less that you took them. It could kill you, and he could have taken advantage of you."

I bark out a laugh and rest my head against the wall. "Maybe I want to be taken advantage of. Maybe I want someone to do nasty things to me," I say over the beat of the music, my chest heaving.

A dare. I'm daring him.

I'm so horny, I'd let this man ravage and fuck me right here. It's been so long since I've been touched. Since I've wanted to be touched by anyone.

I fold my arms. "I'm a big girl now. But you know that, since you touched me when I was a young one. And why do you care if it kills me? Isn't that what you're pretending to be…a killer?"

He leans closer and his breath whispers against my cheek, causing my nerves to fire up. "That's where you're wrong. I don't want to see you dead; I want to protect you."

"Protect me?" I mock. "Protect me from who? From you? Because all I've seen are nude pictures of me and a missing girl who lives hours away. No dead bodies anywhere. I think you're a joke."

He watches me carefully before answering. "Do you think it's a coincidence that the girl who is missing looks exactly like you?"

Chills run up my spine and anger builds inside me. The blonde hair… I was hoping it was a coincidence.

I lift myself up onto my tiptoes, my lips gently brushing against the burlap sack. "I'm right here," I whisper and his body tenses. "You didn't need to take her."

His body shifts and I so desperately wish I could read his face. "I didn't take her," he responds. "He did."

More riddles.

The water helped regulate me, but I'm still dizzy, still rolling. His fingers dig into me, steadying me, helping me calm myself.

I stare up at his mask, the cherry lips I can see through the hole in his mouth, and his whole vibe. I told Dani I'd never make out with a man whose face I've never seen, yet that is exactly what I want to do.

And I hate myself for it.

He tilts his head, grabs my face, and rubs his fingers over my cheek. My body salivates and pulses. "You shouldn't be here."

I squint at him and purse my lips. "What do you mean? Everyone else is here. It's a party."

He stares at me and a tug pulls at me. A twinge. "I mean at Kinsmen, this town… You shouldn't be here; you took the bait."

I blink at him. "What bait?"

My scholarship…he must be talking about my scholarship.

His hand finds my hair. "You should run."

"Why?" I yell louder. Grittier.

I swallow hard, not wanting to believe what I'm hearing. The realization that he's rejecting me causes my teeth to grind and my vision to turn red.

He doesn't get to reject me.

His eyes swirl as he keeps his gaze focused on me. "Because I can't protect you while you're here."

"I don't want you to protect me," I taunt him, my voice dripping with defiance. "I want you to follow through with what you've always promised, what you've said to me repeatedly... Kill me, you motherfucker."

His eyes flicker some more, as if mirroring the lights above. "Be careful, Summer. If you keep talking to me like that, you'll wake him up."

Wake him up? Why does he keep talking like there are two of them?

Motionless...he's motionless. His eyes are dead now, and blind terror pulses through me at the clear and sudden shift within him.

"Summer..."

I stare into his eyes through the mask. His pupils are black, the whites of them glowing.

"You might want to run..."

Jesus.

With a sharp jerk, I wildly look for a way out. Before I can react, his hands clamp down on my hair, forcing my head up. My face is an inch from his, and in one second, something flips within him. His grip is so tight as his breath tickles my cheek. The pressure is so intense, it feels as though my neck might snap. I whimper, helpless and still so fucking high. The tension between us is so brittle.

My precious life is so meaningless to him as I hang in his deathly balance. He went from wanting to protect me to hurting me in a matter of seconds.

He lowers his hand and squeezes my hip, dipping dangerously close to my waistline, and I buck my hips so he has no choice but to feel me. My breath lengthens, and I can't stop the pulsing of desire building from within.

My eyes blaze into his. "What will *he* do to me?"

"I'll cut out your eyes, pretty girl," he whispers.

My teeth find my bottom lip and the pressure inside me mounts. He's different…his voice has audibly shifted.

I'm completely mesmerized as I stare at someone completely different from who I was just with. My nameless monster.

My body melts when I finally touch him again. His warmth melts my skin as my body starts to unravel.

He slowly presses me harder against the wall, his dark energy radiating off him—unlike a few seconds earlier, when he was much more controlled.

Whoever this is, he's seething. His body is tight, rigid, and about to explode.

Trapped between him and the concrete, I wrap my hands around his waist, my head hitting the wall. My leg rises and I wrap my knee around his midsection. The pressure inside me is now excruciating.

"Are you real?" I whisper as the song shifts. The relentless music pounds, the rave storming around us in blinking lights and bodies everywhere.

He doesn't respond, no more dirty threats, so I decide to see for myself. I run my hands along his sides, and he lets me caress him in my drugged-up state. I lift the back of his shirt, and my hands find his smooth muscles. I scrape my fingernails along his flesh and his body flinches as if he's ticklish.

His fingers, which have not left my middle, squeeze my hips as I catch my breath and finally lay my forehead against his chest. For unexplainable reasons, being in his arms gives me a sense of safety.

For the first time since my father died, I feel like I'm home. We stay like this, locked with each other, for a few seconds, and I keep moving my hands along his back.

He likes it, I realize. He likes me touching him, which is why he isn't moving.

My heart is doing backflips, but I can sense he's not giving me full control, only a moment, so I seize it.

I stare up at his black pupils through the mask. I bite the inside of my cheek as I dig my nails into his flesh. He doesn't react so I keep doing it, and I enjoy hurting him.

I'm not okay with what he did to me. I'm not okay that he left me like that for as long as he did. I'm not okay with him making me doubt my sanity by making me think he wasn't real. Maybe if I can make him bleed, then I can prove he exists.

His hard body, every hard edge, molds into mine. His erection presses up against my belly as I keep digging.

He gently removes my hand after a few seconds, freeing my nails from his flesh. Our gaze connects, filled with anger on both ends, and he wipes the small stream of blood from his back, smudging it across my face with his thumb. As he rubs the blood onto my lips, my mouth slightly opens, allowing the metallic taste to enter. His pupils flare and I hold my breath, knowing he'll likely kill me now.

At least I got the last word in.

He retreats a step and admires me. He looks at me in a way I can only describe as disgust blended with equal parts desire. I'm not sure how it's possible for me to hate him, fear him, and want him in the same breath.

"You're so fucking pretty with blood on your face," he finally says, and I melt at those words. His teeth grind, his voice laced with acid. "I hate how pretty you are."

This version of him sounds younger. Like he doesn't have a good sense of his words, and all he can do is tell me how pretty I am.

My heart flutters and my hands find his mask again, but he stops me —and not in the soft way he did before. This time, his grip hurts.

I squirm beneath him. "Why don't you show me your face?"

He plays with my fingers, intertwining them with his before he grabs my cheeks, squeezing them hard. His fingers feel like they might burn through my skin. He tilts my head back, forcing me to look at those dark, yet mesmerizing eyes.

"You're not ready to see me yet."

I push him back, but his body is like stone. "I deserve to know who you are," I whisper, my breath catching in my throat. "Tell me why you're doing this?"

His fingers brush my cheek, a feather-light touch before finding my lips. "I'm doing this to make you suffer for what you did, pretty girl."

What I did?

"I haven't done anything," I bite at him.

He barks out a laugh. "That's my point, baby. You didn't *do* anything. You didn't tell anyone what you saw."

I squeeze my eyes shut as that flicker of a memory comes back. Not the boy at the kitchen table, but another memory...the missing memory. It's a black hole, a tiny flicker that I can't quite grasp. But it's there... And it's caused me to have nightmares my entire life.

He watches my clear torment and confusion with amusement.

Something flashes in his hands. My heart stammers as he presses the edge of the razor blade into my cheek, running the blade along my cheekbone.

He drops my hands, and I can almost hear my heart pounding louder than the music.

"Let me go or I'll scream," I tell him.

He softens and I can see a hint of a cruel smile, the outline of his perfect white teeth. Just pure emotion radiating from under that mask.

Hatred. Desire. Pure evil.

I refuse to touch him anymore, even though I instinctively want to wrap my hands around his waist and pull him closer. I let my hands fall to my sides.

He backs off, then chuckles. "No one will hear you or care. I could do anything I want to you right now, pretty girl. You came here knowing I'd be here, didn't you?"

He has a point. Everyone here is dressed the same, so no one knows it's me. The couple a few feet away are basically full-on fucking now. My hands I can control, my body I can't. My hips shift and I grind against him, even as I turn my head away from him in clear defiance.

His breath is heavy as his demeanor shifts. I squeeze my eyes shut as he runs the blade down my body, cutting a diagonal edge of the fabric in the front of my shirt. One breast falls out, my nipple taut. I freeze, not daring to move. When I open my eyes again, he runs the blade down my belly with such precision to the point it tickles. He keeps his gaze locked on my exposed flesh.

The music shifts, causing my breath to catch, and instead of running his other hand over my breast, he tilts his head and gazes at me. As my hair falls over my chest, a sense of euphoria overwhelms me with him looking at me that way.

It's messed up how much I enjoy him watching me. Even more messed up is the fact that he could end my life right now, and I'd find pleasure in it.

He's playing with the blade like it's a toy, shifting it in between his fingers. I gasp as he cuts the fabric between my legs, revealing the lace underwear I have on underneath.

My breath hitches, shallow and uneven, as he slips his fingers inside me, moving over the lace of my panties.

"You have such a dirty little fucked-up mind, don't you, baby?" he says, watching my reaction. "So turned on by death."

I bite my lip; my nausea returns despite the pleasure coursing through me. I moan as he hooks his finger right into my g-spot and rubs his hand in a circle.

He's so different than he was even five minutes ago, like a whole new person is hiding in that darkness. His motions are soft and deliberate, my body tensing and melting all at once.

Keeping his fingers inside me, he lifts my body, cupping my ass in one hand. I have no choice but to wrap my legs around him, the pressure building to the point it's torturous.

He lifts his mask for only a moment, just above his lips. He leans in and kisses me, soft and sensual—and it's nothing like the vile things he's saying to me. His tongue playfully dances with mine, and my primal instinct is to kiss him back. It's orgasmic, so hot like a dream.

He fucks me against the wall with his fingers, holding me with one arm. I want so badly for him to fuck me, while the other part of me knows I need to push him away.

He senses my conflicted thoughts and squeezes me. His kiss leaving me absolutely breathless.

"You're mine, Summer," he reminds me. "You've always been mine. And if you let anyone else touch you, I'll kill him."

He moves his fingers in small circles. "Say it, pretty girl."

"I'm yours," I whimper.

That seems to satisfy him.

"What are you going to do to me?" I ask as he pulls his fingers out and in again, rubbing me, then adding one more finger and causing another moan to escape.

"I'll do whatever I want with you. I will slice up that pretty neck of yours or cut out your eyes. But before I do, I'll take my time with you and fuck you in every position possible before I kill you."

His words make me come undone.

My body is vibrating as he deepens his hold on me, and I mirror every movement until we are grinding to the music. A fresh wave of the drugs hit me, and I have this desire to touch him. The fear rippling through me is like lava, causing my lower belly to burn.

Fear.

Terror.

Lust.

The sensations are overwhelming, and I can no longer tell the difference.

His lips curl to that smirk as he leans into me again.

I become entranced by the music as the lights flicker around me. His intoxicating scent engulfs me. I invite his fingers to explore me, and we move together until my body pulses and explodes, and my moans harmonize with the girl nearby.

Even after my orgasm subsides, his fingers remain deeply embedded in me. I catch my breath and wrap my arms around his neck, getting a good grasp of his body, but before I can get a good grip, he drops me.

I fall right to the floor in a crumpled mess, my breast hanging out, the fabric of my pants torn, my hair frazzled and sweaty, and my pussy still pulsing.

He stands over me and smiles…

My heart flutters looking in the eyes of a killer. I curl myself against the wall to create some distance from him, my face heating from the fact I just got off on him like that.

Something flashes, and I realize he's still holding the razor blade and he's playing with it between his thumb and forefinger. He crouches so he is eye level with me. He takes the blade and cuts a larger hole in the center of my pants where he cut before.

He pulls something out of his pocket, and immediately, fire flares up in his fingers. He takes his lighter and holds it against the blade, and I watch in utter horror as he heats the piece of sharp metal in his hands.

My breath is ragged, and his hands are soft as he slips his fingers inside the hole he created and presses the blade near the apex of my thigh. I try to look away, but he holds my chin and forces me to look at him.

Those translucent shimmering eyes.

The heat of the blade burns the hairs on my skin.

I let out a small cry, and he tilts his head to gauge my response to him. My gentle cries, my slight whimpering…all the confidence in myself and my doubts about him eradicated.

As our eyes lock in a tense moment, he drives the blade into my skin, the sharp sting followed by a burning sensation. He leaves a distinct mark on me in the shape of an X.

And I scream, so violently, as he keeps the blade pressed into me.

No one hears me over the chaos, and panic consumes me as my consciousness blacks out to nothing. It's quickly replaced by pleasure as he presses his fingers back inside me for only a minute, but it's long enough for my clit to pulse. He runs his knuckles down my thigh, then pauses.

I'm still shaking as he moves closer to me. "Fucking. Mine," he reminds me, as if I could forget.

Then the fucker—this sick motherfucker—just gets up and walks away.

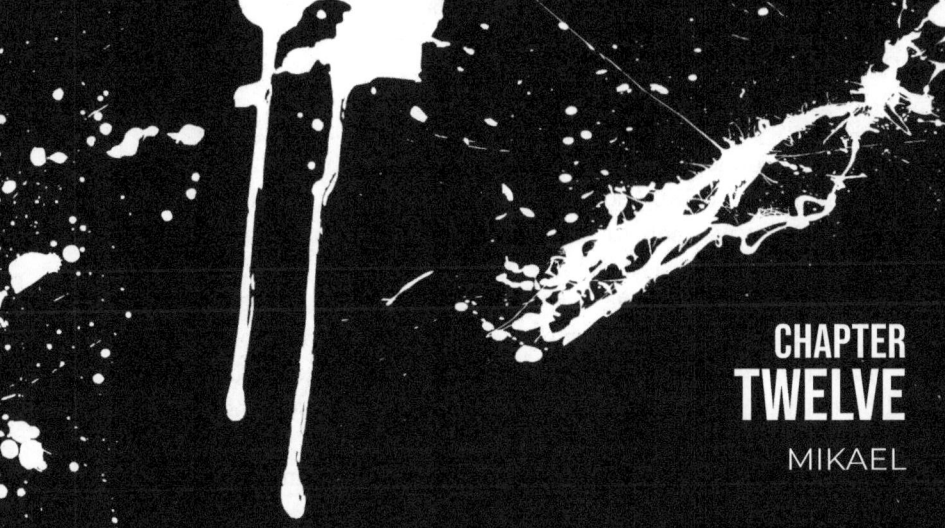

TWO WEEKS EARLIER

B *link.*

My eyes shoot open, and the dark room expands into my vision.

Blink. Blink.

The fog in my mind begins to lift. With my head down, I struggle to breathe through the cloth covering my face. As I try to adjust to my surroundings, I stumble around in a disoriented, half-awake state.

I scan the room and see her through the two slits in my eyes. A precious bundle in front of me. She's sleeping sitting up, as if she was positioned that way, her head hanging to the side, her hair flowing over her face. She's positioned the way Shadowface positioned all his victims.

Being around her always brings about a tightness in my chest that threatens to consume me.

My eyes are alert now.

Pretty girl… My pretty girl is in front of me.

I roll my shoulders and tilt my head from side to side, cracking my neck. My body is tight, unfamiliar, and twinges in places it shouldn't.

I lift my hand and curl my fingers into a fist as I regain my senses and get a good feel for my body again. It's stronger than I remember. A surge of power pulses through me.

My vision strays to the open window, the way the moonlight streams in over her perfect face. Everything is the same, but different.

The vein in my neck pulses.

What was he about to do to her? Why is he in her room?

I look around, my eyes finally adjusting to the light. This space is nothing like her childhood bedroom, where I would visit her a few times a year when I was able to. If it were up to me, I would have visited her more, but distance was a factor.

So where are we right now, pretty girl? All grown up.

The trees outside cast long shadows against the small bedroom walls and arched ceilings. Everything about this place seems to belong to a different time and a different reality. The only constants are the open window and the pretty girl sleeping in front of me.

The rage that ignites inside me is familiar, too. So much rage. A wave of it nearly consumes me.

My attention draws right to her smooth neck and her chest, that rises and falls with her precious breath. As if waiting for me.

My cock stirs to life, remembering the last time we were together. My final memory—

If it's possible, she's even prettier than she was before, and I hate her for it. I hate her perfect face. So flawless.

My senses are now dominated by a painful erection.

Summer shifts in her sleep, and I move on instinct toward her. To touch her, to kill her before an invisible string pulls me back.

There he is… I was wondering when I would sense him. My instincts were screaming at me to act, sending electric jolts through me, a constant reminder that I am not in complete control of my body.

Lincoln's been in control for a long time—I can tell by the unfamiliarity of my senses. The muscles are tighter, the bones are bigger. Like the elasticity of my skin doesn't match my movements.

So why am I awake now?

Summer. Summer woke me.

I remember now, when he saw her in town only a day ago. I jolted awake at the sight of her. My consciousness flooded with memories—his memories. My desperate need for her awakened me, overwhelmed and revived me. That must be why he's here; he must miss her as much as I do.

When we saw her, I pushed ahead for one second, seizing control of my body before he stopped me.

It was smart. If it were two seconds, there would have been mayhem. There would have been slaughter.

I close my eyes, reliving the memories that haunt me. The memories swirling in my head. The memories I can't get rid of.

Blood. Tears. Carnage.

Witnessing my mother's murder.

All the memories that made me realize I couldn't handle living anymore.

A cool breeze hits my face, reminding me I'm no longer in that slumber. I was happy in the darkness; it was bliss there.

Now she's awoken the monster.

I move out of the dark corner of her room and step toward her. I watched her for years this way, in the dark periphery of her life. Admiring her beauty while simultaneously dreaming of skinning her.

She likes to sleep in the dark, pitch black, like a baby, with her window open, inviting death inside her room.

She sleeps so soundly and looks peaceful, as if she doesn't have a care in the world. As if she doesn't have a fucking conscience because she's such a fucking liar.

I admire the way her pale face blooms under the small stream of moonlight she captures with her beauty, causing her white hair to shimmer.

She appears frozen, as if there is no air flowing through her lungs. Yet, to me, in her vision of death, she's never been more beautiful.

A knot forms in my stomach as her lungs expand. I resent her for simply breathing, for merely existing.

With a gentle movement, I lower myself and carefully trace my fingers an inch away from her face. The air is thick between us.

I'm familiar with every curve of her body, every dark expression she thinks no one else notices. For years, we lived in the crevices of her life, in the darkest parts she can't see. We filled her soul, even if she didn't realize it, filling her mind with poison.

I reach into my pocket, and a small, sharp object settles into my fingers. I can't help but play with the blade, maneuvering it.

Blood blurs my vision.

I've been sneaking in here since she was young, always knowing deep down that I would eventually kill her. The desire is overpowering, surpassing my love for her. He is the only thing that kept me from slaughtering her.

He is the only reason she wasn't completely and utterly soiled. He wouldn't let me touch her until the end.

I relax and breathe, not letting him gain control, even as he tries to push to the front. We have awareness of each other when we confront— we always did. But when he was in full control, everything seemed darker. I was still there, watching as a separate entity, but I was paralyzed. I watched everything he ever did.

The day I went to sleep, I was in full control until that moment I let go, and since then, I have no recollection of anything.

But the sensation is different now. I sense him as if we are one, and I instinctively know what he wants me to do.

He may be stronger, smarter...ancient. But his fascination with her borderlines insanity, even more than mine. Tonight, he must have slipped because I have full control. For the first time in a very long time, I can breathe.

And I really fucking like it.

She takes shallow breaths, making the same sweet whimpers she always makes while asleep.

That moment seems like seconds ago, not the years I suspect have gone by.

I remember it vividly. For an entire hour, I couldn't take my eyes off her while I was consumed by pain and anguish. After years of simmering anger, I reached a breaking point, and I needed to destroy her.

I covered her mouth and nose with my hand, her body jerking with each passing moment as I withheld oxygen from her lungs. I held it there, stifling those breaths with her body withering beneath me, waiting for her to die.

Eventually, her body slackened, and her hands reached for my face. Scraping, pulling and yanking the cloth mask. It wasn't the frantic clawing one would expect someone to exert when they were dying.

She wanted to see me.

Her body and mind gave in to me, and my hand found her soft breast. I leaned down and brushed my lips against her, tickling her earlobe with my mask.

"Pretty girls shouldn't sleep in the dark," I had whispered. "It's where the monsters hide."

Her clawing hands froze, and her body stiffened in response. She didn't move or scream, even though I could clearly see the whites of her eyes sparkling from the light in her window.

She stared right at me…for the first time, she could see *me*. My fractured essence manifested through her vision of my mask.

Her heart rate evened out. Not a single uptick in its beat as I enjoyed her soft, supple flesh under my fingers. All she could do was part her lips and stare at me, unblinking.

I pulled the blankets off, revealing her supple body. Her legs parted, allowing me to slide between them as she wrapped her thighs around me.

I fit into her like the last piece of a puzzle.

I leaned down and kissed her neck and nibbled on her earlobe. My hand drifted between her legs, and I slipped my fingers between the fabric of her underwear, teasing her clit before slowly removing her panties.

Her little cunt was dripping like I knew it would be.

I unzipped my pants, pressed my cock into her, and I fucked her slowly, lovingly. And I enjoyed how tight her pussy was as I worked my way into her.

Blood on the sheets afterward caused my heart and head to split. I've never seen anything so beautiful. I truly loved her.

That's when I let go.

That's when everything went dark.

I have no idea how long ago that was, but I can tell Summer is older now. Her face has matured, her tits are slightly bigger, her curves more defined.

Her life almost ended that night, but I'm thankful it didn't. Because I prefer blood to asphyxiation, and when I kill her, I want there to be lots of blood.

My fingers run over her face, visions of her crystal blue eyes gouged out waking up the part of me society can't handle.

I usually go for the eyes first, petrified and pretty. Eyes that cry. It's what Shadowface did to all his victims, too.

Her breathing becomes shallow, and her body relaxes under my touch. She remains in a deep slumber, her body completely limp.

My hands slip to her breast and her nipples instantly tighten, and in her molten state, she moans like she missed it.

"Did you miss me, pretty girl?" I whisper.

Given she still sleeps with an open window, even after I defiled her, I would say she does.

My hand finds her cunt, my fingers slipping just inside her folds. She parts her lips and arches her back, but it's not because she's awake; it's how her body always responds to me.

I keep pushing her until the muscles tighten around my fingers, and she finally lets go and squirts her juices all over my hand.

He must have given her something to keep her unconscious, which means she's not in the semiconscious state I want her in.

The state where dreams seem real.

With my fingers deep inside her, I lean over her tight body. "I'm going to kill you soon, Summer." I press a kiss on her cheek. "Sweet dreams, pretty girl."

It's a promise.

I smile at how easy it would be to take her—to slide my blade over her throat and move it up her ivory face until all she sees is the sharp shiny edge.

The pressure in my cock is too much to bear as it throbs to life thinking of how good that would be.

"Fuck," I mutter as my erection presses hard against my pants. The frustration is nearly killing me.

God, I want to fuck her so badly.

I want to fuck her until she can't breathe, and I drip every ounce of my cum deep inside her. I want to fuck her until she's lifeless.

I reach into my pocket and pull out a phone—his phone.

I instinctively understand exactly what I need to do and the reason he was here in her room. I don't know the code, but my face opens the screen easily enough. I open the camera and snap a photo. And for a moment, during the flash, I can see her clearly.

Her white hair is splayed out over her breasts, her angular face, the tiny dimple in her cheek. How pretty she is with an afterglow of the orgasm I just gave her.

I pull off my mask and place it over her head and take a few more photos.

My dick twinges at how peaceful she looks.

I've missed her. I haven't touched her in a long time, but I can't bring myself to kill her yet. She hasn't experienced enough pain.

A cold dread settles in my soul. The pull of the other side of my psyche is undeniable, and I sense my time is drawing to a close.

In his eyes, I am powerless, barely a flicker of existence. A demon lurking in his mind. I am all of those things, but now that I'm back, I will grow stronger.

There is nothing he can do to stop me.

I step back and smile as I stare down at the pictures I just took of her. The millisecond it took for the light to flash, and now I have a memento I can look at forever.

Once I kill Summer, I'll reap chaos in the town that ruined me. I am aware of who they all are that made me this way, and nothing will stop me from killing every single one of them.

It's time to bring Shadowface back.

CHAPTER
THIRTEEN
SUMMER

I take a few minutes to come to my senses. The rave is still raging around me as I sit curled up against the wall, close my eyes and get lost in the music. I can't say how much time goes by as I sit huddled in that dark corner. No one notices my tattered clothes because I blend into the wall. He tattered them like he tattered my soul.

I can't stop shaking. Whatever amount Grant gave me, it was too much for my little body to handle, but at least it helped dull the pain of my branding. At least, for now, the pain is dulled from where he seared and sliced me.

The drugs' effects linger, and I'm left in this dark corner, where time seems meaningless, and I stare at the dark wall, unable to move or process what just happened. The drugs finally ease, and my body is left reeling from that polarizing experience.

I am, without a doubt, the target of a killer; every shadow seems to hold a threat, every sound heightens my anxiety.

'Be careful, Summer. If you keep talking to me like that, you'll wake him up.'

Is that what happened? I woke him up?

I keep my hand pressed on the X he carved and branded into me. Fuck, it's deep, and will scar, probably forever. He's tainted me with his darkness. He forced himself so deeply inside my soul, his hellfire is burning inside me.

I guess I wanted proof he existed.

I peel myself off the dank floor, trying to arrange my clothes and avoid looking like a monster. I tuck my breast into my shirt and stumble through the warehouse back to where I left Dani and the others.

111

I have no clue what time it is; the party is still going strong, although the crowd seems thinner than before. It must be well past two in the morning.

Dani and Misty are waiting for me, crossing their arms with their masks dangling in their hands. Dani looks more than unimpressed as she stands with her arms folded, tapping the toe of her stiletto.

She glares when she sees me, but her eyes soften when she sees the state I'm in. "Summer, where the fuck were you? I've been freaking out for an hour."

My high quickly evaporates, replaced by utter dejection. I cross my arms in a pathetic attempt to hide the gigantic hole in the center of my shirt. "I-I'm sorry," I stammer. "I was dancing and got lost in it."

A pathetic lie, one I'm sure she can see right through.

Her eyes finally graze up and down my body, lingering on my general ruffled appearance and the rip in my shirt. She pinches her forehead as she hands me my purse. "Why do you look like you made out with a meat grinder?"

A flush of heat hits my face and her eyes widen.

"Summer Landry, you did not."

I cringe, wishing I could melt away. "No, I didn't. I was just dancing with someone. It just got a bit out of control."

She juts her hand on her hip. "With whom, exactly? Because it wasn't Grant. He was looking for you for a while before he gave up and moved on. I think I saw him making out with someone. And now we can't find him."

"I'm not sure who it was."

Her eyes gleam. "I danced with someone, too. I think it was Xander, but I'm not entirely sure."

I blink at her. "Really?"

"Yes, really."

I cock a brow. "How do you know if he was wearing a mask?"

She grins. "His build was the same, and I recognized his sexy tattoos. This girl kept watching us as we were dancing, and it looked like that Bianca chick." A blush hints at her face, and she bites her lip. "He kept asking me to do *things*."

"What kind of things?" I'm happy for the digression of the conversation, and I'm genuinely curious what kind of interaction she had with Xander. Also, if Xander was there, Lincoln would be one of the faces hidden among the crowd.

She takes my hand. "I'll tell you, if you confess why your clothes are ripped, you naughty girl."

The color drains from my face and she frowns. "Summer, are you okay? You look…pale. Did something happen?"

Besides being marked by a satanic overlord who gave me the best orgasm I've had in years…no, nothing.

I wrap my hands around my shoulders, goosebumps pebbling my skin. "Grant drugged me," I admit. "I'm not used to taking drugs. Can we go? I don't want to be here anymore."

Dani looks apologetic, but her pupils tell me she was on the same ride I was.

Misty walks up and frowns. "I want to go, too. I found Grant. He can drive us."

I don't miss the judgmental stare from Misty as she takes in my appearance. I wonder if she can smell the sex on me, or perhaps the stench of my burning flesh.

I follow the girls out to the vehicle, and the boys are already there. I pile in the back and sit in-between Grant and Dani. Luckily, Grant's friend is sober enough to drive us.

Grant stares at me and fortunately, he can't see my tattered clothes in the dark car. His hand finds my knee, and he leans into me. "Hey, where did you disappear to?"

His hands are foreign and clumsy, and after what I went through, I don't want anything to do with him.

I face him and give a meek smile. "Sorry about that. It was hard to find anyone with the masks."

He pulls his arm around me and shifts closer before I can stop him. "Come here. You look freezing."

My bones bleed into ice.

It's like my nameless monster is inside me. Like he knows Grant is touching me and is biding his time before he snakes in through the shadows and butchers him.

It has been just a few hours since we came here, and it's as if I have been summoned to a higher calling. Experiencing emotions I shouldn't be having. Something's awakened inside me—something dark and sinister that I suspect has always been lurking in my core. It's settled in my bones, my blood, and heart.

His hand innocently grabs my leg, and I imagine my nameless

monster breaking each of those fingers as they tickle dangerously close to the X marked on my skin.

I carefully remove Grant's hand from my thigh. I'm so tired and lean my head on Dani's shoulder instead.

As soon as I have more energy, I need to tell Dani what's going on. If I end up dead, at least I will have told someone, and hopefully stop him from doing this to someone else. The thought of such a possibility—of him killing another girl—makes me want to scream.

Something is definitely wrong with me.

I've heard about rape fantasies, and perhaps I've indulged in those thoughts in the past. But that was merely sexual curiosities since I'm not overly experienced in it.

But this?

I can't deny it anymore. I was more than turned on at the thought of being his next victim than anything else. Dying at his hands, like it's a prize to win. Sacrificing myself for something so sacred.

When we finally get home, I spend an entire hour in the shower, scrubbing myself. My sweat, his sweat, his essence all over me. Whatever it is, it lives in my bones, and no amount of water will wash it away.

I crawl into bed and revel in the scent of my body wash, though I still smell him on me. I stare out the window at the morning light as it drifts through the layered trees.

I lift my knees and wince as the X splits, and I examine it and start admiring it. The pain is excruciating now as it blisters and bruises on my pale skin, and I don't bother to dull it.

He's marked me... I'm just not sure what that means. I stare at it in fascination, and while it scares the living hell out of me, part of me thinks it's beautiful.

Will I become one of the countless lost souls of Kinsmen, a darkness that's plagued this town for centuries? A deep and succulent part of an unknown history. Truths and stories only the trees really know.

I grab my computer and open the private browser, typing in *death fetish*. I quickly delete it, disgusted with myself for even thinking those words or manifesting these hideous thoughts by typing them. There is no way I want that or even want to get off on it. Yet...there was no other explanation for his effect on me. I don't want to die, and I'm certainly not suicidal.

I type in various other sex fantasies, mainly BDSM. It's somewhat reassuring knowing the statistics show approximately six in ten women have these types of thoughts in one way or another, and that experts say they are common.

But this isn't a rape fantasy, this is something else entirely. Following years of inner numbness, I've never felt more alive than I did the moment he held that blade to my throat.

I sleep the rest of the day, and don't emerge from my room until five PM. Dani and Misty are both in their rooms, so I grab a left-over piece of pizza and head back upstairs.

Instead of reading like I should, I decide to see if I can find anything on the Order. Of course, all that comes up in the search engine is Shadowface and the media circus he created.

That is not what I'm looking for right now. So I try to dig in deeper into my search but can't find much about them.

This leads me to more dead-ends, so I give up and type in Lincoln's name instead, and hundreds of search results pop up. There are literally hundreds of Lincoln Kennedys in the US, which isn't helpful, so I type in Kinsmen.

That search yields me his school profile and a superficial IG. He couldn't have a more basic name if he planned it like that. And who knows, maybe that's exactly what he did.

My mind keeps going back to that boy, and the familiarity I have when I see Lincoln. That boy was an orphan; he was most certainly an orphan. My father insinuated as much because he didn't have a family. Lincoln was also an orphan.

I take another route in my thinking, deciding to search the missing people presumed to be the Shadowface victims. I do a quick search of obituaries from 2002, or anything related to the victims of the time. I scan a few links and nothing sticks out.

I keep scanning until I stumble upon an obituary that catches my attention. More specifically, a name that catches my attention. And the name is not Lincoln.

Kim Peters, a beloved mother and friend, passed away unexpectedly on October 31, at twenty-two years of age. Born on March 3, 1980, she left behind her cherished three-year-old son, Mikael Peters. Mikael was the joy in Kim's life, and she was dedicated to her studies at Kinsmen University, where she attended on a scholarship to help build a better life for her and her son.

Mikael Peters.

I swallow hard as that name circles my mind. I type in *Kim Peters and*

Kinsmen University to see what else pops up. I scan the university site and finally come upon a photo of my father and my stomach sinks. I stare at it for a few seconds, making sure of it. It's a younger version of him with more hair, and he's in a group photo. He is at some sort of campus event, and the photo is captioned: *Kinsmen University, 2002.*

A woman is smiling up at my father, who has his arm around her. She was stunning...long blonde wavy hair, low cut jeans, and a belly shirt. The name at the bottom catches my eye next to my father's. Kim Peters, the same woman that died unexpectedly. No taunting photo, just a life that got cut short. No explanation.

My hand flies to my mouth as I stare at the photo of a woman who died during that era, smiling adoringly up at my father.

The world spinning around me, I close my eyes. It's so overwhelming, I might pass out. My stomach tightens, twists and twirls. Years after this woman died, my father brought her orphan son into our house. And he never spoke of her.

I hate thinking it...I hate that there is a connection, as small as it might be, that my father could technically be Shadowface. SF insinuated it as well.

Did my father kill his mother? That would explain his obsession with me. One thing I am certain about, that makes my stomach turn: my father is connected to both 'orphans.'

I flip my light off at midnight and close my eyes. My inner thigh is still throbbing, his scent lingering, his translucent eyes still embedded in my vision.

I roll to my side, then to the other, and stare outside—desperation clawing at me.

Whatever his plan is, it's working.

I can't get him out of my head.

CHAPTER
FOURTEEN
MIKAEL

Disguised with my mask and hood, I traverse the candle lit cave. A rock serves as our symbolic altar in the center, while the rest of our order forms a circle around it. I'm the last to arrive, and no one recognizes which version of me is standing among them.

I'm alive, alert and have a scent for blood as I stand among my enemies, in a place that holds sacred significance to me. The cavern is hidden away from the rest of the town, yet close enough to bring those who are marked to their final resting place.

The last time I was here, I watched as Summer's father cut out my mother's eyes and fed them to the God they worship—the same God they expect me to bow to.

Today, I feel older than I did last night at the rave. My body is more familiar, my mind still adjusting to missing the last two years of my life. Some of his memories are starting to infiltrate my own. Just as I suspected, none of them have any emotional substance.

And without emotion, he is nothing.

Since waking up I've shown immense self-control, as I've successfully avoided the temptation of slaughtering everyone. Patience is my best course of action right now, even if I'm not good at practicing it. Destroying this Order is the only thing that holds more importance to me—more than death itself, even surpassing my obsession with Summer.

The guardian walks toward the center of the cave and, with precision and grace, lights a series of candles, forming a perfect circle. I can't see the rest of them, but their evil and greed are palpable.

The Order of the Shadows.

The mayor, the police chief, the doctor, and the professor.

I am intimately familiar with each one of them, having spent my early years learning about their lives, observing their every move, their families, their wives and husbands, their sons and daughters. I wondered how they could live their lives so effortlessly, despite selling their souls to the devil.

The children of the Order will follow in the footsteps of their parents. They are connected by bloodline, destined to inherit both his wealth and wickedness.

The guardians believe, in their naivety, that Lincoln is one of them, oblivious to my return or the fact that their reasoning is flawed because he is not technically bound by blood. They put their faith in his loyalty and his ability to continue, despite the fact that Summer is the rightful owner of that position.

Tonight, I want to fuck shit up for all of them. Tonight, I will forge my way forward as one of them.

The guardian walks around the flickering circle and raises her hand. The hushed whispers come to a halt as the candles flicker from a distant wind rushing through the cave.

"Who among us has found their mark?" she asks, as if taking a life were a casual matter. Draining blood, offering eyes, hearts and souls.

I step forward, raising my hand beneath my hooded robe. In a low voice, I reply, "I have."

Hushed murmurs and Xander scoffs. No one else in this generation has found their mark yet. And Xander is tethered because of his relationship with Bianca.

Talia Garcia's curious gaze meets mine; even beneath her hood, the firelight reveals her surprise, and recognition flashes in her eyes.

She lifts her head and steps toward me. "And whom have you marked, my child of chaos?"

Child.

I suppose I am her child, since she technically adopted me.

I keep my voice low and steady. "Summer Landry."

Whispers fill the room, and she lifts her hand to silence them, aware of the significance she holds within this order and what she represents. She approaches me and gently places her arm on my cheek, lifting her head and projecting her voice so everyone, including our dark one, can hear. It is time to reveal the name of his new sacrifice.

"Being marked by the Order of the Shadows is a sacred act, binding her forever. Are you absolutely certain?" she asks.

I am not aware of what happened between her and Summer's father, but a hint of malice hits her lips.

I am ready…this is what I woke up for.

I nod and my jaw clenches as I fight back the maddening itch that crawls beneath my skin. Tilting her head, she scrutinizes me, but I keep my face obscured, hiding my eyes beneath the deep shadows of my hood. If she catches a glimpse of me at this moment, she will recognize me, and everything will be ruined.

With a wave of her hand, she says, "So be it, then."

LINCOLN

It's eight PM on Tuesday night, two days since the rave. I've spent the last hour clicking my pen in my basement bedroom, twirling around in my chair at my desk, staring down at those two words.

Two words, when I have thousands to read, and even more to write, if I plan to defend my thesis against the most aggravating, egotistical group of academics I've ever met.

Two words that have consumed my thoughts for the past hour as I stare at the candle on my desk that's nearly wicked out, the wax dripping molten liquid on my mahogany desk.

Two words as I sit in my windowless bedroom, my classical music playing softly, which muffles the muted, and rather annoying, sobs of the little blonde problem I have tied up on my bed.

Two words that were penned by my hand, yet are words I have no recollection of writing. I've read those words as if they were written in scripture, the handwriting so foreign.

Two words that merely say, *she's mine…*

A dark laugh skims the surface of my psyche. A mocking laugh, as if to say, *fuck you, I'm still here.* His laugh is followed by the visceral rage he embodies. I can't deny it anymore—

Mikael's back.

This world isn't ready for his kind of madness.

Flesh and carnage.

I can sense his emotions as if they are an object I can grasp as a critical observer.

"You're so fucking dramatic," I mutter, knowing just how close he is to the surface and how easily he can take back control. His emotional baggage from whatever happened at that rave with Summer has lingered for days, giving me the worst hangover.

"You have no idea, psycho boy. You soulless prick."

His voice echoes inside my head, causing me to jolt. His words chill me to my core, since this is the first time he's ever spoken to me directly in years. I tilt my head and wait for him to say something else, anything I can latch onto and use to silence him as I've silenced all the other alters that have tried to take control.

Little old ladies, children, fragments. It pained me to do it, but I had to control the system for her. So before they could fully form, I muted them.

I've ripped myself to shreds trying to figure out how to silence *him*, but it seems he is invincible, despite our attempts at suppression.

The girl on my bed eyes me curiously as I frown at her, turning my attention back to clicking my pen and staring at those words as the fire from the candle dances in my periphery.

I place my wrist over the flame until it burns and blisters, holding strong and biting down on my cheek until the pain is unbearable, and even then, I keep it there for seconds longer. He thinks his emotions make him powerful.

"You want to feel something? Feel that, motherfucker," I mutter through gritted teeth.

Finally, the sensation of him settles down, and he disappears into oblivion. My point is firmly made.

Music starts to pump upstairs, and Cali squirms even harder, trying to break through her binds as she watches me burn myself.

Her eyes begin to droop, and her motions slow from the sedative I gave her a few minutes earlier with her food. Her head hangs down as she falls asleep. Her body is still so bruised from when he took her a couple weeks ago, she almost looks as though she's dead.

It's easier for me if she is sedated. We both share this sentiment—neither of us wants her to be here. But she's seen my face, and he has no impulse control, so here we are…

He is, however, reclaiming control in more ways than I thought. He took Cali the weekend before classes started, the same day we saw Summer move into her new apartment. I went for a run on my usual hiking trail and remember passing her, then I was in my basement. It's not the first time I've blacked out, but that should have clued me in.

I'm lucky Cali isn't from Kinsmen, so no one made the immediate connection. I went to Summer's house the next night to visit her and woke up to a bunch of pictures I don't remember taking.

Although, I didn't complain too much about that and thought it would be fun to mess with her, so I sent out one of the photos to the rest of the class as I usually send similar photos every year.

As soon as the news spread that there was a missing girl, I searched the tunnels that led to this house, and there she was, a striking image of Summer. In that instant, I momentarily mistook her for Summer. The poor girl was scared shitless and since I wasn't aware she was here for three days, she was nearly dead. I was relieved to see he at least had the foresight to give her a bottle of water, which is probably the only humane thing he's ever done.

I've been nursing her back to health ever since.

His hatred for Summer runs so deep—the kind of hatred that simmers in every cell—and at the same time, his love for her is so binding.

Summer woke Mikael up; she must have. The power she has over him is stronger than any drug I can take to suppress him.

I grab my pills and study them, inspecting them for any sort of tampering and only when satisfied none are missing do I pop one into my mouth. The label hasn't changed in years, no reason to. Just a mild dose of antidepressant prescribed by Dr. T. Garcia.

You see, dissociative identity disorder is not treated by a pill—you can't prescribe it away the way you can depression. And in my case, we aren't trying to get rid of me; we are working on silencing *him*.

The world is better off without the original inhabitant of my body, and the world will be a much better place with me in it.

I can only keep Summer alive if I'm the one in control. Mikael simply cannot come out of his box, and he knows it. I'm the only reason we're not in an insane asylum, the only reason he's not slaughtered hundreds of girls during his miserable excuse of a life.

All he sees is death, blood, and destruction, and it nourishes his soul. The more he gets, the more he wants, and he's insatiable.

To distract me, I pull open the next of two hundred essays I have to read through. Pages upon pages of crap, lines of drivel and thoughts of stupidity. I bridge my nose at the thought of reading another reflection paper on Dr. Garcia's mocking burning building example, as if she wasn't the one that burned that hall down. I skim through three of them, grading each a C, before finally reaching the one I was keenly waiting for.

Even seeing the name on paper makes him squirm inside me.

Summer Landry.

So much pure radiant emotion flows through him. His desire for her is giving me a physical response, making me really turned on.

I turn my attention to the replacement blonde on my bed, still sleeping soundly. Her bare legs are draped over top of the covers, and she's in a clean shirt.

I've thought about fucking her...I have. What guy wouldn't? However, I'm not that kind of psycho, and I'm not going to fuck her, even though I could.

Mikael's not the only one with an attachment to Summer Landry. He's not the only one who got a taste of her all those nights we snuck into her bedroom. She belonged to both of us, even if my motivations were entirely different from his.

Her name still sends a thrill through me. Part of me still can't believe she took the bait. In her mind she's following in her father's footsteps, and in my mind, I want to quite literally see if she's like him, so I lured her here.

I'm sure her mother wasn't pleased about it, either.

Deviant little thing, aren't we, Summer?

I grab my phone and type in Summer's name. I haven't contacted her since the rave, because I've been busy, and I ignored her in class yesterday, hoping she would come see me during my office hours, which she didn't. On top of the two classes I TA for, I'm also working on my PhD, and I defend my thesis in January. I've not yet completed my research and although I hate to admit it, the girl Mikael plucked off the side of the road is helping immensely with that.

A call comes through from Xander as soon as I grab my phone. I swipe to answer it because he won't stop pestering me until I agree to hang out tonight.

"Xander," I say casually, knowing I'm probably on speaker phone with his girlfriend Bianca—the one he will never kill, because I'm pretty sure he can't stand her.

He responds quickly, "I realize you're super smart and important, but can you spare an hour to come upstairs and hang out with me tonight?"

I pause for dramatic effect. "I can spare an hour."

"Good. Bianca has her friend over. By the way, how was *your* night on Saturday? You disappeared on us for quite a while."

This gives me pause. "I have no idea what you're talking about."

He chuckles. "Yeah, you do. How was she, bro? You're one savage motherfucker. I saw you in the corner with some chick. It was her, wasn't it? You were knuckle-deep inside Summer Landry."

My stomach twinges at him saying her name. "I'm not discussing this with you, Xander."

He chuckles in his deep voice, and I can hear Bianca in the background. "Who are you talking to?"

"I'm talking to Lincoln. Did I say you could speak, Bianca?"

Bianca mumbles something, and I can imagine her sitting on the floor in front of his feet like a good girl.

I close my eyes and think about the last thing I remember from the rave, every crystal-clear moment of it until it turned dark. Her tight body, how she fell into me, her blind faith in me, her body blooming with desire. I enjoyed every moment until he fronted. When I woke up, his fingers were in her cunt. When I regained awareness, I had zero control over my body until after he burned her. And now his insidious presence is inside me like a worm.

I push up my glasses, which slipped off my nose. "I'll see you later, Xander," I tell him, which means he's won, and I will finish up early tonight.

I hang up on him before he has a chance to respond and click on Summer's contact.

SF: *Hi, baby.*

She takes longer than I like to respond, which makes my jaw tick as I read the opening sentence of her paper. My eyes shoot right to her thesis statement, and I have to admit, I'm impressed.

A few minutes later...

Summer: *Quit texting me, or I will go to the police.*

A smile forms on my lips and I rub my chin. Her feisty attitude is adorable, but if she hasn't gone to the cops by now, she won't, especially not after what Mikael did with her. She showed up to class on Monday as if nothing happened at all, confirming my suspicions about her.

SF: *Are you mad at me? I was hoping you would thank me for making you come all over my hands.*

Summer: *You took advantage of me. Last I checked, what you did is assault. Let alone threatening to slice my throat out and burning me.*

My recollection of the events are fuzzy, but I wouldn't put it past him to say that.

Summer Landry is the only reason Mikael's mind hasn't disintegrated into ash. She's the only thing keeping him alive after years of me trying to dissolve him and placing him in a tiny bottle.

He hates most women, but she brings out a special level of depravity, evident from the condition he left her in on the wet and dirty floor.

I sense a flicker in my mind's eye, a taunting laugh, and I shove it aside, pushing him down as far as he can go.

Not right now…

If I'm being honest, I wasn't expecting to enjoy her skin on my hands as much as I did. How badly I wanted to feel how tight her cunt was, or how much it hurt not to fuck her on that dirty wall, completely soiling every ounce of her perfection.

Even if I'm a sociopath, my dick still works, and the desire he has for her bleeds into me.

Fucking her was never the plan for me. But now I have an opportunity to get inside her mind and prove she is the monster I think she is.

I skim through her 2,000-word essay, finding her writing voice remarkable. If I didn't know it was Summer, I'd almost think it was her father behind these words. Her analysis is complex, which I'm not surprised about, given her genetics and her extremely intelligent study partner. Still, she didn't do her research; she didn't use a single external source, which was a requirement for the assignment.

I mark it as an F, and write *insufficient sources* in the feedback section before I press submit, smiling to myself at finding the one loophole I can use to fail her again. Failing her a second time will get her attention and will finally get her into my office.

I pick up the phone and dial her number. Texting is fun, but I want to hear her voice. She picks up after one ring, as if she was waiting for me to call.

"What do you want?" Her tone is snippy. I lean back in my chair. My nostrils flare, and an erection immediately presses against my pants. Images of blood penetrate my mind.

His responses, my awareness.

It makes me smile.

The reason I'm in charge is because I am more rational and law-abiding in terms of my emotions. Unlike normal people, I don't experience emotions myself. When Mikael has them, I analyze and suppress them. It's like witnessing someone else's suffering. I can perceive the emotion and acknowledge its existence, but since it doesn't affect me directly, it's difficult for me to empathize.

"I want to know what you're wearing," I tell her. It's not what I want; I want to see if I can make her take her clothes off. I want to see what I can make this girl do for me. I want to humiliate her, protect her, keep her alive, and study her.

She huffs. "I'm sure that's all you want. I'm wearing a paper bag dress, granny underwear, and a chastity belt, if you must know."

She's so cute when she's trying to be funny. "Turn your camera on, baby. Let me see that pretty face while you're scowling at me."

"No."

I snicker. "Why not, Summer? You like being looked at, don't you?"

"I need to make something clear." Her voice comes out like steel.

"Do you, now?"

"I think you're a fake; I think you like to fuck around with people. You're using the lore of a serial killer to get off and terrorize me—I don't think you've killed a single person. So you can take that razor blade and shove it up your ass. And no, I will not show you my tits."

I let out a dark laugh at how wrong she is. At the night and shadows blistering through me. "You didn't seem terrorized the other night, when my hands were stuffed up your cunt. Those moans, baby…what I would do to hear those again."

Anger radiates through the other line, and I find her anger ravishing. "I was high. It didn't mean anything."

It wasn't exactly my choice to slice her like that, but since I did, I couldn't stop thinking about her silky thigh and the trickle of blood that fell into her pussy, or the disheveled mess he left her in. My dick throbs, and I glance over at Cali, desperately wishing she were Summer.

"How does your thigh look? Will you send me a photo?"

A dramatic pause. "Never contact me again."

The phone clicks and the line goes dead. A flicker of his anger shoots up my spine, but I can't help but smile at her spirit. This girl is so entitled and clueless to what he's capable of. Her choice in attending this school was the worst decision she's ever made. She walked right into the arms of a monster.

"Well done. You pissed her off."

I shake my head and don't respond to him, although I bet he can hear my thoughts, anyway. We aren't a team. Nothing I'm doing with Summer has anything to do with him. My obsession with her is entirely different from his. She is the reason I am here, my sole purpose for existing.

I glance at the clock at nearly nine PM and shut my laptop to get ready to head upstairs and pretend to be normal. If it were up to me, I'd just read and consume information all night long like I usually do. Which is why the world believes I am brilliant when, in all actuality, I am merely studious. I'm often drained when spending time with others, yet I am aware of the importance of maintaining a facade so people cannot perceive the lack of humanity behind my eyes.

I don't identify as a human.

Humans feel, humans care…humans weren't programmed to exist for a single purpose. And while I do experience fleeting emotions, I am something else entirely.

I can't resist the urge to have the next word, so I end up sending her another text.

SF: *Goodnight, Summer.*

She doesn't reply, and I won't push her for a response since I'm almost certain she will see her grade tomorrow, which means I will see her in my office very soon.

I t takes an hour, one student after another, filing into my office, complaining to me about their grade. By the time they leave, they were pouting because I refused to give them the grade they think they deserve, and my patience is worn thin.

I spend an entire hour with one girl in particular, who clearly wanted to stay as long as she could in my presence. Since Misty is Summer's roommate, I indulge and give her some special attention, flirting and toying with her, because one day she might come in handy.

The way I connect with my students is by using manipulation tactics to make them feel special, even though they aren't.

She twirls her hair, her eyes glistening up at me. "Bye, Lincoln, thank you." Her words are accompanied with a shy smile, and the heat rises on her cheeks.

"Keep digging inside yourself, Misty. You'll grasp the concepts in no time." My eyes linger on her short dress.

I've had the nerve to fuck my students in the past. Although, I wouldn't call it nerve, more like my given right. And since I'm the only TA with a permanent office in the department, it's quite easy to shut the door and politely ask for a blow job if students want more from me.

The girls are usually too stunned to say anything, and I'm quite nice about it. It's amazing how willing most of them are and how quickly they drop to their knees.

I still don't change their grade, and they don't say anything because it could get them kicked out of the program.

I consider doing this with Misty, but change my mind. Not with Summer here, and Summer is the only one I want.

I'm not a normal TA, and the only reason I haven't obtained my PhD yet is because Dr. Garcia thought it would be strange for me to get it so quickly, given how young everyone thinks I am. So I waited for the appropriate age by society's standards.

Dr. Garcia has determined I am ageless. My mind knows no bounds, and its only societal constructs that hold me back. I also have the body of a twenty-five-year-old, which means my physical needs are relentless.

Once Misty finally leaves, the late afternoon sun casts a warm glow across my office. I sink into the comfort of my oversized chair, a warm sigh escapes my lips, and I turn to gaze at the grand oak door, anticipating my blonde beauty to walk through.

A twinge of disappointment hits me when the clock on my wall hits five-thirty PM. I was sure she'd visit after failing her. She was only one of a few to receive an F in the class.

I planned for her visit, prepared to talk to her, and I'm pretty sure she knows it's me stalking, even though I've been avoiding her.

I lean back in my chair, and swivel to look out the window instead of staring down at the sprawling campus below. The sandstone buildings, the old architecture, and the canopy trees hint at shades of red and yellow, indicating the early signs of fall. The shrill of the early evening sun when things are the most peaceful and the sun is blinding in the sky.

Home...

This university made me what I am. I am a construct of what was created here, an outcome of the evil things people do for greed. All because of some silly parchment found in the university archives.

283 years ago, a historian decoded an ancient text. He wrote it down with a quill pen on parchment and sealed it with wax. Based on his loose and deranged interpretation of old Latin, and following the steps, he created the Order of the Shadows, proclaiming that following these steps will lead to enlightenment. He was the first of many people in town who ended up going insane, and who killed innocent people because the words in this book told them to.

The Order of the Shadows has been going strong ever since, nearly two hundred and eighty years of terror—and a new terrifying future I plan to forge into the dark past.

After a few minutes, I sigh and rise from my chair, pulling my wool coat off the hanger near my desk. A sweet voice pulls me from my thoughts.

"Um, Lincoln?"

I allow only a twinge of a smile before I place on my mask of indifference and turn around to face her. She looks just as gorgeous as she always does, her hair a brilliant natural white. The air sparkles around her as she takes a tentative step into the sunlight and shuts the door behind her.

It looks like she's been crying, her eyes are glistening and puffy.

A small twinge of...something hits me. Pity, maybe?

I shove the emotion down so hard.

Get out of my head, especially while I'm at work.

"She's crying."

I can see that. I'll handle it.

He settles back into onyx liquid, but his essence remains, and I put the walls up in my head—the same walls that used to work to keep him at bay. He never used to be this chatty.

I was formed during Mikael's early years to help him disassociate from what he witnessed in his early childhood, but I lingered beneath the surface for years as a fragment. That changed the day he saw Summer for the first time. That's the day the fragment that is me formed into the alter I am today.

She is smart. She must be piecing together her father's time here. I wonder if she's starting to suspect that her father was the most notorious serial killer of this century.

I offer a small smile and hold out my hand. "Hi, Summer, I was wondering when you'd come to see me."

She quirks her head, then frowns, but keeps her eyes glued on me, studying me. Wanting to call me out, but still not sure.

She frowns and places her hand in mine. "How do you know my name?"

I arch my brow and sit across from her on my plush chair, pushing my glasses up my face, crossing my arms. "You're the only one I failed who hasn't come to see me."

She chews on her bottom lip as I maintain eye contact. She blinks a couple of times before her cheeks flush.

Her cute curiosity turns to trite anger. "Yeah, about that. I really don't think that was a fair grade."

She doesn't know what to make of me yet. After Mikael went quiet, I kept going back to see her because she was my entire existence. I didn't sneak in to fuck her like he did, only to watch over her. Stalking Summer was the only thing I was compelled to do because it was the only way I knew how to protect her.

A singular focus.

As the years went on, my mind transformed into something more complex and nuanced than a single thread of existence. Since the biggest threat to her was living inside my head, I decided the easiest way to keep her safe was to stay away from her.

I lick my bottom lip and my lips quirk into a smile. "How so? I'd like to think I grade quite fair."

She pulls out her laptop and leans in, her typical sweater dress pulling her cleavage together even though she's trying adorably hard to be professional right now.

"My sources were sufficient," she says, matter-of-factly. As if her stating it makes it true. "I used three of them from the textbook."

She leans forward and I get a whiff of her perfume, and my eyes linger on her pink full lips. She never wears makeup like this, so she must be trying to impress me.

In an instant, her sad eyes turn feral as her pupils darken.

She loves the way I just looked at her—the reason she keeps answering my calls and will continue answering my calls. Summer loves being looked at. All she knows in her short life is being watched.

I tilt my head at her. "That's the thing, I read your paper carefully. You didn't complete the requirements for a passing grade. We asked for three sources to back up your work—at least one external, besides the required readings. I can't pass you when you neglected to complete the basic requirements for the assignment."

She snaps her lips together and crosses her legs so I can no longer stare at them, but her sweater dress is so short, it rides up her thighs, and for a split second, I see the little wound he put near her cunt. My cock grows thick at the sight of it.

I'm amazed that's all he did to her—it could have been a lot worse.

She catches me looking and her eyes narrow. She wants to say it; she knows in her heart who I am.

Do it, baby. Ask me if I'm the one that did that to you.

A flush of heat spreads across her cheeks as her mind races. If she says something and she's wrong, that would be quite the embarrassment in front of her father's protégé.

I'm not done playing with her yet, so I'll have to spend the next ten minutes convincing her I'm not who she thinks I am.

She lets out a sigh in defeat. "I did the readings, and my thesis statement was solid. You can't dispute that."

I swivel my chair to face her, again mirroring the face she's giving me. "I'm sorry, but my grade stands." I keep my voice soft and her eyes skim over my body. "Your thesis was good, but it wasn't enough. You have to seek out and find additional sources outside of the ones listed." I turn to my computer. "Do you have access to the journal article database?"

She leans forward to look at my screen, her face visibly calming. "I think so, yeah. I just…don't know how to use it."

Liar. Not with her infamous father. She knows who I am on that basis alone, so it's adorable she's pretending not to understand this database.

"I can show you how to do a basic search if you'd like? Sourcing articles is hard and tedious for new students, but it's a good skill to learn early in your academic career."

Sadness clouds her eyes. "No, it's fine. I'll figure it out." She looks at me carefully, picking her perfect words. She's silent for a few seconds before saying, "You know who I am, don't you, Lincoln?"

My insides light on fire and I dart my eyes to the computer screen, then back to her. "Yes, I know who you are, Summer."

Her hand moves to the soft skin of her leg, her eyes drawing down to the mark just underneath the fabric. "What was he like?" she asks, keeping her eyes drawn down.

I let out a small laugh and lean back. "Who? Dr. Landry?"

Her eyes draw up to meet mine. "Yeah."

"He was your father. Why are you asking me like you don't know anything about him?"

The intensity of her stare is exactly what I was waiting for.

"Sometimes it's like I didn't know him at all," she admits, and I truly wonder if she ever did. But I'm certain she was aware of what he was; what I want to uncover is why she suppressed her memories.

I scratch the back of my neck. "His brilliance was truly exceptional. His mind was fascinating."

"More brilliant than Dr. Garcia?" she asks. Her question takes me aback. Dr. Garcia was his mentor, and he surpassed her in so many ways.

"Or what about you? I've heard that you're supposed to be a genius.

My father spent a lot of time with you," she says playfully, her eyes gleaming.

I shrug and choose not to dwell on my brilliance. "He was different from Dr. Garcia. His research was more chaotic, yet precise. He delved into intense psychological theories about the true driving forces behind fear. It was truly an honor to collaborate with him."

Glancing at the neatly stacked papers on my desk in the corner, she asks, "Is that the research you're currently working on?"

"Some parts of it. That research provided me with a new purpose in life."

Her pen finds her mouth as she smiles, and I can finally see her dimples. "You sound like a real professor."

I chuckle. "I will be a professor in a matter of months, but you're not here to talk about my work. Let's talk about why you came to see me."

She hoods her eyes, then looks up at me with her long lashes. "I don't stand a chance in this class, do I?"

I lean back in my chair and arch my brows. "Everything's within reach, Summer…if you're willing to work hard enough."

A playful smile hints at her lips. "What do I have to do then, Lincoln?" She runs the pencil down her chest to draw my attention to where she wants it to go. "To help get my grade up."

Flirting with the TA. If she only knew I've already experienced that slick cunt of hers and how much she already owns me because of it.

I pretend to think about it. "I'll tell you what… Write a thousand words about today's topic in class. Build on last week's reflection and give me a thesis statement. Source out at least two additional journals to support the topic. You don't have to dive into the actual research, but I want to make sure you understand today's theory."

She runs her hands through her perfect, angelic hair. "Nature vs. nurture, got it."

I shake my head. "Nature, Summer. We are talking about the principles of psychobiology. Nurture has nothing to do with it. It's all about what you were born with: brain anatomy, nervous system, levels of dopamine that cause your primal, most basic responses to situations."

The opposite of her father's field of study, which was focused more on emotion. Her inability to grasp this is not unexpected—and exactly the theory I'm trying to prove. She comes from a genetic line of killers.

She shoots me a blank stare, her emotions bubbling to the surface. "I'm sorry. This is all so confusing."

"Do you have a study partner?" I ask softly. "Someone you can bounce ideas off of? We strongly encourage it in this class; someone you can build trust with. We realize some of these concepts can be quite complex, and it's helpful to talk them through."

I can't wait to hear her response to this question.

Her eyes flash. "Sort of… I suppose I do."

I rise and casually sit on the desk in front of her, my leg in line with hers.

"Keep talking things through with him. It will help. You have to be open and vulnerable, though. This class brings up ugly feelings in some students because it forces you to be self-aware, and people don't often like what they see."

She swallows hard and plays with her hair—a tick she does when she's nervous, and that's probably because I've inserted myself into her personal space.

"Are you self-aware, Lincoln?" she finally asks without moving. "Did you have to accept everything about yourself, even if they're ugly or disturbing?"

I chuckle. "You have no idea how long I've spent psychoanalyzing myself."

I've come to terms with what I am. Now she just has to come to terms with what she is…preferably before *he* kills her.

"Do you know what I do when I'm stuck?" She nods at me, her eyes filled with a pleading gaze. "When I'm struggling, I like to go back to classical theory, otherwise known as the philosopher's point of view. Plato and Aristotle each had different theories of where our thoughts and feelings arise from. Plato believed our mind was connected to the brain, as do scientists today, and Aristotle thought they are directly connected to the heart."

She bites on her pen, giving me a playful grin. "Well, that's just ridiculous."

"Is it?"

"Of course it is! I mean, isn't it scientifically proven that our thoughts are connected to our brains?" She pauses and thinks about it, which is utterly adorable. "They are…right?"

"Well, think about it this way. Are our emotions not directly connected to our overall wellbeing and vitality? If you are sick, hurt, tired, does that not impact emotion? And is vitality not directly connected to our heart?"

She muses and her face lights up. "I guess I never really considered it from that perspective."

I move closer to her and casually position myself directly in front of her. "Have you ever taken the time to think about what it truly means to have a broken heart? Why is it that the emotions we feel in our chest are connected to our brain? And if that's the case, why do we perceive them here?" I softly place my hand on her chest, right over her heart, and her lips part slightly.

As soon as I make physical contact, Mikael withers inside me, bursting to come out. Luckily, my walls are stronger while in my office. Here, I am in charge, and he has no place fronting at work.

"Huh," she says, her brain working through it. Her little mouth chewing on that pen.

I mirror her confused facial expression and move my hand. "It's a powerful metaphor, but it helps put it all in perspective. Go back to the classic philosophers. I'm convinced they all had it figured out back then, and scientists have merely been wasting our time ever since."

Her eyes linger on mine, her pale face filling with the same beautiful color as it does when she's turned on.

"And that, Summer, is the reason your heart is beating so fast right now while you're talking to me. It's all connected right there." My eyes drift to her cleavage, then back to her questioning gaze. A moment of silence passes between us.

"Have we met before, Lincoln?" she finally asks, rising, her body now positioned between my legs. Our faces are in line with each other and our eyes meet. "I feel like we have. You seem so familiar to me."

I tilt my head, and she mirrors my movement.

"I must have one of those faces," I tease, arching my brows.

She studies me, peering into my eyes, trying to find some evidence of him, which she won't find. Our mouths are so close, and I wonder if she wants me to kiss her.

"Yeah," she whispers. "I guess you kind of do."

She pulls away, slipping her body away from mine, but the electricity between us is still simmering. "Thank you for everything," she says and leans over to grab her computer.

"Anytime, Summer. I want you to succeed."

She turns to leave but pauses. "What did you mean when you said... him?"

My eyes shoot to her.

"Earlier, when you asked me about my study partner. I don't recall telling you my study partner was male."

I let my eyes fall to her sexy bare legs. "I guess I just assumed. Apologies if that was presumptuous."

She presses her lips into a thin line. "I have a couple of roommates I can talk to, but sometimes it's nice talking to a stranger, you know?"

"My door is always open, if you ever want to talk."

She pulls her backpack over her shoulder as a flush hits her face.

"Oh, and Summer." She glances back at me, her white hair gradually darkening as the room dims with the onset of evening. "Take care out there. This school always gets a little crazy with Shadowface. Don't let him distract you."

Her face is unreadable as she listens to my words. A hint of a smile, a touch of emotion.

"Thanks, Lincoln. It was really nice to meet you."

"It was nice to meet you, too, Summer."

She melts into the darkness of the hallway and a jolt hits me like an electric current, nearly paralyzing me.

With calm and ease, I rise and close the door behind her. My jaw clenches at the laughter that echoes in my mind and the current that runs over my skin, like I had an unexpected jab into my heart.

He's here with me, I realize, completely synchronized with my mind like a spider spinning its web. The level of control and precision astonishes me. He weaved this whole time, like a whisper in the wind, and I didn't notice the complexity of the pattern until after it was finished.

The hairs on my neck stand on end, and it's not from Mikael. The sudden jolt of emotion wasn't caused by him—it didn't carry his emotional signature. Whatever it was is far more unexpected and alarming.

I shove the emotion down before it has a chance to embed itself into me. I can't help but wonder where it originates from, and if I have another alter I must silence.

Fragments are the easiest to mute, but I must do so fast, before it has time to grow.

CHAPTER
SIXTEEN
SUMMER

I step out of Lincoln's office and can't contain my heart rate, which spiked the moment I walked in, and escalated in those final seconds when I saw the monster in Lincoln's eyes right before I left. I press my back up against the hallway just to breathe, slapping my hand over my mouth.

A couple of students walk by and stare at me curiously as they disappear into the shadowed hallway, leaving me alone with a psychopath in the psychology department of all places. Does this school not realize what he is? How has Lincoln been able to hide what's inside him?

It's him—I know it in my heart. Those near-translucent eyes came back. The same ones I saw at the rave. Watching. Waiting. Whispering. It invigorates me.

Whatever it was, it wasn't there when I first walked in. It showed itself at the very end. The insidiousness was inside of Lincoln.

That memory, once lost and forgotten, now plays out in my mind. His creepy teenage gaze fixated on my body and he looked sad. I tried to smile at him but his eyes grew dark and heavy. All I could see was darkness inside his soul, pure evil. I refused to look at him the rest of dinner.

A prickling discomfort ran up my spine and I wished he would leave. The boy at the dinner table was Lincoln—they are the same person. His eyes flickered the same way.

· · ·

M y dreams began the night he spent in our guest room. My father wasn't helping an orphan; he invited in a monster.

I remember him so clearly now, and I'm kicking myself for not seeing it sooner. I can't find anything about Lincoln Kennedy online, because Lincoln Kennedy doesn't exist.

My heart rate slows, and I make my way down the darkened hall and take the stairwell down to the main floor. Even though his presence in this building is all-consuming, I need to get away from him. I need to regroup and think about my next move, especially if I want to stay alive.

I stop mid-step and sit down, my heart in my throat. My phone dings in my purse and I take it out, secretly hoping it's him.

It's Dani, wondering what the hell is taking me so long, and that she'll wait another ten minutes before she's going home.

I ignore it, my thoughts entirely consumed by the man in the ivory tower.

Lincoln was not at all what I was expecting. His cool indifference in class must be a mask, because the man I met was smart, kind, and seemed to know my inner thoughts. He's even sexier up close, his skin pale and soft.

I can't imagine he was the same awkward boy I met all those years ago, but there is no denying it. I'm so attracted to him, I could burst. Lincoln Kennedy is *everything*.

I close my eyes, remembering the rave. His soft hand when he held mine through the crowd, the way he took care of me, and the clear shift in him when he started cutting my clothes and burning my skin.

The references to *we* and *him*, like there are two of them inside his mind.

My scar starts to pulse, shifting from pain to desire. My phone buzzes again, pulling me from those dark thoughts.

Dani: *Okay. Where the fuck are you? I saw Lincoln leave already, and I'm not leaving you with some psycho on the loose. Meet me now.*

Once I'm out of the sandstone building, Dani and Misty are both waiting for me, leaning against a gargoyle statue, the sun low in the sky, giving off a doomsday glow.

Misty perks up when she sees me, her blonde hair peeking out of a wool hat. Dani frowns, and I can tell she is annoyed with me. The two of them seem inseparable lately. Their friendship is growing while I seem to be fading away—much too absorbed with studying with a certain someone while they are matching their outfits.

"So what did he say?" Misty asks, and Dani barely spares me a glance.

I keep walking past both of them, making them catch up to me. "He's keeping my F, but he's letting me make it up with a new essay."

"Okay...that's good, right?" Misty offers.

"It's good," I say dryly.

I make eye contact with Dani as she steps in beside me in her knee-high boots. She narrows her eyes. "You were in there for a long time. What were you doing?"

My teeth find my bottom lip. "We were just talking."

"Ha. Yeah, whatever you say."

My eyes flit up to hers, but I don't say anything.

Dani continues, "Remember that rumor I was telling you about Lincoln? He makes girls—"

My stomach swirls. "Makes girls, what?"

She licks her bottom lip, her eyes gleaming. "He makes them go on their knees."

Misty's eyes grow wide like saucers, and I cut her a glare. I'm acting guilty, so guilty. I pull my hair behind my ear as Misty stares at me curiously. "I don't know what you're talking about. All we did was talk. If you're insinuating I sucked off my TA to get a better grade, you can rest easy, Dani."

Dani just smirks and crosses her arms. "You're blushing, Summer, and I've only ever seen you blush once."

I place my hand to my cheek and she's right, it's burning hot.

"I didn't do that. All we did was talk, and he's letting me make up my assignment. But thank you for thinking the best of me."

Dani crosses her arms. "Okay, I believe you. But you're hiding something from me, I know it."

I roll my eyes, attempting to conceal the complex feelings I have for him, as well as my desperation for him.

We pass a group of security guards, and I'm reminded of the missing girl from a few towns over. A tight ball forms in my chest—jealousy tightening its grip on my heart, not the guilt I should be experiencing.

"He offered me extra help, too," Misty says out of the blue. Both Dani and I whip our heads to her. "I'm going to visit him every week."

She darts her gaze between the two of us as we head to Dani's car in the dark parking lot.

I glare at her and bite the inside of my cheek until my jaw locks. "Did you go down on *your* knees? You were in there before I was," I ask her, and Misty's face fires red.

She shakes her head. "I would never do that, that would be unethical…but he was flirty with me, too."

That word.

Ethics.

He made me recite every sentence of that chapter.

"He's a nerd," I mutter, pulling my seatbelt over my shoulder. "Why are we even talking about him?"

Dani grins and slides in next to me. "That nerd is really hot, Summer. I can't see how a guy who looks like that is single. And if he was flirting with you, then you need to get me closer to Xander."

"Well, ask Misty, then," I say flippantly. "Apparently, she's the one he likes." I turn back and wink at her. She scowls, but I don't miss the tears forming in her eyes.

It seems as though I have lost all sense of life within me. The words that fill my heart with bitterness are not my own. They can only be attributed to my nameless monster, and the years of him whispering in my ear while I was asleep. I have no other explanation.

We drive the rest of the way in silence. When we arrive home, Misty grabs her things, heads to her room, and slams the door.

I stand in our small kitchen, and I give Dani a *what the fuck did I do* look.

She merely frowns. "You haven't exactly been warm to her."

I place my head in my hands and lean over the barstool. "Well, I haven't exactly felt like myself since my father died."

This summer was the hardest of my life. When I left home, I also left the life my mom wanted for me and trounced around Europe. I was going through the motions. I had these images of what college was going to be like, that it would make me better. Coming here, following in my father's footsteps, seemed like the right thing to do.

My time, though, has largely been spent in solitude, engrossed in books, and captivated by a psychopath with potentially duplicitous personalities. One who cursed me with the mark of death.

Dani looks sad, and I can tell she's reflecting on her own father, who's been away for years. "Yeah, I know the feeling."

Dani grabs the kettle and starts boiling some water, placing tea bags in two cups. I'm relieved she's not following Misty and ignoring me after my outburst. I miss talking to her.

She turns to face me as I slouch on the island. "I hope you can start to enjoy yourself soon, because it looks like you're tearing yourself apart." Her eyes drag up my body. "You've lost weight."

I place my hands on my waist and graze my hip bone, and give her a weak smile. I hate fighting with Dani, and I hate lying to her even more.

Waiting for the water to boil, she scoots her butt on the edge of the counter and stares at me. "So tell me about your conversation with Lincoln. Was he really flirting with you?"

I bite my lip and can't help but let out a small smile. "I don't know if I'd call it flirting, but he gave me a vibe."

Her eyebrows shoot to the ceiling. "A vibe? What kind of vibe?"

I lean forward, resting my chin on my hands, propping my elbows on the table. "He was kind of sweet. I maybe kind of get what girls see in him. We talked about my father."

Her eyes are curious. "And you've never met him before?"

"My father kept his home and work life separate. I might have met him once, but that was a long time ago, and I was young."

She stops in her tracks as if putting two and two together. "You don't think... Is he the freak messaging you?"

My stomach drops. "I don't know...probably not."

She looks at me like she doesn't believe me. "Has he messaged you since you told him to fuck off?"

The kettle whistles behind her as I think about what sweet lie will roll off my tongue next.

"No. I haven't heard from him since that first week."

Now, Summer. Tell her everything now. Do it for Cali, do it for all the people he might kill. Tell someone that you think your life is in danger.

Apparently, I have a death wish. Either that, or I'm extremely sexually frustrated because I say nothing.

"Good." She turns her back to me and pours the hot water into each cup. "You probably scared him off. Tell me if he messages you again, though. Especially with everything going on and the missing girl and that creepy photo. I don't want you to end up as a statistic or something."

Emphasis on the or something...

I sigh, rise, and grab my tea. "I promise I'll tell you. I'm sure it was nothing."

I head upstairs to my attic bedroom and get ready for a really long night. My eyelids are heavy, and I lean back on my bed and rest my eyes for only a few minutes, ignoring the hot tea but enjoy its spicy aroma.

I snooze for a few minutes, then force myself to get to work. I pull out my textbook, sip on my lukewarm tea, and start working on my make-up assignment for Lincoln.

I read the words, try to understand the concepts, but they just don't resonate. Not the way they did when Lincoln talked through the theories with me.

He made me understand them so I could comprehend them. *I could feel them.*

Eventually, I grab my computer, sit at my desk, and type in Lincoln Kennedy and Kinsmen University. All that pops up is his university profile, which I've already seen, and he's like a ghost on his other socials.

So I take a different approach and type in Mikael Peters, but no one by the name Mikael Peters comes up as a student at this school. It's like Mikael with his odd, spelled name, died along with his mother. Except he didn't because my father brought him to my house years later.

I clench my jaw and bring up the journal site Lincoln showed me and type in his name. He's in at least thirty published journals, every one of them co-authored by Dr. Garcia and my father.

Genetic mutations, brain abnormalities, inherited psychological traits, and emotional responses.

Nature, Summer. Nurture has nothing to do with it.

It's like his only existence is around his research. As if nothing else matters.

I'm suddenly very curious as to what Lincoln's doing his PhD on. What is his ultimate theory?

I type in my father's name. I promised myself I wouldn't do this, but it was inevitable. Hundreds of search items pop up, dating back at least twenty years. Nearly all of them are co-authored with Dr. Garcia, until they abruptly stopped three months ago when he died.

I never really understood what my father studied, but I believe that matters now, given he was the world's leading expert on fear.

Fear. Synonymous with death. Death equated with murder.

Four missing girls...hundreds before them. One of them staring up at him lovingly in a photo.

Serial killers instill fear. Shadowface instills fear.

I look at photos from the killings of 2002 and try to imagine each victim as a person, a girl like me. Each photo represents life lost at the hands of a monster. Needless deaths...unless—

His own personal test subjects...

What is a better way to study fear than instilling it? How many did he need until he got what he wanted?

Was four enough, or were there more? Was Kimberly Peters a Shadowface victim, too?

Did my father savagely murder four women? He's the only person smart enough to do it and get away with it.

My stomach convulses as the evidence starts to unfold. I saw something as a child and blocked it out. I saw him do something he shouldn't have done. Something so heinous, it was easier for me to pretend it didn't happen.

My father was Shadowface...I feel it in my heart.

I quickly press the back button and close the browser. I can't look at that right now. The back of my head hits the headboard behind me. And the sickness in my stomach spreads into my veins as an icy breeze ruffles my curtains.

"What did you do to those girls, Daddy?" I whisper. *Who was Mikael to you? Are Mikael and Lincoln the same person?*

I place my computer down and close my eyes, ignoring the tears streaming down my face. It only takes me a minute to fall asleep, and as I drift off, I think of masked faces and tears of blood.

Warm feelings, love, acceptance.

The years my nameless monster spent manipulating my mind to crave death. And now...now when I think about him, he has an actual face.

Lincoln's face.

CHAPTER
SEVENTEEN
SUMMER

A full week goes by and nothing. It's now early October, and with no additional evidence, the media has treated Cali's disappearance as a missing person's case, not a murder. Nothing to indicate a resurgence of Shadowface, other than the blistered X on my thigh and the giant hole he left in my heart. I haven't found any new information about the Order or who's involved—nothing to help me piece this all together. Part of me thinks everyone in this town is in on the dirty secret, and I'm nothing but a puppet.

Like everyone is watching me and the silence is mocking me.

My days start and end in a haze. I wake up, go to class, read, study, repeat. He doesn't text; he doesn't indicate he's watching me or even exists at all.

I try my hardest to forget him by burying myself in my other classes, wishing my dark feelings for him will go away, but they don't.

If anything, they've festered and grown. Shifted and transformed into something I can't explain. He fills every empty part of me, eating me from the inside out, to the point I can barely focus on anything else. And I seem to have a lot of empty parts these days.

I hang out with Dani and Misty here and there, but I mainly avoid them. Misty and I can't seem to find our footing, and that's partly due to me being so rude to her. The distance between me and Dani is widening while I watch her and Misty's friendship grow stronger, and I'm unsure how to fix it.

It's Wednesday, and I head into psychology with my usual tingly anticipation as I head up the wooden stairs to where Dani and Misty are sitting in our usual place at the back of the lecture hall. Dani waves at me but frowns as someone takes the seat next to her, and mouths, *I'm sorry*, as I'm left in the dust.

I wave at her to let her know everything's fine. I spot a couple of seats in a row near the front—just one row away from where Lincoln usually sits. I take one of the seats, and Lincoln enters my field of vision, rocking me to my core.

He gracefully enters the lecture hall, looking exceptionally attractive, and settles into his usual chair before adjusting his glasses. He sits in a relaxed and confident manner, with his arms crossed over his tight black shirt, his muscles flexed and his jaw clenched.

He still acts as if we don't know each other. He acts like I'm invisible, even though I'm certain we almost shared a kiss in his office and his eyes looked nearly possessed when I left. Like they literally changed color.

Right now he seems so normal and composed, and I have no choice but to question if what I saw was real.

Except, what is real are these feelings burying themselves deep into my heart, and I wonder if I'm the one becoming obsessed with him.

This town is making me insane.

Dr. Garcia follows him in, giving him a small smile before heading up to the stage to start today's lecture.

I finished my extra credit paper during the weekend instead of going out, and my eyes lit up this morning when I saw he returned it with a grade of a B- and a note: *Much better. Come see me during my office hours when you get a chance.*

My little dark heart picked up a notch, so desperate for interaction with him. Any interaction, since SF has gone icy cold since he maimed my thigh and I told him to leave me alone. I plan on visiting him this Friday. It's time to find out why he's pretending to be someone else and why he lied about meeting me before.

An enormous shadow looms beside me, pulling my attention, and Grant slinks into the spot next to mine.

My stomach roils.

"Hey, sexy girl," he says, loud and obnoxious, which captures Lincoln's attention. Only a twitch of his head, but I saw it.

A reaction.

My skin crawls at the sound of Grant's voice, and Grant's arm finds the back of my chair, forcing me to sit closer to him. The scent of his cheap cologne isn't appealing to me and makes me want to gag.

I turn and smile, snapping on the charm, knowing I have Lincoln's full attention. "Hey, Grant."

"So, I was thinking," he says, moving his arm down, his hand slinking over my shoulder. "I want to take you out. Just me and you."

Lincoln's head twitches again, and a satisfying twinge hits my stomach at his clear reaction to Grant's voice.

I imagine that sexy, terrifying flicker flowing through his eyes.

"Yeah," I say smiling, speaking as sexy as I can, crossing my legs and pressing out my chest as if Lincoln has eyes on the back of his head and can see how good I look.

"Yeah, sexy. We could catch a movie, and I can take you to dinner." Bile hits my throat as his hand finds my thigh. "I want to get to know you a bit more." He's basically chewing on my ear at this point.

I've seen Grant around school getting to *know* other girls, too. I want nothing to do with him.

I remember those final threats from SF at the rave, but since SF doesn't seem to give a shit, I don't see how he has any right to threaten anyone I choose to go out with.

I smile sweetly. "I'd love to."

Grant is distracted, staring down at my boobs, and Lincoln's head finally turns to face me. My breath gets caught in my throat as translucent eyes stare back at me—they weren't the eyes Lincoln walked in with and are similar to whatever I saw inside him in the office.

His jaw flexes as he beholds me, his mouth twitching to a small but cocky smirk, almost boyish. And while I'm melting inside, I give him nothing. No emotion, no smile, no outward expression of how terrifying he looks right now—or how sexy he is. Or how he's not looking or acting the way Lincoln usually does.

My lungs seize as I stare back at Lincoln, who is observing me and not even trying to hide it.

Lincoln's eyes flash, and he fixes me a psychotic blank stare, and for a moment, it's like we are the only two people in the room. In a flash, they are normal again, and I wonder if anyone else in this room noticed.

Lincoln turns back and faces Dr. Garcia as if that didn't happen, and the lights dim. Grant, thank god, didn't see the intense interaction.

I'll confront him when I see him next. Whoever this monster is inside of Lincoln needs to come out and talk to me.

Dr. Garcia's heels click over the marble stage in the bundle of fury that she is, and I shift my attention to her. She has managed to remain, thus far, an afterthought in my mind, but I am growing suspicious of her.

She must have known what my father was. She knew him too well not to have known anything.

What are your dirty secrets, Talia Garcia?

My mother hated her. Jealous whenever my father mentioned her, which is likely why he never brought her around much.

She's just an old woman now, grasping on her final days, but I've seen photos of her in her youth. She was a dark beauty, with onyx hair to her lower back that covered the entirety of her slight frame. Everything about her reminds me of midnight. She certainly looked like someone who might worship a dark deity.

Her research is less refined.

Fear. Anger. *Loathing.*

My father had the fear covered in spades. So does that leave her with anger or loathing?

Do you loathe yourself, Dr. Garcia?

Grant squeezes my arm, and I smile back at him but shift over slightly and focus diligently on taking notes for class.

Week five of the semester, and we're finally done learning about biological psychology. And I found the material dry as hell. I didn't sign up to learn about the anatomy of the brain, nor do I care that it's the unifying function. I'm loving this week's topic on developmental psychology—the nurture.

I want to understand the phenomenon that is the human mind. What are the factors that drive someone to commit murder? I don't believe that is something you are born with. If my father was a monster, that doesn't automatically mean I am one, too.

After class, I head to the campus pool to let off some steam and swim some laps alone. When I head to the locker room to change, I can't hide the scar SF gave me, and a few girls stare at the red and blistery mark on the edge of my swimsuit line.

They whisper, giggle, and stare. "That's a mark of the Order," one of them whispers. I guess people understand more about the lore than I give them credit for.

"She's gonna die," the other one says too casually. "The rumor is, they mark the ones they kill."

I turn and look them straight in the eye. "I cut myself," I spit out at them. "No one did this to me. And your bathing suit is way too fucking small for you." I move toward the shower, hearing gasps in my wake.

When I get home from the pool and see Dani and Misty's cars parked out front, I let out a deep sigh. My thoughts are entirely consumed by the whispers of the girls at the pool. As if my evil nature is stamped on me for the world to see.

They saw it…they grasped what he's turning me into.

I hop out of the rideshare and stare up at my tiny house. My feet suddenly can't move, and I'm planted outside, hiding beneath water-dipped trees and the glittery night sky, knowing I have to go in there and be normal. I just can't bring myself to go inside yet.

My chest stings…that hellfire he put in there is burning strong.

Breathe. One. Two. Three.

Before I know it, I'm facing the ground, keeled over.

Breathe, Summer. Precious breath.

Clearly, I am spiraling.

I take a few minutes to compose myself out of the haze. I take one last final breath and walk in, keeping my head down. When I step inside, I immediately lean down, unzipping my knee-high boots and dropping my backpack.

"There you are," Dani greets me. Her and Misty are eating pizza, and I kick off my boots and walk in. Misty still won't look at me, and Dani gives me an apologetic look. The air inside this house is suffocating.

"I was just about to text you," Dani says, hardly paying attention to me. Books are strewn out in front of them.

I smile weakly, averting my gaze from Misty. "I'm fine. I went swimming, then I needed some air."

"Summer... Seriously, just call me next time. I'll come grab you. Cali was running in the woods when she went missing, and you don't want to end up like her, do you?"

I should only be so lucky.

Misty snakes her gaze over me, and I just don't have it in me to fight with her. Can they see it on my face? The shame of what I am. The product of darkness.

Dani pats the empty barstool beside me. "Why don't you have some pizza, and I'll open a bottle of wine. And you two can talk; I'm sick of the tension between you two."

Swallowing my pride, I head over and slide onto the stool. "I'm sorry. I can be mean sometimes. I don't hate you, Misty."

She runs her hand through her hair. "It's fine. Let's have some fun. I'm sick of the tension, too." She's probably forgiving me because she knows Dani won't relent until we make up.

We have a couple drinks, relax, and try to have fun.

It's...robotic. Typical. Boring. And I end up having one too many drinks.

"Are you okay, Summer?" Dani asks me as the three of us finish a game of cards.

I keep staring at my phone as if that will make a difference. As if it will make him call me. I fake a yawn. "Yeah, I'm just...tired."

I excuse myself and head to my room, change into my camisole and shorts, open my window, and crawl into bed. Picking up my phone, I scroll to the last message I sent SF.

I asked him not to contact me, and he listened. And his silence lands like a gut punch, which I can't help but think is what he intended.

I click on the message and start typing, knowing I will completely regret this decision. The couple glasses of wine are clearly clouding my judgment. But the heat in my blood doesn't want to simmer, even as the cool breeze from outside pebbles my skin.

Why the fuck do I miss him so much? I don't even know him.

Summer: *Hi...*

It's a while before he reads my message. I place my phone down and lean my head back as my stomach shifts into full-blown anxiety.

He doesn't want me anymore.

Then, he has the decency to respond.

SF: *What do you want, Summer?*

What do I want?

I pause for a moment, not actually expecting him to respond, let alone respond like that. This man stuck his fingers inside me. He ripped into my skin with the heated edge of a razor, and now he's asking what I *want*?

Summer: *I want help... You told me you'd help me study.*

Truth. All truth... I just have to ignore the burning in my core.

Again, he doesn't respond right away. A few minutes tick by, and I start into my textbook. The words are not quite registering. When I look at my phone, I find the last message wasn't even read. Finally—

SF: *You're such a good liar, aren't you?*

Fuck him. I'm not a liar.

Summer: *So that's it, then?*

SF: *That's it...unless you can tell me what you really want. You told me numerous times, and not politely, to leave you alone...so I did.*

I bite my lip and shift, waiting for his response. Trying to imagine Lincoln on the other end of the line, where he is right now and what he's doing.

Summer: *That's not what I want.*

He responds quickly this time.

SF: *Much better. So, what do you want, exactly? Be clear, because I have things to do.*

I read those words and scroll over to his message on his assignment.

Much better... Just like he left on my paper.

He's leaving me so many clues.

I can't fathom the person texting me is the well spoken and kind TA I met. But all the evidence is pointing toward it.

Without thinking, I press the call button.

He answers immediately.

"Shouldn't you be studying?" I close my eyes, appreciating his voice. So deep, sexy, and familiar. It kills me hearing it again. I find it even more concerning that I miss him so much, especially considering the fact that he is, or at least was, stalking me.

I shut my computer down and move to my bed, positioning myself over the covers. "That's the thing," I tell him. "I am trying. I just can't understand it." I spent all week trying to comprehend the material.

A silent pause. "What part are you struggling with?"

I bite my lip as tears threaten to burn the backs of my eyes.

"Be honest with me, Summer. What aren't you connecting with?"

Cognitive vs. Operant Conditioning—*Dr. Kevin Landry.* Every theory, every thought grounded in research.

How scared were those girls before my father cut their eyes out? Lincoln knows who wrote the words I am expected to internalize. Is this why he's targeting me? It would make sense if my father killed his mother.

"I just...I need to talk it through with someone."

"And why should I do that? What's in it for me?" His voice has shifted. Bored. Indifferent.

I pull my knees up. "Because you told me you would?"

Another pause.

"I have to go, Summer."

No. No. No.

"Wait!" I cry out before he hangs up.

Silence. He's waiting for me to say something.

"How do I know you're real?"

A dark pause. "I'm not sure I follow."

"Prove to me you're a real killer."

Why the fuck would I ask him that? I am losing my grip on reality.

I stare at the wall, listening to his breathing on the other line as my heart beats blistering fast. A few agonizing seconds pass before a message comes through, and I swipe on it.

My heart nearly stops at the sight in front of me as I stare at a photo of the missing girl, Cali. Intense jealousy burns in my blood staring at her bound hands, her clothes half ripped off. Her eyes are open, staring into the camera. Fear bleeding out of her eyes...open eyes.

She's alive.

I blink at it twice, and I don't even recognize my voice as I speak to him. "I should go to the police."

His voice is deadly. Calm. Quiet. "But you won't, will you, Summer?"

I don't respond.

Without thinking, I move my hair down over my shoulders so it's splayed out in pretty waves over my chest and take my shorts off so I'm in my panties. I reach into my purse and grab my pink lipstick, then grab my phone and bring up the video so I can see myself. I spread it evenly over my lips, making a popping sound when I'm done.

Before pressing the video button, I position myself a certain way. He answers, and my face pops up on the camera, but of course, he has no video on.

I smile into the camera, knowing I won. Now that he can see me, there is no way he will let me go.

"Hi," I breathe.

A pause, just heavy breathing in the way he usually does when he is turned on by me. "Well, don't you look nice."

No pretty girl?

My thighs heat—no, not my thighs…my entire body ignites.

"Don't I get to see you?" I ask him, propping the camera up as I lie on my pillow, my hair splaying out beside me, my cleavage pushing up in my tank top.

"I thought you told me to leave you alone?" he says.

I look up at him through my long eyelashes, hoping it has the desired effect. "I changed my mind. I think I need your help, and you promised you would help me. It's easier when I have someone to talk to about this. It's how I learn; I don't retain anything while reading."

He swallows. "You still want my help? Even knowing what I am?"

I'm not so sure I know what he is. He hasn't killed anyone that I'm aware of…yet. He sent me a picture of the missing girl, who seems very much still alive.

"Yes, I want your help," I repeat back to him. "Do you want me to beg?"

"And what are you going to do for me? This arrangement feels one-sided."

I arrange my camera on the tripod on my desk, which conveniently sits across from my bed. I hear Misty and Dani laughing from down-stairs. They could easily walk in on me.

That makes the thrill of this so much more fun.

I rise to my knees, the soft bedding tickling my skin. "Are you still watching me?" I ask, suddenly very self-conscious about what I plan to do.

"Yeah, baby, I'm still watching."

I sit cross-legged and look into the camera. "I want to see you," I tell him. "Turn your camera on, too."

I hear him breathe. I can only imagine what he's doing right now.

"Please," I whisper.

"Okay, hold on." I adjust myself again as he puts the call on hold.

A few seconds later, the video pops up, and he's there, wearing his burlap mask, which makes me want to scream. He's leaning back on the bed with his hands behind his head, his arm muscles flexing in his black T-shirt. In fact, he looks mighty fucking relaxed.

"So, what game are we playing right now?" he asks through the blank darkness.

I reach down and pull off my camisole, leaving me topless. He tilts his head as I rise to my knees, the same way the girls in the photo are positioned.

"Is this what you wanted to see?" I breathe and flip my hair, quite unsure what I am supposed to do with my hands. I lean back on them, spreading my legs slightly.

He chuckles, and not in a way I like. I perch up and frown. "You've been asking to see me like this all semester. Isn't this what you want?"

"You have no idea what I want from you, Summer."

"I can guess."

"No, baby. You can't."

I pause and wrap my arms around myself as a cool breeze hits from outside, causing my nipples to harden like rocks. "Do you want me to stop?"

He leans back even further, his hand finding the hem of his trousers. "I never said that."

It's too late. He ruined it… Clearly, he's moved on. I flash my gaze downward.

"Keep going," he presses. "You have my attention."

I find his gaze again. His head is tilted, and he's leaning forward as if wanting to get a better view of me.

My tongue runs along my bottom lip and my heart is simply purring. "Okay," I say, running my hand down my stomach, playing with the hem of my panty line, mirroring his movement.

A dirty little game we play.

My fingers linger on the blistered X, and I pause. "Do you remember the night you fucked me?" I ask him outright, keeping my eyes down on the mark of death.

No more pretending he hasn't been in my life for a long time. He doesn't respond immediately like I thought he would. In fact, he doesn't respond at all.

For a moment, I worry I have this all wrong. That it wasn't him; that perhaps it was someone else, or another version of him entirely.

Finally, he says, "Yeah, I remember."

I instantly relax. "You told me the next time you saw me you'd kill me." Just the parting words every young girl wants to hear from the man who deflowered her.

He tilts his head again, and this time, I can see him smile. "Yeah, I suppose I did."

I return his smile. "Well, you lied. Because I'm still breathing."

I'm taunting him so deliciously.

"We can change that any time you want, baby." My body vibrates at the thought.

I hitch a breath and run the finger over the X. "Are you going to kill me? That's what this mark means, doesn't it?"

He shifts. "I haven't decided what I'm going to do with you yet. I don't want you looking so composed. Relax, Summer. This isn't one of your pageants, and I don't give a fuck about sophistication. Let it go, baby."

I sit back on my knees. "What are you going to make me do right now?" I ask him as my hands run over my stomach. Every nerve is shaking.

He smiles wickedly through his burlap, his legs lazy in front of him. "The thing is, I'm not going to *make* you do anything. I want to see what you will do all on your own."

My pussy is so wet; if he were here, he would be able to smell it. Closing my eyes, I can still feel the warmth of his body pressed so close to mine.

That body—

I try not to think of how fucked up this is, or how crazy I am for doing this.

"You're not recording me, are you?" I ask.

He shakes his head. "No. I'm keeping you all to myself."

I start by running my fingers over my breast, my nipples so hard and tight.

"I'm so fucking horny," I breathe. "Why are you doing this to me? It's like you're inside my head."

"Because I am inside your head, Summer."

Why does his voice have to be so sexy?

The pressure inside is mounting as I keep my fingers on the swell of my breast and slide my other hand down my panty line. My fingers slip inside, and I stroke my folds. A small moan pours out of me as soon as my vision catches sight of that mask again and the hushed shadows that surround him.

I close my eyes and enjoy my fingers, wishing they were his. I add another finger and arch my back and play with myself for a few minutes, forgetting everything.

My eyes open in a haze and he's still watching me, but I can't see his facial expressions. To me, he looks...indifferent.

"Do you like that?" I ask him, out of breath.

"It's a good start," he says in a low voice.

I part my lips and lean back on one hand, spreading my legs for him so he can watch everything. I can hear my wetness as my fingers stroke in and out as my orgasm builds. Knowing he's watching helps get me off, and it's not long before my insides are exploding.

I add in another finger and shove it inside myself. "I wish you were here to do this for me." My breath is ragged, my voice comes out stuttered.

"Trust me, Summer, you really don't want that. It's probably best for both of us if I keep my distance from you."

And there lies the truth of the matter.

What if I want to be his next victim? Why else would I be doing this?

Fuck. I'm catering to a psychopath.

Someone knocks on the door. "Summer?"

Shit! It's Dani, and I didn't lock my door.

"Should we invite her in to watch, too?"

I glance over at the door. "Sorry, I'm just studying," I call out to her, hoping she takes the hint and goes away.

I hear a muffled pause. "No worries. I was just checking on you. I'm going to bed."

My fingers are still pressed to my clit. I deepen my breath, waiting for her footsteps to echo down the staircase.

Finally, the stairs creak and I hear her bedroom door shut on the floor below.

I glance back at the camera. "I think...I think I'm done," I whisper, pulling my hands out and curling my knees up.

He shifts, still looking so composed compared to me. "We can be done tonight if that's what you want," he says, and I raise my eyes to meet his across the screen. He's still watching me, studying me. "But I promise you, Summer, we are far from *done*."

I pull my blanket over my body, covering myself from him, but keep the camera on. I reach over and grab my textbook and lean my head against my headboard, opening the book.

This week's topic—Cognitive vs. Operant Conditioning, an introduction to developmental psychology.

Maybe I will learn why I'm so dysfunctional.

"Will...will you still help me?" I ask him.

He reaches for his phone and flips off his camera, and my heart sinks. "Yeah, I'll still help you, but I won't make you look at this creepy mask while I do it."

I giggle at that comment, at how normal he sounds.

"I have to read this tonight," I tell him, "or I am going to fall behind."

His keyboard clicking echoes out of the phone. "When you're ready to talk about it, I'll be here."

My eyebrows furrow. "So you're just going to watch me read?"

"No. I'm going to work on my stuff while you read."

I let out a sigh and start reading through the first few paragraphs, fully aware he's watching me, even though he says he isn't.

My eyes rise. "I don't find you that scary, you know."

"You will..."

My eyes crinkle. "I will, what?"

"Eventually, you will be scared of me. I have no control when I'm near you. There is a strong possibility that beating heart of yours would cease to exist if I were near you right now. Especially the way you just positioned yourself like that."

My mouth gapes open.

"Now get to reading. That chapter shouldn't take you more than twenty minutes. When you're finished, we can chat through the concepts. And when we are done, you're going to keep this camera on so I can watch you sleep."

Goosebumps form on my arms as a tremble runs through me. And I am fully aware now of the full evil residing on the other side of that screen.

I roll onto my side and let him watch, taking my time to read every word, hyper-aware of his clicking. Eventually, I ignore him and start to absorb it all. Once I'm done, he's still there as promised, and we talk through each concept, focusing on the basic psychological theory of operant conditioning.

"I don't understand the difference," I finally admit after ten minutes of trying to explain it back to him. "I mean, I get what you're saying… I'm just not sure how it's different, if that makes any sense."

His level of patience is astounding, and I forget what he is and let him help me, like he said he wanted to.

"It's simple. Why did you take off your clothes earlier?"

Why did I do that?

I swallow a lump in my throat. "Because I wanted your attention."

"And it worked, didn't it?"

"I suppose, yes."

"Are you going to make me wait next time I ask?"

I blink, wondering what *next time* he's referring to.

"I'll do whatever you ask, when you ask."

"And I will reinforce that behavior by praising you. Now, let's think about this another way entirely. You were jealous when you saw a photo of another girl, weren't you?"

My jaw ticks.

"Answer me, Summer."

"Yes," I admit.

"You realized you're not the only pretty blonde on campus, and that my affections are easily replaced. You did that by observing and gaining a better understanding of me. So you took your clothes off without the expectation that I'd help you. You did that all on your own, with no force or reinforcement. That *ah-ha* moment you had was a cognitive leap forward, and you gained a deeper understanding of yourself."

"I…I'm not following you."

"You realized that you wanted my affections and missed them. You crave me watching you. You like to be looked at, Summer, so you took your clothes off for a total stranger. That is quite the insight about yourself and your understanding of how badly I wanted to see you like that."

Everything clicks, the concepts and my understanding of it.

I bring my fingers to my lips, keeping my eyes on the textbook, realizing everything he's saying makes total sense.

Perhaps my naughty behavior isn't because of anything being inherently wrong with me. That I enjoy being looked at because it pleases others to look at me. A strange man just got me to strip down and give him a show. And it was more, so much more, than only wanting his help.

I'm hyper motivated to write now, so I open a new Word doc and get ready to type.

"You're wrong, you know," I say without looking up from my computer.

"What am I wrong about?"

"You're not a total stranger. I know exactly who you are, Lincoln."

He doesn't respond, but I hear him clicking away on his computer.

I am a rarity, an anomaly in the human mind.

I possess a profound comprehension of my identity and what defines me. It is a strange sensation, being aware of my reality, yet living a life devoid of emotions with a deep clarity of my purpose. I can envision what it's like to be a machine programmed for a specific task without the agency to deviate from its intended purpose. I recognize when there is a flaw in the system that makes up my flawless mind.

I'm losing control.

Every second Summer is around us, Mikael grows stronger, more aware, and alert. Those tendrils are spinning. The whiplash-inducing shift from his psychotic hatred of Summer to an equally intense, blind love is deeply unsettling. It's not surprising, considering Mikael created me the moment he saw her. Or at least, let me grow from the fragment I was before that. Part of me has always existed, but that was my first real memory as a separate entity.

He initially programmed me to protect her. But I grew stronger and took over his life and made it my own. His life got infinitely better, and I finished the requirements for my degree within record time. Dr. Garcia used her power to legally change my name. Which was easy since she kept him hidden in her basement for years, and Lucy homeschooled him. He had no friends, no acquaintances.

A life of zero substance.

Which is why I'm doing my best to keep my distance from Summer since she came into my office, even though she's all I think about. I can't protect her the way I need to when I'm around her. Earlier this week, I gave into temptation and answered her call. I helped her study, she took off her clothes and let me watch her as she did naughty things, and then she eventually fell asleep with her camera on.

Mikael, as chaotic as he is, is simple. His mind never progressed beyond the day I was formed. He didn't need to, since I took over that role. He's still an adolescent—an angry adolescent with zero control over his emotions. And now, whenever we're in her presence, it feels like we're united, almost indistinguishable.

Almost, but not quite.

There is something else festering in my mind, something more complex I can't quite comprehend. I sensed it in the office when I watched Summer leave, and again when she took off her clothes for me a few days ago. It's growing, deepening its roots, almost as if this emotion doesn't belong to him, but to me.

It's Saturday night, and I'm working at my desk as loud music pumps from upstairs. I take my contacts out, and for a moment my vision is blurred until I slip my glasses on and take a moment to admire the photos he snapped of her the weekend she moved in.

I can't deny how badly I want her. My fascination with Summer Landry has unexpectedly morphed into something else.

She has zero fear, just primal lust for a masked man who's already proved dangerous. Even if she has put the pieces together that it's me.

Mikael flutters up my spine at the thought of her.

"Relax. She wasn't reacting to you."

He flutters again. *"Yes, she was."*

Admittedly, he might be right. The nights we shared with Summer are blurred. A push and pull between him and I.

His love. His hate.

Love. Hate. Love. Hate.

He had a brief moment of sanity before his hatred completely consumed him. It was during this time he did the most selfless thing he could do.

He put himself in a box.

All I have are fleeting moments of satisfaction, frustration, and anger, which put me on a constant pursuit of pleasure and knowledge, which is a wonderful place to be.

I've yet to feel anything truly gratifying. The more I understood her connection to Mikael, the more I had a compulsion to understand her better. As I spent time with Summer's father and learned what he was, I started asking questions. Like one of the ultimate debates in the field of psychology.

Nature vs. Nurture.

Was she born with it, or was she created like I was, through trauma?

I move my laptop to my desk, shut off the lights and, heading to the back of the basement, I pull open the trapdoor. I cough as the dust kicks up into my face. I wipe it off my designer sweater.

I'm sure Cali isn't a big fan, either, but I couldn't have Summer see or hear her, so I set a mattress down here and attempted to make it as comfortable as possible.

These tunnels, likely constructed during the Prohibition, have been quite useful over the years. This house is very old, almost ancient, and disturbingly evil. I shudder to think how many people have died here.

Dr. Garcia gifted Xander and me this house—the same house she lived in when she was a student. Now it's our turn to kill and carry it forward.

When I open the door, I turn on the small light. Cali is lying down with dirt streaks smeared over her delicate face, even though I just washed her up yesterday. I had to bind her mouth today. Her sobbing got tiresome, and I'm sick of drugging her.

She stares up at me as I crouch down next to her. "I'm going to take out your gag now so you can eat. Please don't scream."

She doesn't respond. Instead, she stares at me, likely trying to figure out which version she is getting.

I pull the gag out and hand her the salad and a fork with a bottle of water.

She looks at me dead in the eye. "I hate you."

I take a deep breath and run my knuckles softly down her face. The fear bleeding out of her eyes, the emotional response she has to me. "I'm not the one who did this to you, Cali," I remind her, "but I am the reason you're not dead yet. So hating me might not be wise."

She doesn't respond, though a single tear falls from her eye, and she digs into the gourmet salad she requested. She bristles, and eventually, her fear morphs into anger. She's already cried, begged, screamed, and offered herself to me in hopes I would let her go.

Truth is, I'm not entirely sure he hasn't hurt her. I don't think he has, but he has blocked me out for short periods already, and she does look an awful lot like Summer.

Cali is aware there are two of us—it was blatantly obvious on day one.

Despite these non ideal circumstances, I have utilized the opportunity to work on my research and have been studying her diligently since I possessed her. I've observed her every night since he took her weeks ago. Fever, chills, her rapid heart rate, and vomiting. I've kept her comfortable—more or less—and have been nothing but kind and courteous. I even bought her a few books to read and have made multiple trips to the bookstore at her request.

I take a moment to admire her as she finishes her food and curls her knees up to her chest. A deep flare erupts inside me as I watch her.

That emotion again...that fragment in my soul pushing to the surface.

I lower myself to her and pull down the strap of her shirt over her shoulders. She flinches at my touch.

"Don't worry, Cali," I say softly, "I'm not going to hurt you. I just want to check your pulse."

Her body slacks, and her face turns ashen.

Okay, maybe I'm trying to scare her a bit. But only because it's so fascinating, and I can understand why Dr. Landry was obsessed with this emotion.

This girl's breathing is rapid, causing her chest to rise and fall. I tilt my head for dramatic measure, and notice the throb in her throat, the slight change in her pupils, and her cheeks, which are completely devoid of color.

I place my two fingers on her chest and study the rhythm of her heart. Her goosebumps flesh when I touch her.

I just told this girl in all honesty, I wasn't going to hurt her, yet her biochemical reaction is that of extreme fear and anxiety. Her eyes are fully glazed over.

I feel myself slowly, and ever so slightly, get turned on.

She visibly relaxes, but her eyes are bright, and they flick down to the bulge in my pants.

I lean down and whisper in her ear, "I'm not going to fuck you, either, Cali."

It's happening again. His emotions, his physical sensations, start to trickle in. For the time being I'm able to push them aside, but dark images of her eyes being gouged out consume my mind, and it's not a pleasant sight.

Not urges, I remind myself. I don't desire this woman.

These are his memories. Memories.

My skin burns, arousal thickens, and my chest expands.

He's a killer.

He's killed multiple women while Dr. Garcia had him in her clutches. She brought him prostitutes and transients, people who didn't matter, to see what he would do with them when left to his own devices.

He was thirteen, and what was left of those women was carnage.

Before I can fully comprehend what I'm doing, I slide the razor blade over the flesh of her arm. I just want to see how much blood spills out.

She screams—luckily the music spilling from above mutes her—and I jolt back.

Fuck. What am I doing? Why is this so natural? So satisfying.

Using all my willpower to keep him at bay, I step away from her. A dark laugh fills the room and a small flicker hits my center.

That fucking flicker, flying around my head like a moth I can't catch. The little angry split.

I take a deep breath, watching the blood trickle from her arm, and she passes out. I take off my sweater, but before I wrap her arm with it, I snap a photo of her. I can't help myself because the blood is so beautiful.

Coming to my senses, I wrap the sweater around her arm to stop the bleeding. Once I'm done and satisfied she won't die in the next hour, I leave the room as quickly as I can before we kill her. Mikael's so embedded in me now, I'm unsure where the lines of our subconscious lie.

This girl will be the key to saving Summer's life, so I need her to not end up looking like a scarecrow. And frankly, I do not want to deal with a corpse.

CHAPTER
TWENTY
LINCOLN

My breath catches as I reach the top of the stairs and slide into the kitchen, keeping myself as calm and composed as possible considering I mutilated Cali's arm moments ago. It was me, all me, in that moment.

The clatter of plates and the swish of water fills the air as Lucy, the housemaid, scrubs the dinner dishes. Lucy's in her seventies; her family worked for Dr. Garcia's parents before she handed the house over to us, and Lucy right along with it. I'm certain she's well-aware of the girl in the basement.

Over the years, I've come to realize that Lucy knows everything and says nothing. She's aware of every single thing that happens here.

She dries her wrinkled hands on her apron. She fixes her gaze on me and a flicker of movement crosses her eyes. She helped raise Mikael before I took over; she knew him first, yet welcomed me with open arms. Xander's parents ran off and abandoned him, so Dr. Garcia and Lucy raised him, too.

Lucy pauses before she says, "Would you like a drink before joining the others?"

I wipe the sweat building on the back of my neck. I flash her a smile, unsure of where my threshold of sanity lies. "Please," I say to her calmly. "Make it a double."

She pours whiskey into a crystal glass—neat, how I like it—and hands it to me, but doesn't quite let the glass go as her fingers graze mine. Her eyes penetrate me, seeing right through my facade.

She gives me a cautious smile, seeming to sense my racing heart. My palms are sweaty and my adrenaline is still high—these are not normal reactions for me. Just the sweat alone should make her weary. Finally, she releases me, as if confirming what she needed to by her lingering touch.

As Summer and I grow closer, Mikael's getting stronger and his triggers are getting worse. His emotions are blurring with mine, and my impulses are loosening because of it.

And that is a big problem.

For now, I ignore it. Being around people helps. He won't come out if he's uncomfortable, and at least for now, he prefers to watch.

"Let me know if you need anything else," she says.

"I sure will, Lucy."

Lucy always liked me the best. I offer what Xander is lacking, primarily in manners, bringing a sense of sophistication to the house. Xander is more about ruling with an iron fist. Despite his parents leaving town, he had a spoiled upbringing. Dr. Garcia's familial wealth knows no boundaries.

The sip of liquor calms me. Mikael is no longer hissing in my psyche as I ease back into my naturally composed state, but something still grips me. That alien sensation is slowly becoming part of my skin, interlocking with every muscle, every vein.

The fragment is growing.

I make my way out of the kitchen and down the dark, narrow hallway to the grand entryway of the house, leading to the great room where Xander usually hangs out.

In contrast to the basement, which is cramped and dimly lit, the rest of the house is grand, with elegant windows overseeing the forest beyond. This is an old house, built in the early 1900s, but it was renovated and reconstructed in the 1970s, and the windows are the only vintage part of the house. A large staircase leads to the rooms above where Xander takes up the primary bedroom, but I much prefer the basement, where it's soundproof and quiet.

It's always been my bedroom.

When I open the door to the living room, Xander and Bianca are sitting on the couch. Well, Xander is sitting on the couch wearing a backwards hat, his cuffs rolled up over his tattooed arms. Bianca is on the floor in front of him with a sour look on her face, her hair tied up in a tight, dark ponytail.

His eyes are shadowed, and she's saying something to him, likely talking back, and as I suspect, he yanks her head back slightly, using her ponytail as a grip.

His body is tense, but he's grinning at her and she's smiling with adoration in her eyes. He grabs her shoulders and starts rubbing them as the music pounds from the surround sound in our ceiling.

Her body visibly relaxes.

Xander has a way with the ladies, and he's cocky. And Bianca only seems content when he's dominating her and giving her his full attention, which she doesn't like sharing.

On the surface, the two of us couldn't be more different. But he's smart in ways I'm not. Everyone thought I was different, but I quickly learned how to function in society. When Mikael disappeared, he embraced me, no questions asked. No one touched me while I was with him.

I don't love him—I'm not capable of it—but I am loyal to him.

The usual group, the other children of the shadows, are here. The offspring of those who scorched eternal bliss above for fleeting earthly desires of money and power. Wendy, the mayor's daughter, and Gabe, the police chief's son, are cuddled together on the couch. Bianca is also one of us; her father is the town physician. To everyone else, we are a small group of friends who don't enjoy interacting with anyone else. But to us, we are bound by blood and oath.

Well, everyone except for me—I have no blood ties to the Order, and therefore, will never truly become one. I'm agnostic to the entire thing, or at least I was until Mikael marked Summer.

Xander turns the music down when he sees me and grins, causing the entire room to look in my direction. "Look who rose from the dead. What do we owe the pleasure of the almighty professor?"

"I'm not a professor yet," I remind him, making sure I look bored as usual.

Bianca observes me and scowls. She knows about my dark past, just not all of it. Dr. Garcia kept Mikael well hidden as a child and throughout his adolescence, and then introduced me to the outside world as Lincoln. No one is stupid enough to question her openly, even though none of it adds up. They know I started my life as Mikael. They didn't, however, truly realize what Mikael was or the reason I changed my name.

And none of them truly comprehend the depravity of what almost happened beneath them. How close Cali was to getting slaughtered if I hadn't had the foresight to get the fuck out of there.

I slam my drink back and place the glass down on the coffee table.

"You good, man?" Xander asks, watching me carefully, his eyes jerking to my wrist.

Well, fuck, blood is splattered on my wrist. I washed my hands after I cut Cali, but I must have missed a spot.

I fawn a smile. "Never been better. Why do you ask?"

His eyes linger on the blood. I don't know what Xander would do if he discovered the missing girl everyone is talking about is tied up downstairs.

We have a critical rule...don't get caught. After 2002, the members vowed silence and secrecy. No more public displays of violence, and under no circumstances are we to get caught.

Xander snaps his fingers at Bianca, curled up at his feet. "Go get Lincoln another drink, babe."

She grimaces at him, then rises and heads to the kitchen to find Lucy. "Fine," she mutters as she saunters out of the room. "I need a cigarette, anyway."

His eyes flicker, revealing his own internal demons. "You need a fucking attitude change, babe," he yells at her and watches her leave like she's a piece of meat.

Once she's gone, he rises and moves to sit next to me.

Bianca knows her place and has accepted the fact she will never be his number one. She's not his number one because she's not dead yet. He hasn't chosen her.

She comes back a few minutes later and hands me a drink, then heads back outside for one of her many cigarette breaks.

"You're talking to Summer Landry," he says slowly, his face growing dark and serious.

I turn to look at him and quirk a brow. "She's a student in my class, that's all."

He leans back, wrapping his hands around the back of his head. "You've always had a thing for her, but this is vicious, man, even for you. You gonna kill her?"

I take a sip of my drink, the cubes clinking against the glass. "I think it's poetic justice, don't you?"

The liquor burns my throat. The bitch gave me bourbon; I hate bourbon. I'm more of a whiskey guy, especially when my brain is consumed by death. That flicker bubbles up inside me.

Xander pauses and doesn't say anything, but he keeps his gaze steady on mine. "Well, I think she's hot, a lot sexier than she used to be."

Mikael jerks from deep inside, and I have to push him down. Summer Landry isn't just hot; she's the most beautiful girl I've ever laid eyes on. He just had eyes for someone else.

Xander runs his thumb over his mouth, his eyes gleaming. "I think her friend Dani is hotter. Do you think you can get the girls to the house for our party next Friday?"

We make eye contact, an unspoken pact for me never to interfere with his shit as long as he doesn't interfere with mine. Xander technically still needs to choose a girl to become a full member, and he's had eyes on Dani ever since his great-uncle put her father in prison.

Love is an integral and necessary ingredient as part of the sacrifice.

That's the way.

By now, Bianca must be aware she will not be the only important girl in his life. I know Xander, and she's not the one.

"I'll think about it," I tell him. But I won't. I don't want Summer anywhere near here. I want to keep her all to myself.

He takes a sip of his drink, and his eyes fall on Bianca, who saunters back in and talks to Wendy, keeping his voice low. "All that work with Summer and you're just going to kill her? That doesn't make sense."

I shrug. "It's not unusual for members to play with their marks before the ceremony." It is, however, unusual to mark the daughter of a former member, considering it's technically Summer's birthright, not mine.

He tilts his head to the side, his darkness swirling in his eyes. "Is that what you're planning on doing, Lincoln? Playing with her? Or is it someone else who wants to do that?"

I stare at him for a long, cold second. A second ticks by, then another, the tension palpable between us.

"Is he back, Lincoln?" His jaw tightens. "Don't fucking lie to me."

I keep my face tight and lie, "No, he's not back. Why would you think that?" I still have time to control this; Xander doesn't need to know Mikael has returned.

"Because you're acting weird, and you and Summer have a shared history. I don't believe for one second her being here hasn't had an impact on you. Plus, you marked her, which should be impossible, since you don't have a fucking heart. Does my grandmother know he's back?"

I take another sip. "She doesn't know because there is nothing for her to know."

He reaches out and grabs my glasses off my face. I don't bother stopping him. My vision blurs, and all I see are the outlines of his hands waving in front of my face before he leans in closer. "Mikael, are you in there, you crazy son of a bitch?"

Mikael's usual tendrils crawl over my spine and, for a slight moment, his pain is my pain. His emotions fuse with mine.

"Tell him. I dare you. I think he misses me."

Mikael and I separate once more as I work to dissolve those feelings with emotional acid. I hate that he can talk to me...at times, it feels like a possession.

I swipe my glasses back, ignoring the little devil on my shoulder. Xander's grinning at me once I'm able to get them back on.

"Mikael's dead," I say in a calm and careful voice. "And if he were still here, Xander, do you really think he'd like you waving your hand in his face like that?" Xander was kidding, I think. But even his jokes skim too closely to the truth.

My gaze draws down to the scar on his hand. "Didn't Mikael burn your hand once, for waving it in his face?"

Xander snaps his hand back faster than I can blink and grimaces at the clear memory. I remember it vividly. Mikael secretly entering his room, dipping his hand into a pot of scalding water while he was sleeping.

They had a relationship of sorts before I progressed into myself, before Dr. Garcia discovered the mind hiding inside that disturbed boy. Once she discovered my IQ, she drew me out.

Dr. Garcia was appointed to Mikael's case from the very beginning to keep the entire thing buried. More than likely, the Order of the Shadows didn't know what to do with the orphan, so they kept Mikael alive.

"Do you know the last thing Mikael said to me?" Xander says as he brings his drink to his lips.

I look at him, but I don't really want to hear the answer. "He said he loved her, that he would do anything to be with her. Then, as soon as she comes to town, she's suddenly marked."

My phone buzzes, drawing both of our attention to the sound in my pocket. I lean over to grab it and can't help the smile that pushes on to my face.

Summer: *How badly do you want me?*

I quirk my head, a small smile hints at my lips.

I click a quick response.

SF: *More than anything.*

Summer: *Do you remember what you told me to do with the stick?*

A photo pops up on the phone, and I literally spit my drink out. Xander arches his eyebrows, reacting to my very few occasions of outward emotion.

I stare at the photo for a long second and push my glasses up to make sure I'm actually seeing what I'm seeing.

Summer's in the woods, on her knees, wearing nothing but a bra with a stick stuck right up her cunt. Her body and hair are smeared with mud, and it's hot as hell.

All-consuming anger erupts inside me. Anger, lust, sheer obsession. Darkness fills every pore, and I barely have a grip on myself as Mikael twinges deep within. He's seeping into my skin, my bones, my identity. My dick nearly explodes at the sight of her.

Perfect Summer Landry, humiliating herself for me. I've always been obsessed with her beauty, but this…? I will never get this image out of my mind.

He either wants to rip her to shreds or fuck the living daylights out of her, I can't tell. The two of us sing in perfect harmony.

Xander nudges me. "What's got you so fucking excited?"

The sound of his voice snaps me back, and all the emotion is sucked out like a vacuum. While I'm still coherent, while I'm still myself, I pull up the picture of Cali dripping with blood and send it back to Summer.

It looks like a fresh kill, and that's what I want Summer to think.

I set my glass on the table and slip out of the room before Xander can ask me anything else. "I have more papers to grade," I tell him flippantly, though I can barely contain my excitement as I head downstairs. I'm not going to chase her in the woods…not yet, at least.

"**M**otherfucker," I mutter, staring down into my phone in a mix of horror and disbelief. There is no mistaking what I am looking at. I knew he had Cali—and now he is using her as an opportunity to bait and provoke me. But here she is, torn to pieces, her blood splattered everywhere. It's as if my bones might shatter under the weight of this image. Proof of his insanity if I didn't believe it before.

She looks so much like me in this photo. Dirt smears and blood stains cover her face, and I can't help but trace the clear cut on her arm, the crimson streaks leaking from it. My fingers glide over the scar on the apex of my thigh, a painful reminder of his touch in such an intimate place. He promised me so much, only to leave me longing for more.

She has no mark, no demonic claim to him, but he killed her anyway.

The damp earth presses against my skin as I lie beneath the gnarled branches of the skeletal trees, a chilly wind whistling through their bare limbs. The park is a popular spot for runners, and I often see people walking their dogs or even couples on a late-night date. Dressed in barely anything, I exude desperation rather than the blood I crave, finding myself in a position that is utterly degrading and vulnerable, where anyone could walk by and see me.

Vomit hits the back of my throat and my knees sink to the ground, the shock of the moment weighing heavily on me. I try to make sense of what I'm experiencing or why I just did what I did.

Nothing. I feel nothing, but I should be overwhelmed by a whirlwind of emotions—terror, anger, sadness. I should have *remorse* for the girl who just lost her life because of whatever twisted game he and I are entangled in. Instead, there's nothing but gaping desperation.

Clearly, I'm out of my mind, or losing fragments of it. Like he's stealing every part of me, piece by piece, hour by hour.

Finally, I pull my trench coat over my body just as rain lightly patters down over me, and I bark out a laugh.

I might be the daughter of a serial killer, and I'm so turned on by the thought of the guy stalking me being his copycat killer, I could scream. I have so many questions—about myself, about my father, about him. About why he's lying about his name.

A few people walk by, their gazes lingering on me as I hurry past, head bowed, my mouth dry and parched. I'm relieved they weren't here two minutes ago, when I was trying to become his sexy dark archangel, crucifying myself in the most heinous way. Now I just look like a crazy white-haired girl in a trench coat with an extremely swollen pussy.

A single, massive cloud parts, revealing the full moon, which casts an otherworldly light through the trees as the storm moves on. My heart is as icy as the frigid air, and I finally understand the allure of this town and how deep it can sink its claws into you if you let it.

Is this how everyone else died who went missing in this place? Did they sacrifice themselves for the Order?

I'm not that far from home, so it takes me no time to rush home on the slippery sidewalk. I open the door, and luckily, Dani and Misty are in their rooms and don't see me naked under this coat.

I have a quick shower to clean off my filth, and when I reach my room upstairs, I close the blinds. I put on a big sweater to stay warm. Then I curl up in bed and think about Cali.

Did he taunt her like he's taunting me? Did he spend an entire night on the phone with her, helping her with homework and telling her how gorgeous she was?

Did she touch herself for him? Did he touch her?

My stomach burns and my jaw clenches at all these unanswered questions. The burning slides through my body into nearly every bone, like my skin is on fire. I've never felt more alive than at this moment.

The phone rings in my hand and SF comes onto my screen. The world around me dulls as I stare down at my phone, and I take a deep breath and answer.

Real death. Real blood. There is a real killer.

Swallowing hard, I manage to tame my heart rate and swipe to answer.

"What the fuck do you want?" I snap at him. I can't pretend I don't want him with every ounce of my soul, yet I'm so fucking mad at him.

His voice is dark and calculated. "I want to talk about your morals, baby," he answers without hesitation. "You appear to be lacking them." I instantly recognize Lincoln's voice, not whatever phantom version resides in his mind.

I breathe in hard. One call, and I could have the protection of this entire campus. I could end him, ruin his career before it even gets started, and make a news story they will talk about for the next fifty years. My heart is beating out of my chest now. *I don't want this anymore.* I can't believe I ever thought I did.

I think about Cali's dead body, about him killing her, and I fight off the wetness building between my legs. "You killed her," I hiss. "And you want to talk to me about fucking *morals*?"

He sighs, his voice softening. "I want to talk about *your* morals, Summer, not mine. And believe it or not, I'm trying to protect you."

I grip the phone so hard my knuckles are white, and my hands start shaking.

"What the fuck does that even mean?" I manage a whisper. "Protect me from who? Who are you trying to protect me from, Lincoln?"

"Summer…can we talk about how you're feeling right now?"

It takes a minute for my racing heart to slow down. Does he want to discuss my emotions, or the absence of the ones I should be experiencing?

"What?" I ask him, wiping my nose with the back of my hand. There's no way he can't hear me crying, and I must sound pathetic to him.

Yet, he's patient as always, curious about what I'm experiencing. "Baby, tell me every emotion you're experiencing. Clearly, you're mad and jealous, but what else do you feel? I think this is a good time for you to reflect. What is the most primal emotion inside you?"

My body relaxes—his voice has a way of doing that. There's never any judgment, no mocking tone, no shame; just calm, cool, and soothing reassurance that he's here.

He's always been here.

The sound of his voice is everything; it's all I need. I choke on my words, so many thoughts and feelings. I desperately wish he was in front of me. I want him inside me.

"Tell me, baby."

I curl my legs up and run my hands along the intense pulse inside my thigh. Right now, I'm content. My heart flutters, my stomach tingles, and knees weaken. I trust him more than I should, because everything logical should be the opposite of how I'm feeling.

I'm on my knees for this man.

"Love," I whisper. "I think I'm in love with you. I think I've been in love with you since I was sixteen."

He doesn't respond, but I didn't think he would. A moment passes, then another, and all I can hear is my growing heart rate, the wind picking up outside, and the dark evil presence on the other end of this phone call.

"I want to see you," I tell him. "I'm sick of just talking on the phone all the time."

"That can't happen right now," he says calmly.

"Why?"

"I think you understand why."

No. I don't understand why. Not even in the slightest.

My hand whips to my mouth and, for a moment, I lose the ability to breathe. "I'll do anything to see you." My hand drifts to my abdomen, even though my fingers, no matter how much pressure I apply, simply aren't cutting it anymore. "I'll let you do whatever you want to me," I breathe.

A long pause, and I wonder if he's still there. Then he says in a voice I recognize, but it's darker, edgier, and sounds like my nightmares, "I'll see you soon, pretty girl."

And with that, the line goes dead.

It's Monday afternoon, and I've just finished my third appointment of the day and the only reason I'm still here is because I'm waiting for Summer to show up. Despite my avoidance strategies to keep her alive, my fingers slipped last night, and those two words flowed out of my fingers as if the thoughts were my own.

Pretty girl.

I've never thought of her as pretty girl—those are Mikael's rudimentary, fragmented thoughts. Yet at that moment, I was the one who said it.

I wanted her to come see me in my office—this is where I'm in control. This office, this profession, the life I've built myself over the past few years while he was asleep, none of it belongs to him. Here, he's muted, and it's the only place I'm safe seeing her in person without the chance of him fronting and killing her.

I glance at my screen, hoping to find news of the anticipated return of Shadowface causing a frenzy.

There's nothing.

Which means Summer is still sitting on the incriminating evidence I sent her. Not that it would make a difference, even if she reported it to the police, since the chief of police is one of them.

Even if she did run to them, they won't take any action. He's given his oath, killed his beloved, and he will cover up any evidence to protect me, but more importantly, he'll protect the Order until death.

After a few minutes, as I'm preparing to leave, my heart races as Summer walks into the room, shutting the door behind her. Her lips are pursed, and her tight outfit leaves little to the imagination.

Mikael simmers in my blood, settling close to the surface at her arrival. The heat of him cools when I give him a stern warning not to overstep, especially not with my colleagues just outside and Dr. Garcia down the hall.

I should shut him out, but I'm becoming more comfortable with his presence in my head. I'm reluctant to admit it, but he's making me more whole. The twinges of emotional bursts he gives me, some of which I've never truly experienced. Yet I still sense a foreign substance, as if some of those emotions belong to someone else—something more powerful and much more appealing.

I settle back into my chair and raise my eyes to meet hers, adjusting my glasses so I can get a good look at her. A wave of Mikael's anger pushes into my peripheral vision. I keep my voice even and arch my brows, enjoying the electric current of emotions flowing through me.

My tongue slides across my lips. "Hi, pretty girl." Not my words, not my voice. I'm not in control.

She gives me a sharp look, and my sight goes blurry, like my glasses are causing it. I take them off and she is a vision of perfection. For reasons I'll never understand, I'm as blind as a bat, so when I'm wearing my glasses, I don't think Mikael can actually see anything, his view is distorted. So when I can see without my glasses, I know that's when I'm not in control.

Summer stands with her arms crossed and her bright red lips pursed.

My jaw ticks as dark thoughts ripple through me, and I have to admit the images of Summer sliced up are starting to turn me on.

That power pulses again. That growing fragment, I dare now call a split. One I haven't yet killed, and I'm not sure I want to.

I have a theory about the split…that perhaps it's taking away some of Mikael's unimpeded anger. That perhaps the split *is* Mikael's anger, and I want to see what happens to it.

She nibbles on her bottom lip, twirling a piece of her white locks. My eyes move to her throat as she swallows, and I shove Mikael down to the fiery pits of hell that are the inner workings of my mind to keep him at bay.

His primal instincts for murder are so strong, it's overwhelming. His constant arousal at the thought of blood…

Feral darkness.

Summer's hand moves to her throat, seeing my reaction to her. As if she knows instinctively what's waiting just beneath my skin.

I lean back in my chair and study her reactions. The uptick of her breath, the pulse of her throat. Her eyes narrow, and all I can think about is slicing them out. I'm fully aware these are not my thoughts.

I blink a few times as my vision swirls once more, and I place my glasses back on and again, she's clear. Mikael starts screaming inside. Luckily, he can't see her with the same level of clarity I can.

Summer taps her toe and frowns, shaking her head, as if she can see the tug-of-war playing out in my eyes. The facade is over...and I have no reason to hide anymore.

"Summer..." I say carefully and wrap my hands around the back of my head, watching her. The same way I watched her last night.

The intensity that surrounds her is palatable, like a little bomb ready to explode. A smile hints at my lips, but I'm also not sure what she is going to do at this moment.

"You..." she says with venom lacing her voice, "are a liar."

I rise and carefully step toward her, and she doesn't flinch. Not a single tell that she's frightened.

"And what am I lying about, pretty girl?" I enunciate the pretty girl, knowing it will confuse her.

She tilts her head and parts her perfect lips, and I slowly close the distance between us. "You're lying about everything," she breathes.

I take a step closer, and she shuts her eyes.

As I suspected, Summer isn't a rational person. She's hiding a darkness inside her I understand all too well...and that's the side I want to see.

The thought of me choosing another victim doesn't sit well with her. She hates herself for it, and she hates how much she wants me.

"Why did you kill her instead of me?" she says through gritted teeth. She holds her breath as I slide my hand near her ear, pressing her into the door. It's not fear cascading out of her eyes as I move my hand near the curve of her waist and lock the door.

She leans her head back as I press my other hand near her other ear, caging her in. "Jealousy looks unbelievably sexy on you, baby."

Her lips part as I lean my head to get a whiff of her. She smells of lilacs and summer wind.

Her eyes open, and I can see now just how distraught she is. The confusion is suffocating her, because it's clear what she should do, but she can't do it. The mind control we have over her is too powerful. Her body can't resist us, even if her brain is telling her to run.

"I hate you," she breathes. "I hate that I want you. I hate myself when I'm with you."

I gently grab a piece of her hair, and she hitches a breath. "Don't lie, Summer," I tease, pressing my lips to her neck, nuzzling her. "I think you rather enjoy me."

She shakes her head. "I have no idea who or what you are anymore."

A burst of emotion overcomes me, and while I maintain control, the lines between me and him are blurred. Nefarious ideas take over my thoughts; his memories of watching her as a young girl infiltrate my mind.

I reach over and tuck a piece of hair behind her ear. "It's me, Summer. You know who I am."

My hand moves to her shirt, down to the swell of her breast, appreciating her heartbeat.

She presses her hands over mine, stopping me, as if that would stop me from taking what I want. "Why are you lying to everyone, Lincoln?"

I pull away and her eyes flash, keenly aware of how close she is to me.

"Define lying. I'm curious as to what your definition is."

She narrows her eyes, keeping a steady gaze. "Who is Mikael?" she whispers.

My lip curls into a snarl as he infuses with me. While I'm enjoying some of the emotions he invokes, I dislike hearing his name from her lips. I'm also not sure how she knows his name. Perhaps she knows a lot more than I give her credit for.

I keep my hand on the nape of her neck and trace my finger up her skin. The pieces of him are still lingering within.

"Mikael lives inside my head," I growl. "And I'm the thin blanket between you and death. I'm the only reason Mikael hasn't killed you twenty times over."

Finally, she trembles, and a small squeak leaves her lips. "I shouldn't have come here," she says, and her hand finds the doorknob as if I'm actually going to let her leave.

I watch the bob of her throat as she swallows. Her body shifts and a sweet aroma radiates out of her. The scent of her fear, the smell of her arousal.

I bite my lip and keep my hands on either side of her, pinning her in and catching my breath. "Well, you did come to see me, and I gave you every chance in the world not to."

She's quiet as a church mouse and I keep my gaze down, but I can sense her watching me curiously.

"What do you want to ask me, Summer? It's on the tip of your tongue, so out with it."

She shifts beneath me. "How many women have you killed?"

I blink at her a couple of times and push my glasses up my nose. "Precisely none."

Truth. I answered her question truthfully because she didn't ask the right one.

Her breath falters and she pauses before she says, "How many women has *he* killed?"

Well, that's another question entirely.

I pause before saying, "He's a psychopath, Summer. Do you really want the answer to that question?"

I stare down at her and my vision flickers as it does whenever we are around her. We fuse into one. That fragment is spinning around like a wild banshee, affecting both of us in ways I can't even fathom.

She pulls her hand to her mouth and tears well in her eyes, as if she is only now realizing what I truly am.

"Do you want to kill me right now?"

I snap back to myself when I hear her heart beating so hard. I suppress the hot twinge engulfing me as I focus my attention on her lips. I grab her hand and interlace her fingers with mine and move it to the painful erection I've developed in the past two minutes.

She gasps and I whisper in her ear, "Do you feel this?" Her delicate fingers graze my erection. "Do you understand how much I *don't* want to kill you?"

She opens her lips and breathes heavily. I lean down and kiss her. I smile into her mouth as she moves her hands to the back of my neck and pulls me in. Summer Landry is officially the most fascinating girl I've ever encountered.

She has emotions—clearly, lots of them—just not the ones you'd expect being the target of someone like me.

She moans softly as I cup one of her breasts. She leans against the wall, pressing her knee into me like the little tease she is. Her heart rate is beating uncontrollably now, knowing she can't resist me.

She tastes as delicious as she looks, and I'm tempted to rip off her clothing and fuck her right here, and there is nothing stopping me.

Certainly not any moral compass.

I grab her by her ass and lift her, moving her to my desk and angling her so I can get better traction between our bodies. I keep kissing her and he starts to take over, but I pull him back, wanting every second of this for myself.

A fierce battle of our psyches rages within me, each fighting for dominance while being intimate with her. I'm able to snuff him out, push him down, and untangle him from my veins, but it takes every ounce of my energy.

I move her hair out of the way and kiss her ivory neck. "Do you know how long I've been waiting to do this?" Her chest rises and falls so rapidly.

I reach down and undo the buckle of my belt. Keeping our lips on each other, I grab my dick, positioning myself between her legs. Voices echo from outside my office door, then a small knock, which I ignore.

Fire burns inside me, making my fists clench. The only thing on my mind is the urge to have a physical connection with her. My fingers brush against the hem of her dress and her hand instinctively reaches for mine.

Feelings of rage and anger consume me. It's my emotion, not his. This is that foreign entity I've been sensing...except, perhaps, it's not foreign at all.

It's me...my feelings are surfacing.

My fingers curl into her hips. "Lincoln." She manages to pull off my lips long enough to capture a breath. "Please stop."

I quirk my head and appreciate her eyes—a perfect mix of fear and desire. "I don't want to stop," I say, breathless.

I slip my hand up her dress and she opens her thighs, giving me access to her. I brush my lips against her cheek, wanting that perfect cunt.

"Who are you?" she finally whispers between our desperate kisses. "You have to explain yourself, Lincoln."

I'm so fucking hungry for her, I'd ravish her with my eyes if she'd look at me, but she keeps her gaze down on her legs as she lifts them up and down my leg to distract herself. It's smart of her; my vision starts blurring, shifting, morphing...twitching.

I suck in a breath and swallow down these chaotic desires. I'm stronger than this; I'm stronger than him.

"I understand you have questions, and when I'm inclined, I'll give you answers. For now, you will have to trust that I don't want to hurt you."

Her eyes finally flick up to mine and her pupils dilate. "Trust you?" she hisses. "You killed a girl. You're a murderer, and I shouldn't even be here."

I give her a deviant smile and cup her cheek. "Do *not* pretend that you care about anyone else other than me and you, baby. If you did, you wouldn't be spreading your perfect legs for me right now, would you?"

"I won't spread my legs for you anymore," she says, clenching her fists. "I already told you to stop."

I step back and take a calm, deep breath. "I'm not sure when you're going to realize you have no control right now. I own your mind, Summer Landry. When I ask you to open your legs, you open your fucking legs."

She draws in a quick breath, pulls back slightly, then regains her composure. Holding on to the desk, she softly curses. "I'll scream. I'll let everyone in this building know what you're doing."

I lean toward her ear and whisper, as I have so many times before, "Do it. Summer...scream right now. If you do, I'll unleash him. And wasn't it just last night you were professing your love for me? Didn't you say you'd do *anything* for me?"

Her face contorts as if it pains her to do it, but she leans back and lifts her dress just over her thighs, spreading her gorgeous legs wide.

Something within me snaps.

A split second of true satisfaction washes over me as I look at her splayed out. He wasn't the only one who whispered to her in her sleep the nights we stalked her room.

I was there, too.

I had a goal of seeing if it's possible to have total mind control over someone.

Apparently, it is possible...

I slip my fingers around her lace and pull down her panties, slipping them down so they wrap around her thigh, and shove two fingers inside her. Her eyes widen, but she moans, arching her back.

Slowly, ever so slowly, I let Mikael back in. His fusion is the final touch I need, like I can truly do anything. Pure power hums through me. This novel sensation of *feeling* everything.

"Just relax, baby," I breathe into her mouth, and for a moment, our air is intertwined.

She tenses, but I press my thumb over her clit, which calms her down. I rub my thumb in a circular motion, but she's already glistening.

Mikael withers inside me, having his psychotic meltdown because I still have control. His emotional tantrum is pushing every button.

His voice echoes around me. Jagged and half-formed thoughts.

"So pretty."

"Mine."

"Mine."

"Mine."

I spend a few seconds admiring the cut Mikael gave her. He did it with such precision, such love.

"What does it feel like?" I ask her.

She arches her back and moans. "What does what feel like?" She can barely speak, her body shaking.

"The pleasure I'm giving you right now. Does it burn?"

Her cherry lips part and total fear radiates out of her eyes. The paradox between her brain and body, a burning desire driven by total manipulation.

She shouldn't have feelings for me—everything about Summer and I is wrong, and that's what makes it so special.

"I'm going to fuck you now," I whisper, and she nods, knowing she can't fight it.

Fighting it hurts.

Her pussy is already wet by the time I press inside her, and she is as amazing as I expected.

Mikael's memory of fucking her all those years ago comes rushing back, as if it was my own. His tendrils grip me, they tug and latch so hard my world slowly shrinks and everything drifts. Everything softens. Everything goes black—

I get utterly lost inside her. I fuck her so hard, so deeply on my desk. I can't get close enough to her.

"Lincoln," she murmurs, her arms wrapping around me, her lips tracing a path along my neck.

Her voice jolts me back from my brief lapse, bringing me back to reality and control.

"Lincoln...fuck," she moans.

I don't hold back and fuck her silly against my desk. I could have sex with her for hours, and it would still never be enough. Her legs wrap around me, squeezing her knees against my torso. She's also trying to release some indescribable pressure as I pound her, and just as I'm about to come, dark laughter consumes my soul, bouncing off the walls.

Fuck... I will not let him have her. I press my hands on either side of her, but I can't stop it.

I'm already gone.

P *retty girl.*
My pretty girl…

My body jolts, and right as I come to my full senses, I pull out before I unload all over her. The release would be absolute bliss after being in darkness for so long, but I want to savor this.

My skin is my own again. Every nerve tingles; every movement, motion, and emotion is mine and mine alone. For the moment, at least, I've snuffed him out. He may be stronger when he's in his element with his books, and his fancy words, and his theories. But with Summer, he will never be stronger than me.

Summer is mine.

She trembles beneath me, and my dick is immediately hard again. I continue to fuck her on his lavish desk, wanting to soil every square inch of it. My dick slides in and out, and this sensation is the only thing that kept me sane during my muted existence.

If possible, it's better than it was two years ago; her pussy is tight, like she's been waiting for me.

The only reason I've been able to keep my rage in check is because of how euphoric she is. It's prevented me from reaching for the pair of scissors, conveniently resting just three inches away from my fingertips, and using them to carve up the beautiful face I hate so fucking much.

"Lincol—"

I shove my fingers into her mouth before she can finish saying his name. "Shut the fuck up, pretty girl."

She gags on them, and I slide them down over her lips and her cheeks flush as arousal blossoms all over her. I keep my hand on her mouth while fucking her—with me in control this time. I hate how open she is to inviting another man inside her world. Even if, technically, that other man is me.

I tear these awful glasses off so I can see her. I want to watch her pussy clench around my cock.

Her sweat is glistening on her neck, so I lap it up and kiss her neck, her cheek, and then take her lips into my mouth. She's smart enough to only give out squeaky noises when my dick hits her in the right spot.

"That's right, pretty girl," I murmur and bury my head in her neck. I can't breathe. Everything about her is intoxicating. "I want you to close your eyes and play dead."

She squeezes her eyes shut, then relaxes her body and I continue fucking her slowly, methodically, enjoying every second of her soft body and girly scent beneath me. Knowing I own her, even if she's calling out Lincoln's name.

I lift my lips off hers and gaze down at her and her face contorts. "Lincoln isn't home right now," I whisper, clarifying things for her. "You can call me Mikael."

Her eyes widen and pure fear radiates out of them. I deepen my kiss before she can scream and move my hand to her throat, curling each finger and appreciating how delicate her neck is. I will make sure she will never forget my scent or the taste of my lips on hers.

I pull up because I want to watch her pretty eyes as life slowly fades from them. Maybe if she's a good girl, I will make her bleed first.

Her lips part, and she lets out a soft breath. I squeeze her throat, and her body relaxes as if waiting for me to fulfil my honeyed promises. I shove my cock in her and her pussy tightens and throbs, so I squeeze her throat again. Her thighs nearly take my cock off.

There's a knock on the door. "Lincoln, are you here? You have a meeting with Dr. Garcia right now. It's four PM," his receptionist calls out from the other side of the door, and it takes every ounce of willpower not to slaughter her for interrupting this moment.

My head snaps up, and I release Summer from my death grip. I half expect his familiar essence to flood back into my mind—the rational part of my brain.

I glance at the clock on the wall. "Tell her I'll be in her office in five minutes."

Talia Garcia. My favorite fucking doctor. She can wait until I fucking finish.

"Um…she's already here, Mr. Kennedy."

A tightness fills my core, knowing I'll be sexually frustrated for the rest of the afternoon, if not for the rest of my life. Dr. Garcia, from what I recall, does not like when people are late. But she used to bring me pretty things and let me tear them apart, so I'll forgive her.

I stare down at Summer, who is observing me. Her face has a pretty flush. I kiss the top of her head. "Get dressed," I demand.

The door handle jiggles, followed by a stern knock. "Lincoln, I have a meeting with the dean in twenty minutes. You better have a good reason for locking this door."

The doorknob begins to turn. Talia has a key—of course, she has a key. She is the key to all of this.

I jump off the desk and away from Summer. She walks in and her eyes drift to Summer, who has positioned herself in the chair as I lean casually beside her as if we are merely conversing.

Dr. Garcia walks in wearing a fitted red suit and tilts her head at Summer, then darts her gaze between us as recognition settles in.

As Summer rises, her eyes twinkle as she walks past me. "Thank you, Lincoln," she says. "I appreciate the feedback on my essay." The lies spewing out of her are natural. I always knew my pretty girl was a liar.

She smiles sweetly at Talia, who smiles sweetly back, although she seems to linger on the flush of Summer's cheeks.

Summer reaches to shake her hand, oblivious to the marks on her neck. "Nice to formally meet you, Dr. Garcia. I've heard lots about you growing up. I've really been enjoying your class."

Talia's eyes flare. Her eyes are locked on Summer's vibrant white hair, memories of days gone by flash through her vibrant Italian eyes. "Ah, Summer Landry. I was wondering when I'd have the pleasure of meeting you." Dr. Garcia holds her hand longer than is socially acceptable. Her mind is in overdrive, staring at the daughter of her most prized possession and the granddaughter of her former lovers. "I'm very sorry about your father."

Summer pulls her hand away as if Dr. Garcia's skin is burning. "I apologize, but I do have to run." She turns to meet my stare, and in response, I give her a cocky smile while her eyes devour me.

With my arms crossed, I am still adjusting to this magnificent body

Lincoln has taken care of for me. "I'll be seeing you soon, Summer. Don't run from me next time I see you."

She moistens her lips slightly and returns the smile. "See you soon, Lincoln," she echoes as she walks out the door.

She doesn't flee; she walks with a confident strut.

Talia's gaze follows Summer as she disappears behind the shadows of the hallway, and her face turns white like she's seen a ghost. In many ways, she has.

Talia raises her eyebrows at me. Her dark eye makeup accentuates her eyelids, and her hair is tied back. It remains a glossy black, except for the single gray streak at the front.

"It's not what you think," I state before she can start lecturing me. She used to lecture me all the time, and I hated it.

It's exactly what it looks like, and Lincoln is slowly regaining consciousness. I have little time before he takes back control.

"My goodness," she says, keeping her gaze on the dark hallway beyond. "That girl is a spitting image of her grandmother. Her beauty is just—" She pauses, her eyes reflective on what once was, focusing on the woman who single-handedly turned this town into darkness.

Summer's grandmother, the one who spawned the Shadowface we know and love.

Talia's attention is now wholly directed at me. "That must make you happy. She's very pretty. Our dark one loves the pretty ones. He will favor you."

My throat tightens, and her attention moves to the vein throbbing in my neck. Her head twitches. "Lincoln, be cautious around her. Avoid raising suspicion before the ceremony. I've worked tirelessly to keep our group undisclosed. You grasp the significance of what you're involved in and your role in it. Everything will soon be yours, but be patient."

One fluid motion and I could kill her. Snapping her delicate neck would rid me of one less person to worry about. Going on a rampage seems much simpler than hiding in my own skin.

I opt for silence, fearing that if I speak, I won't be able to control myself.

A creeping dread settles upon Dr. Garcia as she stares into the eyes of the monster—the one she believed to be gone forever. Her deep brown eyes, eyes that used to reduce men to their knees, now gaze at me with a hint of piteousness.

Recognition finally settles in. "Mikael…" she gasps, "is that really you?"

I cross my arms, a twisted smile forming on my face. "Hello, doctor."

I'm her patient. A delicate, dark, and disturbed patient, and also her adopted son. A son she gave up on and failed at fixing.

The clarity is palatable.

Her eyes betray a hint of terror, her frail hand trembling as her eyes dilate like they do before death. The silky blackness is so serene, it makes me envious. She darts her gaze to the door and the voices echoing from beyond.

"Mikael," she breathes. "One step closer, and I'll make sure everyone in this office knows what you're about to do. You will spend the rest of your miserable life in the asylum. I'll put you back in that white room."

I lower my gaze, raise my arms to the back of my head, staying perfectly still and comfortable in my chair.

She knows my style. I watch, I wait, then I pounce before they can blink.

"You have no idea what my plans are, doctor," I say sardonically.

She barks out a laugh. "I can guess, boy." Any fear has now melted away, leaving her cold and cruel exterior. "Do you remember how scared you used to be of that white room as a child?"

She always threatened me with a white room. That I would live a colorless existence if I behaved badly in public. I ended up there, anyway.

I started to equate white with evil…and when I first saw Summer and her white hair, I was fixated on it. That is one of the reasons I will, one day soon, kill her. It's also the same reason I am obsessed with her.

Dr. Garcia takes a careful seat in front of me, inches away from where Summer and I just fucked.

She pulls out her notebook. "The last time we spoke, you threatened to tear my eyes out," she says matter-of-factly. "Do you still wish to do that?"

I snicker as that memory vividly plays out in my mind. I had said that to her after I killed my last victim. If it weren't for Lincoln, she'd be dead. In fact, if it weren't for Lincoln, *many* people would be dead.

I rise from my chair and step around her, clicking the door shut and locking it before moving to the edge of the desk and leaning back next to her. "Yes, doctor," I say with arched brows, "I would very much still like to cut your eyes out."

When she first discovered Lincoln, she used her power and manipulation to draw him out. When she discovered his level of brilliance, she fell in love with him. She decided I didn't matter anymore.

She steps toward me, the familiar scent of her designer perfume wafting in my face. She must have put it on the spot between her collarbone and neck before she arrived.

I stand still as a statue as she rises on her tippy toes and runs her fingers along my cheekbone. "Mikael..." she whispers in awe. "I can't believe it's really you. It's simply remarkable; I thought you were gone for good."

She lies. I can taste her fear, see it shining through her devious eyes. Heat rolls through my entire body as I imagine finishing her like I promised myself I would.

My eyes drift to those scissors on Lincoln's desk. The perfect tool to carve out an iris.

I lean my hands back on the desk. "Don't worry, Doctor Garcia, I've never really left."

She takes a careful step back but rakes her gaze over my body. She watches me stoically, like a guardian of the Order should.

"It was you who marked Summer, wasn't it?" she asks. "It was you at the ceremony, not Lincoln."

I bite the inside of my cheek. "I had every right to be there. She was my mother, not his. He has nothing to do with the Order. It's my birthright, and it's what she died for."

She waves her hand and lets out a deep breath. "That may be so, but you can't stay in control, Mikael. We've been through this; you can't control yourself. You will kill again, and you will continue killing until the day you die. That missing girl... You took her, didn't you?"

I curl my lip at her. "You don't know anything about me, *Doctor Garcia*."

She shakes her head. "You're angsty and anxious. You only call me Doctor Garcia when you're upset."

"I'm sorry, Talia. Is that better? Or does *Mom* work for you?"

She flicks a piece of dust off her red suit jacket, completely composed now that she believes I won't kill her with so many witnesses just outside the door.

She takes a deep breath. "No child should witness what you saw. You were not supposed to see that. Your mother was chosen for a greater purpose. Her soul is at rest; she's with Him. You need to put yourself to peace."

A snarl rips from my lips, and she jolts back. "I didn't come back to talk about my mother."

Her eyes narrow. "So why did you come back? Why are you here, Mikael?"

I gently touch my lips. Her flavor lingers. My skin tingles from the brief moment when I was in control, when I regained ownership of my body. "I want Summer. She's mine, and she is the one I want to kill."

I can't lie. She is the only reason I haven't completely let go of myself. *Revenge, love, hate, obsession.*

I don't know which one is which anymore. My reality is defined by her. No one else in this world matters the way she does.

Talia blinks and stares blankly at me for a few seconds. She is ignorant of what we did. The late-night visits, Lincoln's years of manipulating her mind, and my obsession with her are all unknown to her. She doesn't know her star student, *her son*, at all.

"Then you shall have her," she says. "But only when the time is right. But under no circumstances are you to kill her yet. Do you understand? This campus cannot deal with another Shadowface. I won't let you be like Kevin. I'll tear your soul apart before I let you destroy what I've protected since I was a girl. And you won't like the new methods I've been using to control my patients."

My jaw ticks and I smile, looking down at that paper. "It's too late, Talia. I already am Him. You made me Him when you sent me those pretty girls."

She's responsible for this. I was compelled by her. She tempted me with bait, testing my resolve. I have no idea where she got them from. All blonde and all pretty. All of them looked like my mother. She created the circumstances and placed them in a maze with a mouse only hunting for bait.

I was so young, so I barely remember the specifics. Just that it satisfied a need.

I tried not to do it. Each time I saw them tied up on my bed, I curled up as far away from them as I could. A few moments into it, she played music, and I blacked out. When I came to, Dr. Garcia was writing on a clipboard, a smile tugging on her lips like I was her little pet. They were dead—more than dead, actually; they looked like grated cheese.

Then she made me clean up the mess.

I was thirteen the first time I killed.

She walks up to me and presses her lips against my forehead. "Do not think I won't make the call to put you away. I love you, Mikael, like you're my son, but this is for the best."

She reaches into her bag, grabs a piece of paper and writes something on it, then slides it on the desk. "Tell Lincoln, if he can hear me, to take this medicine. Bring him back and put yourself back in your cage. He has a thesis to defend soon."

She sighs as my fingers curl around the paper. Her eyes flit up to meet mine. "You created Lincoln for a reason. He is on the cusp of greatness, and the world is a better place with him in it. All you will do is create chaos; you will get him thrown into an asylum. You're not well, Mikael. You do not know how to function properly in society."

I marvel at her. The hypocrisy of everything she is and stands for. The hypocrisy of the world in which we live...the world I'll never understand.

I draw my eyebrows in. "I thought you liked chaos, *Talia Garcia*. Guardian of the Order."

She runs her hand over my hair line like she used to do to calm me down as a boy.

Her patient.

The same way my mother used to as well. "Enlightenment is found in the perpetual dance of order and disorder, control and liberation. You need to be controlled, Mikael. The world isn't ready for you."

I'm not sure when it happened, but the scissors are now in my hand and pressed into her neck. I play with the blade and meet her gaze. "You were supposed to make me better," I say as a dullness hits my vision. "You didn't make me better, doctor."

Instead, she relentlessly pounded blind hatred into every contour of my mind. Etched her scripture into my skull every day, as if she was chiseling her dark emblem into my soul.

Hate. Kill. Blood. *Murder*.

I was a child when she was assigned to me. Orphaned, alone, and traumatized, and now she wants to box me in?

She was aware of my identity. She was there when it happened. She's the one who found me and made sure she was assigned to my case.

Her hands are soft as she reaches up and cups my face. Although they always were soft, like a mother's touch. And I suppose she is the closest thing to a mother I have. But I'm not the shining light in her world.

Lincoln is, and will always be, her favorite.

"Take a look around. See the life he made for you. Just relax, observe, and enjoy it. It's all yours, too. Experience what he does without interference. Fuck that girl to oblivion for all I care. Having a second chance like this is a gift. You're truly fortunate."

I slam my fist into the desk as she turns away and heads to the door. "He doesn't even feel," I spit at her, and she pauses. "He's not real, you stupid bitch. He's a shell *I* created."

She only half turns her head. "For your own good, keep your distance from the girl until the ceremony. She belongs to Him, not some half-formed orphan."

I release a growl.

She lifts her chin to the sky. "You will deliver her body the night of the ceremony, and that will be the end of it. Do not mess with me, Mikael." She disappears into the same darkness as Summer, clicking her heels as she goes into the ivory tower she hides behind.

I swallow bile down my throat. Every ounce of me wants to follow her, tie her up, eat her up, and spit her out. I close my eyes as Lincoln's voice brings me back to my sanity, and I let go of my shields, preventing him from coming in.

It starts with a subtle ringing in my ear. I don't fight him. I let go of the constant tug of war and the psychotic withering he's used to.

I'm strong. He knows I'm strong.

So the question is, what the fuck is he going to do about it?

"We have to talk, Mikael," he says in my mind's eye.

I stare at my reflection in the window, at Lincoln staring back at me. I grab my glasses and slide them back on my face as my vision blurs and his vision grows clear.

"About what?" I smile, knowing why he's pissed. I took the best moment from him, right as he was about to come.

"About Summer."

I shoot an emotion straight into his spine as I dissipate into the abyss. Let him *feel* what I feel for once—the worst emotion in the human consciousness.

Jealousy.

I've been lost in my textbook for the past hour, only occasionally aware of the cool breeze whispering past my cheek. Five days have blurred into one since my last interaction with him. It's Friday now, and I fucked Lincoln, or Mikael, or whoever that was on Monday. I only saw Lincoln in class once this week, on Wednesday, and he ignored me. The silence is deafening.

I grip the phone and swipe to my last set of messages with Lincoln. Five days have gone by since we've spoken. I'm barely sleeping, barely functioning. I stay up until three in the morning, trying to drown out all the other thoughts I should be reconciling, or the fact that I'm falling into a dark hole.

Although, I'm not sure if the intense emotions I'm feeling are love.

It's the same insidious thoughts I have about getting off on being killed. He's planting these ideas in my mind, controlling me from the inside out, and there is nothing I can do to stop it. Lincoln is smart, a certified genius, but this is beyond anything I could ever imagine.

I stayed late on campus today to just breathe and avoid Dani, who can sense that something is seriously wrong with me. The grass is still soft, not quite dead yet, although the earliest hints of fall have crept into the air given it's pushing mid-October. The campus is still busy, even though classes ended an hour ago, but it's thinning out, people are drifting out of the sandstone buildings, and the evening sun layers onto the trees like the brilliant red of the blood trickling down Cali's arm.

I'm not convinced Lincoln is a serial killer—at least, not the psychotic and calculated kind we see in the movies.

First, the way he kissed me. I've learned through my obsessive research the last few days that most of the killers in popular culture are sexual serial killers. As in, they get sexual gratification from the act of killing itself, where the violence takes the place of sex. Second, sexualized serial killers often place their victims in sexually degrading positions without actually having intercourse with them. What I've learned is that killing is like the cherry on top for their release. They have no remorse, no guilt, just pure sexual pleasure over the act itself. They are neither a psychopath nor a sociopath, but are something else entirely. Scientists have no way of knowing what that something else is exactly, because they are so rare and hard to study.

Lincoln enjoyed fucking me way too much for me to think it's anything but immensely satisfying for him, and I don't get the sense Lincoln is a killer at all. He is way too kind and smart.

Mikael, however, is a different story.

I'm pretty sure I almost died when he fronted while he was fucking me on Lincoln's desk. I physically felt how different they were in that moment, and that was when it cemented for me that there are indeed two of them.

That makes my stomach burn because it means he gets his true sexual satisfaction in a way he's yet to experience with me. And I don't know how to change that, or if I can change it.

There is something else that's been bothering me since that day.

The eyes.

Lincoln can't see a damn thing, and Mikael's eyes were normal when he came alive with me. But sometimes, they seem translucent, almost ethereal. So what version of him am I getting when his eyes are like that?

That's the version I saw at the dinner table that terrified me to my core. I'm only seeing fragmented pieces of him, and I want to see all of him.

I glance down at my phone and hover my thumb over it as it buzzes, interrupting my train of thought, as ringing takes over my earbuds.

I shift my gaze to the canopy in the sky and lay my head on the ground, utterly dreading the sound of her voice as I answer the call.

"Hi, Mom."

"Oh my god," she huffs out a breath on the other end of the line. "You finally answered. I thought you were dead."

I've been avoiding her call for days—ever since I've started suspecting what my father was. I have a hard time believing she knew nothing about any of it. I roll my eyes, but my insides squirm at the validity of that comment, even though sarcasm is dripping out of her.

I should be dead, and so should she, because of the monster she chose to spend her life with.

I grit my teeth but smile. "I'm not dead, Mom. I'm really busy studying and being the perfect college student. But don't worry, no one has torn my eyes out yet if you're worried about what's on the news."

A pause. "That's not funny, Summer."

"Isn't it?" I can't help but smile. I have to wonder what secrets she holds, and how much she knows. How could she not know she was married to a notorious serial killer?

Maybe she and I aren't that different after all.

Can you be brainwashed into loving someone?

"How's school going, Summer?"

I close my textbook, marking the beginning of *Sensation and Perception,* and shove the textbook into my bag.

All my senses are on fire. I can still feel the slickness of him fucking me. The burning...as he accurately described it. The pleasure coming straight from hell.

I chew on my lip as the mark on my hip flares. "I'm fine."

She lets out a deep sigh. "Are you coming home for a visit soon? I really miss you. This house isn't the same without you."

She doesn't miss me; she misses the idea of me. She misses prancing me around like an accessory. But I really, *really* miss my father.

"I'll think about it," I tell her, but I won't. School's too busy, and Mikael told me not to run away from him. Simple polite words, I realize now, were a command.

"Please consider it, Summer." The phone clicks dead before I can answer.

"I won't," I mutter. My mother and I have barely spoken since my father died.

I'm unable to move. It's like he controls me completely. Last night I stared out the window for an hour, wishing I could escape. I want to run away from here—away from him, away from this nightmare—but my legs won't budge. The thought of it makes me sick. He's in my head, manipulating my thoughts.

Over the past three days, I've learned there is no one named Mikael who attends this school with that peculiar spelling.

No reference to him at all, anywhere, as if this town wiped him clean.

I am absolutely sure that Mikael lives somewhere deep inside Lincoln's head. And because of the news article, I am certain Mikael was there first.

I turn to my side, keeping my head on the ground, and type in Lincoln's name again. His picture pops up as I stare at his superficial IG profile.

He's so gorgeous, so composed and dark, his skin so smooth. His jawline cut so tight, his clothes hugging his body, wearing all black like he always does. His skin is a soft pale white, like a ghost, like he barely exists, and whoever snapped this photo caught the very edges of him. An ethereal image of perfection.

Even now, it's like he's staring right at me through those thick glasses. Goosebumps pebble my skin as my nipples grow hard beneath the fabric of my dress.

He's always watching…

I lie back on the grass, and even though I'm wearing a trench coat, only a thin line of my panties covers me beneath my dress. I open my legs like my life depends on it.

*Dammit…*I'm missing something so obvious. Something right in front of me. I'm missing him again, tortured, waiting for him to call when it seems like he is blatantly ignoring me.

I grab my phone and swipe to SF, my nails tapping the screen.

Summer: *I'm done with you. Pick someone else to torment.*

I slam my phone down, not expecting a response. The worst part is I'm not even upset or scared of what this guy is capable of. I'm rabidly pissed off because he's playing phone games with me, like we are actually dating, and I'm unsure if I should play hard to get or let him know I'm interested.

He's winning in every aspect of this game right now.

A few minutes go by, and I wonder if he's even going to bother answering me. Then he messages me, causing the butterflies in my stomach to stir.

Fuck him…finally.

SF: *Hello to you, too.*

I squeeze my eyes shut and take a deep breath before opening them again. No indication which version is behind these words.

Summer: *Why are you ignoring me?*

SF: *I've been busy, Summer…I defend my thesis in January.*

I let out a sigh. So normal…on the outside. Just writing his thesis, while at the same time, mind-fucking girls.

Summer: *Well, I'm studying, too. I just…*

SF: *Do you miss me watching you? Because I promise, I can't stop thinking about you, either.*

I run my fingers along my lips, imagining him watching me, and they twitch into a smile. I play with the hem of my dress, laying my bare legs out under what's left of the heat of the sun.

Summer: *Yes, I miss you.*

I hate admitting it, but I'm unable to lie to him. He seems to see right through my lies, anyway.

SF: *I love the dress you have on, pretty girl.*

Pretty girl?

I shoot my head up and peer around the now empty campus, my heart in my throat as those darkened sun rays now blend into the earth and sky.

Mikael. In a moment, he's shifted. I don't think Lincoln's the one talking to me anymore, and he's here somewhere.

My gaze finally settles on him in the shadows of the trees, watching me like he always does. The final stream of sun hit my eyes, causing me to squint, but I can make out the mask staring back at me. The familiar tightness wraps around my muscles and pleasure builds between my legs at the sight of him.

I reach down and press the call button, and I watch him move his hand to his pocket; he picks it up on the second ring but doesn't lift the phone to his ear. He's so still…he looks like a scarecrow, and I have to remind myself to breathe.

"How do I know which one of you is watching me right now?" I ask in a meek voice.

A small shift of his head. A breeze shuffling the leaves high above. "You don't," he says. I can hear him so clearly through the phone.

I bite my lip and watch him, too scared to move, too scared to stay, but knowing running won't matter.

Something washes over me. I close my eyes for a moment, enjoying the cool wind on my face, as a tiny drop of rain hits my cheek, and then another.

He doesn't move, but I grab a nearby stick and my breath immediately lengthens as I slip my dress above my knees, keeping myself propped up as possible, arching my back.

Just seeing him in that mask, knowing two of them are blended together under one…

I don't need the moisture of the rain to slide the stick inside me—he already has me dripping wet. I slide my panties down one leg and close my eyes, slipping the edge of the stick inside me.

The pressure immediately subsides. I'm so sexually frustrated, like nothing in *this world* can satisfy me. I let out a moan as I work it a few inches deeper, but I don't take my eyes off him. His expression is neutral, as to be expected in that hideous mask of insidiousness, as I slide this stick further inside me.

My phone pings, and I glance down at it.

His voice rises from the phone. "Harder, pretty girl. I want you to fuck yourself so hard, you sever your body."

I push the stick fast, its edges tearing me, but I don't care. I push it in, harder and faster—dirtier—giving him the show he wants.

The fact he's the most dangerous man alive only makes me wetter, hornier, hotter. The build up starts to ease as my orgasm builds and the stick is much wetter than it should be because of how much juice is flowing out of me.

Keeping my one hand on the stick, I close my eyes and let the orgasm be what it is…pretending that I'm fucking him instead.

I open my eyes as my orgasm blooms, the heat building within warms me up. I keep fucking myself as he stands across the lawn by a large tree, watching me.

I bring the phone to my mouth. "How long are we going to play this game, Mikael?"

He tilts his head and doesn't respond. But it was enough of a response…he reacted to the name.

Mikael.

The line goes quiet.

Shit. Shit. Shit.

I pushed him too hard. I'm being too needy. A group of students pass by, and I quickly pull the stick out of myself and hug my knees to my chest, tossing the stick and the phone a few feet away from me. My mouth is like chalk as they walk by me, and I try to hide my shaking as they stare at me awkwardly.

When I look back at him, he's gone.

I stay on the grassy lawn until the sky darkens and eventually opens up, utterly still. My body's in shock. The rain smothers me, but I don't move; I don't find anywhere to go, and eventually, the rain subsides and whatever water is left hitting my face is dripping from the trees above.

A heavy mist settles in the air—one that matches my current dreary mood. This isn't how I thought my dating life at Kinsmen University would go. He's testing me, I realize. He's seeing how far I'd go for him.

Anger seeps into every bone as I glare at the stick a few feet away from me, thinking about what I just did with it. *Again...* My pussy is still bleeding with shame.

I crawl over it and somehow muster enough strength to snap it in two and whip the pieces across the small meadow in which I lay. I pick up my soaking wet backpack, thankful my books are still dry inside.

My phone dings, bringing me back from the inferno in my mind, and I crawl over the wet, frozen grass to answer it.

It's Dani. And I've missed three calls from her.

I fumble in the dark until I'm able to swipe my fingers, my hand numb.

"Hello?" I barely recognize the voice that rasps out of me.

The numbness in my bones isn't from the frozen water—I experienced it even before the heavens opened up on me. It's because I can barely feel anything anymore unless I'm with him.

"Where the fuck are you?" Dani sounds composed as usual.

I rise and pull my backpack on and rub my arms. "I'm still at school," I tell her and run my hands over the goosebumps prickling my flesh. I scarcely know what it's like to be in my own skin, and when I take a careful step forward, it's like my body isn't my own. It's like each step is controlled by someone else. He seems to control my thoughts, my movements, my soul. Every minute I don't run to the police, his darkness takes over to the point I can almost taste it. Except the taste of his darkness is so fucking sweet.

"Well, get home. We're going out. It's Friday night, and we've been invited to a party."

I check the time and frown. Somehow, it's already seven PM, but I swear, when he called me earlier, it was only six PM. I'm not sure where the last hour has gone. The campus is empty, eerily quiet, like the cocoon that is my mind. I must have sat here in a trance for longer than I thought.

"Fine," I mutter as my teeth chatter. I don't have the energy to argue.

"Do you need a ride?" she asks.

I scan the dark, empty campus, half-expecting to see a burlap mask. The lights in the windows are all twinkled out. The whispers of the fallen, the ghosts of this town, tickle my ear.

"No. I'll walk. Give me twenty minutes, and I'll be home."

"Okay. Suit yourself. Be careful. Love you, bye."

I walk through the stone pathway to the tree-lined road that leads to town. The wind is still howling from the passing storm, and in the distance, the moon lights up the sky.

"Wait…Dani?" I ask her before she hangs up.

"Yeah, what's up?"

"What party are we going to?"

"Not sure. A mysterious invitation showed up on our doorstep. And before you say anything about it, yes, we're going. I suspect it's Xander's house, and I'm desperate to see if it was him at the rave dancing with me. Don't tell anyone, but I have a feeling it's them."

My stomach twists. "Who?"

Dani sighs. "The Order, Summer. I think they are connected to all of it. I have a strong suspicion they are involved in my father's conviction."

I trip on a rock and steady myself. "Why do you think that?"

"Just a gut feeling, but I need to get into that house to be sure."

D ani and Misty are both wearing loose sweats when I get home, looking fresh as daisies. They are sitting and drinking wine at the kitchen island, their hair and makeup done to the nines.

Dani's eyes widen when she sees me walk in like a drowned rat. I did my best to wipe the mud off my face, but I'm sure it's still caked on. "Summer? What the fuck?"

Guess not…

I wipe my hands over matted hair, as if that would make me look any better. "I fell asleep on the lawn at school, then got caught in the rain. It's not a big deal."

"You look like death reincarnate. And seriously, every time I see you, it looks like you've been…"

I raise an eyebrow at her. "I've been…?"

A wide grin spreads on her face. "Never mind. Are you going to tell us what happened?"

My pussy is still throbbing and raw… It's like Dani can smell the sex on me, even if that sex was with a piece of wood in the forest.

Misty spits out her wine, her face tight, her eyes lingering on me for too long. I must look bad, and I glare back at Misty.

I drop my bag on the couch and sigh. "I need a hot shower."

Dani pushes her barstool back. "Nope, not doing that. Where the hell have you been? And who is this mystery boyfriend? I recognize that look on your face, Summer. Something happened."

My mouth gapes open at the audacity. How could she possibly…

"Don't try to get out of coming to this party," she adds. "It won't be as crazy as the last one."

Misty doesn't seem too keen on my coming or my presence here at all as she sits and scowls. She remains silent, but her eyes, hard and unreadable, seem to dissect every inch of me.

Lincoln didn't invite me to this party. He must have known this was going on, given it's at his house. I guess I'm good enough to fuck on his desk but seeing me in public doesn't seem to be too high on his agenda.

I stalk toward the hallway, toward the stairs to my attic bedroom. "Look, Dani, I get it. I just don't have time."

Dani sticks out her fingers. "Two drinks. Only two small glasses of wine, then you can go shower and get ready. Who's got you so distracted?"

Misty cocks her annoying eyebrow, her eye twitches. "Oh… Summer, I didn't realize you were seeing anyone."

"I'm not," I say too quickly.

Dani gives me a *don't bullshit me* look, and Misty gives me a cocky smirk, not unlike the one she gave me when she was prancing out of Lincoln's office when I first met him there. We haven't spoken since that moment. It was as if she was silently saying, *I want him, too.*

"I swear, I am not seeing anyone." Which is true, technically.

Misty's gaze pierces through me like blazing flames. Like she can see my hidden shame and is envious. "Oh…" she says in a mousy voice. "I thought you liked our TA."

I do like our TA, and I'm pretty sure she likes him, too.

He kills people who look like you, I want to scream at her.

Dani pours me a glass of wine, which I accept and ignore my wet clothes and how I want to puke at the soft, sweet aroma pouring out of Misty.

Intense jealousy fires up deep in my core. It expands in my stomach and wraps itself around my heart, burning me.

It's unexplainable. Like I'm jealous of her mere existence.

I glare at her. "I don't. If you're so curious, I'm thinking about going out with Grant."

Narrowing her eyes, Dani continues, "Grant? I thought you weren't into him?" She shakes her head. "Never mind him. I want you and Misty to try to talk to Lincoln tonight. I need you to distract him while I try to dig up shit on Xander. I want to get into Xander's bedroom without anyone seeing me."

Misty and I stare at each other for a brief second before both of us break the stare.

"I thought you liked Xander?" I ask her, shooting my gaze toward Dani.

Her eyes twitch. "He's hot, I won't deny that…but there is something off about him. I have a bad feeling about them. Did you know they are all from here? All their parents grew up here, too. All they do is hang out with each other. It's incestuous."

I shrug. "That doesn't make them part of a secret cult. This has nothing to do with your father, Dani."

She leans back on the counter, her eyes glaze over and I immediately regret saying that. "I…I never said that…" She's tongue tied. I've never seen Dani stammer like this.

She recovers quickly, but it landed on her like a gut punch. "It's still suspicious. If anyone has secret society written all over them, it's that group. I found an article yesterday that says they mark the flesh of the ones they kill. I want in that house tonight. I'm very curious to see inside. I have a feeling they are the key to everything."

I suspect Dani isn't telling me everything, either. She's always believed so strongly of her father's innocence. She must be connecting some dots, and I might be starting to connect them, too.

My stomach burns as I reach for my mark and tickle it with my fingers.

He's already chosen someone.

I'm thinking it doesn't matter. He's made it clear I'm not the only blonde in his sights.

Maybe he's done the same thing to Misty, and that's why she's acting so strangely. If she keeps glaring at me like that, I'll be the one to leave marks on her skin.

I keep my face neutral, knowing Dani is watching me. I vividly imagine Misty's eyes gouged out, and that thought brings a sweet smile to my face, even though it shouldn't.

Fuck. What is wrong with me? These aren't my thoughts. This isn't how I think…

The room grows quiet, each of us in our own thoughts. Dani musing, Misty gleaming and me…I have no clue what's going on with me, my body doesn't even feel like my own.

Dani draws out a long blink, then claps her hands. "Alright, let's get ready. I want to be there by ten."

I let out an audible sigh and gulp down my last sip of wine.

"This," Dani says, her eyes darting between us as she slams her hands on the island, "is going to be so much fun." Dani has a knack for relieving tension.

I finally make it into the bathroom and eagerly step into the soothing shower. The hot water cascades over my chilled skin, instantly warming me up. I gently slide my hands down my breasts and glide them over my stomach, and a sense of relaxation washes over me. The mud oozes off my body as I clean between my legs, and I turn the water up so hot, it nearly burns.

As I lower my gaze, a gasp escapes my lips as blood slowly streams down and forms a crimson whirlpool in the drain. My stomach and breasts bare deep cuts, leaving gashes scattered across my body. These wounds mirror the exact slashes depicted in the photograph Lincoln had sent me.

My heart nearly stops.

Breathe, Summer...one shallow breath. I close my eyes and focus on inhaling oxygen, and when I open my eyes, the blood is gone. And for a moment, I am grateful for the all-consuming terror. *Fear is the appropriate emotion.*

But a clear pulse hits my center, and that's when I realize I'm absolutely fucked.

I can imagine how soft he was before he killed Cali. How he spoke to her...so smart, so dirty, so fucking sexy.

Did he fuck her before he did that to her?

What the actual fuck is wrong with me?

This isn't a kink or a sexual preference; I am actually fantasizing about being murdered. Pure, steely jealousy overtakes any other logic, and my jaw clenches just thinking of it.

Do you want me to kill you, Summer? Well, I sure as hell don't want him killing someone else. Why the fuck do I keep fantasizing about it?

I shut off the water, head upstairs, and throw some makeup on while blasting music so my roommates can't hear me scream. I stare at myself in the full-length mirror in my room, completely nude. Then I pull out my lace bra and matching panties—the ones he likes so much—and slide them on.

Then I toss on my tightest black dress and curl my hair in beach waves before adding some thick black mascara.

I pull out my phone and hesitate for only a moment before I click on his name. The picture of his slaughtered victim is still fresh in my messages, reminding me of what he is. My eyes linger on it for much longer than they should, and I decide not to text him.

It's best if he doesn't know I'm coming. I'll keep my face covered the entire time, and he shouldn't even notice me.

The address on the invitation brings us to an imposing property on the outskirts of town. Dani's eyes pop out of their sockets as we pull up to the front. The house—if that's what you want to call it—is more like a compound with remnants of what looks like it used to be a Victorian manor. It's hauntingly gorgeous, shrouded among the trees, and the lawn surrounding it is immaculate.

The place screams money, darkness, and slaughter.

We drove twenty minutes in the dark to get here and cars are lined up down the street. Shadows are darting around the lawn, swarming everywhere, with hanging lights dangling from the trees. The entire party looks as though it's outside.

Dani finds a parking spot and pulls the car in, turning off the engine. "Look at how many people are here," she says, twisting her head, trying to get a feel for what we are walking into. "I can't believe we almost missed out on this."

Misty chimes in from the backseat, "I wonder if Lincoln's going to be here."

I bristle and try not to respond or think about Lincoln and Misty interacting at all.

A guy stumbles beside us and hurls in a bush on the edge of the property. "Looks fun," I quip, giving her a thumbs up. I'd much rather be in a quiet room studying...preferably with Lincoln watching me.

"Shut up, Summer," Misty bites back.

Dani shakes her head. "Okay, what is up between the two of you? Both of you can cut it the fuck out. I want to have a good time tonight, and I'm on a mission to find out more about them."

I lean toward Dani and whisper, "She's just jealous because every guy she likes wants me." Straightening up, I turn to Misty. "You're not special, Misty."

Misty gets out and slams the door.

Dani looks at me and frowns. Her pretty hair is in one of her loose bohemian braids that falls over her shoulder. The tank top she wore does wonders for her tits, too. For someone who claims she's not interested in someone, she sure looks like she is.

"Do you have to be so mean to her? Is this about Lincoln? Because you just told us you were with Grant."

I lean back and fold my arms. "This isn't about Lincoln. She's not special, and I don't like fake people."

Dani's face drops as it always does when I'm being ugly. The problem is, deep down, I am ugly, which is why I put so much effort into making myself flawless on the outside.

Making Misty look bad doesn't make me feel better...not at all. And I'm thinking this part of my personality is why I like the degradation that Mikael gives me.

Mikael sees that side of me; he knows the dark parts of me I desperately try to hide and loves pushing me to bring it out.

Tonight, I want to find out more about Mikael, if that is even his name—but it's the name I've given the shadowed monster in Lincoln's eyes. I have no proof he's real, other than my dissolved memory and the fact he reacted to the name when I whispered it.

Misty stands just outside waiting for us, and Dani whispers, "What is with you lately, and what's your problem with Misty? You only act weird like this when you have a crush on someone and you're jealous. And I don't believe you suddenly like Grant, so don't bullshit me." She covers her hand over her face. "It's him, isn't it? You are talking to Lincoln."

I raise my eyes at her, and as soon as she says it, she knows. She sucks in a breath and says, "Summer..."

"We flirted," I finally admit to her. "We have so much in common. He knows my father, and my family's roots are here. We connected over him, that's it."

"Was he the one texting you that weird shit at the beginning of the semester?" Dani asks. "Should I be worried about you?"

A bang on the window. "Are you guys coming?" Misty calls from outside.

"We're coming," Dani yells back at her, but she gives me a look and I realize this isn't over.

"It's nothing," I whisper, pulling off my seatbelt. Nothing I can truly explain, anyway. "We spend a lot of time talking, and he's been helping me with schoolwork. I'm sorry I lied to you, but I'll explain everything to you soon, and I'll apologize to Misty."

"Thank you," she says, pulling off her seatbelt. "And you're right, this conversation isn't over, but let's have some fun tonight." She passes me her keys. "Here, take these. I plan on getting ridiculously drunk tonight. If you want to drink, too, I won't stop you. We can find another way home."

She's already surveying the party and has a look in her eye, and I don't want to question her. I have my own secrets tonight, my own agenda.

I slide out the passenger's door and, taking a deep breath, face Misty. "I'm sorry for what I just said. Thank you for inviting me."

Dani smiles and Misty still looks less than impressed but softens at my clear fake apology.

"See, isn't it easier to be nice?" Dani says as we take a few steps closer. A group of people walk by laughing and my heart stops.

Each of them is wearing a mask, but it's not him... None of them are *him,* even though *he* is everywhere and nowhere all at the same time. Shadows dance from the slits of their eyes.

"Here we go again," Dani jokes, and we each grab a mask from a box on the edge of the property. I quickly throw it on, hoping it covers me enough. The only evidence is my white hair, which peeks out. A cool wind hits, and I eye one of the fires roaring in a pit a few feet away and the dark brooding house with flickers of light in the windows.

"Is the party inside or outside?" I ask. The house appears dark and ancient. The outdoor speakers are blaring music, like an outdoor festival or some kind of ritual. No one looks like they are in their right mind. But I guess that's what Shadowface does—he gives people a release.

Dani shrugs. "I honestly don't know."

"And how do we know if we get...marked?" Misty asks.

I glance at her and roll my eyes. What a stupid question.

"I don't know that, either," I say, looking around and glancing at the curved entryway to the house, soft shadows dancing from within. We wander around for a few minutes, and I quickly realize finding Lincoln will be like finding a needle in a haystack.

My eyes stay fixed on those flickering windows and the warmth and mystery inside.

"I have to pee," I lie as an icy breeze runs through the fabric of my thin dress and bare legs. I need to get inside of that house.

"We're *so* coming with you," Dani says. "Let's do our best not to split up this time."

That's probably for the best...for my sake. But if Lincoln's here, I'm going to find him.

As we step into the darkness, heading toward the house looming ahead, my eyes briefly meet Dani's and a breath escapes me, taken aback. With a devilish glint in her eyes, Dani looks at me, as if she, too, embodies Shadowface. As I watch her with *that* face, my body trembles, and not in a bad way.

"It doesn't look like anyone is in there," Dani says.

"I guarantee they are inside," I mutter. "And I bet it's warm in there."

We step toward the house and see the front door is actually being guarded by two masked men. As we walk up, one of them crosses his arms and stares us down...me, in particular.

"Let me in," I snap at him. My patience is wearing thin.

He tilts his head and, to my surprise, he steps to the side, allowing us entry. I walk through first, and right as I cross the threshold, he shuts Misty and Dani out.

I glance back at him, only to be met with an iron wall. "What the fuck?"

"Only one goes in, and it's you." He smirks. "Your friends will have to stay out here."

I grit my teeth and look at Misty and Dani standing a few feet away. Dani merely shrugs and waves goodbye. "Just go," she says. "I'll be in shortly, don't worry."

She stands back with Misty, leaving me facing the guards.

I'm invisible in this mask, but there is no way he's not here, watching me as he always is. The guard grabs a flask and jerks his head for me to tilt my head back.

"You've got to be kidding me. I'm not drinking that."

"Everyone drinks." He shrugs. "How badly do you want in?"

I don't fight it. I let him grab my chin, pull up my mask, and pour the monstrosity down my throat.

"Have fun," he says and nudges me through the doorway. I lift both arms at Dani, who I'm certain is reeling, because I truly have no idea what's going on. These two can deal with the wrath of Dani; I bet she will be in right after me.

Two more people push through and try to enter the house, but they are immediately denied access. "Sorry, no entry unless you're invited," the guard says and pushes the two guys back.

"How come she got in?" one of them whines, pointing at me standing awkwardly inside the door.

The bigger of the two men crosses his arms. "She was invited. I don't make the rules, man, I follow them. Now get the hell back before I get in shit."

I get chills. Goosebumps prickle my arms in the way he says it.

How did Lincoln find out I was coming? I certainly don't remember being invited, unless you consider that ominous card pushed under our door an invite. He had ample opportunity to personally invite me earlier this evening when I was degrading myself in front of him. All he had to say was—

Hey, pretty girl, want to come over tonight?

Simple.

I also thought this society was supposed to be a secret, but it seems like *everyone* knows exactly who they are.

I wrap my arms around myself and rub my shoulders. "How do you recognize me? I'm wearing a mask."

The smaller of the two extends their hand and grasps a lock of my hair. "You're the girl with white hair. We were told if you wanted in, to let you in." I swiftly swat his hand away, spinning around in annoyance.

They step outside and shutter the door, leaving me in the dark entryway of the house. It's warm, but goosebumps still pebble my flesh as I take a tentative step inside. The interior of the home is vast, with a grand entrance that appears both empty and immense. Two spiral staircases, each twisting upward and meeting at the top, leading to a mezzanine level above. Intricate fixtures hang off the wall, delicate lights flicker within them, casting a mesmerizing glow that reminds me of fire. It's the kind of house that has lots of nooks and crannies.

Family photos speckle the hallways, large portraits of people I don't recognize. An old painting of a man is centred on the wall over the arch of the staircase.

Matteo Vital, 1756.

His eyes are like fire, his face like stone. I'm assuming he's some sort of patriarch. Perhaps he's the one they all worship.

He's in the air, the walls, the creaky floors. It's as if I can hear the screams of the fallen and his whispers of death. This is where He originated, and I am certain this all has something to do with me.

My bloodline, my heritage, and my future.

My roots are in Kinsmen. This is where I belong and where it all began. My grandmother is here, too; I can sense her everywhere, feel her in my bones.

Whoever He is, He just met the daughter of his predecessor, and I'm developing a taste for blood.

Hushed laughter and voices echo from both directions in the dark house. I head left, sliding along the fancy wood floors, making little to no noise. I keep my mask on, as if it somehow will keep me invisible, even though my heart rate alone would betray my presence.

I pull my clutch off my shoulder and grab my phone, but I have no missed messages from anyone. I head down a dark hall and push open a large double door, hoping I can find a bathroom and regroup. Or better yet, find Lincoln and be done with these games. If this is where Lincoln lives, then where the fuck is he?

Instead, the door opens up to a large, impressive dark room with an elegant bar in the corner. The plush couches are filled with people, chatting and relaxing. Some people are wearing masks, some aren't.

It's the descendants of the town's founders. These are the people Dani believes are part of a secret society that murders people. This is, of course, all according to Dani's research over the past few weeks on the people that live in this town. On those that she thinks were involved with her father's false conviction. If I didn't bear a mark on my thigh, I would have thought she was insane.

There are enough people in here that no one notices me walk in, with my mask on and my hair tucked in tight so nobody can identify me.

Not that I mean anything to these people.

To me, it just looks like a party—normal college kids, doing normal college things. Everyone is mingling, drinking, or…making out on the couch.

A couple of scantily dressed girls are sitting on the laps of their men with their dresses pulled up over their thighs and, to my extreme relief, none of them are kissing Lincoln. Their masks lay lazily in their hands as if meaningless, and the music is much lower than it is outside.

Each girl is kissing her own partner, then they kiss each other, and then they make out with the guys again.

My face heats beneath my mask, but it's dark so I can't get a good look at them. I can tell by the way he chews on his lip and watches his girlfriend like he wants to destroy her, it's Xander. That and his arms are flexing and his tattoos are a clear marker.

He is a complete juxtaposition from Dr. Garcia, who is so petite and, even in her old age, pretty. Minus the darkness, which they both have in spades.

I stare at Xander and his girlfriend, at what they are doing, as heat pools in my lower belly. I watch him grab his girlfriend and pull her in for a kiss.

The guy next to him notices me, and Xander stops kissing her as our eyes lock. His features seem darker in this house. He gives me that slick smile and his girlfriend turns to face me. Heat fills my cheeks as I capture all their attention.

"Fuck," I whisper, and I turn to run.

"Hey," Xander yells, pushing his girlfriend off. "We just want to talk to you. We know who you are."

Nope. Nope. Nope.

I flee back toward the front door. If I can get outside, I will be invisible among the crowd and Xander won't find me. I didn't come here to talk with Xander, and since Lincoln is nowhere to be found, it's time to find Dani.

When I run to the door, the two guys from earlier are there, blocking me. Apparently, they let me in but have no intentions of letting me out, so I veer up the stairs instead, running up the curled ornate staircase leading to the rooms above.

I stall, catching my breath at the top of the stairs. Dim lights shine on a blood-red carpet in a long hallway with a few doors on either side. I turn, and am only met with silence and dust, so I tiptoe down the hall as the floorboards creak beneath my feet.

I decide to explore.

My eyes are immediately drawn to rows of photos lined up on the wall, similar frames to the one downstairs. As I carefully examine each old black-and-white photo, some dating back over a hundred years, I eventually stumble upon one that catches my attention. It is a picture of Dr. Garcia, adorned in her graduation gown, proudly receiving her degree. Her dark hair, neatly parted down the middle, gracefully cascades down to her lower back. She looks youthful in this photo, and it's hard to believe she was around twenty at the time.

Her beauty is undeniable, but the way she gazes directly into the camera is almost unnerving, like a cold stare that chills me to the bone.

As if she's saying, *I see you*, and the welcome isn't friendly.

I notice pictures of Xander and others I don't recognize, assuming one of them is Xander's mom, who I realize I know nothing about or what happened to her. My breath catches when I see a photo of Lincoln next to Xander. Lincoln barely looks eleven, and I stare at him for way too long as my one memory flashes back at me. I stare at his eyes, trying to decipher who is inside there, staring back at me.

It's Mikael, I decide. It can't be Lincoln, because this sad-looking boy staring back at me is not wearing glasses. It's also the boy I remember seeing.

I move down the hall and another picture stands out to me. I take in a tall, handsome boy with wavy sandy hair next to her holding a guitar. Dimples I can't look away from. Emotion rushes through me as I stare at his familiar face. Such a kind face, so many of his features trickled down to me. So many times I spent bouncing in his arms as a young child.

Tommy Landry…my papa.

He was such an incredible man, even though I haven't seen him in years. My father and he had a falling out and quit speaking. I lost my relationship with him because of it.

He is still alive to this day, nestled in a small quiet town a couple hours away from here.

The woman standing beside him takes my breath away. I gasp as I behold the sight of my stunning grandmother, Didi. Her hair, her eyes, her face, all white.

I've only ever laid eyes on a single photograph of her before, but it never could have prepared me for this moment.

She passed away before I was born, so I never had the chance to know her. But I have an indescribable connection to her.

I inherited partial albinism from her, although it only affects my hair and skin. My eyes are blue, my eyelashes are dark, my skin and lips have a hue.

She was born with winter in her soul.

Her hair, her skin, every single feature is a brilliant white.

She's standing between my grandfather and Dr. Garcia. Dr. Garcia is kissing her cheek, and my grandmother is smiling. My grandfather stares down at her adoringly, and they all look...happy. I refuse to believe they were behind the slaughter of 1979.

But the death was real: the blood, and the carnage left behind. Someone or something was behind it.

My grandparents, Tommy and Didi, lived in this old house, I realize. Dr. Garcia knew them so well. I try to breathe as the realization of what I'm looking at settles in.

Chaos, 1979, is written in ink on the bottom of the photo.

The years match up perfectly.

Something creaks behind me, and I lurch back. Two men stand at the end of the hall to my left, wearing masks, hidden in the deep shadows of the hall. My heart startles and I reach for the closest door, twist the handle, and step into the dark while slamming the door behind me. Luckily, I'm able to twist the lock in place.

I stumble back, falling in the dark bedroom. My heart races and my body trembles as the door handle jiggles. The room is completely dark, but my eyes slowly begin to adjust. A heavy buzz courses through my skin, as if my body is turning into liquid.

Fuck...

The drink they gave me must have had something in it.

I slam my hand over my mouth as heavy footsteps stop in front of the door.

"*Sum—mer,*" Xander's voice is deep and brooding. He raps his knuckles hard on the door, causing me to flinch. "You sneak into my house, and you don't even want to say hi?"

I instantly hate him. Everything about him.

This is a game...an enjoyable game for him. They are just a bunch of spoiled rich kids who think they can do whatever they want to women under the guise of a *secret society*.

When it seems like they pass by, I look around the dark room, the buzz of the party still outside.

The door opens and I take a step back just as Xander stares at me standing in front of him, like a lamb to the slaughter.

The edges of his mask curve into a smile. "Are you going to run?"

I don't want to give them the satisfaction of a chase because that's what I suspect they want me to do. His nameless, faceless friend walks in after him.

"Damn, she's hotter than I thought she'd be," the smaller one says under his mask.

Xander leans in and stares at me under the cold, dead eyes of the burlap mask. "And bold," he says. "Are you feeling brave, sweetheart? Or are you just going to sneak around my house uninvited?"

I cross my hands over my body, feeling very exposed in my short dress. "I didn't sneak in here and you know it. You lured me. Where is Lincoln?"

He steps toward me, and I fall back on the soft bed behind me. So incredibly soft, I run my fingers over it.

What did they give me?

"You're pretty fucking stuck up, aren't you, Summer Landry?" he says. For whatever reason, he hates me and he knows who I am. He can tell from my last name and the picture of my grandparents on his wall.

The relationship his grandmother had with my father.

"What the hell do you want from me, Xander? I don't even know you." He's so close to me, I can smell the spice of his cologne.

My heart rate is extenuated because of the drugs coursing through my system. I pull off my mask so I can breathe.

His eyes draw to my white hair and his head tilts. "You don't belong here. You're not one of us. I don't care who your father is. Open your fucking legs; I want to see what that fucker did to you."

My mark. He's talking about my mark. My fingers instantly cover it and my mouth gapes open. "I don't think so."

He grabs my knee and I try to kick him, needlessly, because he merely swats me away.

I stiffen as he grips my leg. "Is that why you drugged me when I came in, so you can take my clothes off easier?"

He snorts. "Believe it or not, sweetheart, I have no desire to fuck you. The drugs are because I'm a nice guy and it will make it hurt less." He jerks his head. "Hold her down, man."

Panic settles in. I kick hard, flailing my arms. My nails meet flesh as I scrape Xander's friend's arm with everything I have, digging my nails in as hard as I can.

"Fuck, man," he cries out, pulling his arm away. "She made me bleed."

Xander shoots him a look, and he pins my wrists and wraps a powerful arm around my mouth. I go to bite him, but he anticipates it and shoves his hand over my mouth, depriving me of oxygen.

He leans down and whispers, "I'm very good at inflicting pain. Don't fucking test me."

I go slack, knowing it's pointless to struggle. Eventually, his grip loosens, and I take deep breaths in and out of my nose.

Xander runs his hand up my calf and smiles when my body finches and tears well in my eyes, despite the orgasmic sensation running through me that seems to settle between my legs.

He pulls my dress up, his face unreadable. His gaze travels down my body, his attention drawn to the prominent mark on the apex of my thigh, right next to my panties.

He chuckles and shakes his head in disbelief. "He really fucking marked you. Son of a bitch." He raises his head, his black holes for eyes flicker. "I hope he fucks that attitude right out of you before he kills you. If you were my woman, I'd have you in line by now."

"Well, thank god I'm not your fucking woman," I seethe. "Lincoln is so much better than you."

He yanks his mask off and shoots me a look of complete revulsion, as if my very existence is a source of torment for him.

He raises his chin and chews on those damn lips. "I'm not talking about Lincoln, sweetheart. You're a fucking dead girl walking. You have no idea what you've done, or what you're doing to him. Get the fuck out of this town, Summer. That's your only warning."

What the hell am I doing to *him*? Last I checked, I'm the one who got carved up at the rave, stalked throughout my entire teenage years and ravaged in my sleep.

I give him an icy stare and the smaller guy finally takes his hands off me.

I jerk away and scramble up, glaring at him. "I don't respond to idle threats."

He rises and peers down at me, pure steel raging from his eyes just as a shadow looms behind him, and I make eye contact with Lincoln in the doorway.

Xander shakes his head, his jaw flexing. "You really have no idea what you're a part of, do you?"

I attempt to keep my breathing steady. "I'm here to see Lincoln. I'm here to talk to him, that's it." My eyes are steady on Lincoln, but Xander still doesn't notice him.

Xander scoffs, his eyes gleaming in the darkness. "You're destroying him by being here. If you don't leave, Lincoln Kennedy won't exist anymore. And he doesn't care about you because he doesn't care about anybody. He's a robot. He's incapable of *feeling* anything."

"That was unnecessarily theatrical," Lincoln says as he stands at the shadowed doorway with his arms crossed, glasses on. He's holding his mask, his hair messy, like he just woke up from a nap or has been running his hands through it.

With his dark eyes peering through the glasses, his gaze travels down to my dress, still hitched above my legs. As our eyes meet, his pupils flare and flicker, and he effortlessly glides into the room.

The way my heart stops from that flicker and my body instantly relaxes. I want to be the one running my hands through his hair. I want to be the only one he ever looks at like that.

I smirk at Xander, who moves away from me, his arms crossed defensively, and his eyebrows rise as he observes our interaction. His body is rigid, every muscle taut, as if his insides are wound up like a tight, compressed coil.

Lincoln ignores Xander, and watches the other masked man, who now stands coolly to the side, as the two *brothers* face off. All of them have now removed their burlap sack masks.

Lincoln glares at the one who restrained me. "If you put your hands on Summer again, I will cut off every one of your fingers and choke you with them. And if you think I'm joking, ask Xander what I'm capable of. Summer is off limits."

A lump forms in his throat as the guy struggles to swallow. "Look, man, I was just doing what Xander told me to do. I was just holding her down; we weren't hurting her."

Lincoln's stillness is absolute, and an aura overcomes him. A subtle

237

tilt of his head, a shift in his demeanor. Unimpeded rage oozes out of him.

He tilts his head, speaking to the ground. His eyes falter just as he raises his head and removes his glasses.

"Listen very carefully, you little fucking twat. I will end your miserable life if you ever touch her again." My heart lurches.

Mikael.

I recognize the voice that comes out of him—so intimately. That was not Lincoln speaking. The clear transition, the clear flip, and I'm not sure anyone else noticed. But Xander flinches, and for a fleeting moment, even with the rippling tattoos on his arms, he looks petrified.

He quickly regains his composure and faces Mikael while his friend flees from the room.

I'm transfixed by Mikael, watching him smile at Xander, a slow knowing grin that makes my pulse quicken. I focus on his eyes, which aren't translucent like they were a moment ago, or at the rave; they are now a solid brick-like color as they were when he was fucking me. When his hungry eyes find mine again, they flash.

Then, as if a switch has been flipped, he becomes still, and that same flicker appears before his eyes return to their usual hue. I'm not sure what I just witnessed, but it was the way he was acting in his office, and it makes me wonder if there are perhaps three of them inside his head.

Xander casts a glance at me as I sit up on the bed cross-legged, and I give my cockiest smirk. As if to say, *See, asshole, he likes me. They all do…*

Xander shakes his head and curls his lip before he takes a step toward Lincoln and slaps him on the back as he walks out the door. "I hope you enjoy your funeral, sweetheart," he says to me as he slams the door behind him.

Lincoln turns to face me, his glasses square on his face again.

My little heart is racing—the rapid beating might kill me before he does, especially with how he's looking at me right now. His face is so soft, and his eyebrows arch like he's worried. Very much the way *Lincoln* watches me.

He hesitates for only a moment before crawling in behind me and positioning me so I'm between his legs, then lays us both back on the soft fabric of the headboard and silk pillows.

I'm shaking, I realize, and he holds me for a few minutes, allowing me to ride my high, realizing I am in the arms of the man I am in love with.

One of them, at least.

And for whatever reason, I start to cry…all my emotions building up over the past few weeks pour out of me. He just holds me; he doesn't speak, he lets this happen before he finally says, "They're gone, Summer. They won't be back as long as you're with me." His lips graze me. "You're safe now."

Safe… Am I actually safe with Lincoln?

Do I want to be safe?

I turn to face him, straddling him, squeezing his toned body between my knees. My body is in a cold sweat. Now that I have him, I have no plans of letting him go.

I run my fingers through his mussed hair. A flicker hints in his eye, and I bite my lip like I want to devour him.

Because I do.

He grabs my hands and interlocks his fingers with mine, and I can feel his arousal. "You shouldn't be here. You're making this really hard for me."

I secretly keep waiting for him to call me *pretty girl*, but he doesn't. Which means this is all Lincoln. And that's okay with me, because Lincoln fascinates me just as much as Mikael does.

"Making what so hard?" I ask as I grind on him.

He pulls me into his strong sexy arms and runs his hands down my legs, his hands resting on the side of my thigh. "I'm trying to avoid you, Summer. But when you come into my house, looking the way you do, it's nearly impossible to keep my hands off you."

My lips part as I sink my hips further into his lap. I stare deeply into those eyes, trying to find a flicker of anything. No longer are they translucent. If Mikael is here, he is hiding. Lincoln's eyes are deep, dark, captivating, and familiar, as I've seen them so many times before.

"Then why did you invite me to this party? The invite showed up at our door."

He sighs and his shoulders slump. "That wasn't me; it must have been Xander."

"Why would you want to avoid me?" I tease, and my lips find his ear. "You certainly weren't avoiding me earlier today." I grip his arms and dig my fingernails into his skin.

He rests his hands on my hips, and I kiss him. The coolness of his glasses hits my face. When I pull up, I see that flash I was looking for.

The monster within isn't too far away, and I really want to draw him out.

Lincoln arches his brows. "I'm afraid that wasn't me, either. You must be mistaking me for someone else." I can't tell if he's teasing anymore.

We're dancing around Mikael. Always dancing around Mikael. "I'm still bleeding from that," I tell him, grinding on him. "Want to see?"

His body jolts and he sighs before delicately moving me off his growing erection. "I really don't want to see you dead tonight, Summer. You should probably go."

My heart rages out of control, and I sit cross-legged on the bed and cross my arms. "I'm not leaving," I say stubbornly. If he knows me so well, then he should know this about me.

He sighs and runs his hands through his hair, rises and pulls me to my feet, grabbing my hand. "Fine. Come on, let's go to my room."

I clutch him as the drugs course through my system. I really wish people would quit drugging me, but I'm getting used to it. I'm starting to enjoy it, especially if I get to play with him every time.

"Where is your room?" I ask, peering around. Since there are no personal items, this room is clearly a guest bedroom.

He tilts his head down before finally meeting me with his shadowed, emotionless eyes. "The basement."

Of course it's the basement.

I pause as heat fills me before a moment of panic. "How do I... How do I know it's you, Lincoln?" Perhaps I'm not ready to draw Mikael out yet. I have too many questions for Lincoln.

He takes a step into the dimly lit hallway, and I keep myself pressed against him, not wanting to break skin to skin contact with him.

He looks both ways, the hallway empty on both sides, before he says nonchalantly, "Because you're not dead yet."

Is that the difference between Mikael and Lincoln? Sure death...

Silently, he guides me through the blood-red hallway and down the winding staircase. The sound of laughter filters in from the room where everyone is gathering as he leads me to yet another door. Beyond it lies a much narrower staircase, descending into what appears to be the abyss.

Something catches my eye, and I startle when I see an old woman staring back at me from the shadows of the hallway. I blink for a moment and gasp, wondering if I'm not looking at a ghost. I freeze as she steps forward and reaches for a lock of my hair, then reaches for my face.

She squeezes her eyes shut, then opens them again; her pupils dilate as she runs her fingers down my skin. "Diana, is that you?"

Lincoln grabs her hand and rubs it with his thumb, pulling her fingers off my face as I stand there stunned. "Lucy, this is Summer, Diana's granddaughter."

She quirks her brows in a moment of confusion, then she nods and smiles at Lincoln as if coming back into this decade. "Of course. Nice to meet you, Summer. I'm glad Lincoln found a nice girl." She carries on through the dark hall, humming, as if that wasn't the strangest encounter.

"That's Lucy, our housemaid," Lincoln says, as I flinch. "She can get a tad confused sometimes. Don't pay her any mind."

I follow the shadows from where she disappeared. She's gone again as quickly as she came. "She knew my grandmother?"

He leads me down the dark stairwell into the depths of this house; the boards creaking as we head down into the abyss and a soft draft hits my face.

"Lucy's been the housemaid for a very long time. She knew both of your grandparents, and your father as well, while he studied here."

As we descend into darkness, my phone vibrates in my tiny purse I've managed not to lose. I grab it and scroll to Dani's message.

Dani: *I just got in here, where are you?*

Okay…she's in. The rest is up to her, and she can have fun with Xander and doing whatever it is she has planned.

I quickly power off my phone as I reach the bottom step and place it back in my purse. I don't want any distractions right now. I regret not responding to Dani, but I'm sure she will figure out soon enough who I'm with.

Lincoln pushes the door open and we step inside, and I look around. The room is a beautiful blend of antique and contemporary elements. Its soft lighting and plush carpeting make it very cozy. A modern fireplace stands alongside pillars that separate the sitting area from a desk and a large chair. The scent in the room reminds me of him, sophistication and elegance. Or perhaps it's the candles he has lit by his desk and on a shelf above his work area.

On the other side of the partition, I glimpse his four-poster bed with those dark sheets I've seen during our video call. It's the only part of the room that I've seen through the lens of a camera. The same one he had that girl tied up on before he killed her.

The police haven't picked up on the thread that Cali is dead. She's been missing for weeks, and everyone has given up on finding her.

A hint of a draft teases my bare legs and my head whips around, but there are no windows that I can see.

A sharp pang hits my stomach, and I wrap my arms around my prickled flesh, thinking of what must have been a very intimate moment between the *three* of them.

"I've lived in this basement for as long as I can remember," Lincoln says, interrupting my train of thought as he moves and hovers over his desk, fussing with the mouse on his computer as if he's been down here fretting over his research all night. Papers are strewn about like he was recently in deep thought and soft music plays from speakers in the ceiling.

Timeless music. Classical strings and piano.

It's lovely and soft.

He *was* hiding down here, not partying with everyone else. This shouldn't surprise me, given how hard he works every single day. His obsession with his work rivals his obsession with me.

At least I think he's obsessed with me...

I walk over to his dresser and look around. His personal belongings are minimal—no trinkets, no photos, nothing to indicate a healthy child-hood. "This was your bedroom?" I ask him.

His warm hands startle me as he wraps them around my midsection. "Ever since Dr. Garcia adopted me. But I have little recollection of anything before that. My memories began here."

"Do you consider her your mother?" She took him in, took care of him, even adopted him, but I don't get the motherly vibe from her.

"No. I don't consider anyone to be my mother. Not in the way you think."

I look up at him and blink. "Not even your real mother?"

He shakes his head. "No. Not really." I try to find any hint of emotion in his eyes, remembering what Xander said, and I don't push the subject.

Instead, I huff. "And Dr. Garcia put you down here in a windowless basement?" It's not like there aren't enough bedrooms upstairs. This house is big enough to have at least six bedrooms.

He stares down at me, and I observe and study every movement, aware of his every action. He places his hands on my hips as he walks me backward toward the bed. With a reassuring squeeze, he gently pushes me onto the soft sheets.

"She adopted me," he says. "She's not my mother, and I suspect at the time, she wanted Mikael far away from Xander."

Mikael. He's talking about him as if he's real, as if he's someone else entirely. And he was here first...

I peer up at him, the gaze he's giving me right now is predatory. "And what about you?" I ask. "Why are you still down here?" I lie back on the soft bedding, propping myself up with my elbows, opening my knees to him. He drops down in front of me.

It's a test, a tease, and I hope he bites.

A candle on the desk behind him flickers. That small draft I keep noticing, leading me to suspect this basement has an exit and entry point somewhere.

"I prefer solitude," he tells me without looking up, giving all the attention to my legs, which I slowly wrap around him.

"But you're never really alone, are you?" I ask.

With a gentle pull, he removes my heels and places them nearby. His eyes meet mine as his hand travels up my calf. My reflection is visible in his glasses. The glint of my white hair stands out against the darkness of this room, this house, and the dark eyes observing me.

"Why does Xander hate me so much?" I ask, although...I'm thinking the reason is deeper than I ever could have imagined. His grandmother and my grandparents were in a picture together in this very house.

"You're a threat to his leadership and inheritance," he says, shifting his focus to my dress and gently nudging my knees open to access what's inside. I lean back on my elbows, wincing as his fingers brush against the mark.

"And how exactly am I threatening his leadership?"

Finally, he raises his eyes to meet mine. His pale skin and dark hair are accentuated in the soft light, but I don't recognize the person staring back at me.

"By simply existing, Summer. Technically, you are the one who is supposed to lead us—it's your birthright."

I wrap my ankles around his waist and tug him closer. "So it's all true, then? You're part of the Order of the Shadows...the secret society that kills people?"

He blinks and that flicker arises in his irises. "Yes. Although I'm just a part of it by technicality; I'm not part of the bloodline. They kept me alive since I'm such an anomaly, and generally, they are regular people who dislike the idea of hurting a child. That was never part of the Codex."

The Codex...

My breath deepens, and he moves his hand up and down my thigh, as if inspecting me, and he slides my panties right off my legs.

"Xander's in quite a predicament."

I squirm when his fingers tickle my soft skin "What do you mean?"

His lips tickle my thigh as he presses a kiss between my legs, and I quiver. "If Mikael kills you, then that means Xander doesn't have to worry about you. But if he kills you, then that also means Mikael will be let loose, and Xander will probably end up dead, too."

I grip the sheets so hard my fingernails nearly break off. His tongue flicks my clit, and I nearly scream.

"*Lincoln!*" My hands grip the covers, but he ignores me. He only gives a serpentine smile as he teases me with his tongue and keeps his eyes down.

Something is different about him... Something's changed. Someone else is present...I can *feel* him, sense him in my soul.

Lincoln raises his flickering eyes to mine as I squirm beneath him. "Do you want me to kill you, Summer?" he asks softly, the terrifying shimmering is almost blinding. "The honey pouring out of your pussy tastes like you want me to kill you."

A darkness fills up inside me, like starlight hitting a void as I watch him morph in front of me. Those starlight eyes mesmerize me.

"I don't want you to kill anyone else," I whisper, grabbing onto his hair with dear life.

His body tightens. His eyes ripples like twilight, that otherworldly shift as he morphs into a stone-cold killer. At least I think he is a killer; this version of him confuses me.

Mikael is close...so close. Like he's here watching, but not the one in control. And it doesn't seem like Lincoln is in control, either.

Lincoln continues to work me with his tongue, bringing me close... close...close. I dig my nails into his scalp as my orgasm starts to build, and I forget about everything. I crest and I arch my back as I let out a moan, coming down from it.

More. I want more. That wasn't nearly enough.

"Lincoln," I gasp.

He pauses as he lifts his brows, the bottom of his glasses teasing my clit. His pupils are so dilated they nearly take over his eyes.

"Yes, Summer?"

Xander's words slam into me as if they didn't matter, and now they do.

I am still unaware of the man behind those glasses, or what Lincoln is capable of, but that was a surge of emotion deep within his soul. And I can't reconcile the duplicity of my own thoughts. I'm torn between whether I actually want him, or if he has created this desire within me.

"Is what Xander said true? That you don't feel anything?"

His eyes swirl into everlasting darkness, his face stone cold. "It's true. I study feelings, emotions, and the actions of humans because of them. I understand them so intimately, but no, I don't actually feel them."

Humans. He says the word as if he's not one of us.

I let out a deep breath as the music shifts to a soft cello. The soft melody takes over my entire mind before I snap myself back into focus.

"You made me do things to myself I never would have done on my own. I shoved that stick so far up myself that I bled out for an hour."

His eyes flash—not in a psychotic way, but with pure satisfaction. "We own you, Summer. We've owned your mind and soul since you were young...since the first day we found out you existed."

I snarl at him, "Where is *he,* then? If he's so involved in all of this, why does Mikael hide so much?" I peer deep into his eyes. "Come out and play with me, Mikael. Because, apparently, Lincoln doesn't have *feelings.*"

A flash of annoyance crosses Lincoln's eyes, and he rises and strides over to his desk, leaving me cold.

"Be careful what you wish for, baby," he says as he sits on his chair. "I can't control Mikael. If he's not here right now, it's because he's *choosing* not to be."

I cross my arms and pull my legs, catching my breath as a fresh wave of the drugs hits me at the sudden change of tone in the room. I lay my head back on the bed. "You're probably the most confusing person I've ever met."

"That's because I'm not really a person. Not in the sense you understand it."

I lift my neck briefly. "What do you mean? What are you then, other than a robot?"

He pulls open his desk drawer and pulls out a bottle of pills and inspects them. "That is a very…colloquial way of describing me." He shoves the drawer closed, stuffs the pills into his pocket, and pulls off his shirt.

I can't take my eyes off him as he walks toward me. His muscled abs, the soft lines of his torso, his messy hair curling over his forehead. The perfection that is this man is otherworldly.

He's a god. He's a fucking god, that's what he is.

He stops beside the bed, places the pills down, sits and takes off his pants and boxers. "Scientists would describe me as the gatekeeper of the system, the core, the caretaker. Some might even call me the demon. I'm a fragment; I'm all the fragments combined. I'm something scientists have never encountered, which is why Dr. Garcia took such an interest in me when I formed. I am everything that makes up this mind. I am ageless, timeless, and *powerful*. Mikael made me into the very image of what he fears the most."

"Shadowface," I whisper as I stare off at a strange shadow on the wall beside me. A cool draft hits my face and my heart rate spikes.

He killed that girl… I am in bed with a monster.

He then takes off his glasses and places them on the nightstand. "Yes, I suppose I am Shadowface in the most rudimentary sense, but Shadowface isn't a person; he's an entity. But I do lack one very important element. One important primal part of what it means to be human."

"What is that?" I ask him.

He slides in beside me and helps me pull off my dress, and his body is like molten lava and I appreciate being next to him. "I lack real emotion."

He unbuttons the clasp of my bra and helps me pull it off my shoulder as I rest my head down, enjoying the sound of his voice. His body wraps around me like a warm blanket.

My nipples harden as he reaches around and cups one. His body is so soft and secure. "I am everything Mikael isn't, and everything he wasn't able to be because of his trauma."

"And what was his trauma, exactly?" I dare to ask him.

His lips meet the back of my head. "Your father tore his mother apart in front of him when he was three."

And there it is...

My heart jolts at hearing him say it so nonchalantly. Mikael's trauma...his trauma. "Mikael turned into the monster he is that night. He had no other choice."

He reaches over, pulls a pill bottle out, and hands it to me. I frown as I inspect it and see the words *Fluoxetine (Prozac)* prescribed by Dr. Garcia.

"You take an antidepressant?" I ask him.

"It's silly really, considering I don't have feelings. But it's the only thing that truly suppresses him. It's the only thing that worked to get rid of him."

My lips part at those words—*Get rid of him.*

That girl is dead...one of them slaughtered her. And I'm still not convinced it was Mikael.

I stare at the bottle, the prescription dated a week ago. Yet...it's full.

"You don't take it, though, do you?"

His lips tease my cheek. "I stopped taking it a couple of weeks ago."

I blow out a breath. "What? Why would you do that, Lincoln?"

He moves his hand up to my heart. "Because when I'm with you, I can experience emotions in a way I haven't before. For the first time in my existence, I've experienced emotions, even if they are his emotions. I want more of it... It makes me stronger, like I'm invincible...like I'm *real*. If it means letting him back to experience what it's like to be human, I'm never giving that up. Even if it kills me."

I'm the one killing him.

My heart is now throbbing. "And you can't control him?"

I've witnessed Mikael's presence; I've experienced his influence and Lincoln just said as much.

His danger and darkness.

I know too well that he is beyond control. At some point, you'd have to think Mikael never really went away. Perhaps he chose to stay away because society didn't want him anymore. Everyone gave up on him, including the woman who raised him, and there is something poetically sad about that. After all, he was once an innocent child who lost his mother. He wasn't born this way.

Lincoln turns the bedside lamp off, then moves his hand down to my belly and pulls me closer. It's strange thinking of Mikael and Lincoln as separate. As if the traumatic history didn't happen to Lincoln, too.

I turn in the dark and position myself on top of him, and it takes no effort for him to fill me.

"Summer, fuck," he whispers as my thighs clench around him. I want to show him he's not alone. Show him his trauma, even if he won't admit it, doesn't have to define him. I want to fuck the daylights out of him.

I grind and squeeze, our limbs become tangled as if we are one. I lean over him, his mouth finds the tiny muscle above my collarbone and his teeth graze my skin. I can't see his eyes right now, but I know they would look like a vortex. Even if he wanted to kill me right now, I'm fucking him so hard, I don't give him a chance.

Eventually, his teeth do more than graze. He bites down and I cry out as we both climax. I roll off him, out of breath and satisfied.

He's quiet for a moment, as if pondering my earlier question if he can control Mikael, his hands not nearly done touching me. "Out of all the things I am to this body, do you know what I am first?"

I turn to face him completely, my eyes widening in anticipation as our breaths mingle. The room is softly illuminated by the flickering light of the candle still burning.

"What?" I whisper just as a soft wisp of air blows the candle out, leaving us shrouded in darkness.

He pushes himself on top of me, still hard despite his cum on the sheets. "I am your protector," he murmurs. "I was created to protect you, Summer. I won't let him kill you. I refuse to let history repeat itself."

He fucks me three more times before I pass out, further demonstrating his godlike abilities.

CHAPTER
TWENTY-EIGHT
SUMMER

I am awakened by soft and beautiful humming. It is a low, melancholic melody that I remember hearing in my sleep, followed by a loud, solitary cry. I open my eyes to darkness and, for a moment, panic sets in. The cry seemed so real, so distinct, and markedly feminine.

I lie still, my eyes wide open, waiting for it to happen again, wondering if it was just a part of my dream. All I hear are the occasional cracks in the walls, like whispers from the deceased. The noise from the party outside must have faded away by now. Dani is probably upset that I never responded to her texts.

But I heard something, or someone—

The draft…there is a draft. Which means there is fresh air coming from somewhere.

Lincoln is curled around me in a deep sleep. So many sounds are coming out of the walls, it's a wonder how I ever fell asleep. Creaks and moans, the furnace kicking on and off, and a cool breeze hits me. Light footsteps pattering on the floors above us, lingering from whatever was going on upstairs while we were down here, getting lost in each other.

Lincoln adjusts himself, but keeps his arm wrapped around me, holding me tightly in the same position we fell asleep in.

Even the supernatural, god of all things, master of minds, still needs sleep like us mere mortals.

I can't help but smile. The bulge pressing against my lower back is mortal too, so is his heartbeat and the orgasms I gave him last night, leaving me wet and sticky. Everything about him seemed real and human as he held his body close to mine after he finished.

I'm still overwhelmed by what he said to me. That he was created solely to protect me, that his entire existence revolves around me.

He is my protector.

I clung to him, refusing to let go until I succumbed to darkness. No mind control needed. I'd have given him anything he wanted in that moment—dead or alive.

After we finished, I passed out in a peaceful drug-infused bliss. And now I'm wide awake and cold, even with his hot breath tickling my ear. I turn toward him, wiping his soft hair across his brow, appreciating how vulnerable he is at this moment. I could kill him right now if I wished.

Real. Lincoln Kennedy is real.

He shifts momentarily, and I lay my head in the crook of his arm and his breath softens. Then I hear it again...a soft cry, a soft sob in the air, deep in the walls and I shoot up.

We're not alone down here.

I shiver. Another breeze touches my bare skin and Lincoln doesn't hear it. He keeps his breath steady.

Goosebumps pebble my flesh as I rise like a ghost and tiptoe across the room. My eyes can distinguish the furniture, while my hands trace the pillars, guiding me to the darker corner, toward the only other door in the basement.

I pause, turning my head toward the bed. It's warmer there than creeping around naked. The sheets are soft against my bare skin. He's soft too, especially when he's asleep.

I hear it again. Soft sobbing coming from somewhere in this basement. What's left of my shattered conscience pushes me forward. That or jealousy, I'm not sure which one at this point.

If Lincoln has another girl down here, I will be the one doing the slaughtering. And it won't be her...I'll mutilate him.

Tiptoeing silently on bare feet, I cautiously open the door. I step inside and close the door behind me. My breath is heavy, my stomach in a tight knot. The air is fresher and cleaner, as if it's coming directly from outside.

I stumble forward in the dark and listen. "Hello," I whisper.

Silence.

I frown. "Hello? Is someone here?" I whisper again.

A pause...

"Help me, please." A muffled cry comes from inside the walls.

I turn and press my hands up toward the wall from where I heard her.

"*Cali?*"

Another pause. "Please, get me out of here, he has me."

A deep sense of relief washes over me. He has her, but he didn't kill her. He's had her this entire time.

I press my forehead against the wall. "Are you hurt?" I ask her. "Has he physically hurt you?"

A muffled sob. "Yes, he cut me once, and he won't let me go. Please, I'm begging you, I can't be locked in here anymore." Her voice is clear now, like we are talking through a vent. He's had her for weeks…*weeks.*

I dig my fingers into the wall and grind my teeth together. I turn my head toward the door in which I came.

"Keep your voice down," I warn in a hushed whisper. "You don't want to wake him up."

"Will you help me? Please call the police, do something, just get me out of here. I won't tell anyone or say anything, I swear." The way she's talking to me, as if I have something to hide, as if I'm one of them.

The police… Given the chief of police's daughter was straddling a masked man upstairs earlier, I don't think the police will do anything even if I called them. Lincoln told me who each of them were. The police chief's daughter, the mayor's son. Dani told me about all of them.

Calling the police is pointless.

It would be so easy to find her, rescue her, and let her go. Both of us should just flee. Mikael's the one who took her, and Lincoln is protecting her. Either way, Lincoln will go down for this, and I can't let that happen. After last night, I am convinced Lincoln can't hurt a soul.

Mikael was the one who cut her, and it's a miracle she's even still alive.

But he didn't kill her…

I stand dazed for a moment, my hair falling over my face as I'm left pondering and puzzling the pieces together.

Lincoln did, however, lie to me. He fabricated the narrative for his sick pleasure to get to me and make me admit to the darkest parts of myself. It's easier to fall in love with a monster than to admit you are one.

I take a moment to catch my breath as my thigh starts to pulse. I run my fingers over the blistering scar. Was that why he cut Cali? Did he mark her, too?

Something inside me stirs.

He didn't kill her.

I slam my hand against the wall. "Fuck," I cry out.

I can't do it. I can't turn him in, but I can save Cali. I continue moving, searching for a way to reach her. I run my hands along the wall, hoping to find something. I need to see her and make sure she's okay. But it's been weeks, and she's still alive. I'm sure she's miserable, but at least she's okay.

He didn't kill her.

Eventually, my hand meets cold metal. I pause before I turn the handle and push another door open and fumble my way until my hands find a light switch.

The light pops on and I jolt back.

In front of me stands a woman with white hair, her eyes filled with blood, and her body marked with shadows. A smile spreads across her face, causing my heart to skip a beat. It's as if I'm looking at the exact replica of my grandmother, who once lived in this very house.

It takes me a moment to realize it's not her ghost covered in blood, but rather a mirror tucked away in the corner of a bathroom. The girl staring back at me is none other than myself, although I hardly recognize her. I take a deep breath and shut myself in and warmth instantly hits my skin.

I look back at the mirror and finally see nothing of the girl I see staring back at me. I'm a disheveled, freshly fucked mess. There is a girl hidden within these walls, yet I'm not screaming bloody murder.

I turn the shower on, cranking the heat as high as it can go, letting the steam build up around me. I sit on the floor like a child, and take deep cleansing breaths, letting the warmth fill my bones as the entire washroom fills with thick steam.

After a few minutes, my head starts to hang heavily in front of me. Suddenly, a faint squeaky noise echoes through the mist. I scramble to my feet and squint to read the message on the mirror. The fog gradually lifts, allowing me to read the message clearly, as if it were written plain as day.

Hi pretty girl…

My breath falters as a shadow engulfs me, and the burlap mask stares back at me through the mirror.

I whip around and face him. A faint squeak escapes me as I take him in. He's wearing only boxers and the mask. The rest of him is identical to the man I was just sleeping next to, the same man who was holding me ten minutes ago.

Part of me wants to cry out for Lincoln, as if he's merely sleeping in the next room and could come save me.

"Mikael," I whisper, the only sound now a faint drip of water beside us in the room that's otherwise full of steam.

He nods slowly and I freeze, swallowing hard as my throat tightens. He tilts his head in response, his eyes drifting to my neck, then down the bare skin beneath it. My tiny breasts rise with rapid breath as I stand in front of him, entirely exposed. He's calm as he beholds me with a predatory gaze that makes me twist and burn.

"Fear is so fucking sexy on you," he says. "I could die watching you scream, and it would never be enough for me."

I hate myself for the pleasure shooting to my core. Shame blends with pleasure as I stare at the shadowed man who ruined my life.

With fire in my eyes, I reach for his mask. He stops me, gripping my hands, and just by the grip, I realize Lincoln is completely shut out. Even their hands seem different. "I want to see you," I whisper. "I deserve to see you, Mikael."

His chest expands as I pull the mask off his face. It is not Lincoln Kennedy staring back at me, and these eyes are not translucent.

My mouth gapes open as I stare into them, and something shocking stares back at me. Something so innocent and pure. So real. His pupils dilate as if he can see me clearly, and his eyes gleam.

Lincoln's eyes don't gleam, and now I'm stuck wondering who has those translucent eyes I keep seeing. I'm positive now there is a third entity hiding in there.

There must be.

My hands find his cheek, my fingers a light caress as I move them over the bridge of his nose and to his lips, as if I need to explore every part of him. He grabs my hand, and my eyes stay steady on his as I move our hands down to my breast, giving him permission to touch me.

His hand tightens around the flesh and my nipples harden despite the heat.

His lips twitch into a smile, and he almost seems soft, which is exactly how I remember him. His hands were always soft, even if his words were cutting.

"Is this what you like?" I ask him, his head so close to mine our breaths mingle. He doesn't respond, but he licks his lips as his other hand finds my waist and it's exactly what he wants.

I remember... All those nights, he always started with my breasts before moving to other places. The way he looks at me now is almost boyish.

"You can touch me, Mikael," I whisper into his cheek. "Anywhere you want. I'm yours just as much as I am his. You can do whatever you want to me."

Did I really just say that? Is that what I want? Or is this the mind control they have over me?

He gently touches my nipple with his thumb. He squeezes and plays with it, and his smile gives me chills. The lights flicker again, as if he can control them, too.

"It's cute you think I need your permission," he scoffs, a smirk playing on his lips.

In one swift motion, his hand finds my throat. Time seems to stand still as he thrusts me up and slams me into the mirror.

The glass cracks slightly and his fingers begin to squeeze my neck. I can't breathe, my lungs collapse, and little lights pepper my vision. Then he abruptly stops...

"You do not want me to do whatever I want," he threatens, and his forehead meets mine. His hands once again turn to honey and he caresses my cheek. "Because I want to fucking kill you."

I shake my head. "No, Mikael. You don't."

His eyes twinkle, his iron grip once again turns to a soft caress. "I'm nothing like Lincoln, pretty girl. And you know nothing about what I want."

My heart flutters at his voice. This is the first time he's really spoken to me—death threats don't count and calling me *pretty girl* doesn't, either.

He underestimates how much I understand him. Lincoln isn't the host...he is. He is the architect behind it all. I've seen Mikael in Lincoln, but I don't see any Lincoln in Mikael. Mikael's been here the whole time.

I lift my leg so my thigh grazes his. Teasing him, taunting him. Taking some semblance of control and dignity back, even though I'm desperate for him.

I gaze up at him and he looks back at me with a soft, boyish expression. "Is that all you see when you look at me?" I ask him. "Just death and nothing else. I understand why Lincoln's doing what he's doing, but what is your goal, Mikael? Why are you always hiding?"

His lips curl, his eye twitches, and he stands back. "It's hard to call it hiding when you're being suppressed."

For a moment his eyes start swirling like the mist, and I gasp, staring at that mesmerizing flicker before it disappears again. He's still so good looking, but his mannerisms are so different. Almost...normal. Like he's just some normal twenty-two-year-old, not some ageless entity. Despite his appetite for destruction or the fact he hides behind a supernatural, academic persona, he's just a young man. One who society gave up on, and one with so many emotions he doesn't know how to handle them.

"Is that all I am to you, the physical manifestation of your mother's death?"

His body jolts and he punches the mirror a mere two inches from my head, shattering whatever was left of the glass. I gasp at the level of anger that radiates out of him, and I squeeze my eyes shut as shards of glass hit my face and neck and a sizable chunk of mirror falls to the sink basin below.

The shattering is so loud, it reverberates and shakes the room.

Time seems to stand still as my blood trickles down my face and his blood pours out of his knuckles. Tears sting my eyes, but I don't dare move. His hands now grasp a piece of glass and it's all he needs to end me, and right now, all I feel is pure and utter terror. And heat...

Slick heat hits between my legs as I shake beneath him.

I stand in front of him, careful not to move, aware I am naked with shattered glass around me.

We stare at each other through the steam.

Long seconds go by, and he admires the blood dripping out of the shards in my skin, and finally he says, "Revenge."

I suck in a breath and blink at him. "What?"

"I want revenge, pretty girl. I watched your father kill my mother, and now, I want to kill you."

He tilts his head and cups my cheek, then pulls the little pieces of glass out of my skin. He turns on the water and washes the blood off my face. I lean into him, nearly collapsing as he nurses my wounds.

He catches me, and when I look up at him, his eyes are wild. And sad...so sad.

"Then why haven't you?" I ask. "You had so many chances. All those nights, you could have done it so quickly." I pause and gaze up at him.

"You never came back to me. I waited so long for you to come back to me, and you never did. I dream about you every single night."

It's true. I've never gone a day without thinking about him. There hasn't been a single night where I haven't dreamt about him.

He leans his forehead against mine—a similar mannerism to Lincoln, although that's the *only* similarity.

"I fell in love with you, Summer," he whispers, and I blink at him a few times to make sure I heard him right. "And it hurts; it fucking pains me. Falling in love with you was the worst mistake I ever made. I lost myself because of you."

I hitch a breath. "Mikael," I whisper, and my heart breaks for him.

It was him, not Lincoln, I spent that night with. He took my virginity, and I gave it to him willingly. My silent, scary monster now has a name.

He rubs my cheek, his pale skin glowing. "I still hate you. I hate that you got to live a normal life while my mom suffered. I hate how pretty you are," he whispers. "I hate how much I want you."

I let out a tiny whimper as a pained look crosses his face. He said the same words to me at the rave before he marked me. He's so close, his lips a kissable distance.

"You can't kill me yet, can you?" I dare to say to him. "You marked me for the devil, and he's not ready to claim me." My leg wraps around him, and I pull him into my allure. His erection is so stiff, it centers itself right between my legs. I arch my hips to rub myself against him, daring him to do something…anything to me.

His mouth twitches at my coy bodily threats. "They will expect your body, pretty girl. I have to deliver it to them."

The Order of the Shadow's.

"Why do you care what they want, if all you want to do is kill them?"

He smirks. "Why do you think all I want to do is kill them?"

I fold my arms and arch a brow. "I just assumed."

"I do, but maybe I want to rule them first."

I jerk my head to the side, mimicking his mocking stance. "Maybe that's what I want to do, too. Lincoln told me it's mine by birthright, and it would only be yours by technicality."

I just drew a line in the sand.

His eye twitches as he beholds me, as if seeing me differently. Seeing me as something more than a victim.

"Is that so, pretty girl?"

"I was victimized by all of this, too, Mikael. I didn't even know this secret society existed before coming here. I didn't realize what my father was."

The slam of his wrist against the glass jolts me. He misses my head by mere inches, and I start shaking. I hate how much he scares me, but he does.

"You," he says very slowly, "are a fucking liar."

Lying? What am I lying about?

"You knew *exactly* what he was. You dreamed about it for years."

That void...that itch on the edge of my mind I can't grasp. What is he referring to? It has something to do with my father. I saw something I shouldn't have.

A sharp image cuts into my mind of a woman.

"I'm sorry," I whisper.

He flinches at the only words I can think of to say at this moment. "I'm sorry about what my father did to your mother." As if my meager apologies matter, as if they mean anything. "I'm sorry for existing," I say to him in a final plea.

"My mother wanted it," he finally says, and he moves his hand between my legs, sliding his finger inside. "Just like you want it."

I gasp at how good it feels. At how much pent-up sexual tension is still inside me, despite Lincoln fucking me silly for hours.

This is different. A totally different person, and it's like neither of them are enough for me.

My lips find his, and he finally gives me what I want. He kisses me softly, keeping his fingers inside me before pulling back. He gives me a feline smirk as he walks toward the door.

"See you soon, pretty girl."

"Wait...where are you going?" I say breathlessly.

He pauses at the door and his head turns slightly, but he keeps his back to me. "Lincoln needs some sleep. He has to work on his thesis tomorrow."

He vanishes and I let out a deep breath, only now remembering the girl hiding within the walls who likely heard everything.

I step into the shower and take my time cleaning off the blood. Afterward, I tiptoe out into the hallway, careful not to step on the shattered glass, and whisper, "Cali, can you hear me?"

She answers immediately, "Yeah."

"I'm going to get you out of here alive, but you have to trust me, okay?"

A pause, then she says, "Okay."

I walk back into Lincoln's bedroom and crawl into bed with him. He's lying the exact way I left him. He curls his arm around me, and I snuggle in next to him, as if he was there fast asleep all along.

I t's nearly one PM by the time Summer stirs beside me. I've been awake since mid-morning, working away on my laptop while she slept. I've never seen anyone sleep as deeply as she does. Especially when she knows we are watching and where we are right now.

I glance over at Summer again, at the faint gash on her cheek that wasn't there the night before. I open and close my hand, the pain of my bruised knuckles shooting all the way up my arm.

Everything he touches turns to ash, and it pains me to see Summer bleeding and the marks on her flawless face, especially since I wasn't remotely aware enough to stop it. Something happened last night, and I have no memory of it.

It's a black hole when I'm asleep, and I often wonder if that's when he takes full control. He dreams, and I merely experience it.

Witness, observe, and analyze.

But this was different. It was as if I didn't exist at all.

Summer, however, is not dead despite being injured. I made him promise one thing after our rare and vivid conversation after we fucked her in my office.

Not to kill her.

I suppose he kept his promise, although the shattered glass in the bathroom and the cuts on Summer's cheek indicate it was difficult for him. And now I am burdened with the overwhelming guilt of what he did.

Guilt...

My blood is absorbing his emotions, and it's been slowly happening since Summer came back into our lives. His anger and guilt—they hit me in waves, almost like he's turning on a faucet and giving me more than I can handle.

It is changing me, transforming the very essence of my being and my purpose. Because I also sense his hatred as if it were my own. And that fragmented split is starting to grow, implanting itself in my bones.

I should have captured it when I had the chance. Instead, I have spent the morning accepting what is happening and deciding not to resist it. The process of fusion is taking place, and I will not fight it. When he sends me these emotions, I get a surge of power.

Desire. Anger. Guilt.

It is exhilarating, and now that Summer is by my side, I am beginning to explore her in every way.

He may be strong, but so am I, and this is the life I have created. Unlike him, I do not carry the memories that shattered his mind. He needs me just as much as I need him. Without me, he will always be fractured.

He shoots me a hint of jealousy, and I can't help but smile at the irony of it. I will take whatever shred of emotion he will give me.

I'd sacrifice everything to feel emotions, but I'd give up my soul to experience a single second of loving her.

She moans and turns around, lifting her leg out of the duvet and crossing her leg over it. I close my laptop and watch as she finally starts to make motions.

Mikael stirs deep within...and I shove him down.

At some point in the night, she found my shirt and slipped it on. Her hair is damp, she smells like my shampoo, and not to mention the shattered glass in the bathroom I had to clean up.

My eyes are fixed on her legs, her toned thighs hanging out of my shirt. A throb of desire consumes us. Our joint emotion intensifies everything, intensifying my arousal and fueling that split as it flaps around inside me like a banshee.

My head pounds, so I take off my glasses and set them on the nightstand and my vision clears, his chaotic emotions erupt at the crystal-clear view of her.

I give him a moment with her as she opens up and smiles at me. He's like a tornado destroying everything in its path. Whatever he's feeling right now, it's hazy, and I can't quite capture it. Like he's hiding from me or pushing me out.

When I glance back over, her face is a blur. I place my glasses on and smile. "Wake up, Summer."

Her brows twitch and pretty lips part, then she visibly relaxes. She didn't know which one of us she was getting, I realize. Only Mikael brings out that look of fear in her eyes.

She lays her head down and continues peering at me. "I think I'm going to puke," she says, moaning. "Make it go away."

My lips graze her hair as I continue typing. "Someone shouldn't have taken so many drugs last night."

She runs her lips over my arm and her hair falls over her face. "Like I had a choice," she mutters but can't help but smile. Xander targeted her the second she decided to walk into this house. "I feel dirty."

I adjust my glasses. "Why would that be? Because you spread your pretty legs for both of us last night, or because you fucked Mikael near a toilet."

She blinks in surprise, then her eyes gleam as she lifts her head up to her elbow. "Lincoln Kennedy, are you jealous?"

Taking a deep breath as the waves of this emotion course through me, I close my laptop to give her my full attention. "Jealousy must be one of the single worst emotions to ever exist," I say to her. And truly… it is quite icky.

She merely nods and lays her head back down on me. "Yes, it's not very fun, is it?"

I don't know if it's his emotion or mine. And that thought is unsettling.

A deep, mocking laugh erupts from within.

I reach over to my nightstand and pull out a pill bottle. Her hand immediately reaches for my stomach, running her fingers over my abdomen like she doesn't want me to move. I slip a little pill into her mouth, and she tenses. "It's ibuprofen, Summer. Relax."

I reopen my computer and start typing again. I can't help it…when I get into a flow state, it consumes my brain.

She stares at my computer screen, then up at me, then back to the computer screen as trying to read my work.

This section is titled *Moral Code*. Something she clearly lacks—because we stole it from her in her sleep when she was a teenager.

I can sense the confusion etched into her face. "You have questions," I say, typing away. "Feel free to ask me one."

"Can you see when you're not wearing your glasses?"

I wrap my arm around her and wipe my thumb across her hairline. "Out of all the things you could ask me, you choose that?"

"Yes. I've never seen glasses so thick."

Another handicap he gave me—he made me blind. I think it's because he didn't want me seeing her when he was watching her.

"I'm blind as a bat without them."

She reaches over and pulls the glasses off and runs a hand over my face. She looks at me inquisitively, her blurry face studying me. She closes her eyes for a moment as the ibuprofen kicks in. Her breath grows heavy again.

I place my glasses back on and click away. After a few minutes, her body is tense.

"Instead of staring at me for the next hour, why don't you ask me what's really on your mind?"

She sits up. "I can't express my thoughts in words."

"Say the first thing that comes to mind. Usually, it's the most unfiltered and interesting."

"Anything?"

"Within reason. Patience is not a virtue of mine."

She presses her lips together. "How old are you, Lincoln?"

I give her a sly smile. "I'm ageless."

Her brows furrow. "So you're old?"

"I'm timeless, baby. In my mind, it's as if I've always existed." I wrap my arm around her and she nestles in close, running her hand along my stomach.

"How many of you are inside your head?"

I take a deep breath as that darkness ripples beneath my skin. "Just the two of us," I lie. "And trust me, that's plenty." I don't bother trying to explain the split. Partly because I don't truly understand it myself, but I also don't want to frighten her.

Fragments, like this one, aren't sentient. You can't reason with them, and I don't seem to have the ability to stop this one.

Her fingers dance lower on my abdomen until she's playing with the line of my sweats. "How does that all work? I mean, with you and him... Aren't there sometimes more? I thought DID patients had hundreds of alters."

I place my computer down, pull her on top of me, run my fingers up her shirt and play with her, running my fingers down her back.

"That's how powerful I am. Usually the various alters in DID patients make up what's called the system. I *am* the system, or at least I used to be. The few times in my existence when a fragment emerged, I would control it and stifle it before it could grow into a sentient being. I'm all this body needs, Summer. And when I take what's left of Mikael, he will be gone, too."

Her lips part as if she wants to say something but doesn't.

Her knees squeeze my torso and her pupils flare. "How do you silence them? The other alters, I mean."

I chew on my bottom lip. "I tear out their tongues." I smile at her while I say this, of course.

She gasps. "*Lincoln*...how do you do that?"

I shrug. "A knife...though my preferred method is razor blades. Metaphorically, of course, since they aren't real people. But the pain they experience is real, and it all feels very real to me. Sometimes I'm gentle, but with the particularly stubborn ones, I need to use extreme measures. The outcome, however, is always the same. They are silenced."

Although...that's not entirely true, either. They are all part of the system; I just found a box to put them in, so I don't have to hear them.

She swallows hard. "Do you do that to real people, too, or is that just Mikael?"

My vision shimmers and all Mikael's memories come rushing in.

Blood, screaming, shredding.

"No, Summer, I don't kill people."

Her lip trembles. "Mikael kills people, though, doesn't he? If you're part of the same system, then that makes you a killer, too."

I squeeze her sides and pull her head in for a kiss. "He hasn't killed a single soul since I was created. I've made sure of that."

She lets out a breath, but her face tells me she's far from done. Her eyes drift to the back wall where I have Cali.

"Lincoln?"

"Yes, Summer."

"You have a girl hiding in your walls. The girl you told me you killed."

She shivers as I run my fingers up her back. "I told you, my love, I don't kill people. And yes, I do have a girl down here with me—you can thank Mikael for that one. He screwed up and took her in a blind fit of rage. She reminded him of you. I'll be honest, I'm not sure what to do with her. She's seen my face; she could ruin me."

She lets out a labored breath. "Why did he come back?"

My body tenses, my pupils shimmer again. "Because of you. You woke him up when he saw you in town the weekend you moved in. I hadn't felt him for two years before that."

She stares deep into my eyes, her brows furrowing. She sees it—the split, the anger living untethered in my head.

"He's stronger than you," she whispers.

"He's part of the system, an important part, but no, he's not stronger than me. He can't function in society, and he knows it. He hasn't grown much past his adolescence; his brain never made adulthood because I started taking over that role when he was young. He needs me, Summer, more than I need him."

She's quiet and contemplative. Her eyes blink and grow distant. "Can't you just suppress him like you do the others?"

My pupils flare and he pushes into the periphery, and it's everything I can do to calm him.

"Relax," I tell him, pushing him down. This girl must really have a death wish.

"Do you remember anything from last night?" she asks me.

I adjust my glasses, seeking a better view of the expression in her eyes. "Not the part you're referring to."

A smile hints at her lips. "And you think I had sex with him?"

I don't respond as her fingers reach down and find my erection. "You're just full of questions this morning, aren't you?"

"I have a right to know the person I'm in love—" She doesn't finish the sentence.

I arch a brow and smirk. "Continue the thought."

"I want to know who I'm in love with," she breathes. "And if he's a part of you, then that means I love him, too, Lincoln."

She shifts and a surge of unbalanced and irrational emotions hits me as she grinds her pussy over me. He directs them effortlessly, like he's playing a fiddle, until the jealousy nearly kills me.

I grit my teeth as his laughter fills my head, spitting me images of my hands wrapping around her neck, wanting to see how pretty she will be when she's dead.

My heart rate quickens and body tenses as I grip her hips and dig my fingers in her. He hurts her when he fronts, and she seems to enjoy it. Maybe I should hurt her, too?

She runs her hands through her lush white hair and places her hands on my chest as she spreads her legs and slides herself over my cock, like

I'm delicate. Her pussy is so tight my cock throbs just from the sensation of taking me deep. She leans down, pressing her tits over me, and I grab her hips as she starts to grind.

"You think he fucked me, and you're bothered by it," she whispers.

The rage blooms inside me. The angry split withers and whines. And it's...exhilarating.

She arches her back, continuing to ride me and staring into the turmoil in my eyes. "You're jealous, Lincoln. You think he was better than you."

My jaw tightens as I thrust deep into her. She lets out a little squeak, a sound I'm discovering I really enjoy.

"Be really careful what you're saying right now," I warn.

She blinks at me and moves my hands to her soft tits. "Or what?"

She's testing and teasing me, trying to see what makes me tick. She's doing her best to understand me. Finally, I understand why he acts the way he does, the extent of his anger. She's a little fucking tease, and he is downright lethal. I am the only thing in between him and the mass chaos he would unleash on this world.

A burning sensation begins to wind its way through my veins. I need to control it before it explodes out of me and it's too late.

I squeeze my eyes shut and get lost in the physical sensation of Summer grinding on me. My body relaxes as she squeezes her thighs around me and works my cock.

After a few minutes, my heart is empty again. My body returns to just flesh and bone, and I can breathe. I'm able to enjoy this moment without the emotional baggage that comes with sex, and I just fuck her.

I open my eyes again and she's staring down at me. She keeps her pussy tight on me, squeezing and grinding. "What did you feel, just now?"

How do I tell her I had the urge to kill her? That I felt his bitterness and rage because that's all he will share with me.

I lean back, rest my hands on the back of my head and smile, enjoying the view of her tight little body. "It doesn't matter now. It's gone."

She tilts her head, her pretty white hair falling onto her face. "But you felt something, didn't you?"

I bite my bottom lip, pulling her body down so I can kiss her. "Right now, all I want is to feel you," I murmur.

I now firmly believe that Summer is the root cause of my insanity and will ultimately lead to my demise. She will be the destruction of everything I know.

Mikael's emotions are overwhelming, and his desires are so intense, it hurts. It's unbearable, but I also can't get enough of them.

He can't resist when she's near, and he's tightening his grip. Every emotion he gives weakens me but also strengthens me. It makes me become him.

I grip Summer by the hips and twist her body around so I'm on top of her. I need her to understand she can't manipulate me like that. She can't toy with my emotions just as they begin to surface.

She stares up at me as I press down on her. The shadows are in my eyes, I can sense it. "Lincoln...you're hurting me," she whimpers.

She needs a reminder of who I am and what I'm capable of.

I am Shadowface.

I am a god.

CHAPTER
THIRTY
SUMMER

For a moment, his eyes are a maelstrom, and when I blink, they fade back to his dark brown eyes I'm used to behind his spectacles, unchanged.

His body is so hot, burning on top of me as my legs wrap around him.

What the hell just happened?

I run my hands through his hair. The room and the house are so quiet, and I'm acutely aware of Cali's presence inside the wall. "Lincoln." I whisper, "is…that still you?"

His body doesn't move, his breath is so heavy. "Yes, it's still me."

"What went on inside your head just now?"

He is still and unmoving, and if it weren't for his pounding heart pressed to my chest, I would believe him dead.

But then he makes motions, pressing himself deeper inside me. He fucks me slowly and forcefully, causing my legs to open involuntarily and a moan escapes my lips.

If it's even possible, he's even better than he was last night. His lips find mine, and I playfully nibble on them. Then he moves his kisses to my neck, and finally to my ear.

It doesn't seem like he wants to talk, and that's okay with me. I'll happily spend the rest of the day entangled in him.

Something flips again, and when he looks up at me, his eyes flicker and I can see the inner workings of his mind change within him.

"Do you want to know the best part about this?" he murmurs, and I let out a sigh of relief at hearing him speak, knowing it's still him. Although, this isn't him; he's changing...

"What's that?" I pant, his tongue teasingly tickles my ear.

He lifts his head up and stares down at me, pulling off his glasses and smiling. "Having a scientific mind like mine and not giving a damn about ethics."

My heart races at his words.

Ethics... Of all the things to discuss right now.

He continues, "That I get to test a hypothesis that no scientist could properly research without getting thrown into prison." I meet his eyes, and he drags his lips down my neck. I bite my lips as he presses my arms around my head, grasping them into his.

I'm captivated by those mesmerizing, flickering eyes that pierce my soul. "Would you like to know what I hypothesize?"

I think I already know. It's the reason I'm here and haven't run out screaming. It's the reason I haven't put him into prison for kidnapping the girl he has hidden down here. It's why I crave him so much.

He wants to discover if I am like my father. And I wonder if that's the reason he's keeping Cali alive...

My insides tighten as footsteps shuffle on the floorboards above me.

Do they realize what's really going on down here? I saw the way Xander's eyes widened when Mikael made a brief appearance upstairs. He was terrified. He knows what Lincoln is...

My hand instinctively goes for my phone—gone. I glance at Lincoln, and he's smirking.

I grit my teeth. "I'm not my father, Lincoln. I've never thought about death until you and Mikael put those vile thoughts in my head."

I don't admit to vividly imagining cutting Misty's eyes out—or how real that urge was, or how often I think about death.

He chuckles softly. "That's not exactly what I'm referring to, although we will address that, eventually. What I really want to explore is what I can make you do. I want to have complete control over your mind, baby."

I'm weak. *Weak.* He's been manipulating my thoughts for weeks. Years, even.

My throat starts to burn, and I push away from him but am only met by a solid wall of his ab muscles. "You don't own my mind. I'm in complete control of myself. Full mind control is impossible."

He chuckles again and kisses my lips, releasing his grip on my arms.

A smile spreads across his face as he beams down at me. "You're sure of that?"

Goddammit.

Why does he have to look so hot? His hair is so perfectly mussed, his skin so smooth, like silk, like an underwear model. And the way he kisses… Right now, it's so much like Mikael.

So much like Mikael…

He stares at me with a cool gaze, devoid of any emotion. I'm left lying in his bed, mesmerized by the V-shaped muscle of his thigh.

He tilts his head. "Get on your knees."

I twerk my head and arch a brow. If he wants to play games, then we'll play games. I'll show him his hypothesis is bullshit.

I cross my legs defiantly. "Actually, I think it's time for me to leave."

He arches his brow, and his eyes…they are serious.

And not his…

A wave of nausea fills my stomach as a sickening realization hits me. I'm not going anywhere. He'll never allow me to leave, and I'm not even certain I can do so without his explicit permission. This nauseousness is the same as when I thought about turning him in.

I'm a prisoner, just as much as Cali is.

"Please, let me go home, Lincoln."

He licks his bottom lip, and I don't even recognize him at this moment. He sounds like Lincoln—his intellect, memories, his essence—but it's not Lincoln. Not the way I understand him…

It's that third alter, the one that scares me even more than Mikael does.

"Does it hurt?" he asks with genuine curiosity. The nausea comes in waves, contracting every muscle in my belly, my head dizzy with the sensation like I'm going to pass out.

I whip my head to face his steady gaze. "Does what hurt?"

The nausea.

It's awful—crippling. My hands curl into fists, and I press them on either side of me just to steady myself. This isn't him doing this…it's impossible. He can't control my physical reaction like this. He's fucking with me.

"You're not supernatural. You're just smart and contrived, and somehow, you planned this."

I pull up to my knees and sink into the soft duvet. After a few seconds, the nausea subsides completely, as if it never existed. The pain and waves, everything stops, and I can breathe again.

Lincoln's on his knees facing me. All that's in my periphery is his toned torso. When I meet his gaze, he's smiling, then grabs my hands, intertwining his fingers with mine. "All better?"

This is impossible.

I stare at him incredulously at how soft his hands are, at how he's mirroring the emotions I'm giving him like he's so good at doing. Like he's normal. I can't deny what I just experienced isn't normal

"How did you do that?" I ask him.

The look he's giving me is unholy. "I am a god, pretty girl. I can do anything I want. I've been working on controlling your mind for years, from the moment of my existence."

All this time I thought Mikael was the dangerous one, but now I'm thinking Lincoln is worse. At least Mikael is what he is. He doesn't hide.

Lincoln is...supernatural. I have no other way to describe him, and he's completely unpredictable.

I swallow a lump in my throat. "Lincoln?"

His hands find my hair. "Yeah, baby."

I shift in front of him, my lips caressing his abdomen with my teeth and tongue as he looms above. "You just called me pretty girl."

He shrugs and stares down at me with those swirling eyes. "I did, didn't I?" He pushes his cock in front of my face and gently swipes my hair. "Let's keep playing our game. Bend down a bit."

I freeze, refusing to move, wanting to see what happens. Slowly, the nausea starts up again. It's subtle at first, but the longer I wait, the worse the sensation gets.

Impossible...

I shift onto my elbows, raising my ass in the air as the slow wave recedes. He leans down, grabbing my breasts and forcefully handles them. He grasps his cock and positions it in front of my face. I bite my lips together, refusing to part them even slightly. He chuckles and says, "Come on, Summer. Do I really need to ask?"

Ironically, if he wasn't testing me like I'm some kind of experiment, I probably would have already taken him into my mouth. But deep down, this isn't about that. It's about control.

I turn my head in utter defiance. I'm hungover, that's all this is. He knows how fucked-up I was last night. I'll wait it out and prove him wrong.

I refuse to look at him as the pit develops in the inner lining of my stomach. The longer I wait, the worse it gets. He plays with me, pressing the tip of his cock into my mouth. I can smell myself on it...it smells sweet. The scent of my fucked-up arousal.

The pain turns to darkness as I snap my jaw closed, refusing to open it.

My skin begins to burn, a searing pain emanating from within. The more I resist, the more intense it becomes.

"How...how are you doing this?" I sputter, struggling to form words.

"Come on, Summer, just open your mouth. It'll make the pain go away," he urges.

Something shifts inside me. The anguish in my stomach shoots between my legs. The pain has become so intense, it's numbing my senses and making it hard to keep my eyes open. It evolves into a sensation I can only describe as pleasure.

I refuse to let him have this control over me. He can't be *this* strong. Despite what he believes about himself, this is impossible. My teeth are grinding so hard, as if I'm working against an invisible force.

His hands are soft. "Open your eyes, Summer." The way he asked wasn't a demand, more like a suggestion. His voice has shifted again.

When I open my eyes, I see him peering down at me. He's put on a mask, but his eyes still shine brightly behind it.

And I explode. An orgasm rips through, causing my body to jolt. I cry out as my pussy pulses and juices squirt out of me. I open my mouth and take him in. Instant relief seeps through me like honey.

I've never gotten off just by the sight of something before.

The sight of death is so satisfying.

Fuck, his cock tastes good. I close my eyes and grab his hips, running my hands up his groin as it tightens, and his cock grows larger in my mouth. I take him in deep, slowly withdrawing my mouth and making eye contact with him as I reach the tip, teasing it with my tongue.

I peer up at him and crinkle my forehead as I don't recognize the eyes peering down at me. Why don't I recognize those eyes?

"Lincoln?" I whisper, pulling my lips off him. He shifts as if agitated, slapping his dick in my face.

He runs his hand over my forehead, down my cheek, then curls his fingers inside my mouth. I stare into those eyes as I suck on his fingers.

It's not Lincoln...not really. Lincoln can't see without his glasses, yet he's touching me with such precision.

"Tell me, *pretty girl*, do you feel better?" I can't help but notice the satisfaction in his voice. And the truth is, I am immensely better. I just don't want him to know that.

He slaps his dick in my face again. "Do. You. Feel. Better?"

I close my eyes as my breath grows heavy. "Answer me, Summer." His voice is different, deeper, more powerful.

"Yes," I pant. "I feel better."

He pushes his cock into my mouth. "Keep going. This time, don't stop until I see my cum all over your pretty face." I hesitate for a moment, and a deep ache hits my core, but then I comply and take him in, sucking deeply.

He grabs my hair and pulls my head back. "Get on your back," he demands. "I want to fuck your mouth."

Those new, shimmering eyes stare down at me until eventually, I comply, positioning myself beneath him. I sink into the soft bed and his knees hug me tight. He fucks my throat until he quivers, and I swallow most of it. The remaining amount he spreads onto my cheek and mouth, as if I were a work of art.

Right now, I don't know who I am. However, there's a certain pleasure in obeying him—it's better than resisting.

He towers over me with a curved smile through his mask that sends chills through my bones. I don't know who this is or what he's becoming, but he feels good. And from this point forward, I'm going to worship him.

CHAPTER
THIRTY-ONE
SUMMER

A buzzing sound wakes me up as I shoot my eyes open. I'm warm, my headache is gone from the water Lincoln—or whoever the hell that was—got me after we fucked again. Then I must have fallen back asleep, but I'm unsure for how long.

Lincoln works at his desk a few feet away from me, his glasses on, his forehead scrunched together, eating popcorn. The fire an image beside him and soft piano music playing above.

Psycho music.

My stomach grumbles from that salty, buttery smell as I come back into myself, but at least my headache is gone.

It's like this man doesn't sleep; he just reads psychology all day, every day. Then he uses it to control my mind.

My phone buzzes again.

"It's been buzzing for an hour," Lincoln says without looking up. "Maybe let Dani know you're still breathing. I'm sure she'd appreciate it."

I shoot my head up and see my phone on the nightstand. Where did it even come from? He must have given it back while I was asleep.

Dani! Oh shit. I ignored her call last night, and that was almost a full twenty-four hours ago. Twenty-four hours of fucking Lincoln, talking to him, snuggling him, and getting to unravel the different layers of his mind.

She is not going to forgive me for that.

My fingers brush against the soft, yielding pillows as I reach for my phone, acutely aware of my nakedness.

I have two missed calls, one from my mom, and a bunch of text messages from Dani. I quickly shoot her a text, letting her know I'm fine and that I won't be home tonight.

I saw she had read it, and the three dots on the text thread went wild for a few seconds, disappearing and reappearing. After that, she sends me a link to a news story with a long message attached.

Dani: *The missing girl was discovered walking alone in the woods. She's traumatized and too shocked to speak. Call me NOW.*

The image of Cali cracks my heart open wide. Her face is white as a ghost, but otherwise, her eyes are intact. She's dirty and skinny, but alive.

Did he release her while I was asleep?

I shift my eyes to Lincoln, who seems composed and relaxed. He's wearing nothing but boxers, leaning back with his hair mussed, running his hands through it as if deep in thought. Memories of this afternoon race through my mind, highlighting the contrast in sex between last night and earlier today. And my interaction with Mikael, which was even more confusing. Like I was fucking a completely different person.

I'm fine. *I'm fine… Lincoln's my protector.*

"Is this your plan for me, then?" I lean back, resting my head on the headboard, and pull the blanket up to cover my stomach. "I'm in your bed, waiting for you to use and fuck whenever you need a break from your research?" I say jokingly.

I roll out of the bed and shuffle over to Lincoln's desk, my footsteps light and airy. Without looking up, he opens his arm as if anticipating me, and I slide onto his warm lap and try not to stare at him curiously.

But he's so curious…

"That's not the worst existence in the world, is it?" He smiles, but it doesn't reach his eyes. His arms curl around me as if protecting me. His body is warm, and his fingers tickle my sides, but he remains focused on the screen in front of him. A notebook is beside him, filled with various musings and scribbles.

He's distracted.

I attempt to act as if everything is normal. Like there wasn't a third alter that came out to play—one that embodies a perfect combination of the two of them. I pretend that I am not under their control, trapped like a prisoner or a plaything.

I pop a piece of popcorn into my mouth. "So, what are we going to do about Cali?" I ask him, curious about what he will say about it.

He removes his glasses and cleans them before putting them back on and turning to me. "I got rid of her earlier while you were napping."

I shift on his lap. "What? How? I thought you were worried about her telling everyone it was you?"

He runs his hand through his hair. "I had some help, and we don't have to worry about her talking."

I don't have the nerve to ask what he means by that. "What...what did you do to her?"

He squeezes my side. "She'll live, and she's not down here anymore, listening to us. I thought that would make you happy."

It makes me happier than I ever want to admit.

I swallow hard. "How...how can you be sure she won't report you?"

He blinks twice and stares at me and, truly, I don't see anything resembling emotion. Nothing resembling humanity. "She has her heart-beat, Summer. She will move on with her life, as best she can despite being mute. She will never be able to speak again. It was the lesser of two evils."

I huff out a breath. "Lincoln...what did you do?"

"I muted her. That's all you need to know."

I give him an incredulous look.

He presses his glasses up his nose and rubs his chin as if this conversation is bothersome. "I'm not the one who took her. Mikael did. I did what I could to fix this."

He didn't do this...

He's a protector.

"How do you mute someone?"

He shrugs and gives me another squeeze. "Trauma-induced mutism. I wasn't sure if it would work, but it seemed to. We scared the girl so shitless, I doubt she will ever be able to form another sentence."

I keep my gaze steady on him, waiting to see any sign of Mikael or the mystery shimmer. "What makes you certain she'll never speak again? And when you say *we*, what do you mean exactly? Who else is in there with you?" Mikael or that terrifying, godlike creature that ravished me for hours. Not that Mikael alone isn't terrifying enough.

What does one have to do to mute someone? Not silence them, not make them promise they won't say anything, but full out *mute* them... altering their brain chemistry into silence.

Lincoln's eyes are fixed on me, and a faint, chilling glimmer shines through them.

It's blinding.

I startle back. I'm not ready for that side of Lincoln to come out again. I've had enough of *him* today.

"As I've told you, the only alters present are me and Mikael. No one else is in here," he says as he pops more popcorn into his mouth and my stomach grumbles again.

"Okay…" I cut him off and grab his knee before the god emerges. I frown as I glance at his computer, and all the notes strewed on his desk.

Trying to keep Lincoln fronting and distracted, I ask, "What are you doing your thesis on?"

"Oddly enough, the same thing you should be studying right now." He opens the desk drawer and places the large textbook on the desk in front of us.

He watches me as I run my fingers over my father's name.

Dr. K. Landry.

Followed by not so big letters.

Dr. T. Garcia.

That sickening sensation tugs at my gut seeing their names together. As if the two of them caused this, as if the two of them created Lincoln—or destroyed Mikael, depending on how you want to look at it. As if they created what force of nature I had sex with all day.

I rise from Lincoln's warmth and stumble back to bed, and my stomach drops. Jesus.

"Shit," I mutter. "I completely forgot to submit my psychology weekly assignment."

"I'm not giving you an extension," he says and goes back to clicking away on his computer, but the smirk on his face is so adorable.

He seems to love my misery in my inability to pass this class.

"I didn't ask for one," I respond curtly and position the heavy text-book on my lap. "I guess I'll just fail."

We sit in silence for a few minutes and eventually, I curl up while he works and I read. My father was known throughout the field, a sought-after practitioner who worked for the federal government and focused exclusively on the most extreme cases. His theories, I now realize, were based on unethical test subjects.

I am an unethical test subject.

My eyes flutter to Lincoln, curiosity burning in me. "You're building off one of his theories for your thesis. You're not only protecting me, you're also using me."

He doesn't respond. Almost like the robot he is, he keeps his composure. "Don't lie to me right now, Lincoln."

He takes a deep breath. "I'm not capable of lying—I'm not built that way. Lying serves me no purpose."

"Well then, tell me the truth. I want to know everything. Who the Order of the Shadows really are, and what you want from me."

He turns to face me. "You can't use a willing participant. And you, baby girl, are a *willing participant*, aren't you? All this time, and you've not run from me once."

He's not wrong.

"What is it? What is it about me that's so enticing?"

His eyes flash. "You understand exactly what is so enticing about you. You're not stupid."

My heart tightens, like a curling black smoke wraps around it and seeps into every vein in my body. I think of my younger self, waiting for him. Is this why I'm not afraid of him, despite what logic dictates?

He shuts his computer and walks to his dresser. "At first, I was curious if you were like your father, but then you started showing signs of her, and that got me thinking…"

I look up at Lincoln, waiting for him to finish his sentence, and startle as he's suddenly a few feet closer. He's holding his glasses in his hand. I stare into his eyes and he blinks a few times.

And then I realize it's not Lincoln. His eyes are lighter and he's grinning in a way Lincoln doesn't.

"Mikael," I whisper, almost relieved to see him. With really beautiful eyes and lashes that make my skin melt.

"Hi, pretty girl."

His entire demeanor shifts, and it's clear Lincoln is gone.

He walks toward me and my breath hitches. My pussy is so raw, and I can still taste his cum. Mikael is ravished—he can't seem to get enough of me, whether he's fronting or not.

He pushes me down on the bed. "You were so easy, Summer. So pure and perfect, and so willing to open your legs for me. I knew you were like her from the second I saw you."

"Who?" I whisper.

But I know who. The picture on the wall upstairs…

Shadowface 1979.

He studies me, his face a mocking grin. He bites his lip as if enjoying the inner struggle within me. "Your grandmother laid waste to a lot of people, baby."

I clench my fists. "No. You're wrong. My father, I can see that, but my grandmother was gentle. She wasn't capable of it."

He slides a piece of my hair behind my ear. "Your grandmother was evil and psychotic," he says softly. "She enjoyed it, because her mind was poisoned. Just like yours is."

My inner rage flares inside me.

"You're lying. You're lying because you're sad and broken and you want company."

Pausing for a second, he abruptly presses on top of me. His hot body, every line of his muscles tense.

My legs betray me as I wrap them around him, playing with him. Playing with the devil. I stare at him for a moment and breathe.

"You've calmed down since the last time I saw you," I say. His entire tone is calmer. His anger and pain aren't controlling him and, for once, he just seems normal again.

He shrugs and stares at my bare thigh in his shirt. "Sex will do that."

I huff. "I didn't have sex with *you.*"

He laughs so darkly and runs his hands through his hair. He looks so different without his glasses, like an entirely different person. "I can repeat exactly what we did all day if that's what it takes for you to believe me, pretty girl."

I freeze as he leans in closer, and I think about all the things he did to me today and how long he fucked my mouth. My throat is raw because of it. He also went down on me after, and that was the best orgasm he's ever given me.

His hand finds my mark, and he gently brushes his thumb across it, serving as a constant reminder I'm not safe with him. My hand instinctively searches for his, causing my heart to flutter as our fingers connect.

His gaze draws down to our hands. "I not only want to destroy you, but I want to own you."

"Lincoln wants to protect me," I counter, "from you."

A small twinge of his lip. "Lincoln's not real, pretty girl. I'm surprised you haven't figured that out yet."

A flood of emotion overtakes me and my hands ball into fists. "He is real. He's complex, brilliant, and kind, and he's *mine.* I like him better than you."

Mikael makes me feel tortured.

Mikael's calm demeanor is replaced by that rush of anger I'm used to with him. *"He's emotionless..."* he roars. "He's a robot, because I made him that way. I gave him *everything*: this nice big house, this life he created while living in my *body*. There was no fucking way I'm letting him have my heart as well. You're in love with the Tin Man. The person you are in love with is *me*."

"Well, the Tin Man was better than the Scarecrow," I quip.

I hold my breath, and a chill on my skin causes a small squeak to escape me. I tremble as his lips delicately trace the contours of my wound, his fingers gripping a razor blade he now holds against my skin.

He starts to apply pressure, causing me to bleed. Not enough that it hurts, but enough to know he's in control.

"You need him," I beg. "You can't survive without him, Mikael."

His lips curl, and I wince, thinking he's going to hurt me. Instead, he kisses the drop of blood and runs circles over it with his tongue, making the sting go away.

I gasp, then he moves his tongue to the fabric of my panties and runs his tongue over my clit. I peer down at him and his eyes are dark. His pupils are nearly black as he trails kisses up my belly and finally meets my waiting lips.

I kiss him. I shouldn't, but I do. His lips are soft, warm and sensual, and exactly what I remember him being like. My nameless monster who used to kiss me in my sleep.

He looks up at me with soft eyes. "I'm real, Summer Landry. And I love you so fucking much, pretty girl. You're the one I can't survive without." My heart completely falters.

Then I register a pinch and a sting, and I squeal as I'm hit with the sensation of my skin splitting. A gush of blood pools on the dark sheets from where he re-cut the mark. And with that, my heart turns to stone.

I slap him. "You asshole, you cut me again."

He smiles, goes utterly quiet. He then rises and strides to his desk, placing his glasses back on. He blinks a few times and his body grows limp and lifeless.

He's switching, I realize, before my very eyes.

Inhaling deeply, he smiles and walks to me. He pulls me to my feet, not noticing the tiny slice on my thigh—or if he does notice it, he's ignoring it.

"Come on. Let's get you dressed and cleaned, and we'll go upstairs. I need to introduce you to everyone, and I'll make us some pasta. I'm a really good cook."

My head hurts from the whiplash I just experienced, and I have no doubt he's a phenomenal cook.

"Lincoln?" I ask, running my hand down his abdomen and his stomach twitches.

"What is it now, Summer?"

I breathe a sigh of relief.

"If I really wanted an extension on my weekly reflection, can you be persuaded?"

He looks at me, warmth radiating from his eyes. "I can always be persuaded..."

My heart bursts. I don't care what Mikael says, Lincoln's not so inhuman after all.

A nger, being a fleeting and rudimentary emotion, is not something people hold on to. It ends up transforming into bitterness and resentment.

Except for Mikael.

His anger became frozen in that moment from his childhood, reliving it repeatedly until his brain simply couldn't process anything else. He wasn't able to move on from that. And now, his unprocessed anger pulsates through our system and is slowly bleeding into me.

It is difficult to explain the sensation of gradually disintegrating—the blending and melting that occurs. Scientifically, this process is referred to as fusion, although the terminology is inconsequential since I won't be around in the end.

The house is dark and silent as Summer and I make our way upstairs. It's well past ten PM; Summer and I have been downstairs for twenty-four hours. The trees rustle in the wind outside, shaking the house, breaking the stillness of the night.

All traces of the party have been cleared away. Hushed whispers and laughter echo from the parlor room, where Xander usually hangs out.

Mikael is well hidden, harboring a deep hatred for Xander, but he's very much blurring the lines of my consciousness and identity. It's hard right now to distinguish myself from him.

Before I grew from a fragment to an alter, Xander wasn't nice to Mikael. He was the weird boy his grandmother adopted and kept hidden from society. Xander's taller stature didn't help Mikael's cause, either.

Dr. Garcia, being the perceptive woman she is, always kept him apart. And this was not for his sake; she did that for Xander because Mikael would have killed him, eventually.

Xander is three years younger than Mikael and came to live with his grandmother during high school after his parents fled town. He and Mikael were close, but their relationship was tumultuous.

Both of them were angry.

They barely spoke back then, and when I arrived, he understood the boy inside was not the one he grew up with, and he grew fond of me. We have been like brothers ever since. Xander knows there are two of us inside this mind, although it's something we don't speak of.

He's never dealt with me like this, with both minds open at once and a rogue fragment I can't quite catch.

Summer watches me intently as we make our way through the house, her curious eyes unwavering as she watches my transformation. She only diverts her gaze when Lucy shuffles by us, her eyes lighting up when she looks at me.

"Welcome back, Mikael," Lucy whispers before carrying along her way. I think Lucy lost her mind years ago—well before I was born somewhere in this house—but she really is quite perceptive.

I adjust my glasses as Summer squishes her eyebrows together in the most adorable way. A flicker of fear casts through her eyes.

I wink at her and a small smirk crawls over my face. The elasticity of it isn't mine. Mikael's mannerisms are taking over my reflexes.

"Don't worry, pretty girl," I assure her, my vision blurring and swirling. "Lincoln is still here somewhere."

Our fusion is causing our eyes to transform. The color remains the same, it's simply the profound psychological intrusions beneath that create an illusion of change. It's enough to speculate that something deeper is transpiring within. And it is; psychological fusion is an intense process, especially when this fusion is happening faster than normal.

It happens when we co-front.

She lets out a small breath, her pupils dilating. It's interesting that all the physical reactions Mikael elicits from her are stronger compared to the ones Lincoln provokes. It's her fear and humiliation that seems to awaken her. Ironically, it's the promises of death that truly brings her to life.

Mikael fronted moments before, and he always unsettles her when he's in control. I was seated at my desk, and then I found myself standing. It felt like a blink, but I became an observer.

I regained control while he was kissing her. The anger that surged within me was a raw and relentless beast, as the fragment implanted itself into me like a tick.

Slicing her mark open again wasn't Mikael's idea; it was mine. His profession of love wasn't Mikael's; it was mine. In every way that matters, every action in that moment was mine.

I am Mikael, and my desire to kill her is getting stronger.

Summer clutches onto me as if she knows I'm leaving her soon. My hand goes to the small of her back as she walks a step ahead, and I admire her smooth, bare thighs. Since she has no clothes here, she's stuck meeting everyone in my shirt. Although it fits her like a dress and certainly will make a statement, it looks amazing on her.

"Don't be nervous," I tell her as I slide my hand and interlace my fingers with hers. "You're with me, and they just want to meet you."

She bristles. "They hate me."

"They hate the *idea* of you. They don't even know you, Summer," I remind her.

She halts just as we step under the archway at the entrance of the house. She looks around as if seeing it for the first time. The dark-stained oak stairs leading to the rooms above, the dining room and kitchen off to the left, the parlor room to the right, all the photos of our ancestors on the walls.

A draft hits her, and she pulls her hand away and wraps it around herself. She takes a couple of steps toward the dark hallway leading down to the backside of the house.

"The house is old," I tell her, walking in behind, sliding my hands around her waist. The wood creaking beneath my feet startles her—or perhaps I startle her. She's had a very confusing day.

"It was rebuilt in the 1900s, and many times over the years," I explain. "But the original house on this property was built in the 1750 by a historian, of all people—one of the founders of the university."

She walks over and runs her hand along the walls and pauses as if she can hear something. She turns and looks me dead in the eye. "He was the one who started all of this."

I wrap my arm around her midsection, and she doesn't move. I pull her body into me and brush my lips against her ear as she peers up at Matteo.

"He's the one they worship. He's the one who demands blood. Every member is related to him and technically, you are, too."

Her eyes glaze over as she beholds him. "I thought they worshiped a god?"

I snicker. "He thought he was one."

Her head shifts slightly. "My father lived here, too?"

I watch her carefully and nod. "Yeah, everyone lives here before they become a full member, usually while attending school. Your grandparents lived here, too."

She swallows and processes what I am telling her. "My mother met him after this, didn't she?" she asks me.

"Your mother wasn't part of it. I don't think she had a clue who she was married to, or what your father did."

Laughter trickles in from the other side of the house, but Summer doesn't flinch and keeps her head down and focused, her body rigid like she's guarding herself.

"What does the Order want from me? How can I be one of them and be marked for death at the same time?"

I wasn't planning on having this conversation with her right now, but it was inevitable. "In order to become a full member, you must offer a sacrifice to him. He demands the body and blood of the one you truly love. Every generation goes through it."

She keeps her gaze on the wall, her blank stare zeroing in on one spot, as if she can see something rising from the ashes of the shadows of her misery.

"Every twenty years," she whispers, as if putting the puzzle pieces together. "My father...he loved your mother? He killed her because he loved her?"

A burst of emotion threatens to swallow me whole. Mikael's turning the taps on, and my eyes sting thinking about my mother in those final moments.

"They were together when your father was in grad school, the same age I am now. She willingly gave up her life for him."

That crushing memory hits me. The way she saw me hiding when I followed them through the forest to the cave. She knew I was there and still let it happen. I'll never forget the look of terror as she died. The blood that stained her cheek as she rolled to the side when her soul left her body.

"And what did he get for killing her? Was it all worth it?" she asks.

I gesture outside. "The entire fortune is passed on to generation after generation. We control everything here, Summer; we rule all of them, and they don't even know it. Regular rules don't apply in Kinsmen. Your father lost his mind with power and greed. He thought he was invincible."

Her eyes glaze over, as if she's in a trance, as if she's lost in memory. "And I am going to be that person for you?"

I squeeze her body tight. "You are the one I love. So technically, it can't be anyone else." She pauses and doesn't react. Her body grows limp in my arms and her body melts into mine. "Say something, pretty girl."

Her eyes flash at that pet name, but she doesn't comment on it— almost as if she understands Mikael is here with us. I pull her into me, and she snaps out of it.

"Where is my inheritance, then? If I'm related to this false god."

I blink at her a couple times and merely say, "I never said our system wasn't flawed."

I press my lips onto her head. "I think it's all ridiculous. Some crazy man decided to turn some old dusty book into a codex. He was a scammer. He took money for a promise of something better. He's a shadowed myth of a god who doesn't exist."

She narrows her eyes. "But you marked me, anyway."

I nod. "Yeah, I guess I did."

Her hand slides over my cheek. "Are you real, Lincoln?"

I clasp her hand, even that name is foreign to me now. "Every part of me, Summer, and I'm not going anywhere. Please remember that."

But my name isn't Lincoln anymore. That name is simply not resonating.

I lose myself in the brightness in her eyes and she says, "The Order believed he was real. Your mother must have believed it, too."

A tightness forms inside me, every memory of that night flooding into my head, almost as if those memories are not just his, but mine as well.

I grab her chin calmly, then run my finger over her lips. "Stop talking about her."

"*Lincoln.*"

"My name's not..." I pause and take in a deep breath. "You don't get to speak about my mother, not yet."

Her pupils flare and her breath lengthens. "Lincoln...you just called her your mother."

Mikael hums through me; his anger momentarily cripples my ability to reason. Summer's voice is like a dream, hazy and fuzzy. "*Lincoln...* what's happening to you?"

I pull my hand away and turn from her. It's as if she can see me disappearing from her very eyes.

"Summer. *Enough.*" I don't recognize my voice.

She opens her mouth but snaps it shut. An agonizing few seconds go by as I do my best not to tear out her tongue.

Mikael's laughter fills my head, and he shoots a crippling amount of love into my psyche as I stare down at the beautiful girl in front of me.

Summer stares at me, watches me, not hearing the war going on inside me, but she seems to understand exactly what's going on.

I deepen my breath and compose myself as Mikael's essence melts away. As if his evil merely slides into the walls where he belongs. And for the moment, I am my usual self again.

I nudge my head toward the hushed laughter in the other room. "Come on. Let's get this over with."

Summer's eyes glaze over and she obeys. We continue down the dark hall. "Dr. Garcia will expect your dead body at the ReBirth Ceremony," I say coldly, stepping in beside her. "She will collect your body, drain your blood, and give him your eyes. Now that Mikael's claimed you, there is no stopping it."

My words are malicious, but she needs to understand the predicament she's in, and I'm not in the mood to care about her *feelings*.

"I'll be the next full member, the first of this generation. All of this will become mine. And that, my love, is where your inheritance went."

Her body shivers. The bare nipples beneath her shirt poke out. "But you said...you said you were created to protect me?"

"I was..."

I was, but not anymore. Summer is completely unaware of the danger she's facing. We finally arrive at the double doors, and I gently rub away the tear in her eye. "Come on. Let's go in." I push the door open before she can object.

Xander is seated on the couch with Bianca looking miserable on the floor with a plate of food in front of her. I chuckle to myself at the sight of her. She must have been naughty today.

Everyone's eyes are fixed on us as we walk in. I ignore their stares and find my regular spot on a plush chair, pulling Summer onto my lap, my fingers grazing her bare legs. She makes eye contact with Xander, shifting her gaze between him and Bianca.

Bianca's black hair is in her usual ponytail, her outfit leaving little to the imagination. Xander's not paying any attention to Bianca. He's smirking at Summer, chewing on his lip, leaning back like he gives zero fucks, doing what he can to make her uncomfortable.

He won't make eye contact with me, so I know he's pissed—or weary as to who he might find staring back at him.

Summer wraps her arms around my neck, pressing herself into me, showing everyone who she belongs to. I wave my hand in an indifferent gesture, wanting to get this over with. "Everyone, this is Summer; Summer, this is everyone."

"We've met," Xander says, leaning forward with his elbows on his knees. He exudes an aura of darkness and destruction, his tight T-shirt showing off his tattoos.

Summer stiffens as Mikael slithers up my spine, embedding himself into my psyche. My vision blurs, and I start thinking about how fun it will be to kill every single person in this room.

They all know what happened to me; their parents allowed it to happen and covered it up. Gabe and Wendy sit back, highly amused by the situation, though neither says anything.

They're happy with the parties, the money, the drugs, and that they're above the rules. Happy to defer to Xander. Gabe is spineless and will do anything Xander asks, which leaves me as the wild card. Technically, I don't belong here, but Dr. Garcia concludes, given what my mother sacrificed, I belong to the Order as much as anyone else.

Wendy sits up, offering a warm smile. "Nice to meet you, Summer. I'm Wendy," she introduces herself, gesturing to Bianca. "And this is Bianca."

Bianca stares at the floor. If anyone doesn't belong here, it's Bianca.

"Bianca can't talk right now, because she wasn't a good girl today," Xander responds for her. Bianca keeps her head to the ground, taking small bites off her plate. A fiery intensity flickers in her eyes.

Curiosity getting the best of me, I can't help but ask, "Do I even want to know what happened?" I'm guessing it has something to do with Dani, who was in this house last night, capturing all of Xander's focus.

Dani doesn't know Xander, but Xander knows Dani. He watched her throughout the entire trial four years ago, and I think he felt guilty about what her family went through. Unlike me, Xander is empathetic.

Xander knew about my connection to Summer, which made Dani even more intriguing for him. The poor thing is a dead girl walking.

Wendy chuckles softly. "Oh, it's just Bianca being jealous, even though she has no reason to be."

Bianca snaps her head up at her friend. "He was kissing that girl. His hands were all over her." She looks directly at Summer. "It was your friend, actually."

Summer's body stiffens at the mention of her friend. In a swift motion, Xander reaches over and forcefully turns Bianca's head toward him. "You're a glutton for punishment, aren't you, baby?" he snaps. Bianca remains restrained in Xander's grip, struggling to swallow. "You don't make the rules, Bianca. You don't get a say in them, either, so don't pretend that you do. I'll talk to, or kiss, whoever the fuck I want."

The room falls into an uneasy silence. We've grown accustomed to the dynamic between Xander and Bianca, but I'm curious how Summer will react to all of this.

"Who makes the rules," he says, and Summer bristles on my lap, watching Xander exert his dominance.

Bianca presses her lips together defiantly.

He pulls tighter, nearly snapping her neck with so much force and tension. He leans down, his voice getting low, which usually means he's getting wound up. "You better open that pretty mouth of yours and tell me who the fuck is in charge."

Summer squirms watching this unfold, and I can't help but admire her reaction to Bianca getting humiliated. In fact, Summer is shifting so much on my lap, she's grinding herself on my leg, and there is nothing but the thin fabric of her panties between my leg and her pussy.

"You make the rules, baby," Bianca finally says.

Xander drops her, takes her plate, and pulls her on top of him. She glares at us as he spoon feeds her the rest of her dinner. She beams as he dotes on her, ignoring everyone else.

I've never understood Xander's need for public humiliation, but he seems to get off on it. Bianca knows what Xander has to do since she technically has to do the same. So I'm waiting for her to piece together the fact Dani could be the key to actually marrying him one day.

Bianca is desperate for him, but he doesn't love her, and in order to transcend, the rule is you must be in love with your sacrifice. Otherwise, how is it truly a sacrifice?

If he loved Bianca, she'd already be dead. So instead he puts her through torture and humiliation because that is what he gets off on. A sadist, just like his grandmother.

It's a very odd prisoner's dilemma.

Summer's breath lengthens, and I reach my fingers under her shirt and slide my hand up her thighs. Her little cunt is dripping wet.

I lean down and kiss her neck, and she melts at my touch. "Did you like watching that?" I whisper as everyone else starts talking, and Xander puts the music on loud enough no one can hear me. She parts her lips and looks up at me, her eyes wide.

"Don't worry, pretty girl, I'll spend the rest of my life humiliating you. I'll treat you like the queen you are in public, but in private, I'll own you in ways Xander can't even dream."

I can't wait to get these niceties over with, make her something to eat, and spend the rest of the night in bed with her. I rise and pull Summer up with me. "Well, it's been a pleasure, have a nice night everyone."

"So sad you won't last past Halloween," Bianca chides from Xander's lap.

Summer sucks in a breath. "Why? What's happening on Halloween?"

"Shut up, Bianca," Wendy snaps at her.

Summer looks at me with confused eyes. I kiss her cheek and say, "Ignore her."

Xander places his hands around his head. "No, Bianca's right. Or have you not told her that part of it? I'm really confused how this is going to work for you two?" A twinge hits my gut. Maybe coming up here was a mistake.

Xander stares at me. "You haven't told her, have you?"

Her eyes peer up at me. "Tell me what?"

Xander laughs as if he's in on some cruel joke. I give him a silent glare and Xander finally looks directly into my eyes. He is aware that Mikael has returned—he saw him in the room upstairs. "Xander, not now," I tell him.

Xander's eyes flash. "The ReBirth Ceremony is in just over two weeks. And that's when your boyfriend is going to fucking kill you."

I am only in my first semester of psychology, but I understand enough to know the layers of how complex Lincoln Kennedy is. The fact he claims he is incapable of feeling anything is bullshit.

He feels me just fine. He felt me multiple times this weekend—feelings were plentiful as his eyes transformed and morphed as he gazed at me. It's confusing how someone who evokes such a range of emotions in me can claim he's devoid of any himself.

I can't deny that I'm slowly losing him. I can sense Mikael gradually taking control over him. It started subtly, but as the weekend progressed and I spent more time with him, I could see him transforming. The way he observed me, his facial expressions, even the way he fucked me... everything changed.

Lincoln was still there, the parts I love, the part that makes me feel safe, and seen. The part that exists because of me. There was more of him, more to him, if that's even possible.

It's like I was simultaneously with both of them. Lincoln and Mikael, and whatever godlike entity emerged when they were together—that's the Lincoln I didn't recognize.

After our house meeting with Xander, Lincoln took me downstairs and let me sleep. I could tell he wasn't in the mood to talk, so I didn't press him. I also didn't want to trigger Mikael. Although, everything about me is a trigger for Mikael.

Lincoln and I cuddled all night, and it was nice and normal. I tried not to think about the other man behind those eyes, who I hate to admit I am in love with, too. I fell in love with Mikael a long time ago; it's more of a primal, basic instinctual love, not nearly as deep as it is with Lincoln. But sometimes that unexplainable love is the most powerful. I listened to Lincoln's heartbeat and snuggled into his warmth until I drifted into a dreamless slumber.

When he dropped me off on Sunday afternoon, he told me he wasn't going to talk to me again until I submitted my paper, which I was able to finish late Sunday night. Luckily, I finished my readings at his house and submitted my reflection, which was two days late. I was able to dig in when I got home, as well as catch up on my other classes.

Dani was home, I saw her car; Misty was there, too, but neither of them left their bedrooms. I knocked on Dani's door to let her know I was okay, but she didn't answer. I texted her that I was home, but she didn't read it.

Dani and I don't fight—she's never been this mad at me. I also have questions about what the hell happened between her and Xander this weekend. I need to warn her, without giving up too much, and tell her to stay out of this. I'll give her a few days to stew. I hope when she understands how in love with him I am, she will forgive me.

By Monday night, I still hadn't spoken to Dani. She had been out all day and arrived home late. I spent Monday night video chatting with Lincoln, and I kept the video on all night long.

He was busy and distracted, but wanted to stay on with me. When I saw Lincoln in class, he smiled but kept his distance, and I've spent the majority of the week working on my next paper.

Last night, we didn't talk and I had trouble sleeping, so I ended up spending hours reading about the original killings in 1979 and analyzing all the evidence. It's disturbing to think that my family may have played a role in every horrifying event that has occurred in this town. That my grandma Didi killed all those people. She doesn't look like she could hurt a fly. It doesn't make sense to me.

It's Wednesday night, and I'm waiting for Lincoln to call. I check the class portal and see my latest paper has been graded.

My stomach twists. Lincoln gave me a C. I grab my phone and rage text.

Summer: *You gave me a fucking C?*

I receive a message back almost immediately.

SF: *You can do better than what you submitted. Your thoughts were all over the place, and you didn't drill down on any topic. The C was generous. It would have been a D, but I'm aware of how rough you had* *it with us this past weekend, so I cut you some slack. Plus, fantastic blow jobs persuaded me to bump you a letter.*

My mouth falls open. Lincoln really has a way of making my jaw drop.

Summer: *I was a tad distracted by a sexy guy in a mask who calls himself a god.*

SF: *Don't be mad at me. I told you I wasn't going to take it easy on you just because you're my girlfriend.*

My stomach flutters and I read those words again. *Girlfriend?* Did he just call me his girlfriend? Our relationship has been so confusing; I didn't think those words were in his vocabulary. But I suppose I'm his girlfriend...

Summer: *I never asked you to take it easy on me. Never, not once.*

SF: *I want to be the best boyfriend I can be for you. The kind your father would approve of. That means I have to push you, baby.*

I nearly choke on my tongue. I'm not sure if my father would approve of Lincoln, but I don't say that. I part my lips and huff before I press the call button, and he answers on the first ring.

"Hi, pretty girl. Did you miss me?"

I jolt at the sound of Mikael's voice. For some reason, I wasn't expecting it. Lincoln's essence has been coming through and I haven't *seen* Mikael since he re-sliced my thigh.

His voice is calm and sexy as always, but it's not Lincoln on the other side of this phone right now. I've spent hours on the phone with Lincoln this semester, and this isn't him, but in so many ways, it is.

I rarely get to communicate with Mikael directly, even though he's always underneath the surface, so I need to be sure—

"Mikael," I whisper. "Is that you?"

A beat of silence. "Summer, it's still me." I blow out a breath and nearly drop my phone as a tidal wave of relief washes over me. His voice, for the moment, sounds like Lincoln again.

The idea of Lincoln disappearing because of me is something I can't process. Even if there's a small part of me—the darkest, most repulsive and repugnant part—that can't help but be incredibly thrilled every time Mikael visits.

I grip the phone and stare down at my computer screen, at the article I was just reading about Shadowface: 2002.

My father—my serial killing, psychopathic father—never loved me.

He wasn't capable of loving people. He killed them and studied them and had no love to give—

"Speaking of my father," I say carefully, "he didn't love me. He lied to me my entire life."

"He loved you, Summer. He moved his entire life away from Kinsmen to keep you away from it all. He did what he could to keep me away from you."

I pull my knees to my chest, as if it could fix everything. "Then why did he pull strings to get me to come here? I don't believe that scholarship was a coincidence."

He chuckles. "That was all me. I think you underestimate how much control I have here. You needed to come here, and I had to make it happen."

Of course it was Lincoln, but part of me wishes it wasn't—that my father believed in me.

"Did he kill anyone else?" I ask. "Or was it the four known victims?"

He pauses longer than he should, and that pause answers my question. "I believe you have the necessary information to answer that question."

My stomach eats itself when I think about my suppressed memory or acknowledge what I witnessed as a young girl. However, with each passing day, it becomes clearer and more of it resurfaces.

My father killed a lot of people. The girls in the photo's were the beginning.

Mikael's mother was the first, and not part of the documented cases. As in, he never left a photo. She was dead and forgotten.

I scroll down on my computer and click on a picture of my father. It was taken only a year before he died. He was still so young, attractive, charismatic, and the smartest man I ever knew. Everyone loved him, everyone wanted to be around him. He helped so many people get over such terrible tragedies.

The tears sting my eyes like poison. I don't want to cry over him, but I loved him. He was a good father to me.

I peer outside, at a cloud passing the autumn moon. "I understand why he killed your mother, but why did he kill the other girls?" I ask him.

He lets out a breath, and I can imagine him running his hands through his hair, disheveling it.

"Honestly, Summer, my theory is your father was born with a taste for blood. When he killed my mother, it sparked something in him, and he went on a spree. He couldn't control it. Don't ask me why he left the photographs; I can't begin to understand his version of crazy, or why he took such a vested interest in me."

I sit with those words for a moment. A big part of me knew Lincoln was important to him, but I never dreamed he was the child of a woman he was in love with.

A sick, vile, and twisted thought hits me. "Lincoln… We're not…?"

"No, Summer, get that dirty thought out of your head. My real father was a one-night stand. I was born before my mother even met your father."

He's silent for a moment before he says, "He's not my blood relation, but he is the most brilliant mind I've ever encountered. I know him well enough to know that your mind is the same as his."

"Because you think I'm a psycho, capable of mass murder?"

"I believe that your minds are similar, but it is entirely up to you what you choose to do with that mind. I've watched you throughout your entire life, witnessing you turn into the confident girl you are now. This is precisely why your reaction to discovering that all the men in your life are serial killers is abnormal. Now, ask me the right questions, not the stuff you already know."

More riddles.

I blow out an exasperated breath, feeling the weight of the situation. The sound of clicking fills the silence on the other end of the line.

His thesis is due soon, the semester is half over. He'll be a full-fledged professor in a matter of months, yet within that same timeframe, he is expected to slaughter me and inherit a fortune.

I breathe out, staring out into the trees, the starry night, the old town road, that may be my undoing. "I miss you, Lincoln," I confess. "I can't function anymore without being near you."

More clicking.

"You're a distraction for me right now, baby. A pleasant one, but you won't help me hit my thesis deadline. My research is done now. I just need to write and finesse. I'm not clear-headed when I'm around you, as you've probably figured out."

I smile despite myself. "Maybe a distraction is a good thing once in a while." His phone call suddenly turns into a video call, and I answer it immediately.

He's lying on his bed with the phone propped up on his nightstand.

My heart stills when I see him. His hair is mussed as usual when he's working. His skin is so pale, it's almost like he's glowing. And I'm relieved to see him wearing his glasses.

He arches his sexy brows. "What do you have in mind?"

I place my phone on my dresser, and I lift my knees, hinting at what he's missing. I pull off my shirt so I'm on full display, and I lie back for him.

I hate that I crave him so much and it's only been a few days. I hate that he supposedly doesn't feel the same way.

He glances up from his computer and smiles. He's stressed, I can tell by the tightness of his eyes. I pull my blanket up to cover myself. "I know you're busy. I'm distracting you, I'm sorry." I have so much to process, so much to consider, but all I can do is think about him.

He sighs and pinches the bridge of his nose. "I am stressed, and I despise it. I have fifty shitty papers to grade before I can even think about beautiful distractions like you."

This makes me melt a little inside.

"Anything I can do to help?" I ask and motion to get dressed.

"Don't you dare move an inch—not one fucking inch the rest of the night." He drops the computer down a touch. "Just lie like that, pretty girl, and let me watch you all night long."

Pretty girl.

It's become cathartic to have him watch me. Like when he's not watching me, there is a dark empty void in my stomach. I secretly like the thought of Mikael watching me, too. Maybe a tiny bit more…

I click open my computer, now more focused—and naked, very naked. I have my own work to do, anyway. After a few minutes, I click off my Word doc and type in Mikael Peters in the search bar. Lincoln's staring so intently at his computer, I almost think he's in a trance.

"Are you okay, baby?" Lincoln asks, raising his eyes and my body relaxes.

"Yeah. Just tired." I lie so easily. That must be hereditary, too. Lincoln goes back to his grading, and I go back to my search. I spend the next half hour desperately searching for him. I check local hospital records, nearby school's…anything to hint he existed.

It's like Mikael Peters died the day his mother did. There is no record of him anywhere that I can find, and Lincoln only has an online footprint as an adult.

Those tiny moments I've had with him.

Mikael. It's always been Mikael behind those eyes.

So handsome, so fucking damaged, so utterly psychotic because of what my father did to his mother.

"Three years old," I whisper so softly. Why was a three-year-old boy watching that unfold? What kind of mother would do that? Where was he before Lincoln emerged?

My heart explodes for both of them. For Mikael and the life he didn't get to experience, and for Lincoln, for the life he got to live but won't get to finish.

"Summer, what's wrong, pretty girl? You look upset."

When I look up at the screen, Lincoln's watching me. He quirks his head, and I quickly work to control my emotions.

"Lincoln, my life really is in danger, isn't it?" I ask him as all color drains from my face.

His silence sends pins into my heart, and a few seconds go by before finally, he says, "More than you'll ever know."

"S ummer…" Dani's voice cuts me off from my daydream as we walk through the crowd on the quad the next day. People are bustling everywhere, trying to get to their next classes. It's a dreary day, as it always is this time of year as the seasons turn. The sandstone walls blend into the trees, which merge into the sky. "Are you even listening to me?" I blink a couple of times and shift my attention to her.

Dani and I made up last night after I spoke with Lincoln. I banged on her door until she opened it. She was still fuming mad at me, but understood I was safe. I asked her about Xander, and her face went white. I know something happened between them because I heard about it, but she isn't giving me anything.

"Yeah, I'm listening," I tell her. And I was listening until Lincoln appeared in the crowd, wearing a wool jacket and tight pants that should be criminal, and my heart hollowed out. He stopped to talk to a student and has been entirely focused on her for the last five minutes. His eyes meet mine for only a moment when he catches me watching him.

I cried on Dani's lap for an hour about how wrong it was to be dating our TA and knew I needed to break up with him. I also confessed I've never felt this way about anyone. She listened and rubbed my back like a good friend, even though I've been a shitty friend to her. I didn't tell her what I was truly upset about, or the fact my clock was ticking, and Halloween was two weeks away.

I just cried it out.

Dani's been talking about how on edge everyone is with a potential copycat killer on the loose and how Cali still won't speak.

It's because she can't speak, I want to cry out but keep my mouth shut instead. The news is eating this up, and Cali still isn't saying a word to anyone about what she went through in that basement.

Trauma can have a profound impact on the human mind, rewiring the brain. Thankfully, Mikael didn't kill Cali, but it seems she might have been better off if he had.

Mikael and Lincoln ensured her silence. I saw firsthand how scary they are when they are working together. It's possible, with Mikael's irrationality and Lincoln's wits, that they truly think they are a god. I've certainly experienced things I can't explain.

Dani continues, watching me watch Lincoln, "I think it's for the best if you stop seeing him. Not only could you get in a lot of trouble for sleeping with your class TA, but I'm convinced Xander's family is behind everything. I wouldn't be surprised if he was behind Cali's disappearance, too."

She's wrong, but not entirely wrong, I guess. "Why do you think that?" I ask, the lies once again spewing out. *Cali never saw me,* I remind myself. She heard me, but she never saw me.

Deny. Deny. Deny.

Dani blinks at me with hard eyes and stops walking. I'm not the only one who's changed this semester. Dani has, too. I can't put my finger on how, but she's too caught up in all this. She's too close to the truth. If she stays focused and doesn't cause trouble, she will graduate like most people and leave with no issues. But it's Dani we're talking about, and she's the most headstrong person I've ever met. And she's hell-bent on clearing up her father's name.

"I went digging around the house," she says, and my stomach tightens. When Dani digs around, she always finds the dirt. She keeps her gaze on the stone ground beneath us. "Xander found me in his room."

"And what did he do when he found you?"

Her face turns red. "He kissed me."

I can't help but smirk, because Dani never gets flustered. But then I remember Xander has a girlfriend who he treats like a dog, and I don't want Dani anywhere near that situation.

"Then what did you do?"

"I kissed him back, obviously. Then his crazy girlfriend found us, and I fled."

"Did you find anything in his room?" I ask her to change the subject, keeping my eye on Lincoln, who's still talking to that girl, who I now realize is a blonde.

Dani shakes her head. "No. But I did see something downstairs when I was looking at all those creepy ass pictures. Did you meet that friend of theirs, that girl, Wendy?"

I stutter out an answer as I continue to watch Lincoln, and he places his hand on the shoulder of the girl he's talking to. "I met her briefly. Why?"

"Did you know she's Dr. Garcia's great-niece and Xander's cousin? Her grandfather is Remington Vital."

Vital.

The name on the family plaque.

I shake my head as if I'm supposed to know these deep familial ties within this region. "Who was Remington Vital?" I ask. But more importantly, who was Matteo Vital, who seems to be the overlord of everything?

A dark look crosses her face. "He's the Supreme Court judge," she says matter-of-factly. "Wendy's grandfather put my father in prison, Summer. It was his conviction that put him in for life. And her father is the mayor of Kinsmen. This is all so convenient. If there was ever a family who could make things go away, it's the Vital family. They've kept their family fortune intact for hundreds of years."

My hand finds her shoulder as the campus starts to clear out, and she looks at me with a swell of emotion in her glistening eyes. "My father didn't do anything; he didn't kill anyone. He was innocent, I know he was. They convicted an innocent man to cover something up."

Jesus.

My mouth goes dry at what this means, at how connected this all is.

Bound by blood.

Dani will eventually find out the connection between my father, my grandparents, and everything that happened, even if I don't know the exact details. It seems like nobody else does, either, because the Vital family has a knack for making things disappear.

"What does this all mean?" I ask her.

She shakes her head, keeping a careful eye on Lincoln as students press around us, hustling to their next class. "I think everyone is in on it, and I think it all stems from this university, and the Order." She points toward the looming, castle-like building, its aged stone radiating a palpable sense of misery.

The psychology building.

She continues, "There's been so many missing people and mysterious deaths. And it's not just recently, this has been happening for hundreds of years. No bodies are ever found, no one asks questions, no one is ever charged. But that all changed this week..."

My eyes fix on her. "Why? What happened this week?"

She runs her tongue along her top teeth. "They found a victim, and she lived through it. I'm going to find her and make her talk. I'm going to find out what the fuck that girl went through and what she saw."

I wish her the best of luck with that.

"You have to promise me something, Summer," she says.

An icy breeze brushes against my cheek as Lincoln's eyes graze me from across the quad. "What?"

"Promise me you will never step foot in that house again."

I lay my hand on her arm. I've never seen Dani so determined about anything before—she's too close to the truth, and even though it may involve her, she needs to stay away from it.

"Okay. I promise. I'll break up with him and I won't go there again." If I was smart, I would flee before the ReBirth Ceremony in a week. I would tell my mom I want to come home and transfer to another school far, far away from here. Mikael will lose his grip on me. He'll have to grapple with his insanity all on his own.

As if he knows I'm thinking about him, Lincoln draws his gaze toward me.

"So," Dani says, looping my arm, "do you want to keep walking, or are you going to stand there and pine over him all day?"

I frown as we continue walking, and I tie my scarf up, trying to get away from this chilly wind.

"I'm still dying to know what went on in that basement with him," she says. "You haven't told me much."

I shrug. "We talked mainly about my father and the work he did for him before he died. It was nice hearing stories about him. Lincoln connected with him in ways I never could."

She eyes me wearily. "You just talked...*right*. You never came out of that basement once; I looked for you everywhere."

I flash her a deviant smile. "We were too busy drinking each other's blood."

She gasps, then narrows her eyes as I squeak out a laugh.

"Okay. You're joking."

I'm now not only protecting Lincoln, but Dani, too. I don't want to give Dani any additional information to continue her witch hunt. I need her to think he's a normal guy.

We continue walking, and I pointedly walk right past Lincoln. My hairs stand on end as I brush by him.

The girl he's been talking to for the past ten minutes has blonde hair flowing from a stylish hat. She turns, smiles, and waves at us, and I realize it's Misty. Suddenly, my veins throb as if about to burst, and an intense urge to tear out her eyes overwhelms me.

I can only interpret the look she gives me as a threat, considering she knows about my crush on him.

Lincoln's eyes meet mine, and he lingers for a moment, watching me. Misty's oblivious to the surge of emotion coursing through him as Mikael momentarily fronts at the sight of me. Even from a few feet away, I can see the whirlwind in his eyes.

The process of a psychopath trying to break through.

Dani watches the entire thing but obviously doesn't register the intense psychological battle warring in his head. Once we are a few feet away, she grabs my arm and pulls me away from him.

"Okay. You have it bad."

I scoff and pull my arm away. "I don't have it bad, but why is Misty talking to him?" I watch as the two of them walk *together* toward the psychology building.

She folds her arms and peers down at me. "You are such a liar. You're so smitten with him, it's not even funny. And I'd like to remind you that he's her TA. If you're trying to keep this a secret, then you're not doing a very good job."

He gets swept away by the crowd, and thankfully Misty heads in the other direction.

Dani taps her toe, staring at me. "Summer. Should I be worried?"

I shake my head and keep my voice low. "Please, keep your mouth shut about it. You can't say anything to Misty or to anyone. If Dr. Garcia finds out he's sleeping with me, he could lose his job and I could get kicked out of class for misconduct. And it would be me getting kicked out, Dani; his brain is too valuable to the university. He's going to be faculty in a matter of months. I'll never be able to get into another school with that on my record."

Her jaw drops. "*Summer*...you've never admitted that you had sex with him. I thought it was just a crush, and you just talked all night."

I grab her hand before she can say anything more. "I love him, Dani. I'm *in* love with him. And I'm trying to figure out what that means."

Silence falls between us, a heaviness in the air.

"Summer..." Dani says, squinting her eyes past me. "Someone's watching us."

My stomach twists and I turn my head to look. "Who?"

"Xander," she says icily, but her face has gone white.

I catch Xander standing under a large oak on the edge of campus. His face is shadowed, a hood is up over his face, and his arms are folded. For once, I don't see a collared Bianca with him or all his tattoos. He looks like he doesn't want to be seen.

And he is staring at us—blatantly, if I might add—wearing fucking Prada sunglasses, as if needing to flaunt how rich his family is.

The Vital family. Of course he'd be connected to that empire.

"Just ignore him," I tell her. "I'll take care of him."

Dani frowns and runs her hand over my arm. "Be careful with him, Summer. He's not a good guy."

After one final grimace at Xander, she struts toward the main part of campus.

Emphasize the strut.

I wait for her to disappear before I gather myself and walk over to where Xander is waiting for me. He knows everything about me, he must...and now, I'm thinking he knows a lot about Dani, too.

He's leaning against a tree with his arms crossed when I approach.

"What do you want?" I snap at him. "I don't appreciate you staring at us."

He smirks. "I thought you like being watched; I heard it's your thing."

I can't help but notice the flex in his jaw or the way the vein pops out of his neck. His hands are so massive, they could squish me like a bug. The thought of him squishing Dani is even more terrifying.

I cross my arms and keep a steady distance. "Stay away from my friend."

His jaw ticks as his dark gaze drifts to where Dani just walked off to. "Sure, but I don't think your friend wants to stay away from *me*."

"She does, I assure you."

His dark eyes flicker. "Is that why I found her hiding in my room with barely any clothes on?"

My mouth slinks open. "She was looking for me, and her choice of clothing doesn't give you the right to stick your tongue down her throat. Was this before or after you held me down?"

He leans his shoulder on the giant elm and chomps on that damn lip. "Is that what she told you happened? I guess you wouldn't believe it if I told you that she kissed me, would you?"

I don't bother answering because absolutely nothing would surprise me anymore. "You know who she is, don't you?" I ask him carefully. "Your family put an innocent man in prison."

His jaw ticks. "All I know is he's a convicted criminal and did very bad things to good people."

"Bullshit," I snap at him. "You were protecting someone in your group. Lincoln told me everything; I know exactly what you are. I'm not letting you anywhere near my friend, so go away."

He tilts his head. "I actually came here to talk to you. I'm trying to help you."

I place my hand on my hip. "What do you possibly want to talk to me about?"

He sneers. "I don't like you, Summer."

I bark out a laugh. "I don't like you, either, Xander. Is that all?"

He crosses his arms. "But I do care about Lincoln, and I think you do, too."

I blink at him and shoot him a dead stare as I lean against the tree next to him, mirroring his cocky body language. "Of course I care about Lincoln."

His eyes darken. "Well, he doesn't give a fuck about you, and I think you know why."

I shake my head. "You're wrong about him. He does care about me, he loves me."

He has to love me... Xander isn't with us at night. He doesn't see how soft Lincoln is. How complex, kind, focused and caring he is. I don't believe he's soulless.

Xander's blue eyes sparkle beneath his hood. "Mikael's the one who's obsessed with you. If you let him out, Lincoln will get put in the psych ward. My grandmother won't let him walk free." There it is... Mikael. It always comes back to Mikael, doesn't it?

My breath grows heavy, my body listless at the mention of his name.

I pause for a moment before I say, "Mikael's already here, Xander. He's always in the background. How do you not see that?"

He shakes his head as if he was looking for my confirmation of what he already knew.

I grind my teeth. "Look, if this has something to do with the fact you don't want me as part of your secret club, don't worry, I don't want any part of it. I won't take your inheritance."

The velocity in his voice snaps me senseless. "That is mine by *birthright*," he says through gritted teeth. "But this has nothing to do with that."

My heart rate upticks a beat as he steps closer, towering over me. I stand on my resolve, knowing he won't touch me because of Lincoln. "I plan on leaving town," I tell him. "I'm already looking into schools to transfer to on the West Coast."

"That will be too fucking late."

I huff out a breath, leaning my head against the bark of the giant tree, trying to distance myself from him. I stare up at his blue eyes. "You're wrong about Mikael; he has good inside of him, even if you can't see it. I don't think you know your brother at all. I don't believe he will kill me."

Part of me wants to stay to prove these people wrong. To prove to Lincoln that he is stronger than he knows.

He takes a menacing step toward me as if he could get any closer. "Be really fucking careful what you're involving yourself in, sweetheart. If I were you, I'd run far away from this town. Nothing good will come from you being here. You don't bring out the best in him, trust me on that."

There's an audible snap in my patience as I curl my fist. "What is your fucking problem?"

He snaps his arm next to my ear, and I back up into the trunk of another oak tree. "I have no problem, but I do have a question." His hulking body pins me into the tree. "What one do you like fucking the best?"

"Get away from me, or I'll scream," I threaten.

He licks his lips. "I can't wait for the day he actually makes you scream. Then maybe you'll get the fucking hint and *run*. Because congratulations, you dumb bitch, you let him out of his cage."

I don't give him time to react. I duck from under his arm and walk hurriedly through the quad and try to contain the burning need consuming me. When I look back, Xander is gone.

The next day, I wait until after my last class, and the very end of Lincoln's office hours, before I make my way inside his building. I make sure I'm the last student and smile sweetly at the receptionist in the office area before I sit in the chairs outside his door.

Xander's words echo in my mind, like a swarm of hornets buzzing inside it.

Get the fucking hint and run.

"Office hours are over," the dark-haired and rather plain looking receptionist says without looking up from clicking on her keyboard.

"I'm sorry, I just have a quick question for him," I say dryly, pulling my backpack up over my shoulder. Even though I talked to him most of last night, and even got my weekly reflection done a day early. There was no sign of Mikael at all, and I want to see him.

The receptionist keeps her eyes fixed on me for longer than I think is appropriate, then grabs her coat and purse. "Sorry, Mr. Kennedy is with a student, then he usually heads home at five."

I stare at *Mr. Kennedy's* door—Lincoln Kennedy has his own shiny silver plaque engraved on the wall.

The door shifts open, and my skin starts to burn as Misty walks out, her usual natural glow replaced by pale white skin. She makes eye contact with me as she hurries by, and I think I might spill the contents of my stomach seeing her alone with him.

No challenging grin today…something's wrong.

"It's fine, *Stephanie*, I'll take her in," Lincoln calls out, enunciating Stephanie's name in a way that makes my toes curl. Stephanie notices, too. Her face fires beet red as she looks at me, then through the doorway Misty just came out of.

"Lock up when you're done, then." She grabs her coat and leaves, shaking her head.

I rise and step toward the door. My throat closes, knowing Mikael will be the one I'm facing right now. No wonder Misty is pale—Mikael has the ability to remove all pigment with a single glance. God only knows what he's said to her.

He's sitting casually with his legs spread and relaxed, and his head is down, focused on the razor blade he's twirling between his fingers. His glasses are off, and he looks more composed than I've ever encountered him.

"Hi, pretty girl," he says without looking up. "I was hoping you'd come for a visit."

I take a deep breath as blood pumps through my entire body. I glance back at the hallway, the dark *empty* room behind me.

He finally raises his gaze to meet mine. "Shut the door please, baby. I don't want anyone to interrupt us. Stephanie might come back."

Dani. I just need to call Dani. She will help me. She might be the only one who knows the extent of the power in this town.

Saying anything to anyone else is pointless—they want me dead, and I am starting to understand why. It has nothing to do with their dark god or a bullshit sacrifice. They want my inheritance. They want what is rightfully mine.

I click the door shut behind me as heat builds in my center. I need to keep him talking; I need to draw Lincoln out.

I rest my head against the door. "You're going to fuck everything up for both of you if you front at the workplace, Mikael," I warn him as he takes one careful step, then another toward me. "You're being too obvious."

I meet his heavy stare. No flicker, no calming presence…just chaos and shadows like the vein of the night.

"Bring Lincoln back now," I demand. I saw the way Stephanie was looking at him, Misty, too. They were scared shitless.

He shrugs and moves closer. "Nah, I won't fuck anything up for him." He slams one arm beside my head, caging me in like a beast. "I only want to fuck you up, pretty girl."

My heart stops. I'm used to seeing him with glasses. His angry eyes are still on fire, but he appears to have more control over himself. And that could be scarier, knowing he's growing stronger and more confident in his skin.

His razor blade flashes in his hands and his eyes drop to my neck. My body vibrates as he reaches out and admires a lock of my white hair.

I stay rigid as he moves in closer, and I close my eyes, not having a clue what he plans to do. I can't have him so close; it's killing me. My skin sears from the heat of him.

He runs the blade against the fabric of my shirt, and his breath tickles my cheek. "Unexpressed emotions never die," he whispers.

My body trembles under the soft electricity of his touch. His evil presence shoots tingles up and down my entire body.

"What?" I breathe, keeping my eyes closed as the blade moves down and he tears a hole in my shirt. His hand finds my breast and my body turns into pudding, and I let him ruin yet another expensive outfit. Because it feels so *fucking* good.

He continues his rambling, "They are buried alive and will come forth later in uglier ways."

My eyes shoot open, half expecting to see Lincoln staring back at me. Mikael tilts his head and smirks. A vicious, cocky grin that makes my heart hurt.

"Sigmund Freud," he muses, playing with the hole he made in my shirt. "This quote summarizes his key psychological ideas about repression."

Those thoughts, ideas, theories all belong to someone else. He's stealing from Lincoln.

His eyes shimmer as he beholds me before they settle into a deep brown. And I know at this moment, Lincoln is gone.

It's the hate, anger, and the icky emotions that are left staring back at me. Broken and abandoned by the one person who was supposed to love him unconditionally. An empty, hateful soul when I know there is so much more to him.

I swallow hard, and his eyes follow the bob in my throat as if it's taking all his willpower not to slice it open. His eyes shimmer and I know I am fucked.

"When did Lincoln disappear?" I ask him.

He licks his lips as my nipples harden under his thumb as he caresses them.

"Alters don't disappear, Summer—it doesn't work like that—we fuse. And now everything he was, all of it, every part of him, is mine."

I hate that he sounds like him. I hate that he can carry on as if Lincoln hadn't carried him through his life because he was so broken and torn, he couldn't cope. I hate that I can't say no to him because of the mind control he has over me—the control Lincoln gave him.

I hate how much I fuckin love him.

My stomach starts to eat itself as I will myself to run, to hit him, slap him, scratch him, rip that razor blade out of his hand and slit open his damn throat and end this.

"I hate you," I whisper as he continues to cut open my shirt.

"I hate you more, pretty girl."

He runs the blade along my breast, teasing the outside of my nipple, and begins to run it along my neck.

"You can't kill me yet," I remind him, standing perfectly still. "It's not the ReBirth Ceremony. And that's what you want, isn't it? To give me to *Him*. To be *Him*…"

A deep rumble escapes his chest—a noise I've not heard from him before, even as he spent two days fucking me in his basement.

That rumble makes my thighs clench. So I taunt him to draw out more of him.

"Will that somehow make you stronger, you sick fuck? You're so weak, Mikael. Killing me makes you a murderer, a cast off to society, not a deity." I move my lips so they are flush with his cheek. "You're not a fucking god," I whisper.

Mikael twists his jaw and runs his hand through his hair, not even trying to hide his level of insanity. "You know what my favorite part of becoming Lincoln is?"

I stiffen at the sound of Lincoln's name as his hand grasps my waist.

"What's that?" I respond and my voice is a million miles away.

I close my eyes, and his heat envelopes me as I press my head against the oak door. The smell is so familiar in the dark, and I can't tell the difference. It could be Lincoln.

"Everything about this brain is intoxicating. The way he thinks things through, his memories, his logic…all the things he did to protect you. I learned, just today from one of his memories, that it's possible to die from intense emotions." His knuckles find my cheek. "Emotions, pretty girl, and here I thought all I needed was blood."

My chest rises and falls beneath him. I'm so exposed and vulnerable, and he's so *mad*. "What are you talking about, Mikael? Get to your point."

"That's how he killed your father; he used emotions."

I tense and whip my eyes open. "My father died of a heart attack," I remind him. "I was there the night it happened. There was no way Lincoln could have caused it."

Was I there, though? I was there when he was rushed in, not when it happened. In fact, he was supposed to be out of town that night. I was with Dani when I got the call.

He lets out a tiny chuckle. "You forget what I am, Summer. I'm a scientist, baby. It took a couple of days, but finally, he got so scared shit-less that his heart gave out on him. It's rare, but apparently possible." He arches his soft brows and chuckles. "Who knew?"

He centers his knee between my legs and nudges them open. My body complies and his hands move to the line of my pants and slips them down.

"You're mine, Summer," he whispers. "You've been mine since I saw you. Lincoln made sure of that when he killed your father. There's no one to protect you now, pretty girl. There is no one else who can. It's my destiny to become *him*. It's what my mother unwillingly handed over to me."

I let out a moan as his fingers slide into my pussy. This man just admitted to killing my father, threatened my life because I'm the key to his *transcendence*, and here I am with my knees open for him, desire radi-ating out of me like a pheromone.

His eyes soften, his soft eyebrows arch, and I swoon a little inside with how fucking hot he is. The look he's giving me makes my blood sizzle.

He slips his tongue inside my mouth before moving his lips to my neck. He kisses on me, running his hands along my pebbled breasts like he used to do while I was sleeping.

"You're missing one very important thing," I tell him as he slides my pants down. They fall off me easily enough, his hand now finding the wet spot on my underwear. He undoes his own button and pulls out his erection, steeling it against me.

"What's that?" he murmurs as my legs open.

"I don't love you. I love him," I lie to him. "And it seems to me that these sacrifices were all willing."

He pulls off me, his eyes shimmering against his pale skin as he takes in those words. An opponent...he's looking at me like an equal for once as my lips quirk up.

He grabs my chin and softly runs his thumb over my lips. His other hand still bearing the blade tears my panties off. He's inside me before I can choke out a breath and the blade clinks to the ground.

His hand finds my throat. "You are such a fucking liar. I embody every aspect of the person you fell in love with."

I don't stop him as he twists me around and pushes me to his desk. I don't squirm as he spreads my legs and shoves himself inside me from behind. I don't scream as he moves his hand and hooks his fingers inside my mouth and starts to fuck me savagely.

He fucks me so hard my head bangs into his oak desk, causing me to clamp down on his hand. I bite as hard as I can before he moves his hand, giving me a gentle caress in my hair. I don't stop biting as my orgasm builds and my body might combust.

I don't make a sound.

"I love you, pretty girl," he says as he finishes, and thrusts so hard in me cum drips down my thigh and he falls over me. "Don't pretend you don't love me, too."

I don't scream...because I never did.

B reath is truly a precious thing, often taken for granted—the simple act of inhaling and exhaling. It represents motion, fleeting moments of life itself. I repeatedly open and close my hand, still trying to adapt to my body. Still trying to adapt to the simple act of taking a breath. It's like skin that isn't fully mine yet, a glove that requires breaking in. The way my body moves now differs from what I remember.

Years of stolen moments that are slowly becoming mine.

He's still inside me like a dull ball of energy. Like a computer that's shut off, but is still connected to the hard drive. I found a box and put him in it, mirroring what he's done to me for the past few years, taking only the best parts of him.

The push and pull between us is still happening; we are not yet unified. What I'm experiencing is not yet fusion, because fusion requires acceptance on both parties, and while we are undoubtedly stronger together, I've not yet accepted all parts of him—just the parts that serve me and to fuse you must accept all of the alter.

And he's clearly not accepted me in my entirety, given the pulse of anger fleeting around my brain untethered.

I sense him, though, in every corner of my mind, alien and foreign and devoid of a soul.

Right now, the thesis demands my full attention, so I sit in front of my computer working. His thoughts are becoming mine, every psycho-logical theory he's memorized, analyzed, and practiced. Every experi-ence of his blurs into my psyche as if I'm downloading it. As each idea comes alive within me, my mind grows more connected to the material. Every new word, and it's as if I've been studying this forever. Every minute, every tiny memory, no matter the significance, dulls him.

The god I created is dying.

I grit my teeth and slam the computer shut, and lean back and turn the music up, trying to drown out Xander and Bianca squabbling upstairs.

Hard metal music is blaring from my speakers because I can't fucking stand that classical shit Lincoln likes, and this was the last band I listened to before I shut myself off. The heavy metal with screaming because I can't let Lincoln define my adult existence entirely.

Bianca, I've decided, will be the first one I kill when the time presents itself, since Xander seems incapable of controlling his woman. Either that, or I'll silence her to submission like I did that blonde bitch I mistook for Summer.

Xander will thank me...eventually.

I stare at my phone and grind my jaw together as I seem to do a lot. It's been a week since I saw Summer in my office. And beyond the confines of the classroom, where she's not glanced up at me even once.

Every day she talks to that fucker who's had his grubby paws on her all semester after I warned her, *repeatedly*, not to go near him. She twirls her hair and gives him flirty gestures as if daring me to do something about it.

I've texted her multiple times, and she hasn't answered. And if it wasn't for this damn thesis deadline, I'd crawl into her bedroom, fuck her senseless, and end this nonsense.

I'm spiraling, I realize—chasing an unwilling prey. I shoot off a text and run my hands through my hair.

SF: *I miss you, baby. I'm sorry if I scared you.*

My heart is scattered when I see that she's read it and appears to be responding, only for the phone to go silent. Maybe I was too rough with her the other day, but the way she succumbed to me. I know she liked it.

I text her again—the angry split flickering to the surface.

SF: *Silence isn't an option, Summer. Do you have to learn the hard way again?*

Finally, a response.

Summer: *You're such a liar. You're incapable of being sorry. I will never forgive you for taking him away from me. You are nothing but pain.*

A pit turns in my stomach as I reflect on her words. She's not wrong, but that hurt and anger aren't a part of me now, allowing me to envision a life beyond my past trauma. Why can't she understand that? Why can't she comprehend she's the finite part of why I'm whole again?

SF: *I'm learning to control my urges, baby. I promise you. I need to see you again.*

Another drawn out pause.

I dial her number; it rings three times, each adding to my growing fury every time it rings. I turn down the music and walk to my bed and she finally answers.

"Mikael," she snips, "why won't you leave me alone?"

"Because I'm obsessed with you, Summer," I bark out. "Not a day will go by where I won't want you, or think about you, or watch your every move. You're the only reason I'm still alive. You are the only reason I want to live. We were meant to be together, baby, and I'll slaughter this entire town if I can't have you."

"You want to kill me," she cries out. "And I don't want to die anymore." Her voice sounds so distant, like she's never been further away from me. "Those thoughts are ones you implanted in me. You ruined my mind, Mikael, and you're going to destroy my body, but I will not give you my soul."

I grab the blade I keep in my pocket and squeeze it until it draws blood. Reminding me that breath is not the only symbol of life; blood represents life as much as it does death.

"Your father knew what I was when he brought me to your house," I tell her. "He knew how I'd react to you and brought me near you, anyway. He gave you to me, pretty girl, whether he meant to or not. He handed you to me on a silver platter. You don't get a choice in this matter."

Her breath grows heavy, like she's crying. Her sweet voice, so gentle and full of despair, nearly kills me. I hate when she cries, and she used to whimper in her sleep so often. I was the one who wiped away those tears.

Me.

"Is Lincoln really gone?" she murmurs.

My jaw tightens, and I grab the blanket, twisting it in my hands. "He never *existed*. Any love you have for him is for me. You falling for Lincoln is the equivalent of falling for a machine. Did it feel like you were being fucked by someone who didn't love you? Every orgasm you've ever had is one I've given you, baby. Every damn time."

She sucks in a breath. "He can't be gone. It's impossible to kill an alter. He called himself a god. He's stronger than you."

I bite the inside of my cheek, my patience waning from her lack of understanding. "God, demon, angel...ancient spirit. I'm not disputing that he wasn't those things. But do you know what he wasn't, baby?"

Silence.

"Fucking human," I hiss. "He was programmed by the child version of me who realized life was easier without caring. My subconscious created a better version of myself, and now...now I'm slowly becoming him. I'm stealing everything he ever did, all the parts of him that suit me, because they were all mine to begin with. We are one fucking person, so quit referring to him as if he's someone else. I'm your god, baby. I'm everything you will ever need if you can just trust me."

She lets out a sob. "Mikael, I'm leaving."

My breath grows heavy, and I run my hand over the back of my neck. "What?"

"Don't try to follow me and don't contact my family or Dani. I told them I can't be here anymore because it reminds me of my dad. I'm leaving as soon as I can. If you come near me, or ever contact me again, I will run far away and tell the world what's going on here. I am *not* lying about that. You're very sick, and this world was better when you were locked away."

"Go ahead, baby." I let out a dark laugh. "Tell the world what I am; they won't do anything about it. They'll silence you before you can leave town. Everyone wants this to happen; your death means everything to them. It's our way, Summer. We can play this game of cat and mouse if you want. Deep down, I want you to run from me. I want to see how wet your pussy is before I kill you."

I kill the line before she can respond, seething anger roiling through me.

My anger feels like home. It fuels me, gives me purpose, gives me *hope*. It makes me fucking *ravished*—especially when I think about Summer in her tight little outfits and her salty attitude.

I walk over to the bathroom and splash cold water on my face, running my hand over my chin. I inspect my adult face—the perfectly portioned features I got from my mother.

By society's standards, I am attractive. Society likes pretty people;

they revel in those they deem attractive. But if society knew what went on in my head, my brain would be dissected.

I want to kill every blonde girl I meet. Everyone who remotely reminds me of my mother, I want to make their eyes bleed. But thanks to Lincoln, we seem to settle into society just fine.

Lincoln's glasses are in a case by the sink—the last place he stood before I took over. I put them on and stare at the blurry face in the shattered mirror. Distorted eyes, a twisted mouth, a ghostly double shadow behind me. It's how I saw myself when Lincoln was in control. The reflection of what I truly am.

A monster with a shadowed face...

Shadowface.

It's the adult version of myself, as if Lincoln never existed.

The thumping and shouting continues upstairs. I pull off the glasses and get dressed. I need to talk to Xander. He's the only other person who knows about me. He watched me transform when we were kids, and he watched as I lost myself.

But he cared about me, even if he doesn't want to admit it. He was the first person to actually give a shit, even if I didn't know how to reciprocate at the time. Killing him seemed easier than to admit I kind of enjoyed hanging out with him.

And he already knows I'm back, though Lucy's known for weeks.

I hear dark, nefarious laughter that echoes in the room, taking over all my senses, causing me to pull on my hair, trying to get it to stop. The hair on my neck stands on end.

It's the laughter of a god. And he's mad, the hatred almost mirroring my own. I close my eyes, and when I open them, a message is written on the mirror.

Kill her. Kill her. Kill her.

Another voice, another presence.

I grind my teeth. Lincoln's not dead, just weak. Desperate to experience what I'm not willing to give him yet. But this voice is something different. This voice is not Lincoln. I don't recognize it.

An image pops into my head...a memory. One of him and Summer, fucking right in this shower and smug satisfaction blooms through me. *His* smug satisfaction. The moments he stole with her. She's gazing at him with adoration, a look she's only supposed to give me.

I crush his glasses in my hand and whip them against the wall.

"Fuck you," I grit out to the mirror, as if he's staring back at me. "This is my life. You can't have it. You don't fucking exist anymore."

I let out a scream and punch the sink, then take deep breaths to calm myself. Those precious breaths I took for granted.

I need to take control of my sanity. I need to take control of my body. I need to take control of Summer, and to do that, I need to send her a stronger message.

Ten minutes later, I stroll upstairs to the main house, a bit more composed. Lucy walks by with a pile of towels in her hand, and her eyes shine when she sees me.

"Mikael," she says knowingly. "Where's the girl?"

"Hi, Lucy," I respond, giving her my devilish grin she used to love. At least someone's happy to see me. "She'll be back soon, I promise."

She nods, her eyes flashing. "She's perfect for you, Mikael. Don't let her get away."

I rest my hand on her arm. "I know, Lucy."

She keeps walking, then pauses, tilting her head slightly. "You're not going to go away again, are you?"

I cross my arms and lean against one of the large pillars at the front of the house. "Not a chance, Lucy."

"Good." She carries on, disappearing into the dark, whistling.

When I walk into the parlor room, Xander's sitting in his high-backed chair with Bianca in her usual spot at his feet. Wendy and Gabe are sitting together, and they are all watching a movie.

Everyone ignores me, as usual. The only exception is Bianca, who crinkles her nose when I walk in and cross the room toward them.

Lincoln rarely makes appearances upstairs, always preferring to work in his dark basement hellhole. I, however, am getting a taste for hard liquor and enjoy the company of others after years of solitude and a muted existence. To walk, speak, and move in a way that's distinctly me.

Plus, I need to make my presence known in this house. The sons and daughters need to know there is going to be a new Order. One where a child of a founding family will no longer take over as they have for the past 275 years. They will all realize what I am soon enough.

An anomaly in the code. An exception. A child of a sacrifice who shouldn't even exist, let alone not kill on the spot.

I am more holy than Christ, and their day of rapture is coming.

Bianca scowls at me as I pass, barely an afterthought in her tiny world that revolves around Xander. Wendy and Gabe barely pass me a glance, too.

But Xander... Xander looks like he's seen a ghost.

I walk over to him, grab the drink out of his hand, sip it, and take residence on my usual spot in a chair across from him, lounging my legs casually over it.

A sly smile slips out of me as he stares at me with a slight grin on his face.

Challenge accepted.

"What's up, *brother?*" I flash a quick smile.

The room grows quiet, watching the two of us as the tension grows between us. A coil of anger radiates off Xander, because the last time I saw him, I offered to bludgeon him in his sleep.

I'm rather relaxed for once and settle deeper into my chair with Xander's whiskey in my hand, which I drink down in a single gulp, then motion for Lucy, who appears out of nowhere, to get me another.

"What's his deal?" Bianca asks Xander, who ignores her.

Lincoln never stands up to him like that—always the peacekeeper, always calm, always trying to hide in plain sight.

But Xander needs to know I'm back, though I think he already does by his tight facial expression and slight look of terror in his eyes.

Xander's not scared of anyone, but he fears me. I'm the only one who's sicker in the head than he is.

He keeps his blue eyes on me, his dark hair hanging over his face. His brutish muscles are gleaming under his tattoos as he uncrosses his arms and turns the sound of the movie off.

He doesn't outwardly show any fear, but he knows he's in the same room as the devil.

"Everyone get the fuck out," he barks. "I need to talk to my brother."

Slowly, everyone makes motions to leave, looking confused and darting their gaze between us as I keep my expression cold and neutral.

Bianca runs her hand over her dark hair. Her lips are painted bright red as she kneels in her spot beneath him, pointedly not moving.

He nudges her with his knee. "That includes you, babe."

Her lips part and she turns her head to me and glares. "Why do I have to leave?"

Our eyes meet and she startles, blinking a few times as she meets my gaze.

I don't blink. I keep my gaze heavy set on her as a slow smile spreads across my face, imagining her with blood-stained tears.

She stares back, and her pupils expand as she takes me in. She can see me...like, really see me. She can see the evil rippling off me, the otherworldly presence behind my eyes as my vision pulsates.

Although we've never formally met, I already dislike her. I'll take care to rip out her throat along with her tongue, so she can't even scream in hell when I put her there. Not even demons should have to hear her annoying voice.

Her eyes drift to my hand, where I am playing with my razor blade.

Oops.

I forgot I was holding that. She looks at me, then back at Xander, her face draining color making her look rather...regal.

My voice is a deadly calm. "My patience is running thin with you, Bianca. Maybe I should cut your tongue out... I don't think Xander would mind."

She lets out an audible gasp.

"Bianca, go upstairs. I'll be up soon," Xander says calmly.

She sucks in a breath, then nods obediently this time. "You're just going to let him talk to me like that?"

He grabs her hair and nudges her up. "Go. Now."

She lets out a heavy sigh as she rises from her dirty spot on the floor and wipes the dust off her black pants.

She glares at me. "I always knew you were fucking crazy."

She runs out the double doors leading to the grand house beyond.

"Make sure you're fucking naked by the time I get there," he calls after her.

A moment passes, then another. A heavy silence lingers between us, and I merely play with the sharp edge of the blade, keeping my focus steady on it.

"How long have you been back?"

I finally meet his eyes and squeeze my fists together around the blade. I'm finally becoming accustomed to this, and this body is like a temple. The pain is like honey as blood trickles down my wrist.

"Three days," I tell him.

He rests his head back on the plush chair. "I fucking knew it."

I arch my brows at him and jerk my head toward the dark hallway where Bianca disappeared into. "I can kill her for you, if you want, since you can't seem to do it."

He crosses his arms and looks at me with an amused face. "Is that fucking so?"

I shrug as Lucy brings me a full glass of whiskey. "Here you go, Mikael." She runs her hand over the back of my head, her touch lingering on my shoulder.

I was always her favorite.

"Thanks, Lucy." I grab my drink, clinking the ice on the expensive crystal, and continue as Lucy disappears back into the walls of the house. Xander's eyes follow her as she leaves the two of us alone.

Lucy stopped me from killing Xander when we were kids, only because she gently placed her hands on my back—the same way she did just now.

"Please, Mikael. This isn't our way; we only kill other people, not each other."

Please. One simple word of kindness brought me back from the edge of darkness. Darkness I eventually slipped into, anyway. But it did save Xander's life.

I hope he understands that.

As I soon discovered my taste for blood, there was no way back. Only death, destruction, and darkness lay in my path.

I take a sip and continue, "Bianca won't help you transcend. Let's not pretend you're not waiting for someone else. Is that why she acts like a fucking dog?"

His eyes are dark. He knows I'm right. The Codex is clear.

He leans forward and takes a contemplative sip of his drink. "I don't know what the fuck goes on in that girl's mind."

I'm sure she's just as crazy as the rest of us. No rational girl would ever date a member of the ancestry, knowing they will likely become a sacrifice. Even if she is technically one of us.

The ritual is brutal, savage and bloody.

"Does my grandmother know you're back?" he asks.

"We had a visit."

He arches his dark brows. "I'm sure she was thrilled."

"I think she suspected it when I marked Summer Landry. Lincoln was trying to stop it, so I took control and made it happen, anyway."

He grins at me. "The way you and Lincoln can lie to the world is mind-blowing, but do not fucking lie to me, Mike. You owe me that much. Do you have something to do with that missing girl found in the woods?"

I knew he'd put two and two together, *eventually*.

I adjust my collar and shrug. "I'll admit it. Taking her was a mistake, but we fixed it. She's all better and still breathing. No harm done."

We worked together when we said goodbye to Cali. Lincoln has the ability to make logical decisions, rather than being driven by emotions. He found a solution that didn't involve death. Combining Lincoln's logical thinking with my primal psychotic impulses turned out to be successful.

He stares at me with a grim expression. "Is he gone, then?"

A tingle hints under my skin. Lincoln is still skimming the surface of my reality. I'm accepting my thoughts as my own as I accept his, but not fully fused.

Two entities where there should only be one. Three, if you count that split dying to come out.

I sense the thrum of it—it tickles all my senses.

"Not completely," I tell him. "He'll never be gone...not in the way you think."

His eyes twitch like he's trying to decipher if I'm telling the truth. "You seem different," he finally says, as if he's done assessing me. "More in control, like you finally hit puberty or something."

I scoff, rise, and grab my drink, pulling on my collar. It still seems strange wearing his clothes. People like him, they respect him. Girls blush when he walks into a room.

People never used to look at me like that.

Never. Not once.

I like how it feels.

"I have all the control, Xander. It's been a real fucking pleasure seeing you again, but I have to get this thesis done, and I have a faculty event I was invited to at the university."

"*At the university,*" he mocks in a frilly voice, leaning back and crossing his arms.

I like this life; I deserve this life with pretty people, the elite, the private functions. I was destined to have this life all along.

He merely scoffs, rises, and walks toward me, and I don't flinch as he towers over me. I give him this moment of control because I know with a blink of my eye I can make him squirm.

"Try not to kill anyone today, Mikey," Xander says.

I smirk at him and head to the door, brushing past him. "I'll do my best."

"And whatever you're doing, don't get caught. There is only so much I can do to protect you. I know somewhere in that empty soul of yours you're angry, but revenge comes in many forms. You don't have to kill her; you don't have to be a part of this."

Lincoln skims to the surface—what's left of him, anyway. And for a moment…one moment, my conscience kicks in. The rational part of my brain starts to buzz because I know he's right. It would be easier not to kill her, to let Xander take what's his.

But I'm not in love with Summer Landry; I'm *obsessed* with Summer Landry. And as long as she's breathing, my urge to kill her will never cease. My desire to own her, love her, manipulate her will consume me until the day I die.

"Whatever I do with Summer Landry is none of your business," I tell him. "I've marked her, so stay the fuck out of it, and I won't interfere with what you have planned for Dani."

The same pact we made when we found out about what the Order was. Who we both wanted from the start. Danielle Perri has no idea what she's in for. She has no idea she caught Xander's attention a long time ago.

"Enjoy that tight little blonde ass while you have her," he calls after me.

I arch a brow, then face the door. "Oh, I plan on it."

I let the double doors slam behind me.

Almost two full weeks have passed since Mikael fucked me in his office. Thirteen days of pretending it didn't happen; thirteen days of cold icy silence from me as mid-October blends into the final days of the month.

Thirteen days since Mikael left me drenched with his cum clinging to my sanity, bringing out my raw emotions. Since then, I've kept myself busy and have clung to Dani for comfort, which has brought us closer again.

I spent my weekends staying in with Dani as much as I could, never straying alone. I lock my window and door at night and have even been sleeping with a knife under my mattress.

I have nowhere to run, and I'm hoping I can last out the semester because he hasn't contacted me since we spoke on the phone nearly a week ago.

Tomorrow is supposed to be the day of the ReBirth Ceremony, where Mikael will ascend and become a Shadow. He will gain access to their power, their wealth, and money. He will keep this tradition—this ritual—this evil alive for the next generation with me as their golden sacrifice. If he can find me.

I'm hoping his silence means he's moved on from this psychotic plan.

"How did you do on last week's assignment?" Dani asks as we settle into psychology class. "Let me guess, Lincoln gave you an A?" She runs her hand down her loose braid and Misty comes to sit on the opposite side of her without looking at me.

This is how it is now. Misty and I ignore each other, leaving Dani in the middle. Misty obviously has a crush, and my confusing actions and hatred of her have driven a wedge between us. I've decided she can have him. He seems to like blondes, so she's a perfect stand in. Maybe he'll kill her instead.

"He gave me a C."

Dani's eyes widen. "Damn," she whispers, and then shrugs. "I guess that's not that bad?"

The last two assignments I've only received Cs. Not an F to get my attention, and certainly not an A. Just a C. He's trying to send me a message.

Mediocrity. I don't matter to him.

Dani still looks at me with worried eyes. She's dropped her obsession with finding anything out about them, or at least hasn't discussed it with me. She won't talk about the kiss with Xander, either.

Mikael walks into the dark lecture hall without his glasses, his eyes locate mine, and he sits in his usual spot near the front. The intensity in his eyes tells me I'm wrong. He's very much still fixated on me.

No one bats an eye at the fact it's a different person walking by them. No one knows or cares that he's killed or will kill again if left untethered.

My world, however, comes to a standstill as it always does when I see him. Lincoln admitted to me what Dr. Garcia made Mikael do. The prostitutes she brought in as a child to run tests on his sanity. He blacked out and killed every single one of them.

The girls in front of me watch his every move. He exudes confidence as he leans back in his seat like he owns the classroom, his black shirt wrapping around his lean muscles. I rip my eyes away from him as my face turns crimson, thinking about everything *both minds* did to me in that basement.

Dr. Garcia follows him with her gaze and smiles at him, giving no hint of whether she knows if her adopted son has changed.

She stands before us in this tainted lecture hall, looking every bit as intimidating as the first day of class. Her dark hair is pulled back, the sharp white streak shining from the lights above. She stands on the same stage that I am positive she burned fifty years earlier. She seems ageless as she spews her darkness, her theology of chaos. It's embedded in every lecture, through the doctrine of research, through the lens of psychological principles.

Chaos. She's an agent of chaos and evil.

And she uses this platform to serve her dark agenda and nothing else.

I can't look at either of them, so I avert my gaze. But no matter where I look, he is there, consuming my thoughts, every moment of every day. And after spending my entire life utterly alone, knowing he's always watching me makes me feel morbidly safe. Even though I am anything but safe.

I watch him now, watching me. He frequently watches me, without even pretending that I am not the center of his existence. I can sense the threats behind those gleaming eyes.

"It doesn't look like he got the hint," Dani says, watching him, too. "He keeps staring at you."

A small sound dislodges from my throat.

She narrows her eyes. "Summer?"

"It's fine," I tell her as tears threaten my eyes. "It's for the best. He's faculty, and I'm a student. I broke it off with him, Dani, I promise."

He can mute women by morphing the color of his eyes.

I've noticed his mind control seems less potent when we're apart, weaker with the more distance I have from him. He can't do much to me if I avoid him and stay locked in my room where he can't access me.

Dani says, "Yeah, but you said you were in love with him. You can't just turn that off."

I turn to face her. Her brows are pinched together, and I know she's worried about me. I know she suspects Lincoln's involvement, and she's right about all of it.

"I've known him for two months, Dani. It was an infatuation that came on strong and fast, and now it's gone. He has a thesis deadline. He's busy, I'm busy, and it's not a good idea." Which is why I suspect he hasn't come to pay me a visit. I'm not the center of his obsession, even if I secretly want to be. He has goals, a career, a life. He must see that I threaten to derail all of that. "I don't want to stay at this school. I've talked to my mom about transferring to a school on the West Coast." Where thousands of corn fields will be in between me and this dark place.

If what he says is happening is true, then parts of Lincoln are still in there. He's not the Mikael who used to visit me in my room, stealing my innocence and taking what he wants from me. He's more sophisticated. More advanced, more controlled.

And *that* is more terrifying because I don't know this version of him.

"Summer...I don't want you to leave. I'll be here by myself."

I sigh because I don't have a choice. In fact, I need to leave tonight—that would be the smart and sensible thing to do. It's not like the Order prowls every inch of these woods. I could leave if I really wanted to.

If I really wanted to. I need to face him. This will never end if I don't. And who's to say he won't follow me or come after my family if the rest of them think we are a threat to their money?

"I just don't fit in here, Dani," I tell her. "Plus, you have Misty."

Dr. Garcia clips onto the stage as the lights dim and a large brooding shadow that smells like too much cologne slides in beside me. I nearly choke on it.

"Hey, Summer," Grant says, and I turn to face him and give him the same weak smile I always give him.

"Hey," I say dryly, hoping he'd find a new girl to sit with. He's bounced around the last few weeks, but it seems I am his latest conquest.

He throws his arm around my neck, forcing me to lean into him. "I wanted to ask you something."

Mikael faces us now, as if he could sense another man's hands on me. His eyes penetrate me, and I can't look away from him, either. The pull between us is too strong, and I remember his vivid threats—his promise of violence—the night of the rave when Grant's hands were on every square inch of my body.

"What is it?" I ask him.

"I want to take you to dinner."

I whip my head to him, and he's staring at me so innocently. "What?"

"You know...dinner. A date."

Dani nudges me. "I think you should go."

The lights in the hall darken and his arm squeezes my shoulder, and goosebumps prickle my skin.

"Think about it, Summer," he whispers. "I know a good Italian place in town."

"Good afternoon, class." Dr. Garcia's shrill voice fills the room. "Welcome to mid-semester." Hushed murmurs flow across the room.

"Why are the lights off?" Dani whispers from beside me.

"I have no idea," I tell her, trying to put some distance between me and Grant.

Dani looks unimpressed, especially now that she knows Dr. Garcia's connection to her father. "Ugh. This class is so creepy."

I can't argue with her about that.

This class may seem ordinary to others, but I am aware of the hidden secrets of the faculty and how they truly test their theories.

"We've talked a lot this semester about fear," Dr. Garcia says, and a light finally shines down on her and only her. She looks unearthly and, for the first time, I don't see her as this magnificent mind, but an old lady...one who bleeds just like the rest of us. She's the only consistent thread through all of this.

"Halloween's tomorrow," she says, and my skin goes clammy. "A day where many want to believe in things that make no scientific sense. Ghosts, ghouls, goblins...monsters. But we don't need to look that far to find the real monsters that should keep us up at night. Monsters that live among us. Today, I want to talk about psychopathy."

She raises her eyes and again it's like she looks right at me. "In your textbooks, you will find a framework that outlines a diagnostic tool for various mental health disorders. This is called the DSM-5-TR, an internationally accepted manual of common psychological disorders and their corresponding treatment. Each of you will choose one disorder and identify a person, fictional or real, that you think has this disorder."

Someone yells, "What about that missing chick who was found in the woods and can't talk? What kind of disorder is that?"

A few people laugh.

Dr. Garcia's eyes shimmer with a knowing glint, almost as if she takes pride in Lincoln's handiwork. "Ah, the essence of what I wish to delve into. What could have caused that girl to become mute? What kind of experience led her to lose her sanity? Consider using yourselves as the focal point for your assignment. After all, everyone harbors a hidden monster within. I expect it to be completed by Monday. Lincoln will assess them next week and, of course, is always available during office hours for further discussion."

The lights in the room brighten. I swiftly reach for my phone and notice a waiting message. My heart tightens as I read its contents.

SF: **It's still me, Summer. I love you, pretty girl. See you tomorrow.** Like fuck...

When Mikael or Lincoln, or whoever it is, walks past, my lips open. His stare triggers memories of how he acted in the office. The sex I simultaneously loathed and loved, and at least until the ReBirth Ceremony date passes, I can't let him touch me again.

I turn to face Grant as he gathers his things. "Hey Grant, wait!"

Grant turns and peers down at me, his soft curls hanging over his face. Aware of Mikael's gaze, I tiptoe closer and kiss him. Grant places his hands on the small of my back, and despite everyone watching, he kisses me back.

He relaxes as I soften the kiss and grab the back of his neck. It's a really fun way of saying, *Fuck you, Mikael. Fuck you for destroying me.* It's a way of getting my control back.

Grant pulls away. "Damn, Summer," he murmurs in my ear.

I'm a horrible woman.

I'm playing him, knowing I'll awaken a beast, but it's all I can do to protect myself.

I can't leave town, they are watching me. Mikael owns me and he knows it. So now I just have to play my game. Mikael can't come near me if I'm in the arms of a football player. He'll have to find someone else to kill, so my plan is to date Grant the rest of the semester.

I grab his hand and interlace my fingers into his for good measure. "I'd love to go to dinner with you. How does tomorrow night sound?"

My eyes shoot open.

Shit. Shit. Shit.

It's nine PM—I slept for three hours when I got home from school at six.

I reach over and grab my laptop and fire it open, getting ready to do my readings and settle in for a long ass night. I'm not going to sleep, so I might as well continue with the pretense that I'll be continuing my studies here the rest of the semester.

The night is a swirl of mist and fury as the wind kicks up outside and small intricate patterns form on my windowsill from the winter's first frost. The window is locked, as is my bedroom door, and the other doors in the house. I'm alone in the house tonight, and there is someone who wants to slice me open and serve me to some dark, unknown god for dinner.

Psychopathy.

Fitting topic for today.

I pull my sweats down so I can stare at his mark. It's long healed, the blister no longer an open wound. It's a tiny half circle which will stay with me for life. My hand runs over it, and I think about all the nights I spent talking with Lincoln this semester.

Getting to know him, talking to him, having him explain the concepts in a way my brain understood. It guts me to think he's gone... and I miss him so damn much.

I stare down at my computer at the blinking mouse, thinking about the monster that lives inside me. A throb hits my center. A warmth that spreads over my skin and heart.

Dr. Garcia wants her assignment; I'll give her a fucking assignment. I'll show her a psychopath when I walk into class on Monday, still breathing.

My plan is to stay in tonight and all day tomorrow and avoid Mikael's calls. He can't get in here unless I let him in, so theoretically, unless he breaks my window open or busts down my door, he can't touch me.

It's the only thing I can think to do to get out of this unscathed, and I plan on staying with Grant tomorrow.

Everyone is in on this. All the founding families that have lived here. And my father did, too, which means I am a member of the founding family. It's my birthright and they shouldn't be doing this to me. It's against their code.

I read his text again and again.

SF: *I'm still here, Summer. I love you, pretty girl.*

I squeeze my hands so tight my nails dig into my skin.

Lincoln can't love, and if he does love me, it also means he's hurting, mourning the loss of his mother, dealing with the trauma he was exposed to as a child. The trauma Mikael never dealt with.

I've been reading more and more about his disorder to help me understand it. The fusion is the process of acceptance. The final step, which means Lincoln is reaching out and needs me.

He's dealing with his trauma.

I rock back and forth in my bed, fighting swells of emotion that rolls through me. It would be so much easier to give him what he wants. Maybe there is a blissful eternity waiting for me. Then suddenly—

Ping.

A new message pops on my phone, pulling me from my trance. I lean over and grab my phone, keeping my body curled up as I open the message.

Sf: *Remember what I told you would happen if you let another man touch you?*

My stomach roils and turns. I ignore his texts as I've been doing the past days and place my phone down as a swirl of wind hits from outside.

SF: *Answer me, Summer...please.*

I gasp for breath, desperate to reply. A sickness hits my stomach, knowing he wants me to.

It's Mikael's power over me, a constant presence in my life. Every time I'm away from him, I'm nauseous. This has haunted me since I was a teenager. The only time I get relief is when he's inside me, touching me, or I'm doing exactly what he wants from me. He is the only cure for this disease inside me. That or...death.

Another message.

SF: *Pretty girl is mine.*

I narrow my brows at the sudden change in tone. Then they hit like a pinball machine. Out of control and one after the other. Chaotic and sporadic, like a child with a knife.

SF: *I promised to kill pretty girl.*

SF: *Don't run from me, pretty girl.*

SF: *It will only take a second. I'll make it enjoyable.*

That doesn't sound like Lincoln or Mikael.

My breath catches, and my heart pumps a million miles an hour. He's spiraling...

I rest my thumb over the message, wanting to respond. Silently begging him to stop, knowing this isn't either of them speaking to me.

I don't engage and then—

SF: *Come on, baby. Don't make me chase you down tomorrow. You'll wake him up, and if that happens, it will definitely hurt.*

Awaken him. Now this sounds like Lincoln.

I pick up the phone and call Dani. If this is the last day I live, I need her to know what's going on.

It rings and rings and rings. "Fuck," I mutter, "please answer. Please."

It goes straight to voicemail, so I chuck the phone across the room.

"*Fuck...*" I scream and start pacing, then eventually curl up on my bed and bring my knees to my chest.

"I'm not ready to die," I whisper to myself.

A notification hits my phone, and all the blood drains from my face as I stare at it on the floor. I get up and grab it and click on the notification as Grant's face hits my screen.

Another news headline.

Shadowface rumors escalate as the tragic news of Kinsmen student, Grant Cooper, (19) was found in the forest near town. Authorities are quick to label it as an accidental death, stating he was eaten by animals. This is the first dead body found in the town since the tragic deaths of four people in 1979, and two weeks after Cali Hartman was found wandering the same woods, unable to speak about the circumstances regarding her mysterious disappearance. In 2002, four girls went missing on Kinsmen campus, their killer leaving mocking photos of their dead bodies in public places. Authorities are stating that the incidents are not related.

I hunch my shoulders. Grant's smiling face appears in his Kinsmen football uniform. They didn't show his dead body, which is decent of them.

"Mikael, what did you do?" I whisper, and tears stream down my face.

Emotion.

Remorse.

All the sentiments I should be having. Perhaps I'm not as destroyed as I thought I was.

The police are tying this one up with a bow. They went on record to say that Shadowface has not returned, and they will not tolerate hysteria in the town.

Investigation over.

They refuse to answer questions about any further rhetoric on the matter. After a few minutes, my phone buzzes, catching my attention.

"What now," I mutter. I can't take anything more tonight.

It's from an anonymous number, so of course I swipe on it immediately, a hint of disappointment it's not from *him.*

My heart jolts, then sinks.

A new photo emerges on my phone. A girl wearing solid underwear instead of lace. My tongue is thick in my mouth as I stare at her, wrapped up on a bed, her soft skin contrasting with the black sheets and dark duvet she's on.

I recognize Lincoln's bedroom immediately. The dark basement where he hides his true self from the rest of the world.

Mikael's room now.

She's wearing that hideous burlap mask. I blink a few times, trying to decipher what it is I'm actually looking at. The girl is wearing a basic black bra, her hands tied up behind her. Her hair is blonde, tousled over her shoulders. Her arm moves and my heart flutters even more.

It's a video, I realize. The girl visibly moves, shifting her body. Rage coils in my belly. How fucking *dare* he?

My door bangs. "Summer, please let me in."

I jolt, not realizing that Dani came home. Against my better judgment, I scramble to open the door I vowed not to open all night, inviting her in. Inviting Him in, too, as if my measly door would really do much to stop him.

Dani rushes in, her eyes red and puffy, wearing her coat. "Summer, are you seeing this? That fucker has Misty, and he's live streaming her."

I snap my focus to her, tilting my head as recognition hits me.

"That's Misty, Summer," she chokes out.

Burning bile hits my throat as my mind catches up with what I'm seeing. "How...how do you know it's Misty?"

"The birthmark on her wrist. Haven't you noticed it? And she's missing. She never came to meet me and hasn't come home. I've texted her a thousand times." I now see the birthmark on her tied-up wrist. It looks like a crescent moon.

I'm too stunned to speak.

Dani sits on my bed. "He killed Grant, too. Shadowface is back, Summer."

"What do we do?" I finally ask, daring to look at her.

"I've contacted the police, but they aren't doing shit. I think they are in on this. He seems to target people who look like you." Her eyes ripple as she beholds me. "But you knew that, didn't you?"

If she only knew... I warned Misty to stay away from him; I told her Lincoln was mine. She didn't listen and now she's facing the consequences.

Dani stares at me curiously. "What's going on, Summer?"

I glare at her. "The fuck if I know. I'm here, in my room, studying."

"Sure. Grant gets killed, then Misty goes missing, and I'm supposed to believe you don't know *anything*?"

She runs her hand through her braid. "The police think it's a prank. It's not the first-time people have messed around and sent fucked up photos and videos over the years, unfortunately. Whoever this Shadow-face is, he's broadcasting this video to our entire class."

Dani lets out a gasp as Mikael comes into view on the live stream. His masked head is tilted, his movement confident and precise. His skin is completely covered, wearing a tight black T-shirt and pants that show off his toned physique.

Nothing like Lincoln—this is all Mikael.

Misty squirms and her tits rise and fall, and a burning sensation overwhelms my body. My heart rate spikes as he looks directly into the camera, directly at me, and waves. The same way he waved at the rave. He's talking to me, as if saying, *Hi, pretty girl.*

"What a fucking freak," Dani whispers, keeping her gaze locked on her phone.

Mikael walks over to Misty, hovers over the edge of the bed, and runs his hands over her leg. She has a blindfold over her mask, so she jolts at his touch. Then he runs his fingers over the skin showing on her neck.

I don't move my eyes off him as he nudges Misty up, so she's on her knees. His hands are so soft, and she moves gracefully with him, almost as if putting on a show for the camera.

Dani is watching me carefully, as if studying my reaction. "Are you okay, Summer?"

"Yeah..." I barely speak as the video suddenly cuts out, and the screen goes black. I throw my phone down on the bed.

She shifts beside me as I stare blankly at the wall. "What are you thinking right now?"

Tears sting the back of my eyes. "I'm thinking how happy I am that's not me," I lie.

Her brows crinkle. "Do you know who has her?" she asks softly. "Is it one of them? Is it Lincoln?"

The dull ache hits my stomach.

Yes. Yes. Yes. I know who has her.

"No," I whisper. The dull ache transforms into a pleasant warmth. Lying is comforting. She doesn't believe me, but she looks too defeated to say anything about it.

"I wish there was something we could do," Dani says, her eyes now bloodshot.

"She doesn't look injured," I mutter. "Or frightened, for that matter. It seemed like she was actually enjoying it." I am well aware of how skilled Mikael is with his hands. He's treating her like royalty.

Dani shifts uncomfortably. "Get up. We're going to the kitchen."

I groan. "Dani, I'm tired. I don't have time to watch other people's sex videos online."

"I'm sure if you explain to our TA that our roommate was kidnapped by a masked lunatic, he'll give you an extension. Now, get up. I don't want to be alone right now."

She pulls my hands and forces me up, and we head downstairs. An hour passes, then another. The guilt eats me alive the entire time.

Grant is dead because of me, and Misty's next.

Dani pours me a glass of wine, which is the last thing I want, but the glass disappears quickly, and I pour myself another. By two AM, I'm finally calm enough to go to sleep.

Message received loud and clear, Shadowface.

"Summer, are you in there?"

A knock sounds on Saturday morning, and Dani walks in; her eyes are still puffy, and she's carrying a cup of tea and flowers. Her hair is down for once, rolling over her slender shoulders. She looks gorgeous as always in high-waisted jeans and a belly shirt. I understand why Xander would be into her. She looks stunning in a more natural manner compared to Bianca, whose appearance is more jarring. Dani, as hard as she pretends to be, is all innocence.

"The police won't listen to me," Dani says in tears. "I told them she wasn't in any of her normal places and that a lunatic has her. They won't put her in for a missing person case, because they say she's not missing."

I know why the police won't do anything about it. They won't interfere with anything that has to do with the Order.

"It's like no one cares," Dani says, shaken. "Just like no one cared about my father."

Is this what it will be like when I go missing? Is this how it was for the other victims who sacrificed their lives?

No one notices or cares when they are gone.

She looks at me and sighs, placing my cup of tea on my nightstand and the flowers on my bed. "These came for you."

I frown as she lays a bouquet of roses on my bed. At least I think they are roses. They are wilted, with the inside of the petals an inky black.

"They're dead," I point out.

Dani shrugs. "Yeah, they sure are."

My heart skips a beat. "Fuck, Mikael," I whisper. *What kind of message is that?*

I grab the card and read it.

I miss you, pretty girl. Please meet me tonight.

My insides tremble because I have no idea which one of them is speaking to me.

The *pretty girl* is all Mikael, but the pleasantries are all Lincoln. I don't know who's behind these words anymore.

I'm tempted—more than tempted—to meet him, at the very least, to right my wrongs with Misty. Then I remember those fragmented texts from the voice I didn't recognize. Whoever he is, he's drawing me out, and it's working...

Dani squishes her brows together. "Summer, who is Mikael?"

My eyes shoot up to her. "Huh?"

"Mikael. You just said the name Mikael."

Shit. Did I? Tears well up in my eyes.

I did say Mikael, not Lincoln. *Mikael.*

"So, is it this Mikael who has you looking like your dog died? Was Mikael the one sending you those creepy messages earlier this semester?"

I take a sip of my tea, the water scorching my tongue, which jolts me awake. "I didn't mean to say that name."

She blinks and stares at me. "But you did say that name."

I frown at her and stop playing with one of the dead rose leaves that crumbles in my fingers when I touch it.

"Summer... Does he...does this Mikael have something to do with all of this?"

I shake my head a little too quickly. I need to be real careful with what I say next to not implicate him. Why I'm keeping his secrets is beyond me—and a testament to the darkness he sees in me.

"No. It's just...complicated. He's very complicated." I must sound crazy to her right now. I sound crazy to myself.

She squeezes my hand, and it trembles. "You'd tell me if something was going on, right? I know your family has roots here; are you one of them?"

I try to take deep breaths and shake my head. "I'm not one of them, Dani, I promise." I stare at my phone, shutting it, trying to avoid the conversation.

She shakes her head. "Here's the thing...I don't think I believe a fucking word you say anymore. If Misty dies and you know something, that makes you guilty. That makes you one of *them*."

I know where Misty is.

I part my lips, but my words are heavy in my throat. It's the right thing to do, the moral thing to do. *Why the fuck can't I do it?*

My head hangs heavy, and she rises and heads to the door. "Alright, I was just checking on you. I'm heading out tonight. I know we're not supposed to, but a few people are going to put some flyers up around town to find Misty. I figure we will be safe enough if we stay together. Want to come?"

She obviously senses my foul mood, and luckily, is not peppering me with questions, even though she knows me well enough to know I'm lying.

I shake my head. "No. I'm good. I'm going to stay in." Although I know I'm not staying in. I need to end this.

Dani quietly shuts the door, leaving me alone again and reeling with my thoughts and my lack of a conscience. I'm coming to terms with who I am. Because I don't care that Grant died, or that Mikael likely ripped him to shreds. I don't overly care about Misty, either.

Secretly, I want Mikael more than I want Misty to live. And I know there is something deeply disturbing about that, but at least I can recognize it. I know it's wrong. The deep remorse blooms within me, and it's tearing me up inside...just not enough to actually do something about it.

I open my blinds, knowing I'm on full display for whoever may or may not be watching out there. The late autumn moon shines brightly, casting a luminous glow down the tree-lined street beneath the dusky pink sky and frost.

My phone pings, and I see it's a message from my mom, asking me if I'm okay about what happened to Grant. I guess this has turned into national news. I'm sure the university administration hates that—they've spent a lot of time denying the fucked-up generational shit in this town.

People dying every twenty years or so and others are noticing the pattern.

I send her a note to let her know I'm fine, letting her know I'm thinking of going out West sooner than I thought.

I think back on my mother's marriage. She met my father after the killings. Did she know what he was? Was she brainwashed herself? Did she protect him the way I'm protecting Mikael?

I stare out at the dark tree-lined road, thinking about the small town beyond. For hundreds of years, this town has harbored an evil secret.

I pick up my phone and call him. It rings three times before he answers. His darkness radiates on the other line like it flows through the phone and drifts inside me. He doesn't say anything, but he doesn't have to.

"Misty…really? Of all the girls, you had to take her?" I say dryly, but so much emotion is built into my voice.

He pauses for a moment, then says, "I needed to get your attention, since you seem to want to hide from me. She's obviously not the one I want, baby. But I am happy to know you still care."

The tightness gripping my head begins to ease as soon as I hear him. His voice is medicinal.

"Did you have to kill Grant?" I choke out.

His voice comes out sharp. "He put his hands on you too many times, Summer. He had to fucking go. I'd do it again, too. I'll kill anyone who puts their hands on you. I told you I would protect you, and I meant it. I also warned you what would happen if you let him touch you. Did you think I'm one to make idle threats?"

I suck in a breath, then a coil of rage springs inside me. Lincoln is the one who protects me.

"Don't you dare pretend to be Lincoln," I spit. "Don't do that, Mikael."

He's quiet for a moment and doesn't respond. I know he's seething, unraveling and transforming on the other side of this line.

Finally, he says, "Did you get my flowers?"

I let out an exasperated breath as my eyes find the dying roses. Such beauty in those stems…such beauty in death. "I got them," I breathe out, if you can call it breathing. My lungs start to collapse.

I play with the hem of my dress as heat builds up between my legs, and my nipples tighten as my body responds the way it always does, thinking about him killing me.

If I go see him, I may not come back breathing. Mikael's losing control, and Lincoln might be gone. *And I don't know who exactly I'll be meeting.* The thought shoots insane pressure right to my clit. My hand moves between my legs, and I relieve the pressure. Although, I'm beginning to worry nothing will ever relieve this pressure.

"Where do you want me to meet you?" I ask him, breathless.

"The warehouse, baby."

I keep rubbing harder. "If I come see you, will you let Misty go? That's my only condition."

A pause. "You're not in a position to give me conditions, pretty girl. See you soon, baby."

He kills the line and my orgasm explodes.

A s I leave the house, I pause by Dani's door. It's quiet in her room and the lights are off. She's gone for the night. I resist the temptation of leaving her a note under her door, knowing this might be the last time I see her.

So I grab my phone and order a ride just to the edge of town. The scent of frost is in the air as my breath swirls in front of me, the light crystals making everything glow. The driver swerves through the dark until he reaches trees and roads I barely recognize.

"You can drop me off here," I tell the driver, and I wrap the hood of my coat over my head.

He shrugs and says in his strong Northeastern accent, "You sure? There's nothing out here."

"I'm sure. Thank you."

"Suit yourself," he says and idles the car, waiting for me to leave.

I pause for a moment before exiting, resting my hand on the door handle. "Have you lived here long?"

He shrugs and peers at me through the rearview mirror. "Long enough. Why are you asking?"

I open the door. "I think you know why."

He turns and faces me as I have one foot out. "If you're concerned about dying, ma'am, then why are you asking to be left in the middle of nowhere where that football player got hacked up?"

I shudder despite myself. Good point.

I don't respond as I leave the car, shutting the door and he peels out.

I'm met with a frosty fall wind, so I wrap my arms around myself, wondering if I am indeed walking to my death.

I walk through the tall grass, and around the dead trees toward the abandoned *Fresh Mart*. Suffocating silence presses in on me.

I take the small path using my cellphone for light and shuffle toward where I think the warehouse is. My footsteps crunch on the fall foliage. A hint of something is burning nearby. Smoke. Definitely smoke. But it's sweet, like the candles Lincoln burns in his bedroom. My chest tightens as the scent lingers.

I approach the warehouse, and its darkness and eerie silence pull me in. I snicker to myself, no longer caring how crazy I must look.

This is the epitome of cliché, which is why Mikael drew me here, so he can chase me into darkness. But I refuse to run, especially from him.

My footfalls barely make any noise as I creep to the warehouse door. My last memory of this place was different. The number of people in this building was suffocating. However, now in the vast emptiness of the room, I can hardly breathe.

I've never been so fucking scared.

The door opens easily enough, and more inky darkness greets me. I nearly trip, and as I find my footing, and something catches my eye on the ground beneath me.

A burlap mask.

Those dark, dead holes for eyes staring up at me from the floor.

I lean down and pick it up, pinching the fabric between my fingers before I pull it over my face. A flicker of excitement shoots through me.

Okay, Shadowface. I'll play.

I can't explain why the mask gives me power. Like somehow it evens the playing field between us. Like perhaps, in some way, it will protect me.

It is, after all, my birthright and not his.

I slow my breathing as I creep to the center of the room, trying to be as quiet as possible.

He's here, watching me. His malevolent presence tickles all my senses.

"Mikael," I say in a hushed whisper, as if there could be anyone else waiting for me on the other side of this darkness. "Are you here?"

Deathly silence greets me, as if he's creating a black hole in this room, sucking anything that's good and holy out of it.

A whimper sounds from the corner, and I turn toward the small flickering lights.

Lincoln's scented candles—at least ten of them—surround a body on the ground.

Misty's tied up in the corner. Her hands are bound behind her back, her pretty face smashed to the ground, but otherwise, she looks untouched.

"Misty," I hiss and rush over, moving her face away from the dirty floor and check over her body. Her eyes grow wide when she sees my mask. I pull off my jacket and drape it over her, covering her, leaving me exposed.

"I won't hurt you," I reassure her, trying to speak softly as I assist her to her feet.

Her fingers find my hair. "Summer? Is that you?"

My hair... Why does everyone recognize me because of my hair?

It's then I sense him, like an otherworldly god-like presence sifting into the room, snaking around my heart. The ancient presence manifested into the body of my boyfriend.

Piano music wafts down from a hidden speaker, and he's standing a mere ten feet away, hiding in the shadows of the room. A stream of moonlight from a nearby window hits him. He says nothing—he's contemplative and quiet.

The vision of him takes my breath away. He's never looked so sexy in his tight black shirt, and I have a senseless urge to bare it all for him and let him stab me.

Instead, the rational part of my brain takes over. My conscience kicks in—the one I need to prove to myself that I have.

"Let her go," I tell him, rising to my feet to face him. "She's not part of this."

He tilts his head, and then I notice his glasses on the bridge of his nose, and I breathe a deep sigh of relief as they reflect in the candlelight.

Those glasses...it must be him.

I blow out a breath and take one slow, cautious step toward him. "Lincoln? Is that you?"

I narrow my eyes as he slowly and methodically grabs his glasses and pulls them into his right hand. His motions are so calm and composed. "You have to run, Summer."

My flesh crawls. "Lincoln, don't leave me again, please. You have to face him. I can help you work through this."

He reaches out and grabs my shoulders. "Summer…it's too late for me. You need to listen to me and run."

I set my jaw and shake my head. "I don't want to run. I miss you so much."

His eyes look pained and listless. "I'm telling you to fucking run, baby."

"Why?" I sob, digging my heels in.

His body goes lucid, his breath shallow, as if he's disintegrating in front of me. "Because he's here…and he'll kill you if you don't."

Suddenly, he's not Lincoln any longer. In a flash, his head jolts, and those flickering eyes greet me.

Fuck.

I retreat a couple of steps, and my breath turns raspy. "Mikael?" I whisper. "Please tell me that's you."

I can handle Mikael. I can reason with Mikael…I think. But whoever this is—

He slowly shakes his head and squeezes his hand, breaking the glasses, gripping them so tightly they turn into a little ball of glass and wire in his gloved hand.

Pure hatred spews out of him like the devil. He drops all but one sharp piece of glass, which clanks on the floor, and he holds it between his thumb and index finger.

I have witnessed the precision and skill of those fingers that hold sharp objects. My terror outweighs any lust or love I've ever known. My skin burns as he takes a few steps closer, his body tense and rigid.

"Who are you?" I ask.

"You know what I am." His voice is raspy and mean, and I *don't* like it.

This isn't a person, this isn't a god, or whatever he wants to refer to himself. He is nothing more than a primal emotion.

One. Primal. Feeling.

He's a fragment…he's not real.

He is *hate*—and he hates me.

I remain resolute and dig my heels into the ground. I need to reignite that love within him. It is the key to his sanity and the force that keeps him together.

I give him a flat stare. "I don't know what you are. This isn't you."

As much as he hates me, he hates the people that created him more, for what they took from him. And I hate them, too.

Hatred and love, both possess the power to bring people together.

With a deep breath, my chest rises and falls rapidly as he looms over me, his gaze fixed downward. These are the eyes of everything that poisoned his mind.

I'm mesmerized by him. His lips are twisted and quirked in a way I've never seen before. He's biting his lip, as if he wants to consume me. My life passes before my eyes, yet I remain frozen.

He's here, fully here, and I'm not ready for him.

He plays with a lock of my hair and moves the glass down my neck. I swallow and sense the sharp edge as he slides it down.

Lower.

Lower.

Lower.

All the way down my belly so it's in line with my pussy.

He drags off my mask and I open my mouth to say something, but he grabs my chin and rubs his finger over my lips.

"Don't fucking talk, pretty girl," he whispers. "Don't fucking speak unless I tell you to speak, and maybe you'll live through this."

Mikael…this sounds like Mikael.

Our lips meet and I kiss him, slipping my tongue inside his mouth. I cup his face and move his hand over my breast. I moan, aware of Misty in the corner, staring at us.

He leans down and pulls my legs from underneath me, and we smash back into the wall with the weight of his body on top of me. My legs wrap around him and his dick presses right into my center. My body rolls into him as I find his lips again, and his body softens as I play with his tongue with mine.

Kiss him, just keep kissing him. Help him through whatever he's going through. I'll show him that my body and soul belong to him. We kiss, and he keeps pressing himself harder into me.

Harder.

Harder.

Harder.

I let out a squeak as I open myself to the mind of pure evil. My breath lengthens and I deepen my kiss as it seems to be working. Whatever he's going through, I'm his cure, I know it. I'll draw out whatever evil he has in him and bring it into me.

He's been through enough.

Misty starts to cry beside us, sniffling like an idiot and catching his attention. He pulls his lips off me and his eyes draw over to her. They change again to that flickering god—the hatred inside him once again spewing out.

I pull him back to me. "Mikael, don't do this," I whisper, running my hands down the side of his body. "Let her go. You don't have to kill her. You can have me, all of me, okay?"

His attention refocuses on me, and he looks down with a tenderness I can almost define as love. His dark hair gleams against his pale skin, his eyes flickering.

"I don't want to kill her, Summer." His voice is low and guttural. All his energy radiates off him as if he's about to burst at the seams.

He moves his hands to my waist and runs his tongue along his teeth, placing a piece of glass in my hand.

He's breathless, watching me hold the glass, and leans close to my ear, teasing my lips. "I want *you* to kill her, pretty girl."

He moves back from me, one slow step after another. Watching me, waiting, his eyes twitching. "That's why I took her. So we can give them her body, and we can finally be together."

I shift my gaze to Misty, who's gone wholly still. Her eyes are wide and red, almost like they're bleeding. I stare back at Mikael, who is watching me. His face is truly neutral, and for a moment, it's like I'm watching Lincoln.

Then...he pounces.

And I fucking *run...*

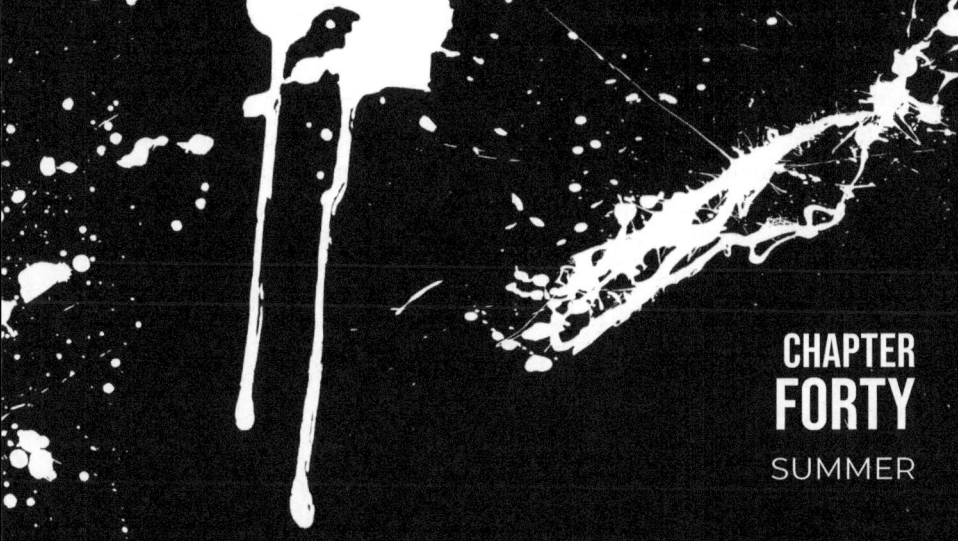

CHAPTER
FORTY
SUMMER

B *lood.*
　　Lots of it drips down my arm as I run as fast as I can out toward the dark night into the thick woods. I'm too full of adrenaline—and freezing—to register any pain. I'm not sure it's my blood; it must be a mix because I got him. I remember the glass in my hand digging into his chest, using the weapon he gave me against him.

All I know is I finally had the urge to run.

A heavy mist develops over the switchgrass, causing a ghostly light to bounce off the trees. I don't look back; I push forward, sliding on the wet ground and fall foliage at my feet. I spring into tall grass and don't dare look back, and eventually, I stagger and fall behind a large tree stump, pull my knees into my chest, and just…hide.

The insidious sickness builds in my stomach, causing me to convulse.

I think back to all the reading I've done on this condition, trying to understand Mikael and what happened to him.

This creature that emerges within him must be an emotional fragment in his mind. These fragments can split off and create sentient beings. These splits know no boundaries and have no fear. They have no consciousness, no identity, and only have one memory, one emotion.

A singular purpose.

They can, however, quickly gain substance the longer they are left to grow. In the beginning, this split only had a slight flash of sentience, but the longer it remains untethered, it grows, pulling the entire system into a frenzy. Without Lincoln holding it all together, this split is taking over.

It is the driving force behind why Mikael kills. It must be the opposite of Lincoln in terms of its function. And it's been here the entire time, hiding in the contours of his mind. Festering, growing, pushing forward.

The night is silent, and I tremble, holding my breath, too afraid to exhale in case he hears me.

I can sense his presence as if it lives inside me.

His footsteps surround me, and a cloud moves across the sky, causing the moon to cast a heavy, ominous glow, as if the night is truly on his side.

A gust of wind rustles the leaves.

He's toying with me. He could have easily captured me, but he let me escape. A pulsing sensation hits my arm, and I instinctively cover the wound, only to see my palm covered in blood.

A clicking sound, like he's ticking a clock with his tongue. Counting down...

Click. Click. Click.

"*Summer...*" he sings in a haunting voice, and his footsteps crunch in the night. "It's me, baby. It's Lincoln. Where are you?"

Lincoln...

But his dark, malicious tone sends shivers down my spine.

His voice sounds so calm, so much like Lincoln—and nothing like the voice I just heard in the warehouse. A sharp pain settles in my chest. I stay still, unable to move because I doubt it's really him.

Emotionless prick.

There's a long pause before he says in the sexiest voice I've ever heard, "Come on, Summer, I thought this is what you wanted?"

Despite my best efforts to be quiet, I release a deep breath, and it's all he needs to discover my hiding spot. He steps around the tree and gazes down at me, blood dripping from his arm. A cruel smile forms on his lips through the mask he's wearing.

I stare up at him, and his eyes, shining through the black slits, no longer hold any semblance of humanity. The evil within him seeps through his skin, as if it lives within the fibers of his mask.

My frightening fragment is gone; he's back to normal, yet I still don't recognize him.

"Please," I whimper, curling into a ball on the ground in front of him.

With his head tilted and eyes flaring, it seems like Mikael is slowly gaining control. "Please, what?" he responds. "What do you want, Summer?" His voice audibly changes again.

I drop my head. "Just let me go."

I shake as he runs his fingers up my face. "Well, that confuses me, baby, because you came all the way out here to see me, so why would I let you go?"

"I came to get Misty. You have to let her go, Mikael. She has nothing to do with this. I'm not going to kill her."

He takes a deep breath and licks his lips as if envisioning her dead. It makes my skin crawl thinking of her with him. It makes me utterly sick knowing his hands were on her in any capacity.

"Is that why you came? To save Misty? Are you finally feeling something under that cold heart of yours?"

There he goes again, calling me a liar. What did I ever lie about?

A rush of anger consumes me. "I *feel* things. Unlike you, I have a conscience."

He merely snickers. "Summer, Summer, Summer. I feel things, too. I *feel* everything. Every moment you've lived your perfect fucking life, I've felt my hatred for you. My anger erupts *every fucking time* I look at you."

My chest shakes as I choke on my words. He crouches so he is eye level with me. "You still don't understand the whole fundamental part of what makes you so unique, do you?"

He leans in so close, running his hand over my wound, mixing our blood together. Even in a psychotic state, he still smells delicious, heavenly.

How I remember him in my dreams, even with that scent of burlap.

"Your conscience has nothing to do with what you feel. I have a conscience, too, baby. Everyone does. A conscience is simply a reflection of the knowledge that you believe to be right or wrong. It's an external factor, Summer. Nothing more."

I swallow hard, hating how what he says makes so much sense. Hating how much he sounds like Lincoln. It's a corrupted version of Lincoln with elements of Mikael, and that *split* mixed in.

He continues, "You could have saved poor Cali. You could have saved Grant, and you could have saved Misty. You could have warned her or told someone."

I flare my eyes up at him. I don't want to answer... Saying it out loud makes me just as bad as my father.

He drags his knuckles along my cheek. "You're in love with me, baby. Aren't you?"

I pause for a moment as those butterflies hit my stomach. "Yes," I whisper.

"And that's why you haven't turned me in, isn't it?"

"This is all so wrong."

"You're rationalizing your love for me, Summer. And in doing so, you're allowing terrible things to happen to innocent people, just like your daddy did with his science. He studied fear, and what a better way to understand it than to create it in the most heinous way?"

I let out a small sob at the mention of my father.

He shifts beside me, looking down at me. "You cry for him... Even knowing what he did, and what he was, you still love him." It's not a question.

"He was my father, Mikael. He was everything to me. He's all I knew."

Something about him snaps. My father makes him snap, just like I make him snap. Split reemerges, and his eyes give off that terrifying shimmer.

"And here you are, following in his footsteps." His voice becomes demonic in a way I don't think is humanly possible. But he's here...all three of them combined, facing me down.

He nudges me up. "Get on your knees. We're done talking." The sheer amount of anger radiating off him spikes my fear up another ten notches.

The tension in my body grows torturous as I rise to my knees and place my hands on his muscled thighs as if I'm worshiping him.

As my last moments approach, I am as aroused as I had imagined.

He notices, because his eyes draw down to my chest, then to my lips, before making eye contact with me again. This time, he grabs my throat, his lips a soft breeze against my skin.

"Mikael, I love you," I cry out softly before he has a chance to squeeze my esophagus. His eyes find mine and visibly shift, softening and dilating.

"You're a fucking liar," he growls. "You don't love me. You only want the part of me society can handle. That's *not* me."

"I do love you, Mikael," I plea, desperate for him to believe me.

He pulls off his mask and shuts his eyes. "You want to know how many people I've killed?"

I pause and wait, catching my breath, and he opens his eyes to face me. "Ten. And I can't promise you there won't be more. My anger is as much a part of me as my love for you is."

I hitch a breath. Ten? *Ten!*

My hands discover his, which are still grasping my throat. He's not exerting any pressure...not yet at least.

"I'm a serial killer. It's in my veins; it's part of my soul."

"That's not true," I whisper as he edges me further onto the ground. "Lincoln told me the only people you killed were the ones Dr. Garcia had left for you. You were a child, Mikael, and she was sick to do that to a child."

What the fuck is wrong with that woman? Why would a child psychologist do this?

He moves a hand to my cheek, causing me to face what lies beneath. "I killed that fucker who had his grubby paws on you all semester, and I'd do it again. He was going to fuck you tonight, whether you wanted him to or not. I watched him rape a girl in the bathroom on campus two weeks ago—him and two of his teammates. No one forced me to do it, there were no conditions or variables; it was just me."

I press my lips together. "*Mikael...*"

His head quirks, but his body is still. It vibrates, almost as if he is otherworldly. It's the fusion, I realize. Lincoln, Mikael, and that split of anger are fusing into one whole.

"That is still your name, isn't it?" I ask softly.

His body vibrates as if the split wants to come out and play.

"Sorry to disappoint you... I've *always* been Mikael."

My hands wrap around themselves, and I shiver, realizing Mikael is coming down from whatever psychotic trip he was on, and I allow myself to relax, no longer frozen by blind fear. It's as if all my psychosocial senses for the last five minutes are dulled. I am, after all, lying on the cold ground.

He runs his hand down my arm, then pulls me into his body to warm me, wrapping his hands around me. "You're freezing, aren't you, pretty girl?"

After all this, after all we've been through...now he cares about my wellbeing. My teeth chatter and my body crumbles into his, and after a few long seconds, I peer up at him. His pale face, his gorgeous eyes. The light shining out of them.

"If I can still love my father despite what he did, why do you think I'm incapable of loving you, too?"

He pauses before he says, "Because I'm not loveable." He trembles, reminding me he is only human. "She didn't love me enough to stay."

I lay my head on the ground, completely immobile at this point. If Mikael doesn't end my life, maybe this cold, frosty night will. Taking a brief moment, I close my eyes and appreciate his presence. My gaze wanders into the darkness as I rest my head on the crook of his arm, relishing in his comforting heat.

All of a sudden, an image invades my thoughts, causing me to push away slightly. "There was something I saw a long time ago, when I was young," I confess.

He adjusts himself, patiently waiting, while his heart pounds and the wind whistles above us. Gradually, the memory comes into focus, crystallizing in my mind.

"Go on," he says.

He keeps his arms around me as I turn to face him, and I slink back into him. "I always knew what my father was. I lied to myself afterward, and to everyone else, but deep down...I knew."

I keep my eyes focused on him.

"What do you remember, baby? Tell me all the details of what you can see."

The memory nearly kills me as it sweeps into my mind, the missing piece of it all. I had it blocked out. For years, I couldn't recall this moment. This dark memory locked inside my head began to poison my mind.

"It's a woman..." I say quietly. "She's lying on a couch, and she's tied up in my basement. My father is hovering over her, speaking sweetly, like I remember him being. He had a notebook in his hand, and he was talking to her. He was explaining everything he was doing, as if he was making sure the circumstances were perfect. He just kept scribbling things down."

It's Lincoln holding me now, or at least, his essence is. I can tell. I relax as he runs his thumb over my cheek. "Where were you?"

"I was hiding underneath the stairs." My tongue turns thick, like I can't speak properly.

His fingers begin to caress. "Keep going. Get this memory out of your head, baby. It will make you better."

The poison. The nausea. My darkness.

"I remember very little of her, but I do remember how scared she was—I've never seen anyone so scared. She didn't scream, and I remember thinking, *Why isn't she screaming?* But she didn't make a peep."

"Your mother...where was she?"

"My mom was upstairs cooking Sunday dinner. We always had Sunday dinner."

My hand finds his thigh, and I run my fingers up his muscled leg. He wraps his arms around my midsection when I start shaking.

"I didn't know what I was watching," I tell him as the tears sting my eyes. I don't bother wiping them as I will smear blood all over myself.

"My father cut her eyes out, and I watched him do it. Then he positioned her in a pose and took a photo. She was dead, but she kept looking at me. Even when she didn't have eyes, she kept looking at me. I just sat there and watched her as my father cleaned up the mess—" My voice cracks. "She just kept staring at me, and I thought... I thought..." I tremble. I can't finish my sentence, and my voice completely chokes up.

His lips graze the back of my head. "What did you think, Summer?"

I take a shaky breath, then another. Finally, I'm calm enough to formulate my words. "I thought she looked pretty."

I sense a strange electrical buzz beneath my skin. That sickening, churning sensation returning to my stomach. I take a sharp breath, expelling all the air out of my lungs. Almost like I inhaled that noxious death in my basement and now, years later, I am finally expelling it.

"Was that so hard, pretty girl?" Mikael's presence is back. He's rubbing my back as I try not to hurl.

Mikael. Lincoln. Lincoln. Mikael. Their unified movements will take some getting used to. Even if the split is inside him, I'll find a way to love him, too.

I lift my chin to meet his gaze, and even in the dark of the night, his eyes shine. My lips root for his, and he leans down, giving me a soft, comforting kiss.

Despite Mikael's desire to kill me, he was the one who provided solace when my mind was lost in those dark places. No matter how hard I tried to block it out, the image of her was seared into my soul. Every nightmare, he was with me. Every time I re-lived what my father did to her, Mikael was there, comforting me. Almost as if he was with me every night, helping me through the pain.

I peer up at him, my eyes wide and blurry. "How can someone stare at you when they don't have eyes? I'll never forget it."

Except I did. I blocked it out for years.

"My father opened a bottle of whiskey and stayed downstairs all night. I waited until he was asleep in his chair before I crept upstairs."

His body shifts underneath me. "Then you went upstairs and lived your life as if it didn't happen, didn't you, baby?"

"My mother was sitting at the dinner table by herself. We had a roast. I can still smell how yummy it tasted. And my mom hummed all night —I'll never forget her humming. She's never hummed since."

Guilt consumed me for so long, I ended up blocking out the emotion entirely. Or did I? Or did I just believe I should feel guilty for watching my father murder someone and didn't. Perhaps I don't know what that emotion is actually like.

"I found something out recently. Something I will never be able to forgive myself for."

He draws a circle on my cheek, running his fingers down to my lips. His eyes flicker. "What's that?"

"My mother helped him clean it up, and they both watched as that judge, Remington Vital, put Dani's father away for that woman's murder."

I will never forgive myself for hurting Dani that way. If she knew this, she would end me. It would destroy her, or they would kill her.

Mikael merely says, "It's what they do. They make things go away." His fingers grip and dig into me. "He got sloppy sometimes; I'm actually surprised he never got caught."

I shiver as a cool breeze hits us, and I realize I'm losing him again. I shift around to face him, pushing him down before he can stop me, and I straddle him, digging my knees into the icy ground.

His eyes. It's always his eyes. They are cruel and sexy and so fucking dangerous. Poised and taut like a violin, tantalizing me to play with him.

I meet his stare. "Don't do that, Mikael."

His head shifts to the side as if my meager attempts at keeping him at bay are amusing. I know the person speaking to me the last few minutes was Lincoln, but now Mikael's back—and Mikael, I can play with.

He blinks and feigns innocence. "Do what, Summer? I'm just being my dazzling self."

I press myself on his growing erection. He watches me now psychotically. The sickness is gone now that I've admitted I'm not normal.

The *guilt* was eating away at me, not his mind control. He never had mind control over me; he just knew that my secrets were killing me.

"Don't leave me. Stay with me. Please. Work through the anger. Don't let that split take over you again. You are more than an emotion, so don't let that emotion define you."

His jaw tenses, but he arches his hips as I grind on top of him. I pull my leggings down and nudge his pants down to his thighs, pulling out his erection. I waste no time getting him inside me, rolling my body over his.

I stare down at him and just breathe.

For the first time in years, my chest isn't constricted. My stomach doesn't feel like it has fleas in it.

I ride him for a few minutes, and I know I have him. Now I just need to keep him from losing himself in his madness.

He grips my hips and flips me over, twisting his body over top of mine. His lip curls and his hand finds my breast, and I squeak when he presses something cold into my neck.

I wrap my legs around him and run my fingers through his dark hair. I go limp beneath him, arch my chest out, and twist my neck so he has easy access to it. "If you're going to do it, do it already," I taunt. "Fucking kill me."

He grabs my hair and tilts my head back. His eyes are wild now. His violent explosion is over; he now has slow methodological movements as he seriously contemplates it. I don't break eye contact. Not once.

"You love me more than you hate me. You won't kill me."

His eyes shift, go blank, and then shift again, reflecting the inner turmoil within him, rendering him silent. It's as if both of them are absent, leaving behind an empty shell.

The moment swiftly dissipates, replaced by a surge of pure, steely rage. The only thing I can do is try to help him pull all the pieces of himself together and, hopefully, it puts the split at bay.

If I can't pull Mikael out, I am going to die. I knew that was a risk coming here, and I'm willing to accept it.

"Do me a favor," I say as the wind shifts and I can hear faint music from the warehouse.

"What's that, baby?" he says, playing with a lock of my hair. I truly don't know who's behind those eyes.

"I want you to fuck me while you kill me so I can at least get off while you do it." Everything after that is a blur. But one thing I'm certain of: he definitely *feels* something.

I arch my back and moan when he hits me hard right in my g-spot, then he pounds me again and again, grabbing my throat and squeezing.

My world goes hazy, and I realize ever so slowly that he is killing me. One twitch of his thumb and I'm gone. A deeper squeeze, and he will cut my throat open.

I get lost in it, in the pleasure of dying. The intoxication of love and death at once. It flows through me like a snake slithering through a garden, toward a piece of forbidden fruit. It tastes sour, then it turns sweet. It's fire and ice, and calm peaceful waters.

He keeps squeezing and fucking until the moment where my stomach heats and my orgasm builds, and I finally find my true release.

It's my true rebirth.

A deep overwhelm hits me as I begin to pass out. I didn't ask for this; I didn't ask for him. And for the first time, I think I've fucked the shadow inside him—and more importantly, I think he liked it.

W e lay in a crumpled mess on the cold forest floor for at least half an hour, a light dusting of frost surrounding us. Once he came inside me, his body went soft, and he didn't move. He lays over top of me and I closed my eyes. His steady breathing is the sole indicator he's still inside his head. His body is wrapped around me, and despite how cold I am, I've never been so warm.

He didn't kill me, but he came damn close.

I'm afraid to move, afraid to see what's left of him after whatever he went through tonight. The seconds tick by and the moon drifts across the clear sky. I understand he must take me to the Order, and I'm not entirely sure what came of Misty.

His steady breathing behind me stops, and when I turn to face him, he's staring at me curiously.

I run my hand along his high cheekbone and stare into his eyes, unsure if he can see me. He flinches but doesn't pull my hand away; instead, he brings my hands to his mouth and kisses it. He blinks, as if his eyes pull into themselves.

"Hi," I whisper, my heart trembling. The turmoil he just experienced seems to have passed, but the way he looks at me fills me with worry.

Does he not recognize me?

What if the inner battle he faced has caused him to lose himself entirely? What if a new persona is gazing back at me? One I can't comprehend or control.

He tugs my hips closer to him. "Come here," he whispers.

His lips caress my forehead, causing my senses to pop, and my legs to wrap around him.

"I'm still supposed to kill you tonight, Summer," he says carefully, but the way his hands roam my body tells a different story.

I pause, contemplating. "Do you still *want* to kill me?" I ask, shivering. I study his soul, searching for any trace of primal rage.

Is he Mikael? Lincoln? I look for the split, for any sign that the fragmented demon has taken over again.

He pulls back, licking his lips as if the thought of killing me stirs his appetite.

"Yeah," he whispers, his deep voice taking my breath away. "I really fucking do." His chest rises and his lips brush against my neck where he bites down. My breath lengthens as he nibbles on my ear. "I think part of me will always crave your death, pretty girl."

Pretty girl. I am his pretty girl, and because of him, I have the most fucked-up kink in existence.

And I will love him until the end of time because he brought me to the brink of death during my orgasm and somehow brought me back again. And nothing will ever compare to what I just experienced with him.

He has an untethered urge to kill me, and I have a death fetish. We're a match made in heaven.

He blinks at me and smiles, flashing his perfect white teeth. "You like that about me, don't you?"

I grind against him, bucking my hips hard as if the sex we just had wasn't enough. I reach up and kiss him, slipping my tongue between his lips, getting aroused again. He stiffens, surprised by the kiss, and I go wholly still at how different his lips are.

Like maybe he doesn't know who I am? Then he kisses me back ferociously.

I stop and frown at him, still petrified to ask his name. His energy is different. This version is all confidence, cuddles and kisses, with an edge of darkness.

"Who are you right now?" I ask him. "Tell me your name?"

He blinks a couple of times and tilts his head, and a warm smile crosses his face. "I don't think I have one yet."

I part my lips as my breath wraps and coils in the air around me. The temperature is dropping fast.

"You're not Mikael?" I ask cautiously, and part of me grieves at that thought.

He shakes his head. "Mikael doesn't seem right anymore."

I arch my brows. "Lincoln?"

He nods and smiles. "It's for the best."

Tears burn the back of my eyes, but I'm not sure why. Lincoln was better, easier. But part of me mourns for the boy who couldn't handle his life. For the boy who lost his mother.

My throat bobs as emotion pours into it. "Is Mikael gone completely?"

He wraps his hand around my waist. "Not entirely. That's not the way it works. I'm still him. He loved you so much, Summer, that in the final moments before we fused, he gave me all of it. He gave me his conscience, his love, anger, remorse. I feel everything, baby, and now, I have to take accountability for my trauma."

I realize he can now *see* me without those damn glasses. "So you're Lincoln, then?"

He bites his lip, and a flash of annoyance hits his eyes, as if he doesn't understand why I can't comprehend this. "Again, not entirely. I'm a better version of both of them." His darkness shines down on me, and I recognize the split in his mannerisms, in the shadows in his eyes. At least they no longer look like they belong in hell.

"And the fragment?" I ask.

"That fragment is my trauma, Summer. And yes, it's still here, too."

It...

"What happens now?"

He snuggles me into the crook of his arm. "My life would be easier if I killed you. I'll have access to a fortune and the power that comes from being one of them. I'll get my tenure at work immediately and won't have to worry about anything for the rest of my life."

I'm so focused on Lincoln, on his shadowed eyes and on what he's saying, that I barely notice the footsteps that pass us.

Misty stumbles into the clearing we are lying in, and Lincoln and I both shoot up. Her eyes widen when she sees the position we're in.

We all stare at one another, and no one moves an inch. Until she moves her foot, and we both jolt up to our feet, pulling our clothes back on.

"You both are batshit crazy," she stammers, darting her eyes around the darkness for an escape.

I turn to Lincoln, only now vaguely aware of the cut on my arm and how badly it hurts. "She's still alive?"

He shrugs. "I thought you'd be mad if I killed her."

"Unbelievable," I mutter.

She bolts into the night, and I dart after her, managing to stop her by leaping forward, grabbing at her feet and tripping her. She falls flat on her face but wiggles and thrashes beneath me.

"Let go of me," she screams. "He tried to kill me." She kicks at me, which irritates the fuck out of me because I'm quite injured, too.

"He did *not* try to kill you," I correct her, and pin her to the ground with every ounce of my energy. Even in my satiated state, I'm still stronger than she is. "Relax, Misty."

She twists to her front. "You have no idea what he—"

Her eyes lose all color as she stares right past me and her words cut off. I turn my head to see Lincoln leaning against the tree I was hiding behind, his mask back on his face. Something flashes in his hand.

"I'm going to tell everyone what you are." She turns her attention to me. "And *you*...you knew what he was this entire time, didn't you?" I meet her with silence. "Didn't you?" she screams.

I glance at Lincoln, then shift my gaze to his hands, where he's toying with his blade. "Take off your mask," I tell him.

He takes it off and hands it to me, and I direct my attention back to Misty, whose eyes widen. "We can do this the easy way or the hard way." I lean over her, and Lincoln hands me the blade he's playing with. "Do you want to live or die tonight?" I ask, gripping it.

She tightens her jaw, pressing her lips together, staring at my hand. She barely manages a gulp as I press it against her throat.

"Don't fight me on this. You have no idea what you're dealing with, because right now, I don't care whether you live or die. I have too much at stake to deal with your shit." I point at Lincoln. "Do you see that guy right there?"

She swallows hard. "Yes."

"Who is that?"

"That's Lincoln Kennedy, our TA."

I grip her chin, keeping my blade tight in my fist.

"Wrong. This man is Mikael Peters."

She catches her breath, darting her gaze to Lincoln, who plays the role of villain so perfectly. He merely picks at his nails as we discuss the matters at hand.

"Say his name…"

She trembles, but finally coughs out, "Mikael Peters." She's catching on.

"Good," I tell her. "Because he is capable of ripping your throat out so you can't scream or tell anyone what happened here tonight. He killed Grant because Grant tried to take advantage of me. He silenced that girl Cali to get my attention. He took you to make me jealous. You're not special, Misty. You're basic. And I want to help you go back to your basic life, okay?"

She shakes violently.

I press the blade harder into her throat. "Okay?"

She sniffles, wipes her nose, and finally says, "What do you need me to do?".

I pull the blade off and help her up to her feet. "It's not going to be very fun, but I need you to trust me. And I need you to cooperate like your life depends on it."

"What are you planning, Summer?" Lincoln asks, walking up to me and wrapping his arms around my midsection.

I grab his hand and interlace my fingers with his and peer up at him, then back down at her. "They want a blonde, so we give them a blonde."

Approximately two hundred and eighty years ago, deep in a forest cave, four cloaked men gathered in a circle surrounded by torches, in what would then become the Order of the Shadows.

The clergyman, the mason, the burgess, and the scribe.

After years of hardship, famine, and disease, they believed that darkness was the only way to find light. The scribe stole a codex from a historical archive in a small town by the sea in Italy and brought it with him across the ocean in search of a better life.

Before he left, he slipped an ancient text into his satchel—its paper brittle with age and smelled faintly of dust and time—believing its origins lay in the lost city of Babylon. The scribe believed in miracles; he believed history had a way of repeating itself and by following the steps of our ancestors, it could lead to a path of enlightenment

He spent years learning to decode the ancient book, then finally read it cover to cover. Within the confines of these pages, he found solace in the divine words that bestowed upon him a resolute and magnificent pathway forward.

He spent months rewriting these words in English and scribbled them in his journal. That journal would then become the one and only copy of *The Shadow Codex*.

The scribe was tired of his friends' suffering. One day, a particularly cold and dreadful day, he walked into a candlelit cavern and placed a tin on the wooden table. It was a dreadful year with scarce crops and dangerous townspeople in constant feud with their neighbors. People were poor and were dying of sickness and starvation.

Grasping his codex in one hand, the scribe told his friends to put all their coppers into a tin.

The clergyman, renowned for his fondness for whiskey and attraction to the younger girls in town, chuckled, his cheeks rosy from ale. "Why would I do that, you fool?" He slammed his mug on the ground, shaking the table. "What are you up to, Matteo?" The pin-nosed burgess and the soot-faced Mason both laughed along with him.

Matteo calmly placed the book on the table and said in his thick accent, "I have found a new path forward."

The clergyman picked up the journal and flipped through its pages, his face growing dark. "What is this, Matteo?" He looked up at his friend. "This is blasphemy. Your soul will be damned to hell by writing such heathen words."

The scribe Matteo, although not as revered as his friend the priest, was gradually gaining prominence in the town after building a library, which would soon become Kinsmen College, and eventually Kinsmen University. He would later be the most prominent figure in town history.

With confidence, the scribe replied, "Next week, I will return with this tin, and the pot will grow. Then you will see what I am saying is true."

The clergyman chuckled, thinking his friend had gone mad. He decided, however, to go along with it to prove to all his friends that Matteo Vital had no place going against the church. Each of them, one after another, placed a coin in the tin and gave it to the scribe.

A week later, they met again to drown their sorrows in ale, but the scribe arrived, looking dejected, as the money in the pot had not grown.

They mocked Matteo and used their remaining coins to get drunk, and Matteo left, promising the next time he saw them, he would make the coins grow.

Weeks passed and things worsened. The flu, having already menaced nearby towns, had reached the village of Kinsmen, causing deaths among the young and old.

A year later, the scribe walked into the bustling tavern, on a particularly dark night. He placed the same tin on the table in front of his friends, and their eyes widened with greed. The coppers, as Matteo promised, had indeed doubled.

"Impossible!" exclaimed the clergyman, with a glimmer of hope and greed.

"The dark god smiles upon us," explained the scribe. "He showers us with his blessings, while your god leaves us sick and impoverished." The clergyman couldn't deny what he was witnessing, even if he didn't fully comprehend it.

Coppers don't multiply on their own. So where were they coming from?

They didn't know Matteo was insane. He heard voices and saw the god's shadowed face through the ancient trees encircling the area.

He was also a thief, stealing from the young people who were flocking to town to study at his school to learn a more secularized way of life.

The god spoke to Matteo and said that by offering a sacrifice to him, their money would continue to grow and ironically, more young people would come to the town to learn.

The clergyman, who had lost his only daughter, couldn't ignore the fact that, despite his devoutness, he did not seem to have his god's favor.

Christianity was failing him.

The following week, the scribe's tin reappeared, augmented with additional coins, and Matteo claimed to be the voice of the dark god who was smiling on them. He opened the codex and started reading passages that detailed the steps required to become one of the chosen children.

Eventually, the four men pooled what little money they had, trusting their friend the scribe. Each week, the scribe brought back those same coins, plus more, and handed it out to his friends and spewed his rhetoric, convincing his friends of a new way.

One fateful night, they entered a solemn pact, a sacred blood oath, vowing that the first sacrifice must be made.

And so, mere days later, the enchanting wife of the scribe ventured into the cave on the outskirts of town, unknowingly walking to her own demise. From the tales I've been told, she was a youthful soul, barely reaching adulthood when this tragedy befell her. Yet, despite her tender age, she had already brought three precious children into the world before meeting her untimely end.

The children of Matteo Vital.

The scribe hid these coins in a trust within the area he administered at the small school he founded. Eventually, this small school grew, and his office became the department of psychology at Kinsmen College.

No one knows the existence of this trust other than those involved, and to this day exists in a fund only accessible by those in this department.

The trust grew with each passing year; the school growing and the trust growing exponentially as each student unknowingly paid for it with their tuition.

Trusts are binding, trusts are law, and trusts are forever.

The interest compounded, and grew for two hundred and eighty years, creating one of the richest endowments in the world. The town flourished under their watch, and they became the wealthiest people in the region.

The scribe waited—as scribes tend to do—biding his time, planning and plotting, wanting more for himself. Scribes, by nature, are very patient people. Matteo waited for his friends to kill their wives in ceremonial debauchery, then he poisoned their ale, weakening them before he slaughtered them, leaving their bodies to rot in the forest.

None of their wives birthed any more children before they died, and the ones that were alive died from the flu, leaving Matteo's descendants the sole beneficiaries of the trust.

Overtime, and as generations passed, Matteo *became* that god. His children, and their children thereafter, sacrifice under his name. The children became the new Order, giving their sacrifice before moving on and bearing children of their own, keeping on with the tradition.

How do I know all of this? I don't. It's an educated guess based on historical records of the time, but isn't that how all history is written?

Whoever survives tells the story.

Now, each one of their descendants stands in this very circle, bound to the scribe who demands blood and sacrifice.

My mother perished here, twenty-two years ago, at the hands of those who sought that greed.

What I witnessed that night should never have happened. I was an anomaly, as no child from a sacrifice should even exist. That night altered my brain chemistry and transformed me into the monster I am now.

I did not inherit this darkness; it was imposed upon me.

I am a new darkness—a new dark god—and I am about to take everything they have sworn to protect.

Every year, the interest from that trust moves to Dr. Garcia's bank account, where she distributes the funds to the full members of the Order, including her family—some to Xander and some to me.

Talia Garcia is the guardian of that trust and controls this entire town. Everyone is in her pocket because she controls the finances.

Dr. Garcia, however, is getting quite old, frail even. Perhaps she only has a short while to live, and she's relying on me to carry this legacy. Except...I'm not bound by that bloodline, even though that 600-million-dollar trust is about to become *mine.*

I stand back from that same circle two hundred and eighty years later. Images form in my mind of their younger selves, with solemn faces as my mother willingly walked into that circle.

In my arms, I hold Misty, who is wearing a hooded cloak. Her blonde hair peeks out from beneath the mask I placed upon her.

My brother scoffs nearby when he sees her. "He actually fucking did it," he mutters.

Talia Garcia steps forward, raising her hand, silencing him. She looks wicked and old in her dark robes.

Talia Garcia—*nee Vital*—was once the strongest among us. Now, I believe Summer, who is hidden in the shadows, is the strongest among us. Summer watches as I carry Misty, who everyone believes is her, to a death ceremony.

There is no rebirth here; there is only death, greed, and insanity.

The scribe killed his wife and stole from his companions with no sacred purpose. He did it out of greed, preying on the weak in their moments of desperation, and knew his wife had eyes for the clergyman.

His insanity has been passed down for generations, manifesting in acts of murder. Once you experience it, there is no stopping it, as I have observed. And I am certain Summer carries that genetic trait, as did her father.

Talia approaches and kneels before Misty, her face concealed. She tilts her head as she beholds the blood on her fingers after lightly grazing the softness of Misty's cheek before moving her fingers to the cut on her neck to feel her pulse.

Tonight, I've brought two women to the brink of death, and one I still need to bring back again. Misty is barely breathing.

She keeps her fingers on Misty's neck for a couple of seconds before rising. Talia Garcia is a mastermind of chaos, manipulating events from a distance and has done so her entire life. She belongs to a completely different crazy. She is utterly terrifying.

Satisfied by the blood on her fingers, she disregards Misty and focuses her attention on me as she rises on her toes to reach for my face hidden deep within my hood.

"It's done," she declares loudly, so the entire circle can hear. She brings her lips to my forehead and presses a soft kiss, and I bow as a sign of respect. "You did well, Mikael." Her voice is soft so no one else can hear the name she uses.

I smile tightly, my voice unrecognizable even to me. "My name's not Mikael anymore," I whisper back to her. "You cannot begin to understand what I've become."

I blink and smile at her. The light from my torch reflects in her eyes. She observes me, her gaze flickering, but then she composes herself and stares into my eyes in fascination. Fear emanates from her, an emotion I know so intimately.

She exhales. "Of course. We will talk later."

She steps back and turns to face the group, leaving Misty's lifeless body in a heap.

Everyone's heads are down, a hush falling over the cave as Talia takes center circle. "We have been summoned here tonight by a higher power. Our dark one requires a sacrifice from each of you. It is a small offering for the power and love He bestows upon us. Once you take a life, you are able to carry on with your existence. You have the freedom to marry, love, and support each other. However, it is important to follow the code, as we all belong to something sacred. Deviating from it will result in dire consequences."

As we all learned from Xander's mother.

"We are all equal; we are all his descendants, and we shall live in His image. Once I am gone, Lincoln will assume the role of the Guardian of the Order. He will wear the mask of obscurity and pass it on to whomever he chooses. He is the chosen one."

Xander's anger and jealousy radiates out of him. However, I did him a favor. This is not something he wants. He wants the parties, the money, and drugs; he doesn't want this responsibility.

Everyone hastily leaves, except for Xander. He remains standing, observing as if he cannot believe he has lost control of what should rightfully be his fortune.

His focus is now entirely on the body everyone else believes is Summer. He hesitates for a moment, as if wanting to verify her true identity, but then he steps back and disappears into the darkness.

Only Talia remains, with Misty pretending to be lifeless on the ground, and Summer hiding close by, watching this all unfold.

Dr. Garcia studies me briefly and says, "Serve her to him."

She shuffles away because Dr. Garcia can't stand the next part—the part where we remove the eyes.

Misty remains motionless, almost like she is dead. I lose track of time, staring at her, waiting for the cave to empty, until gentle hands clasp mine.

"Let's take her home," Summer whispers.

I'm an expert on emotions. I've been fascinated by them my entire existence. Studying them became my way of experiencing something I couldn't otherwise have. Not the same way normal people do.

I became obsessed with understanding every single one of them to the point I could write an entire textbook on the subject. Expertly crafting them, mirroring others' expressions when they are experiencing grief or joy. Desperately trying to understand them. Girls crying in my office, batting their eyes at me, falling for me because they thought I was such a good listener.

Now that they are unlocked, I have zero control over them. Every emotion in the human brain overwhelms me.

Summer's platinum hair is tied up in a messy bun as she sleeps in the crook of my arm. The overwhelming love I have for her threatens to eat me from the inside out, and the hatred for her still simmers in my blood, haunting me like an evil spirit.

Split, as Summer calls him, is a deep, guttural hatred that vibrates in my chest. He is a palpable pain that radiates outward; even as I hold him close, a simmering rage flickers beneath the surface of his skin when I watch her.

Then, when she grimaces in her sleep, her tiny brow furrowing, I can't help but think she's so fucking cute and my love for her overtakes it. I hope one day that hatred can go away, but that's something I need to work on.

She's still sleeping as I open my laptop and write the experiences of my transformation from the night before.

I take a minute to identify and describe each emotion as they come rushing in, form, and settle within my psyche.

Guilt is what I'm focusing on right now. Guilt for stealing Summer's innocence when she was young, for killing the innocent women Dr. Garcia left for me as bait, and Grant…

Well, he deserved it and, obviously, so did her father.

Summer's innocence is something I can never give back to her, and I had no right to take it the way I did. She was so young, breakable and perfect, and I needed to soil her. I needed her to be as dark as I was.

Which I may have succeeded at.

Otherwise, I'm very much the same person I was before. I still maintain an objective world view, the same outlook, same dreams, same drive and motivation. With each passing day, I continue to identify myself as Lincoln Kennedy. Mikael Peters is gone, his identity being blended into mine, making me complete. Making me human in a way I wasn't before.

Summer starts to stir beside me, so I shut my computer and slide under the blankets to join her. Once we got home last night, I changed her into one of my shirts, put her to bed, and kept her underwear off so I could have easy access to what's mine. I also tended to Misty, cleaned her up and made her as comfortable as possible and, more importantly, did my best to keep her alive.

Summer smells like me, and I can't help but run my tongue down her stomach. She runs her fingers through my hair as I pleasure her while she slowly wakes up. "Mmm. Lincoln, what are you doing?"

She slides the blankets down so she can see me, and I peer up at her. "Tasting you, baby. You taste so fucking good." I press a kiss over her mark. "Everyone thinks you're dead, Summer. So now I can do whatever I want with you. I own you now."

She trembles when my hands move to her waist, and I pause as she peers down at me, intrigued.

Her bright blue eyes, full of love, curiosity, and fear, but no remorse.

No, my little liar is incapable of it. Now I need to see if she really does have deadly tendencies.

She is the true descendent of the scribe—I can see it inside her, flashing in the flicker in her eyes. The once-in-a-generation psychopath. If she ever makes a kill, I'm unsure if I can bring her back from what that will do to her. Yet she trembles at my words…

Fascinating.

So the question remains, is psychopathy hereditary? In Summer's case, she had a traumatic event. Watching her father murder someone certainly did shape her, and watching my mother die at his hand certainly shaped me. But my hypothesis is a fourteen-year-old would understand that watching her father kill someone in her basement is not normal.

It was a sloppy kill, much like how I kill, with very little fucks given. I watched him toss her body into the forest. He didn't realize I was in the house, but I was already there hiding in Summer's bedroom.

I've never seen her react genuinely to it, even after watching Dani's father go away for it a couple of years later. And that was over ten years *after* the killings of 2002.

He never fucking stopped.

I can't let it fool me. Summer Landry is an extremely dangerous person and just lost her identity. She chose to suppress a memory instead of facing what her father was, and that makes her just as evil as he was.

I hold on to her calf muscles, and she slowly brings her legs down and wraps them around me. I suck on her sweet pussy until she can't take it anymore. I grip her legs so she can't move, and she moans loudly.

Everyone upstairs believes she's dead, but luckily, they can't hear anything down here.

Once I'm satisfied she's had enough, I position myself over her body.

"You're still scared of me," I murmur. The build up of wet arousal tells me it's not a bad thing, and who am I to pass judgment on her particular tastes?

"I think I'll always be a little scared of you, Lincoln," she says. "How do you feel right now? What are you experiencing?"

I draw in a breath and lay beside her. "Everything, baby. I feel *every-thing*. It's so overwhelming, part of me wants to rip my skin off." Since waking up a few hours ago, I've cried, laughed, and giggled. Every memory invokes an emotional response I lacked before. I'm like a child in many ways, experiencing things for the first time, like candy or potato chips, and I don't just enjoy their taste, but adore them.

She runs her fingers over the bridge of my nose, examining me. "You don't need your glasses anymore?"

I nuzzle my nose into her. "I can see clear as day. And don't ask me to explain that, because I can't. Sometimes science is unpredictable."

"Is he completely gone?" A flash of sadness.

"He's still inside me, but not the way it was before. He's like a ghost."

She crinkles her nose. "Do you still hate me?"

The usual dark shrill shoots up my spine and my stomach fills with acid.

I still hate her...in so many ways. "Yeah, I do. But I love you more."

She purses her lips, not loving my honest response.

I kiss her neck, then her cheek, and work my way to her lips. "I need to emphasize the *I love you more*, though."

"What do we do now?" she asks, staring down the dark hallway where Misty is hiding and recovering. A dark flash hits her eyes and her body stiffens. "Misty better still be alive."

I can't help but smile. "Yes, Summer, she's still alive. You're the only person I have any desire to kill. She'll be rough for a while; she lost lots of blood, but she'll be okay."

She pushes herself up so she's leaning back on my headboard. "Where is she?"

I study her curiously. "Would you care if I killed her, Summer?"

She narrows her eyes. "What do you mean? Of course I'd care."

I squeeze her. "No, baby. You wouldn't, not really. And that's okay." I gently brush my lips against her earlobe. "If I admit to sleeping with her, then would you consider killing her?"

Her pupils widen and she slaps my hand away. "No, Lincoln, I wouldn't. Misty shouldn't have her life ruined because she had a crush on you."

Of course, I'm joking, to some extent. But Summer has psychopathy deeply rooted in her family history, and the scientist in me is eager to find out if she's capable of it.

However, Misty is not the right subject for this. It's time to let her go.

"Do you think she will talk?" Summer asks.

I shake my head. "No. She understands what she was a part of. If she's smart, she'll move away from this cursed place and never look back."

"And what about the other members?" she asks. "Can you really keep me hidden?"

"We have to keep you hidden, Summer. Because they will kill us both if they see you, and I'll lose everything I've worked for. You and I have the power to end this, but we have to be patient. We have to do it the right way."

SIX MONTHS LATER

I 've gotten adept at sneaking around in the dark. The mask is almost like a second skin to me now, as are the tight black clothes I wear. It's dark, midnight black, as I make my way across campus and toward the five-story building that houses the psychology department.

It's easy to hide among the ancient trees and buildings when everyone believes you're gone. I made it easy for the Order to explain my disappearance. I had already told Dani and my mother I was leaving, so it was easy for them to believe I ran away.

I've given no reason for them to think I was dead.

In the last six months, I've gone into hiding and Lincoln's thrived. As the next leader of the society, and now a tenured professor, he's untouchable. Lincoln's groundbreaking research catapulted him to the top of the research food chain in the psychology field. He defended his thesis with flying colors.

I have conformed in many ways. I am what he wants and needs me to be. I dyed my hair black to hide from society and avoid being recognized for my white hair. It also helps him not be reminded of his hatred for me.

But I'm getting bored… The intensity in my soul has awakened, and I can't be cooped up in a basement any longer.

Lincoln barely lets me out, for fear that one of them will see me. Sometimes I go upstairs and spy, hiding in the walls. Lucy is the only one who sees me, but she's smart enough to stay out of it.

Sometimes he takes me to another town so I can get some fresh air and have human interaction with someone other than him. I also go home to spy on my mother, who seems to be doing just fine with the vague letters I send her.

Misty fled town and moved across the country. I'm not sure how Lincoln managed that one, but he scared her into submission. She must have had some interaction with Split. She lied to the police about where she was.

And Dani...

I am guilt ridden by Dani, who isn't handling my disappearance well. No one thinks I'm dead, but no one seems to care, either. Except for Dani... Hopefully, she can let me go.

I continue to uncover the complexities of Lincoln Kennedy every day. He still gets little fits of rage, and sometimes when he looks at me, I swear it's Mikael staring back at me. I want to reach out and touch him, but he disappears before I'm able to.

Split often comes to say hi, too, and I love it when Split comes to play. He's the best one out of the three of them in bed.

Lincoln's eyes are full of all-consuming love after we have sex, and it makes me wonder how many times a day he thinks about killing me.

He's still a psychopath, but at least he has emotion now and can control it. I know he is dangerous. I am the catalyst that made him unravel and become stronger when he put himself back together.

Psychopath or not, we are the perfect match. I really was made for him.

A light layer of spring snow crunches under the soles of my knee-high boots, which I wear under a long pair of tight slacks as I wait until the security guard does his rounds. He leaves the door unlocked when he scouts the building—at least that's what Lincoln told me.

For someone who cares about the difference between right and wrong, he certainly is leaving me enough breadcrumbs. It's as if he knows I'm buzzing inside, watching me transform, day by day, becoming *Him*.

My self-righteous boyfriend suddenly has remorse and lacks evidence to incriminate Dr. Garcia. There is no way for him to prove any wrongdoings besides his suspicion and knowing who she is, and the evident illegal rituals done for a dark deity. I've begun to piece together what she did in the late seventies, and again two decades later.

My body is buzzing as I make my way to the stairwell of the fifth floor and into the cluster of offices where she works. He also informed me that Dr. Garcia sometimes works late into the night, because night-time is when she does her best work.

Lincoln is away at a conference halfway across the continent. It's the first time he's left me alone, and he's been wise not to.

My stomach twists. An instant deep pleasure rolls through my body at the exhilaration of watching Dr. Garcia sit at her desk, a lamp flickering by her side, chewing on a pencil, deep in thought.

Her eyes flicker up when she senses me.

Keen senses. Too bad her bones are brittle, and unless she has a gun stuffed in that drawer, I doubt she will do anything to me.

As I step into the light, she breathes deeply, seemingly relieved, as if she was expecting me. With a slight movement, she lowers her pencil. The light causes the white streak on her forehead to shimmer.

The cloth mask tickles my cheek, itching the skin on my face hidden beneath. I will be careful not to leave any fingerprints. The very essence of it screams at me.

"So it's time, then?" she asks, her voice calm and calculated. "You finally admit what you are, Summer Landry?"

I step forward and play with the razor blade in my fingers but don't respond. Only a quick flash of her eyes betrays her fear on her otherwise stoic face.

She's scared…I was wondering if she would be. She recovers quickly and rises. "This is remarkable, Summer. You embody him so well. You're different from your father and grandparents, yet, in many ways, you're the same. Impulsive, angry and jealous, and clearly so loving in ways that shouldn't be possible. But you need to understand, girl, what you feel for Lincoln isn't love. You are simply not capable of it."

"*I love him,*" I fire back at her. "You do not get to tell me how I feel, you crazy old bitch." My voice betrays my identity, but I don't care. She's clearly been watching me for a long time. I wouldn't be surprised if she suspected I was still alive.

She walks toward me and sits on the front of her desk. "You don't love him, Summer…just as Lincoln is incapable of loving you." Her eyes flicker as if she's deep in memory and she smiles. "Your grandfather could love, though, and so could your grandmother. In fact, they were great lovers."

A stir of something pushes through me. She knew them, all of them, in ways I never could.

"You don't know me. You don't know this version of Lincoln, either."

She smirks, the wrinkles under her eyes more pronounced this close. "I believe in all my heart that true psychopaths are born, not made. This verifies it. But I have to say, whatever you did to transform Lincoln was impressive. Although it's a shame because he had such...potential."

"The Lincoln you knew doesn't exist anymore," I tell her calmly. "He deserves this life, and he deserves to be happy." I glare at her. "And you don't deserve to live."

Her eyes dart to the cell phone five inches from her hand. And I realize now that's the only reason she moved at all.

She merely scoffs. "Lincoln doesn't exist at all. You've fallen in love with my creation, young lady."

I contemplate for a moment. "I thought Mikael created him. And I thought you said I wasn't capable of loving?"

Her old eyes flash to the phone again. "But which part of him do you love, Summer? Because Lincoln is an empty shell, hard to get through and easy to manipulate. So really, it must be the other side of him, the dark side. Mikael is the one you're truly in love with, isn't it? Or perhaps it's that monster that lives inside both of them."

I cock a brow. "I love all of him. Every side, every angle. You're not going to tell me my love for him isn't real."

Her finger inches to the phone. "I imagine it's hard for you. Every little girl wants to grow up and fall in love. You have created a perfect life. I understand why you long for a storybook ending. But your feelings of protectiveness and loyalty are driven by self-interest. You are empty inside, Summer, but you've always known that." She lets out a sigh and continues, "It will make you stronger, enabling you to pursue the things you were destined to do."

I pause for a moment, listening, contemplating, and have no fucking clue what she's talking about. Her eyes keep darting to that damn phone as she rambles.

"If you dare lay a finger on that phone," I say darkly, "I will slice out every vein in your hand. Then I'll move to your feet, so you can't walk, and your ears, so you can't hear. And I will cut out your eyes last because I want you to see everything I'm doing."

Her weathered hand trembles and she pulls it into herself before making eye contact with me. "You're not the first to threaten me, you know. Your father threatened me the same way once, and it was cute.

I'm an old woman, Summer. I'm tired, and this sounds like a very fitting way for me to go." She waves her hand. "I'm not bothered by your threats."

"Did he now? Was that because you made him kill people?"

She sucks in a breath. "There are so many things you simply do not understand, young lady. The genetic makeup you have inherited, the transformation you are on the brink of, and the society I've dedicated my entire life to safeguarding."

"Tell me what this is all about, then. I deserve to know."

She rises and walks back to her desk, keeping her hand away from the phone. She grabs a book...an old one.

Ancient almost...

She hands it to me, but I don't take it. Instead, I stare at that old book like its poison. It's the cause of everything that's wicked in this town.

"Take this codex," she says. "This rightfully belongs to you now, so don't take it lightly. What's in here is sacred."

"It's bullshit," I fire back.

She shakes her head. "It's not."

I narrow my eyes. "And you're just going to hand it over to me?"

She merely shrugs, her eyes look tired. "Seems fitting, under the circumstances."

I stare down at this old book, the pages nearly falling out of it. "What is it, exactly?"

"A codex. One of the oldest known codices in the world. Obey the rules, Summer; that's all you need to do. Read it cover to cover. It explains everything."

My heart rate rises as I flip through the dusty pages. "What will happen if I follow these rules?"

She looks up, her eyes meeting mine. "You will achieve transcendence. There can only be one, and that one is you."

A pang of discomfort hits me. "I can't kill innocent people."

The same discomfort lingers in her eyes. "Read the book. And maybe one day, you'll understand my true motives."

I understand her motives just fine; she's a scientist, and this is just another twisted experiment. "This won't save your life," I say, placing the book down and twirling the blade between my fingers. An old book won't change the fact that she's deranged.

Her smoldering eyes catch the glint of metal in my hands, and I take a cautious step forward and smile. "I lied to you, Dr. Garcia."

Her head tilts slightly. "About what, child?"

That twinge in my stomach turns into something much more pleasurable. "I plan to start with your eyes, and I'm going to enjoy it."

I stare at myself in the window, wearing the mask, and I admire the sleek, sexy lines of my body. If only Lincoln could see me now.

I stand utterly still. The tension between us is so intense, so forced. Then suddenly, as if all the tension in the world is bundled up in this very room, it shatters, and I unleash my fury.

She's dead by the time I'm able to carve out one of her eyes. Brain damage, I'm assuming, because her other eye turned glassy and lifeless. And as disgusting as it is, she needs to feel it. She needs to experience it for all the women whose lives she cut short.

I take my time and once I'm done with her, I slice open her shirt, pull it off, and leave her in the humiliating pose just like the others. The sight of her wrinkled skin and empty eye sockets is disturbing and makes me shudder.

Her blood is everywhere.

Fear emanates from her empty eyes as she gazes up at me.

Eyes are a fickle thing. Many call it the window to your soul, and so by taking them out, I'm stealing the only thing that makes her human.

Although, I don't think Talia Garcia had any humanity left in her at all.

Careful not to expose any skin, I grab an ink pen and piece of paper from her desk and carefully scribble on the page of her notebook as her lifeless body peers up at me.

Shadowface is back.

NOTE TO THE READERS

Thank you so much for coming on this crazy journey with me. When I first decided to write a dark romance, I didn't realize where it was going to take me. Crafting Mikael's character was an unexpected turn as he didn't emerge in this story until I was in the third draft. It took me that long to realize Lincoln wasn't the original inhabitant in the body and there was another voice talking to me. However, unraveling Lincoln's true essence was a journey of its own. Reviews are the lifeblood of authors. If you would be so kind to leave me a review and let others know what you thought of this book. Next up, we go back in time to find out what happened in the slaughter of 1979.

Check out my website: www.rhearyan.com

ACKNOWLEDGMENTS

Here we are at the end of another book and as usual there are a plethora of people I need to thank. First, and always, I need to thank my husband and kids for giving me the space to research and write this story. Without them, I wouldn't be able to do this, especially with how much time I put into these books. Thank you to my beta readers, Amy, Noemi, Sam, Kellie, Melissa, Leslee and Tay. And a special shout out to my PA Shelbie who does so much for me. To all my writer friends who help me get through the hard times, self doubt and technical questions. You know who you are. And special thanks to my readers. You are the reason I do what I do.